A Mischief of Rats

The Dr Nell Ward Mystery Series

A Mischief of Rats

Sarah Yarwood-Lovett

First published in Great Britain in 2023 by

embla
books

Bonnier Books UK Limited
4th Floor, Victoria House, Bloomsbury Square, London, WC1B 4DA
Owned by Bonnier Books
Sveavägen 56, Stockholm, Sweden

A CIP catalogue record for this book is available from the British Library.

ISBN: 978-1-4714-1535-7

This book is typeset using Atomik ePublisher

Embla Books is an imprint of Bonnier Books UK
www.bonnierbooks.co.uk

For Aunty Glad:
Gladys Eleanor Ward.
Regimental sergeant major in WW2; cordon bleu chef;
roof-raiser in the NAAFI.
Your gold standards, moral compass and humour
inspired the best in people.
With your lifetime of adventure, my heroine is named
in your honour for a million reasons.
I'm so lucky to have known you.
'That'll do won't do.'

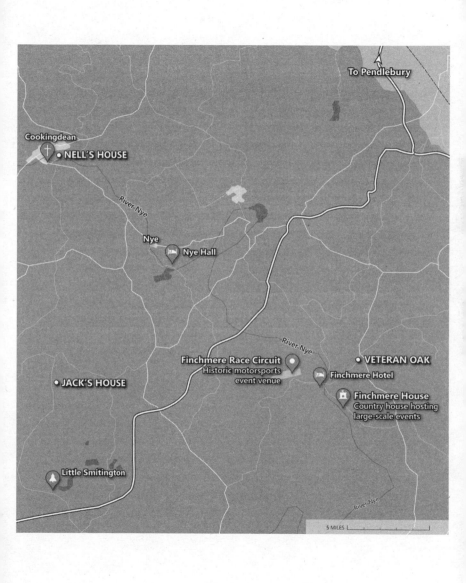

Chapter 1

Knowing she was late, Dr Nell Ward floored the accelerator and whooshed along the swooping country lane in the electric Porsche Taycan. With the window down, the dawn breeze whipped through her pixie-cut hair. She couldn't hold back her grin as she chased the sunrise blazing across the sky.

This was Nell's favourite weekend. The Classics at Finchmere – four days of classic-car racing at her family's estate – was a popular event, and this year she had an ambitious project to oversee, one she hoped would be the catalyst for change. While it hadn't got off to the best start on qualifying day yesterday, the optimism of a spring morning was infectious. A new day, a new chance to get things right.

She inhaled the fresh scent of the stirring morning, her mood lightening with the sky. And over the hum of the engine, birdsong clamoured in the woodland flanking the narrow road. She needed to get a move on, or this morning's survey would be jeopardised, and her favour to Mai, squeezed in before Nell's busy day at the racetrack, wouldn't be so helpful after all.

Even if this visit would be fleeting, it would be great to see Mai again. Nell couldn't help smiling at the thought of seeing her. It had been two years since she'd been Nell's intern at EcoLogical Solutions consultancy, before moving on here to help manage Little Smitington Wood, but the memory of Mai's infectious energy remained sharp in her mind: with her talent for hooking any audience, Mai had brightened everyone's day from the first time she'd burst into the office, with her effervescent greeting, spelling her name out, 'M-A-I, but pronounced like the month.' And she always had a funny tale (survey or dating mishaps) to regale the team with, in her cheerful Malaysian accent.

Nell didn't know what to expect from the morning's survey. The fifty acres of woodland had been in desperate need of restoration for years. Nestled in the south-east downland near her own home in Cookingdean, and close to her family home in Finchmere, the woodland was familiar territory to Nell. But the overgrown tangled habitat had been neglected over the years. The Wildlife Trust had taken it on, but restoration was a tall order, especially on the restricted budget of a charitable organisation, which mostly ran on volunteers and a few employed wardens, like Mai.

Nell had seen occasional signs of progress – the new gate, the hardcore track, a glimpse of a visitor centre being built. Even so, Mai's plea for help with this morning's great crested newt survey was undoubtedly overambitious: the protected species only occupied the most pristine of habitats. And if Nell recalled correctly, Mai had restored the pond just a year ago.

But Nell couldn't afford to be complacent: today's survey involved collecting bottle-trapped newts, and they had to be released before the morning got too warm, or they could boil alive in their traps. Nell didn't need any more excuse to floor the accelerator again.

Spotting the silvering chestnut fencing of the nature reserve, Nell swerved into the track to the visitor centre. Alongside her, the soaring beeches were a mist of unfurling lime leaf buds over an indigo haze of bluebells. In that one glance, Nell saw how much back-breaking brush clearance Mai had done, and the great improvement it had made to the woodland's biodiversity.

She slowed to drive through the open gate at the top of the track, then gaped at the sculptural wood-and-glass visitor centre. The obvious investment was totally unexpected, and Nell's curiosity sparked. The centre's living roof was a curved green swoop, scattered with purple herbs and bright studs of yellow buttercups and dog daisies. An information board listed the roof's plant species and its benefits for thermal efficiency, water management and air quality.

Mai's office extended to the left – her red Toyota Hilux, with its Wildlife Trust logo just visible under streaks of mud, was parked in front of it, next to a shed.

As Nell pulled up, Mai was already dashing over, singing, 'Morning, morning!'

Nell hugged her petite friend in delight. 'So good to see you!'

Mai stood back, eyes wide. 'What's with the glam makeup?'

Nell didn't want to mention where she was heading to next. 'You can talk,' she deflected, taking in Mai's outfit. 'No one told me about the Eighties theme. Bit fancy. For newts.'

In leggings, black Converse and an oversized neon-pink, off-the-shoulder T-shirt belted around her slim waist – her glossy black hair in a high ponytail – Mai wasn't exactly dressed for site work. While Nell's outfit of old T-shirt and camo trousers was more pond-ready, her styled pixie cut, striking red lipstick and cat-eye makeup were perhaps a little overdone. But after this survey, she had to pop home, feed her cat Jezebel, change and dash straight to the track to meet her racing team.

Seeing Mai blush at her comment, the penny dropped. 'Ah. Is someone *else* coming today, by any chance?'

Mai playfully punched Nell's arm. 'Not 'til later. You're the only one I could convince to come for today's early shift. Even if you are late. We better get a move on.'

'True.' Nell dragged her waders from the boot, kicked off her trainers and stepped into the suit. Holding the chest waders' apron across her torso, she tugged the straps over her shoulders, wrapping herself in the odour of rubber and pond, and nodded over at the centre.

'I didn't expect to see anything like this, Mai. Looks like you've made incredible progress.'

Walking to the woodland's edge, Nell crouched to check the bluebells. Across her estate, the native bluebells were losing out to the Spanish flowers and their hybrids. So she was surprised to notice these weren't upright flowers – *bowed raceme and curled-back petals, promising.* Tilting a bell upwards, she examined the anthers. *Cream pollen, not blue.* The rarer native bluebell indicated this was valuable ancient woodland. Inhaling the earthy, dew-fresh scent of forest, she caught the sweet fragrance that only the native bluebells have. Smiling, she peered into the dappled light of the wood, spotting ramrod branches shooting up from wide, gnarled beech trunks – which were wide enough to need two people to encircle them with outstretched arms: *veteran trees, a couple of hundred years old.* The younger, leaner beeches were being managed in the same traditional way.

The coppiced hazel understorey was threaded with honeysuckle and traveller's joy – a perfect dormouse highway. The various boxes on the trees, at different orientations, confirmed that this protected species was present, along with several bat and bird species. Spying faint, narrow paths through the vegetation, Nell sniffed the air. *Fox.* And deer, from the browsing on the trees. Heading back to Mai, she deciphered the birdsong, the intermittent drill of a woodpecker deep in the forest drowned by a distant, bright, bubbling chirrup of a nesting skylark, indicating a nearby meadow. Westwards, she guessed, from the south-facing position of the bat boxes on the trees.

'Mai, this is amazing. How have you done so much, in such a short amount of time?' Nell took the bucket that Mai held out, with a clipboard and two water meters crammed into it. She slid her phone in between the meters, then fell into step with Mai as they walked past the centre and towards the hedge budding with leaves. *Species rich – also ancient?*

'I knew this would be a big project. I've poured all my energy into it. Worth it, though. The wood's about three hundred years old, from those pollarded beeches. I've used the same traditional management for the beech and hazel. After clearing the brush, my volunteers cleared the Spanish bluebells and hybrids. *That* was a task. But I want this to be an oasis of native bluebells. And the biodiversity has rocketed!'

'Yeah, looks like you've got a full house of residents. And I'm guessing some chalk grassland, flora, slow-worms and – with the pond – probably grass snakes and invertebrates?'

Mai shot her a delighted smile as they rounded the hedge into the wildflower meadow. They kept to the edge, avoiding the ground-nesting skylarks, and Mai pointed at the fence. 'We'll climb the fence, walk along the road, then climb the fence again to cross the field to the pond.'

With waders bulging like clown trousers, Nell had to exaggerate her strides. She spied a swathe of magenta lanterns nodding in the breeze: snake's head fritillaries. *Ancient hay meadow? Wow.* 'Seriously, Mai, I can't believe the difference you've made. Has this been just you?'

'I've had a good team of volunteers. They've helped a lot.' Mai's smile faded under a sigh, giving Nell a glimpse of her fatigue. 'They're great – but unpredictable. I do my best to prevent no-shows by enticing them with a campfire breakfast and providing training—'

'Is that the kind of training that happens to get hedges laid, coppicing done, ponds restored, surveys and species lists completed—?'

'A perfect symbiotic relationship!' Mai grinned unrepentantly. 'I knew what this place *could* be. But I had to prove it to get any budget! I had to be imaginative!' Then she side-eyed Nell. 'Though now all the budget is spent on the centre, so I'm still relying on volunteers. And setting up the events is time-consuming. Finding folk to do dawn surveys at this time of year is impossible, even with breakfast bribery. I was glad you said you'd do it. I knew you'd turn up.'

Nell now noticed that Mai's eyes were dark-ringed from lack of sleep, and she sympathised. Two people were always needed for pond surveys: wearing chest waders that could so easily fill with water at the slightest slip, and drown the wearer, was perilous. 'You know me, any excuse to drive on empty roads. But I'm sorry I can't stay for breakfast. Busy day.' She didn't want to give away how hectic her weekend was, and risk Mai's insistence she shouldn't help.

She gabbled on, not giving Mai a chance to ask what she was doing. 'The Wildlife Trust must be pleased, though, to build such an impressive visitor centre. Is that a good sign . . . ?'

Mai practically bounced on the spot. 'I've been bursting to tell you! The restoration has gone so well that,' she whispered, 'we may be designated as a Site of Special Scientific Interest.'

Nell gaped in delight. The national designation wouldn't just afford the site protection; it would also make its management essential. Meaning Mai's work here would be fully supported.

'It's strictly confidential. I applied a while ago. The assessment's next week.' Her last word was an excited squeak.

'That's incredible! Hence the big push on surveys? You need all the evidence possible to show how valuable the ecology is here?'

'Exactly. And I need to keep you onside for another favour.'

'Uh-huh.' Nell stared across the meadow, trying not to smile. She'd known helping out with this survey would be just the tip of the iceberg with Mai.

'I'm monitoring the basic levels, now the pond's pristine.' She pointed at the water meters in Nell's bucket. 'Conductivity, pH, dissolved oxygen, nutrient levels. The biodiversity's *buzzing*. I have species lists of everything. *Almost.*' A hopeful smile lit Mai's face.

Nell bit back a grin, anticipating the question as they approached the fence.

'*But* I don't have any experts who can survey microfauna. I want to show how healthy the ecosystem is. I just need someone who can do microinvertebrates...' Mai shot Nell a winning smile. 'And maybe phytoplankton? How long could it take? They're so *tiny,*' Mai cajoled. 'It's just *so hard* to find someone with that specialised expertise.'

Nell shot her a sidelong glance. 'I *believe* those specialists love your chocolate cake.'

'Done.' Mai stopped walking, pretended to spit on her hand and offered a handshake.

Mirroring the gesture, Nell laughed. 'Got a microscope?'

Mai's brow crinkled. 'No ... But I'll find someone at the university and talk them into lending us one.'

'You astonish me,' Nell deadpanned. 'Just how much free labour have you extracted from students and volunteers? I think your no-shows are more exhausted than unreliable.'

Sticking her tongue out, Mai clambered over the wooden fence, clumsy in her waders. 'God, these things are awful to wear. I spend half my life in them, and they don't even fit. Such hard work to walk in.' She laughed. 'Do you remember that dodgy construction site? Where the security guards threatened to set the dogs on us and we nearly had to run in them?'

'Oh, yeah.' Nell laughed as she swung her legs over the fence, careful not to snag the rubber. 'Not that running would've helped. We'd have been dog food.'

'Slow-moving dog food,' Mai snorted.

'So much for your attack-dog training – you hit the deck!'

Mai giggled helplessly at the memory and hung on to Nell's arm as they walked along the lane. 'Oh, it's so lovely to be surveying with you again. How's the rest of the team?' She nudged Nell. 'How's ... *Adam?*'

Feeling her face flame at being asked anything personal, Nell tried to style it out. 'He goes by Rav, now. Short for Aravindan. He's stopped westernising his name.'

Mai's eyebrows flashed up. 'Good for him. So what's the gossip?' She bounced on her toes again. '*Please* say you got together. *Everyone* could see it coming a mile off. Except you.'

Nell warred with her protective impulse for privacy, then sighed inwardly as she felt her face redden again.

Mai squealed. 'I *knew* it! Hey, maybe you can entice him to help?'

'You and your one-track mind!' They crossed the lane to see around the blind bend. But as Nell scanned along the road, she stopped short. 'What the ... ?'

Black tyre skid marks veered across the road from the far side, towards the reserve's fence. Splintered wood stuck out at angles, a gaping hole caved in.

Nell ran over, finding it was possible in waders if it mattered enough. Urgency and rising adrenaline blurred out her headache, which awoke all too easily since her recent accident, and stirred now as her feet pounded the road. Staring at the tyre marks, she guessed someone had lost control speeding around the bend and shot off the road. 'I didn't hear a crash. Did you?' she panted.

'No.' Mai sounded panicked as they crossed through the smashed fence and raced along the faint tracks – across the dry field, between flayed bushes and ripped rushes at the pond edge – and then down the grassy bank to the waterline.

Dropping her bucket, Nell ran towards the shredded bushes, her heartbeat thudding in her ears. Sweat slithered down her back. She halted, slipping on the slick mud at the water's edge, then righted herself, her head thumping.

A few feet into the pond, a sliver of a car's boot was just visible above the water. 'Oh God.'

Mai collided with her, sending Nell staggering forward. They clutched at each other, side by side, for balance. Mai gasped.

Nell gaped at the sight. The car had nosedived into the pond. The trio of slim rectangular rear lights told her the car was a classic Mustang. But the blue stripes on white paint were a giveaway.

She knew exactly who this car belonged to: *Jack Rafferty*. A wannabe James Hunt who was neither as talented a racing driver, nor as handsome. Nell froze with shock. She'd only seen Jack yesterday at the racetrack, and he'd been busy causing trouble.

'There . . . there must be someone in there,' Mai stuttered.

Nell realised Mai was shivering and wrapped an arm around her as she studied the ground. Nothing was visible on the grass bank around them, and the only footprints in the mud at the water's edge were hers and Mai's. 'No prints.' She scanned the pond. 'No gaps in the reeds where someone's climbed out, except at the far end. Is that your access point for surveys?'

'Yes.' Mai choked. 'It's really deep this side. Too dangerous to access.'

Nell bit her lip. 'So it doesn't look like the driver got out . . .'

'Oh, no,' Mai whispered.

Nell squeezed Mai's hand. 'Call the police and say we may need an ambulance, too. And ask for the fire brigade to pull the car out. I'll see if I can . . .' she grimaced '. . . see any . . . one.'

'Be careful!' Mai reached into her pocket, unlocking her phone with trembling fingers.

Nell took some shaking steps towards the car. Wading into the pond, her feet sank deep into the mud, making it an extra effort to twist and pull her foot out with every step. The sulphuric smell escaping with each footstep assaulted her already churning stomach.

Thigh-deep in water, she bent down, trying to squint through the narrow slice of rear window below the surface. Plunged deep into the pond, the car was full of murky water. Under Nell's feet, the bank fell away sharply. She couldn't go in any further. Desperate to see any sign of someone in there, she crouched as much as she dared to peer into the car.

Suddenly, icy water gushed over the top of her waders. Jerking back with cold shock, Nell's feet slid from under her as her body was dragged down. She floundered, alarmed by the freezing water, the lead weight around her body growing frighteningly heavier by the second. A flashback to nearly drowning after she'd been pushed into the Nye River – hitting her head and ending up in ICU – only five weeks ago, sent fear flaming all over her body.

Slipping underwater, her air snatched away, Nell choked, panicking. Spluttering, hands flailing, she scrabbled to grab the car. The smooth rear wing gave her no purchase as she sank, water burning the back of her nose, terror spiking.

Her fingers found the door handle. *Thank God*. She gripped it, her life depending on it, then fumbled to release the clasp of one strap on her waders. Getting them – and the weight of the water – off her was her only chance of survival.

But her panicky fingers were clumsy, and she couldn't press the clip. She squeezed, desperate to breathe, and finally felt the clasp detach. Swapping hands on the car's door handle, she gritted her teeth and tried to undo the clip of her other strap.

The strap fell away and she tried to kick the ballooning waders off her body. The rubber clung, forcing her to tug, kick. With no air left, her head felt like it was going to burst. She forced herself to open her eyes, in brown, murky water, turbid from silt. Through the gloomy shadows, she made out enough to unhook the waders from her belt and scramble out of them.

But then she saw it – and an unreleasable scream boiled in her throat.

With only the driver's window between them, the bloated, grey face lolled towards her, cheek squashing against the thin pane of glass.

Chapter 2

One Day Earlier: Thursday 18th April – 2 p.m.

Standing in the garage, set back from the racing circuit, Nell fought not to twitch. Jack Rafferty was late. She tried not to check her watch. Again. But everyone on the classic Mercedes-Benz 300 SL 'gullwing' team was present and correct for their interview – except their 'star' driver.

Beside her, murmuring key soundbites, the team's mechanic, Mark Reynolds, absent-mindedly hefted a wrench. Nell bit back a grin at his subconscious, impatient gesture. It might be muscle memory, or nerves . . . or it might be unspoken rage at the person holding them all up. There was no love lost there; Mark and Jack had clashed since day one. But though Nell empathised with Mark – he was the better driver: technical, responsive – he didn't have Jack's star power. And their gamble this weekend needed every ounce of publicity possible.

Nell could see how much this meant to Mark. His overalls were spotless, emblazoned with a new embroidered emblem declaring, 'Mark Reynolds – Reynolds Precision Engineering.' Smart advertising. He needed to realise a decent return from his investment in this team.

Beside him, his twenty-something apprentice, Cassie, chewed a scarlet fingernail. Her overalls were tied around her waist, her pin-curled hair swept into a scarlet headscarf, Rosie the Riveter style. Colourful tattoos wound around toned forearms, and up to the sleeves of her T-shirt. The cameraman was trying to talk to Cassie, but she either wasn't interested, or she was too nervous to notice. Suspecting the latter, Nell shot her a smile.

The film crew were set up, they'd all been sound-checked, and they'd had a couple of run-throughs. Like most people at the event, the presenter had dressed in keeping with the era, in a Fifties-inspired sweater, bouncy ponytail and bright scarf tied in a neat knot around her neck.

Nell noticed that Maxine Armstrong, the team's manager, and Lucio Moretti, the lucky owner of the gullwing, were both chatting to her, as if trying to distract her and the rest of the production team from the passing of time.

Over the small talk, Nell heard the distant growls of the glamorous classic cars roaring past in their qualifying laps, amplified by the racetrack's setting in the downland valley.

Finally, the producer stepped forward. 'Let's make a start. We can get some pieces to camera and if Jack turns up later, we can edit him in. At least that'll help us keep to schedule.'

Maxine, who Nell guessed was in her early forties, smoothed her shoulder-padded power suit and mahogany bob, and strode to the shimmering Mercedes on her vertiginous Louboutins. Nell had never seen her at Moretti's Classic Car Dealership, but she'd seen her office door with the name plate: Maxine Armstrong, Global Director of Specialist Car Sourcing. So she guessed Maxine spent most of her time out of the office. Meeting her for the first time earlier today, she'd admired Maxine's determination to wear heels through the gruelling trackside day. And she'd laughed when Maxine had replied, 'They're giving me right gyp. I can't wait 'til tonight and I can swap 'em for me Uggs.' She'd winked at Nell, making her warm to her instantly, then added, 'It's worth the blisters to make the men around here look up to me.'

And the heels worked: Maxine was eye to eye with Mark, while Cassie came up to their shoulders. The presenter sprang to her mark, a cross of tape on the floor, with a perky smile, and began, 'This year a special car on the track has an extraordinary story. The team is here to tell us all about it. Let's start with Team Manager Maxine Armstrong.'

'You're right – our classic Mercedes has quite the backstory.' Maxine's Mancunian cigarette-and-whisky voice rasped, but her delivery was conspiratorial, drawing you in. She splayed one hand over the gullwing's long, elegant bonnet like a magician.

'When Mercedes first released this car, back in 1954, she was already a model of innovation. Because, *unusually*, it was the *track* car that spawned this *road* car: the fastest production car of her day. And her pioneering racing origins led to the design of those famous gullwing doors, since conventional doors wouldn't fit.'

Cassie stepped forward to open the distinctive rippling gullwing doors.

Continuing, Maxine said, 'So her gorgeous defining features were born of necessity. And it's in *exactly* that same spirit that we've made this conversion. With fossil fuels running out, we've given her a ground-breaking *electric* engine. And, who knows? Maybe electric conversions can secure the future of classic-car driving and racing! And what better car to showcase what electric conversions can do than a gullwing, eh? A historical car that started out as a trailblazer.'

Maxine's pause was the cue for the presenter to move to Mark. 'And here we have the mastermind of this conversion – Mark Reynolds, of Reynolds Precision Engineering. Can you tell us how it's gone?'

Mark took a breath. 'It's worked brilliantly – the original engine was beyond saving, so that made her a perfect candidate to have an electric motor. She's tuned to match her original performance – but she can achieve considerably more!'

'So what *is* she like to drive?'

'She's a dream! But I still find it weird to race a car like this without the smell of petrol and oil, and in near silence.' He looked unsure of the reception of his frank, unscripted comment.

'Yeah, I guess that takes some getting used to.' The presenter's easy laugh made Mark's shoulders relax. 'Classic racing is all about the evocative roaring engines, nostalgic smells of oil and hydrocarbons. But all that will change if this move is successful, won't it, Nell?'

Nell swallowed and smiled into the camera lens. 'The Classics at Finchmere is such a well-loved event, and I still can't believe that people bring their irreplaceable machines to drive them as intended. We host about eighty thousand enthusiasts every day of the event, to watch the spectacle. But we can't ignore its carbon footprint, or its contribution to climate change. So, what are our options? To stop the racing? Consign the cars to a garage to rot? Or give them a new lease of life? If we want to keep them and enjoy them, we need to make some changes. So I've created a special Zero Emissions class within our most prestigious race – the Finchmere Cup, which hosts the most valuable cars racing this weekend – so we can include our converted gullwing. My dream is that if she performs well, then we'll inspire others to follow suit. And soon, we won't just be hosting one or two converted cars in a special class, we'll have a whole race series of sustainable classics.'

'How will that work in practice this weekend, though? Won't she perform very differently to the motors she's racing against?'

'We'll make sure the race is fair by tuning her for parity with her contemporaries,' Mark said. 'Whoever wins the coveted Finchmere Cup will have done so fair and honourably!'

But his smile was tight, and Nell knew he was thinking the same as all of them: she *has* to get pole in today's qualifying lap, and then win her race tomorrow, or all this will be a total embarrassment. And the investments of Mark, Lucio and Maxine would come to nothing.

'But you had to convince the lucky owner to take the leap with a conversion. Signor Lucio Moretti, of Moretti's Classic Car Dealership, what made you agree?'

The camera panned to where Lucio stood, in front of the large black-and-white photos of the restoration that lined one garage wall. When the gullwing wasn't on the track or being tuned, she'd be here as a showcase, for advertising and business inquiries for Lucio and Mark, and hopefully a hub of interested future racing teams with questions for Nell.

Lucio, impeccable in three-piece suit, narrow, shining shoes, and with suspiciously black Brylcreemed hair, beamed, making his tanned, grey-goateed face crease with deep lines. Raising his hands, he announced, 'But this poor darling was neglected, forgotten, for years! See?'

He gestured at the photos showing the neglected classic, minus wheels, on a piled-up wooden platform, her paintwork dull, dusty, patched with rust. Nettles growing from the shed's dirt floor smothered the car, while curling tendrils of ivy snaked through the smashed windscreen.

'It was a lucky day when Maxine discovered this magnificent

machine! Imagine – decades abandoned in a barn. No wonder her engine had seized up.' He gave a flourish of theatrical horror. 'Having to rebuild her from the ground up made her perfect for conversion, thanks to dear Nell – Lady Eleanor – having the idea!'

Nell winced at being named the instigator. Lucio had stumped up millions for the car, and put his and Maxine's reputation on the line. Mark had pivoted his whole business around a new venture of conversions at significant cost. Her part, to include it in the Finchmere Cup, was zero risk in comparison. And that made the weight of everyone else's input all the greater.

The camera panned from the barn-find photos of the rusty wreck to the sleek concours classic gleaming under the lights. She'd been stripped back to bare metal in a nod to Mercedes' racing tradition, and polished to a dazzling shine.

'I must thank the team who brought her to life, Mark Reynolds and Cassie Sullivan,' Lucio announced.

Cassie, standing beside the car like a guardian, shuffled and stared at her feet.

'Now, it is in the hands of Jack Rafferty, who'll be racing her this weekend, following in the footsteps of his father, racing legend and my dear friend, Colin Rafferty. But I must warn our competition: watch out! You won't even hear us coming!'

But Lucio's next sentence was cut off by a very audible, throbbing V8 engine, rumbling through the crowd outside the garage, then shuddering to a halt.

'Cut,' the producer called. 'Great job, everyone. We can use that.'

But the team didn't relax. In fact, Maxine and Mark tangibly tensed. From where she stood, Nell squinted through the open, barn-style door of the garage.

Jack was stepping out of the classic Mustang that had interrupted filming. Despite being late, and having missed the run-through entirely, he didn't hurry in. Instead, he worked the crowd. Irritation flared in Nell as she watched him sign autographs. Rather than looking at what he was writing, he scouted the crowd for the first pretty young woman to pose for pictures with, before winking at the next in line. Press photographers snapped constantly as he bestowed cheeky kisses and joked. At least he was race-ready in his driving suit. Just as well, because he *really* couldn't be late for his qualifying lap.

Nell overheard Mark murmur to Maxine, 'Well, our *star's* here at last. Shame he's not as interested in performing behind the wheel as he is in front of the camera.' Curious, Nell moved to the doorway for a closer look.

At a request for a photo, Jack was folding his arms, leaning against his white 1965 Shelby Mustang GT350, with metallic-blue racing stripes. Beside the daintier exotica on display, the solidly rectangular car stood out as a distinctive example of iconic, rare American muscle.

As if she'd been waiting to claim the focus of the crowd, a tall, lean woman unfolded herself from the Mustang's passenger seat, grey, strappy heels and spray-on snakeskin jeans adding to her loftiness. Though she affected surprise at the press presence, the woman's copy of *Vogue* under one arm was positioned so that her face on the cover was visible. Nell bit back a smile. *Definitely deliberate.* A photographer called out, 'Over here, Svetlana! Give us a smile. How's married life with Jack?'

Svetlana coolly pushed her Chanel shades into her platinum quiff – shaved at the sides, giving the illusion of more unnecessary inches – and struck a few effortless poses. With the attention of the press on her, Jack dashed to her, slipped an arm around her waist and grinned broadly for the cameras. Towering over Jack, Svetlana barely acknowledged him as he shoved on a pair of Aviator shades. Nell wondered if Jack was trying to hide his disappointment at the obvious lack of honeymoon bliss from his new wife.

A small toddler stumbled towards the car, arms outstretched, singing, 'Beep beep! Beep beep!' His mother made a swoop for the little boy but, with a pushchair to juggle, missed. Leaving the buggy and running towards the Mustang, she managed to grab one of her son's arms, just as Svetlana placed her magazine on the roof of the car and crouched beside him. Wriggling free, the boy held up sticky fists near Svetlana's silk D&G shell top, repeating, 'Beep beep!'

'I'm sorry.' His mother grabbed the sticky hands, wiping them on a tissue produced seemingly out of thin air. 'This week's fixation is car horns.'

'Ah! You want to beep beep the car horn, little *milashka*?' Svetlana's tone was as warm as her smile and the boy turned adoring eyes towards her, as she nodded at his mother. Swinging him up, triceps rippling as the boy giggled, Svetlana sat him in the driving seat and turned the ignition one click. She pointed at the centre of the steering wheel, then laughed when he beeped with enthusiasm, bouncing on the seat.

Nell winced at the racket as around her the sound team hastily adjusted their kit. After a few moments, the little boy looked around and reached for his mother, and Svetlana plucked him from the seat and held him sideways, like a rocket, calling out, 'Whoosh!' as she swooped him back to his family. Her smile faded as she waved goodbye, grabbed the magazine from the car's roof and stalked to the garage and the waiting team.

Catching Maxine's eye, Svetlana held up the copy of *Vogue* then walked past the workbench – tools neatly hung up along the far wall – to the corner office: a small but private room with a large window. Leaving the magazine on the desk, she turned and slinked out of the garage, heading towards the VIP area. Maxine had started to follow when Jack appeared, an obnoxious, cheeky grin on his face, his arms outstretched to the team like he anticipated an adoring welcome.

'Here I am! Control yourselves, ladies! Are we ready to get this show *on the road*?' He singled out the pretty young presenter and removed his shades so she could see his eyes roving up and down her body. 'How do you want me, sweetheart?' He smiled suggestively.

'On time would be nice, mate,' the cameraman muttered.

'On the taped mark over there.' The presenter deftly blocked Jack from leaning in to kiss her by pointing. 'We're a little short on time, so let's get going.'

Jack stood in position and shot his trademark cheeky grin at the lens. The presenter waited for the countdown, then smiled.

'Jack Rafferty, what an honour to interview someone with a racing heritage such as yours. How did you come to be involved in this special project?'

Jack's smile faltered. 'As you know, the old man's a racer and a good friend of Lucio's. But Dad's now retired, so I'm honoured to drive in his stead.'

'Of course, Colin's a veteran champion, two-time winner of the twenty-four-hour race at Le Mans. That's some reputation to live up to. And how have you found the car?'

'Oh, she's a terrific ride.' Jack's smile flickered again.

Moving back an inch, the presenter forced a smile. 'Fantastic! So, what can we expect from the qualifier and races this weekend?' she continued valiantly, despite Jack's proclivity for innuendo.

Maxine stepped in. 'We're looking forward to today's qualifying lap giving us a good position for tomorrow's race, when we've got our eyes on the prize!' She slung her arm around Jack's shoulders and squeezed, as his eyes widened in surprise at her strong grip.

The presenter nodded at Maxine, relieved and ready to wrap up. 'Well, tomorrow will tell us how one exceptionally lucky barn find, given a brand-new lease of life, can perform!'

Jack gave a cynical smile, about to say something, but Maxine cut in.

'*Exactly*. People have come to this event to enjoy a nostalgic trip to the past. But *we're* here to give our racing heritage a *future*. And Jack'll do his dad's name – and our team – proud.'

Chapter 3

Thursday 18th April – 3 p.m.

'This is *incredible!*' Rav yelled in Nell's ear, as the cars roared past them. In the VIP stand, with its coveted view of the final chicane, home straight and finish line, he took advantage of Nell's dad looking the other way to trail two brief, soft kisses on her neck. Nell shot him the smile that stopped time: half cute, half pure wickedness, the amber flecks in her brown eyes glinting. Resisting another kiss, he asked, 'How did the interview go?'

'Better than expected. But it's still pretty fraught.' She looked worried and he took her hand, pleased to feel her relax a little.

Between the stands and in the fields surrounding the circuit, the grounds were heaving with the keener spectators who attended qualifying day. They browsed stalls of racing memorabilia, enjoyed the old-fashioned funfair, and bought food from the vans themed in keeping with the celebration of the track's history: from pre-war record-setting twenty-four-hour races, to being requisitioned as an airfield during WWI and WWII, and through its heyday of racing, up to the end of the 1960s. One Airstream van, styled as a Fifties diner, blasted rock 'n' roll music as Teddy boys and full-skirted women jived, colourful petticoats swirling. He couldn't believe the effort almost every attendee had gone to, to dress the part: military uniforms, tweed suits, dresses with matching gloves, hats and heels. It felt like he was in an episode of *Poirot*.

Nell looked stunning, even though she'd opted for practicality in cropped black trousers and sweater, with red lipstick – and ballet flats. But he'd seen how hectic her day was: constantly being radioed to 'just pop over' to somewhere on the other side of the sixty-acre site. The organising team had a fleet of vintage Land Rovers, and always left the key on the front tyre so any of the team could grab the nearest one to help them on their way. Even so, he'd barely seen her.

Out of the corner of his eye, Rav had noticed Shannon Lanner sit up a little straighter at Nell's arrival. As the cousin of Percy – Nell's best friend – she, Nell and Percy had grown up together. But with Shannon considering herself cheated out of the title and castle that Percy would inherit, their relationship had always been competitive. Rav had only met Shannon a few weeks ago, at Percy's ill-fated wedding, which Nell had organised. But already he knew that Shannon was pure trouble. Well, *impure* trouble, actually. Which *also* meant that Rav was slightly indebted to her: Shannon's seduction of DI James Clark, Nell's then boyfriend, had accelerated Nell and James's break-up, and Rav would always be grateful to her for that.

Now, Shannon sat at the back of the VIP area, socialising with a collection of men who Nell's dad, Lord Hugo Ward-Beaumont, had introduced to Rav as the assembled owners of various Ferraris and Astons being raced on the track. As Shannon clinked glasses of Finchmere sparkling wine, chatted and laughed, she made sure she was captured in several photos.

'Here we go!' Beside him, Hugo peered through his binoculars as the announcer crackled over the loudspeaker like a vintage record.

'The qualifier for the popular Finchmere Cup has a twist. Moretti's team make their debut in a brand-new Zero Emissions class, with an electric conversion – created by our own Lady Eleanor Ward-Beaumont, who happens to be an ecologist . . .'

'Your gullwing's just coming up to the starting line, Nell,' Hugo commentated.

Even though she couldn't see without binoculars, Nell leaned forward. Her and Hugo's anticipation was contagious, and Rav felt himself tense.

'Jack's picking up speed,' Hugo said. 'A Ferrari 250 GT's doing well. Oh, the Ferrari's pulling ahead – he must be going for his qualifying lap next.' A tense few moments passed when the cars were out of sight for a section of the lap. As the cars came into view, Hugo confirmed, 'Yes, the Ferrari's going for it – he is *flying*. Hang on. Looks like Jack's also making a move for his flying lap. He's only one lap in.'

'What? He's got an hour out there. The tyres won't be warmed up yet. What's he doing?' Nell gripped the railing, craning her neck to watch where the gullwing would appear. 'We need to get our best time. And he's never going to get it this fresh out of the pits.'

The Ferrari thundered past their stand, then Jack sped around the corner towards the start–finish line where the timers for both cars would start.

'It's poor etiquette from Jack, it really is,' Hugo admonished. 'He's giving the Ferrari no room for his timed lap. And making his own much harder.'

Rav could tell Nell's heart was sinking. This wasn't the glorious show she and the team needed. And one thing he did know after his educational morning with Hugo: the racing code was strictly honourable. Jack's disregard for track courtesy would ruffle feathers.

'OK, they're over the line. Timer's started.' Hugo watched progress. 'Jack's pushing the car hard; he's right on the Ferrari's tail. And now we've got an Aston DB4 GT Zagato coming out from the pit. He's keeping the inside line so the others can overtake him. Ferrari's slicing a tight line around the Aston, keeping as close as he can to the bend.'

The Ferrari overtaking the Aston swooped into Rav's view as both cars rounded the corner.

'Oh, the Ferrari's holding the line very nice—' Hugo stopped abruptly. 'What the—?'

Rav squinted, seeing Jack turn tightly into the bend inside the Aston's line. With the Ferrari tight on its other side, the Aston had nowhere to go. Nell and Rav sprang to their feet, Rav's heart throbbing, waiting for the crash.

A split second before imminent collision, the Aston braked hard. It skidded to a halt, tyres squealing, just as Jack sliced into the Aston's place and accelerated alongside the Ferrari.

Hugo leapt to his feet. 'Bloody hell, that was *close*. Jack charged right for the Aston!'

The smell of vaporised oil filled the air as the Ferrari roared around the chicane, only inches ahead of the gullwing, both keeping a tight racing line through the bends. Jack tried again to force his way inside the Ferrari's line but, unlike the Aston, the Ferrari refused to give way. Jack tried a second time, but the Ferrari held firm, hugging the apex.

Jack oversteered, forcing his way into the inside line. Then it happened. He clipped the Ferrari's rear wing, sending her weaving as the driver struggled to regain control. But the gullwing went spinning across the track, ripping across the grass and shunting into a hay bale.

Nell gasped. Behind them, the Ferrari and Aston owners erupted in outrage.

The Ferrari sped across the finish line as the marshal stopped his clock. But the owner didn't cheer: his car's time – and racing position – ruined due to Jack's lack of sportsmanship.

Jack leapt out of the car, examined the flat tyre, kicked the wing and then hopped, holding his hurt foot. A safety car approached and Jack gesticulated, more in anger than directing the car where to stop, and got in.

'Well, that was certainly a performance, but not the one you hoped for. The team won't be happy.' Hugo's lips set in a line. 'I'd expect a complaint from those drivers and, possibly, disqualification.'

'Oh, bad luck.' The velvet insult and her amber scent told Rav that Shannon had disentangled herself from the knot of Ferrari and Aston owners at the back of the stand.

'Yes.' Nell stood to face her. 'It's a real disappointment.'

Shannon, in a crisp white Sixties mini-mini-dress and knee-high boots, huge shades and wide-brimmed hat, raised her glass. 'But here's to *trying*, darling.'

Nell glanced at Rav. He resisted the urge to look at his watch but Nell grimaced, realising. 'We have to go, don't we? Bye, Dad, hope tonight's dinner goes well.'

'Bye, dear. Have fun with Rav's family. We're looking forward to meeting them this weekend, so please send our regards.'

'Bloody Shannon,' Nell muttered as she hurried down the stand's steps. 'She's never come to the Classics before. Ever. So she would be here to see that, wouldn't she.'

Keeping up, ignoring the twinge in his recently fractured foot from when he fished Nell out of the Nye River, Rav waited for Nell's inevitable question. She asked it before they'd reached the bottom of the stairs.

'Have we got time to go and see the team first?'

They didn't, but he nodded. If Nell didn't check how they were, she'd worry all afternoon. And he wanted her to be relaxed enough to make a good first impression. His mother, who still avidly matchmade him with an apparently unending supply of suitable daughters of her friends, was already set against the idea of Nell, after reading about those unfortunate deaths – well, *murders* – at Finchmere House last month. He knew his mother would be in denial about Nell as a match. That was why he'd decided to just bring her along to today's family barbecue: his parents would be cordial in front of company, giving Nell a chance to charm them. Except . . . *Today, with all this stress, would have to be the day, wouldn't it . . . ?*

Nell felt a pang of mechanical sympathy at the sight of the crumpled gullwing as she parked the Landy near the Moretti team's garage. The tow truck drove off, having deposited the Mercedes in its bay, revealing Lucio's immaculate Ferrari Dino and an incongruous balloon-white Lamborghini Gallardo that Nell assumed was Maxine's.

She and Rav jumped out and Nell studied the gullwing's damage. The front wing had collapsed into a mangled mess above the shredded flat tyre. An ugly travesty on the elegant machine.

Nell had coveted the gullwing ever since its arrival at Moretti's dealership. She and Hugo often visited the local showroom to admire Lucio's latest exotic stock, and spend an imaginary million. On their fortieth wedding anniversary, Nell's parents had spent a real million, on a dainty Miura to tour the Amalfi coast in, in style – but it was still small-fry to Lucio. Only last month, he'd shown Nell a rare Ferrari 250 GTO being sold discreetly (for, he confided indiscreetly, £36 million). Nell had lusted over the Ferrari and its lovingly prepared record of provenance, sworn to secrecy by Lucio, his finger over his lips like an excitable child delighted with his luck.

But to Nell, the gullwing was still the ultimate classic. That she was being driven by someone who couldn't give a damn really stung. And it wouldn't be Jack spending all evening trying to repair the damage by tomorrow: Mark and Cassie would change the tyre and work out the dent, but it would take time, skill and care.

Raised voices made her look round. Inside the garage doorway, Jack ranted at Mark. 'You think you're God's gift and you can do everything. But you're just the grease monkey—'

'Engineer and second driver, actually,' Mark corrected.

'Yeah, right! You might have got lucky on a few test tracks. For all I know, you adjusted the . . . the . . . *performance* somehow so your times would be better . . .'

'Accusing me of cheating, are you?' Mark's voice rose to a yell. 'That's rich, coming from you! That may be your standard MO but we're not all as low as you are!' He hefted the wrench in his hand, his body tense as he took a step towards Jack.

Jack moved back. 'You shouldn't believe everything you read in the papers, mate . . .'

'I'm not your bloody mate!' Mark went to shove Jack's shoulder with his free hand.

Jack dodged, then swaggered towards Mark. 'Fine. But I know this track. *I'm* the star—'

'We don't *need* a star! We *need* a decent driver! Who can show the car off to her best advantage!' Mark swung the arm holding the wrench out towards the gullwing. 'She's a dream! Look what you've done to her, you bleeding moron!' He flung the wrench across the garage. It clattered, with the bright song of metal, into the corner.

By the door, Nell involuntarily stepped back at Mark's unexpected anger.

'Let's get this straight, *mate.*' Jack stepped closer, braver now the wrench was out of the equation. 'This team wouldn't get media coverage without me. Where would you be then, eh? With your investment and your precious—' he simpered '—electrical conversion car company.'

'You're really something, you know that?' Mark raged. 'All you have to do is drive her! She couldn't handle any better! I've given you a thoroughbred horse, yet you give us results as if you're sat on a donkey! Going backwards! How are you going to come back from this? She needs to shine tomorrow, mate. We need that. *All* of us.'

Nell shrank back, hoping to escape unseen. It wouldn't help the team if they knew she'd witnessed this. But Rav was slower to hide and Jack spotted him and stormed over.

'Are you a bloody journo?' he yelled. 'Smelled blood and now you're going for the jugular, are you? I've done all my interviews for the day. You can sod off.'

Rav held his hands up. 'I'm sorry, Mr Rafferty. I'm not press.'

'Yeah. That's what all you lot say until you open the papers and there you are with your private life spewing out of the pages,' Jack retorted. 'Sod off.' He glared at Rav, but when Nell moved beside him, Jack frowned. 'Have you got a photographer sneaking ar—'

'No, Jack.' Nell stepped into his view. 'There's no press or photographers here now. We just wanted to see how you all were. You must be disappointed with that qualifier.'

Behind Jack, Mark rubbed his face and walked over. 'We'll make the repairs. She'll be good as new tomorrow. And the race will go well. Won't it, Jack?'

Before Jack could answer, Cassie pulled up beside them in a vintage truck and leaned out of the window. 'I got one!' she yelled as the truck's engine silenced. She jumped out, walked to the back and hauled the unwieldy tyre off the flatbed.

'Let me help . . .' Mark sprang forward.

'I've got it.' Cassie walked briskly, not seeming to notice the weight. 'I'm used to you two sloping off or fighting. Lucky I'm here, or she'd never be fit to drive.'

As Jack stormed off, and Mark followed Cassie to work on the gullwing, Nell heard mutterings from the office at the far side of the garage, and realised Lucio and Maxine must be in there. Grabbing Rav's hand, she dragged him round the side of the garage, to listen under the window.

Maxine's gravelly voice hissed, 'But Mark knows the car better—'

'*Sì*, but Jack knows this track better.'

'Pfft, you'd not know it from the way he can't keep on it.'

'*And* he is our public figure. We need the press coverage. Mark may be skilful – but, an engineer, I'm sorry to say, will attract less attention than our racing rogue with his model wife.'

Maxine groaned. 'I know today's performance will ensure there's an audience tomorrow. But it's too much of a gamble to let Jack race. He's got no discipline, that lad. Even in interviews he can't help himself. He's only lasted this long because I always clean up his mess. Speaking of which, I need to check what he said in that interview he did with Svetlana, in *Vogue*. Some newly-weds' fluff piece, but I'll have to fine-tooth-comb it to make sure he hasn't dumped us right in it.'

'And this is why you excel as a team manager.' Lucio's tone was dangerously placating. 'I know you've had to break up more than one argument between Mark and Jack.'

'Don't try to butter me up. We haven't got pole position on the starting grid for the race tomorrow; the Aston and Ferrari owners have formally complained; we might even be disqualified. Replacing Jack may be our only chance to compete. Be honest, if *you* weren't mates with Colin, *we* wouldn't be saddled with Jack.'

Nell was surprised to hear Lucio's voice harden. 'I have hired you to do a job. And you are paid handsomely because it isn't an easy one.'

Her heart sank as Maxine hissed to Lucio the truth the whole team were horribly aware of: 'I can't perform miracles, Lucio. If we don't get our best racer in the driving seat, it's over.'

Chapter 4

Breaking the surface, Nell gulped for air, but choked, swallowed more sludgy pond water and sank under again. Shock, panic, and her body's memory of being unconscious and surging along the Nye River made her thrash. A firm hand grabbed her, pulled her upwards. Just like Rav had when he'd risked his life to dive in and drag her out, fighting the roiling current for both of them.

As her body was dragged out of the water, Nell shuddered with sobs, shaking with relived trauma, but thankful to be slithering on solid-ish ground. She spluttered, gasping for breath, until strong hands gripped her shoulders, flinging her sideways so that she didn't choke. Lurching up to her hands and knees, which sank heavily into stinking mud, she retched up puddles of brown water, then wheezed for air.

Her shoulders sagged and rose with every agonising, burning breath, and she collapsed on the mud, crying.

'It's OK.' The voice bubbled from a distance. 'You're OK.' Smart shoes, not Mai's waders, swirled into view as the person crouched beside her, mud caking their suit trousers. A sea-fresh waft of cologne stirred her olfactory memory. Vision blotching, she focused. Mai's worried face hovered over the person's shoulder.

'It's OK, Nell,' Mai said. 'This is DI James Clark.'

Nell groaned, and heaved again, as her ex-boyfriend rubbed her back.

Seconds felt like years as she fought to calm her breathing until she could gasp, 'He's in there. But he's definitely dead.'

'The driver?' James clarified. 'Anyone else?'

'I couldn't see anyone else. But it's too turbid to tell for sure.'

'OK, we've got a team coming. And we should get you to hospital.' His piercing blue eyes were full of concern.

Nell shook her head. 'I can't. I'm way too busy.' Stricken, she gazed towards the pond, remembering her full itinerary.

But Jack was dead. She hadn't liked him, but she hadn't wished him any harm. And this would blow up everything this weekend. The team probably wouldn't race now. Nell squashed the selfish wave of regret for the wasted time, and care, and investment.

How can I worry about that, when someone's dead?

She glanced at Mai, who looked frantic. Nell knew that while Mai would be feeling similarly shell-shocked, as someone with no connection to Jack, she'd also be devastated that the old classic car leaking into her pond was polluting the whole ecosystem – jeopardising her chances to get this place designated as an SSSI – and putting her job on the line, too.

'Thanks, James.' Nell pulled herself up to standing, her feet sinking into cold mud. 'How did you get here so quickly?' Noting his old-fashioned collar and tie, her heart sank.

Don't say it.

'I'm off duty today. I was on the way to your Classics at Finchmere. Just happened to be a road away when the call came in. I heard your name . . .'

Mai looked baffled at their familiarity, and Nell forced herself to explain. 'James is my ex.'

'Oh?' To Mai, that clearly presented more questions than answers.

Nell tried again. 'We got together after he arrested me for murder when I was only doing a bat survey.'

James huffed a sigh, while Mai's eyes shifted between them like she was watching a tennis match.

'Huh,' Mai said. 'Yeah, easy mistake to make.' Then she frowned at Nell. 'What did he mean, *your* Classics at Finchmere? Do you help with the carbon offsetting, or something?'

'Lady Eleanor Ward-Beaumont of Finchmere House, here, runs it,' James sparred back.

Nell rolled her eyes. 'My family run it, and I'm trying to make changes to reduce its carbon footprint.'

Mai gaped, then stared at the – unmistakably classic – car in her pond. She looked like she wanted to say something but clamped her lips with a slight shake of her head and turned away.

Feeling responsible, both for the event that had brought Jack and his crashed car here, and for the disastrous consequences for Mai, Nell reached out and touched Mai's arm. 'I'm beyond sorry for all this, Mai. I'll do anything you need to restore it. I promise. I can do any of the surveys to check progress—'

'Yeah, but you can't do *any* of them in time for the assessment, can you?' Mai gulped back a sob. 'I'm sorry someone's died, but . . . You have no idea how hard I've worked for this.'

Nell ached to hug her. 'Don't worry about your job; I'll cover any costs, OK? And help the Trust's budgets. It'll be OK.'

Mai folded her arms, holding in any reply.

Guilt burned, and Nell was relieved to see the familiar sight of DS Ashley Hollis arrive, wearing the white overalls of the scenes of crime officers. Two of the SOCOs stopped to investigate the fence, taking samples, measuring what tyre marks they could make out and taking photos, while four more followed Ashley towards the pond, along with two people in dive suits.

James intercepted Ashley halfway across the field. Nell knew Ashley's youthful appearance – with her afro caught up in a high bun under the suit's hood – was misleading. Her bright hazel eyes missed nothing: not the slithering gouges in the bank caused by Nell's rescue, obscuring valuable forensic data, nor the muddied state of Nell – and James.

One SOCO began photographing the bank, while a second methodically measured and recorded the flayed vegetation. The third studied the mess they'd made in the mud, while the fourth headed over, waiting patiently to talk to Nell. Across the field, the ambulance and fire engine arrived, keeping out of the way until the team had finished.

With James's permission to proceed, the divers made a rapid assessment, turned on their powerful torches, put their masks on and slipped silently into the pond. Nell shuddered.

Ashley turned to her. 'Dr Ward. We must stop meeting like this.'

Her tone was friendly, and Nell gave a relieved smile. 'DS Ashley Hollis, this is Mai Leen Lim. She manages Little Smitington.'

'Nice to meet you, Mai. I'm Ashley.' She turned back to Nell. 'You must have had a shock. I'll get a paramedic to give you the once-over. And get you checked properly at the hospital.'

Nell shook her head. 'No need. Really.'

Ashley looked offended at her advice being rejected. 'Up to you. I'm guessing your tetanus jab's up to date, since you're an ecologist? And you know about Weil's disease?'

Nell nodded. Most ecologists carried a card to say they were at risk of the severe form of leptospirosis from regularly working in waterbodies that might have been urinated in by various animals. Such was the glamour of an ecologist's life. 'Yes, I'll watch out for any symptoms. And I'm sorry for trampling your scene. I had to see if anyone was trapped in there and needed help.'

'Yeah, I'd've done the same, if I'm honest. And it looks like an RTA. The team at the road say the tyre marks indicate the driver lost control at the corner.'

'No, well, he's not the most careful driver. Even though – technically – he's a professional.'

Ashley froze and stared at Nell. 'You know who this is?'

Nell nodded. 'It's Jack Rafferty. Racing driver. Had a bad day on the track yesterday, so probably wasn't in the best of moods.'

'Yesterday? When was that?'

'About 3.30 p.m.'

'What happened on the track?'

As Nell relayed the events of the previous afternoon, Mai's eyes widened. Nell concluded the account: 'He needn't have crashed out on the track, but he couldn't control even a minor skid.'

When the divers surfaced, and Ashley excused herself to hear their summary, Nell expected questions from Mai. But she was just as keen to listen to the divers' account as Nell was.

'Only one person in the car as far as we can see. Definite fatality. No clear view of the footwells because turbidity is high. But no signs of life. That's all we can do for now.'

The patiently waiting SOCO cleared his throat, interrupting their eavesdropping, and asked Nell and Mai if he could measure and photograph the soles of their waders.

Mai immediately sat on the grass with her feet in the air. The bemused officer took pictures and measurements.

'Um. Mine are still in the pond.' Nell pointed, but then saw that the divers had fished them out.

'Great.' The SOCO went to claim them.

James walked over. 'Nell, can you wait here until we're finished processing the scene and come back to the station to give a statement?'

Nell tried not to groan. 'Can I give it to you here? Now?'

James grimaced. 'Well . . .' He paused. 'We'll have to speak to Jack's team. When do they get to the track?'

Nell gave a long exhalation as she thought. 'Most of them aren't local, so they're staying at Finchmere Hotel. If I call my father, he could gather everyone together and break the news, if that helps? We could put a private room aside for statements, if that's what you're thinking.'

'You read my mind.' He shot her his charismatic, knowing smile, reminding her why they'd dated.

'Good. I'll call and get something arranged.' She automatically patted her pockets for her phone, then felt a swell of dismay, staring at the pond.

Mai nudged her. 'You put it in the bucket.'

Glancing around, Nell realised it was still where she'd dropped it, in the field.

'I'll get it.' Mai hurried to retrieve it.

Making the call, Nell paced the grassy bank, out of the way of the investigators. 'Hi, Dad? I've got some bad news . . .'

After his initial shock as she described what had happened and asked if he could find a suitable room for the police to use, Nell was calmed by her father's pragmatic question about her timetable. 'Er . . . yes, I have loads of meetings today . . .' Nell went through her schedule.

'Then I'll set a room aside for the police and I'll postpone your meetings until after the detectives have been. We may cancel some races out of respect. I'll see what the team thinks. I doubt anything will happen until late afternoon. So don't rush. Help with whatever's needed.'

What will the team do? Cancel? Or would Mark race? And hold a minute's silence?

Hanging up, she watched the industry around the pond. Markers were positioned near the waterline at tyre marks, and at the footprints that Mai and Nell had left. Casts were being taken. Arrows had been spray-painted on the bare soil. Containers of pond water samples were lined up on the bank. Samples of broken vegetation were being bagged up.

James stood beside her. 'You know, our investigations teach us that there's no such thing as a coincidence. I've always felt suspicious of Miss Marple, turning up at every murder, with a plausible reason to pin it on someone else. Now I'm wondering about you.'

Nell shrugged at his deadpan smile. 'You had your chance when you arrested me last year, James.'

'Yeah. But you keep coming back, don't you?' He held her gaze.

'Don't flatter yourself.' Nell shoved him.

'Hey, you've already done enough damage today. Look at my best suit.'

'My heart's bleeding. You'll dine out on that hero story for months.' Her eyes narrowed. 'Is it a coincidence that Shannon asked me for two VIP tickets for the whole weekend?' Naming the woman James had slept with when he'd mistakenly thought Nell was cheating on him – with Rav – made the tips of his ears turn red. Gratified, Nell said, 'Oh, James. You are biting off more than you can chew there!'

'You don't really know her, Nell. You only know what she chooses to show the world. It's not who she really is.'

'Pfft. I've known her all my life; you've met her once or twice. You've no idea what you're up against. Believe me. That woman is a praying mantis in Prada.'

'Maybe that's the fun.' James attempted to shrug. But his smile was irrepressible.

Nell gaped. 'Oh, my God. You're smitten. You're in real trouble, James.'

Mai joined them, in a morose mood, pointing at the firefighters walking across the field. Within a few minutes, a winch from the fire engine was attached to the Mustang's bumper. Nell put an arm around Mai as the Mustang was hauled from the suctioning, silty depths.

The boot and rear wheels gradually emerged, the car creaking inch by inch out of the water. The heavy chain and winch clanked dully over the sound of tearing shoots as plants were uprooted and ripped from the soil by the Mustang's tyres gouging the soft bank. Brown water gushed out from the back edge of the door and the floorpan.

The body in the driver's seat on the far side of the car lurched forward and back, smashing against the window and dashboard, the movement disturbingly clumsy. Lifeless. Mai turned away.

James took Nell over to formally identify the body. She had to stare again at the bloated face; wide, shocked eyes; mud smeared across the cheeks; brown, silty water dribbling from Jack's slack mouth.

As she nodded in confirmation, something on the passenger side of the dashboard glinted in the sun. Recognition slithered. Stepping closer, Nell peered in.

Dread uncoiled in her chest as she recognised the earrings. They weren't just any earrings – these were specially commissioned one-offs, that Rav's little sister, Aanya, had designed for their older sister's wedding. She'd given one pair to Marla, who now lived in India, and had worn the only other matching pair to the wedding as something special to share with her sister. The earrings were elaborate, unmistakable – *unique*. And she'd only seen them yesterday.

Chapter 5

One Day Earlier: Thursday 18th April – 5 p.m.

When Nell and Rav had raced up the M25 to arrive at his parents' 1930s Richmond home – *almost* on time after Jack's outburst at the track had made them late – they'd approached the open door hearing a family argument beyond. Rav's parents were scolding his younger sister, Aanya, despite the gathering of extended relatives for the afternoon barbecue.

'You cannot go to work in that,' Rav's father, Rakesh, said. He was a plumper, older version of Rav, less hair but an extra chin, and much more serious.

'I can. It's fine.' With untouchable, Instagram-ready confidence, Aanya smoothed the short black bodycon dress encasing her curvaceous figure, and flicked back waist-length glossy black hair that shimmered like a mirror. She was startlingly beautiful, with heavily lined brown eyes under perfectly groomed brows.

Picking up her keys and her iPhone in its jewelled case, she started at the sight of Rav in the doorway. 'Oh, you made it, then? Sorry, can't stay. The last-minute hourly rate is too good to turn down. You know how it is.' She eyed Nell, thrusting out a hand. 'I'm Aanya. You must be Nell?'

The muttering between Rakesh and Rav's mother, Neeta, ceased and they craned their necks to see her. Nell felt her face flush at being under such scorchingly curious scrutiny. 'Nice to meet you.' She shook their hands, as they murmured polite greetings. But the sidelong looks they darted at Rav weren't as subtle as they thought. And he, bloody idiot, was beaming too much to notice how uncomfortable she seemed to be making his parents. Maybe they felt awkward at the introduction being mid-argument? If so, it didn't seem to interrupt their exchange with their daughter.

'Wait, Aanya.' Neeta, elegant in a burgundy dress and hair in a sleek bun, held up her hand in a graceful but firm gesture. '*Where* are you working tonight?'

'At an event out at Nye Valley.'

'Oh, nice, that's near me, at Cookingdean.' Nell tried to ingratiate herself in the conversation.

'Oh, yes.' Neeta turned a cool glance to Nell. 'Near where all those murders happened. With those rich people – with all their privileges making them corrupt and lacking morals?' Turning back to Aanya, she waved an elegant finger. 'I don't think so, *Beta*. These entitled people are not nice to mix with. Phone and cancel.'

Nell felt taken aback. The intermittent headache that still throbbed whenever she was tired or upset, since she'd sustained that head injury in the Nye River, began to pound behind her eyes. Rav didn't seem ruffled by his mum's casual insult to her.

'Oh, Mum. Don't overreact. Aanya's working with a team. And Nye's very fancy,' Rav said. 'It's all gated mansions up there. Celebrities and sportspeople. Whose event is it?'

'Jack Rafferty's. Legit celeb! Good tips.' Aanya flashed a dimpled grin at Rav.

Trying not to wince, Nell shot him a sidelong glance. Rav was protective of his younger sister, who was bound to register on Jack's radar. So, if he'd read about Jack's *love rat* reputation in the tabloids, it didn't show.

'How are you getting there? With the others?' Rakesh asked.

'No, the catering team are already there. I'm covering someone who didn't turn up. Their loss, eh? I'll get a train and an Uber.'

'When will you be home?' Rakesh asked.

Aanya shrugged. 'About one in the morning, probably. Depends.'

'Phone when you are at the station and Aravindan will walk you home,' Neeta volunteered.

Apparently unbothered by the time, Rav looked up at Aanya and nodded.

But Neeta frowned at her daughter. 'What are you doing, wearing Marla's wedding earrings, *Beta*! They're too precious to wear for work.'

'It's a glam event, Mum. *Trust* me!'

'And they're too heavy to wear all night. You'll take them out and lose them. Then how will you feel?'

'I won't lose them. Like you said, they're too precious. I'll be careful.'

Neeta tutted. 'And you've barely spoken to our guests and now you're leaving.'

Aanya sighed and beckoned Nell. 'I'll introduce you to the relatives while I say my goodbyes. It'll help me make a fast exit.' She glanced at Neeta. 'I *think* it's Rav's turn to be quizzed.'

As Nell followed Aanya out to the garden, her heart dropped. A group of young men, slightly older than Rav, wore bright shirts, their hair slicked back. *Rav's cousins.* He'd warned her they were competitive. It showed as they postured like preening peacocks. The women looked like bird-of-paradise flowers in tailored, jewel-toned outfits. Seriously glamorous. Her outfit might be described as chic by some, but in head-to-toe plain black, Nell felt dowdy. Seeing the team after the qualifying lap meant she hadn't had time to change, just spritz perfume and refresh her lipstick.

Checking her phone as they walked, Aanya barely glanced at Nell yet seemed to read her mind. 'You look all right.'

Nell wasn't sure if that was a compliment or an insult. But until she had reason to think otherwise, she decided to assume the former. 'Thanks.' Even so, Nell hadn't expected this. Rav had billed it as a casual barbecue with his folks. She knew she was already on the back foot with Neeta and Rakesh, after the murders reported in the papers – and their obvious response to that, which Rav had previously tried to warn her about. The fact that Rav had nearly drowned to rescue her didn't help, either. She'd wanted to make a good impression today. And she had a feeling she was already failing.

'He should have told our folks that he was bringing his girlfriend, though,' Aanya said.

Nell stared at her. 'I . . . I thought *they'd* invited *me*. To get to know me.'

Aanya laughed. 'Uh-oh. Well, not only is this a reunion of all the women Rav's turned down, who settled for a less interesting cousin, Mum's even invited another potential match.' She pointed at a gorgeous woman in magenta silk. 'Chaya's a corporate lawyer and a triathlete.'

Great.

'Obviously, she's Hindu, keen to start a family, understands the expectation for idolised Number One Son to have his parents live with him – and his own family – once Mum and Dad are older.' Aanya gave Nell a pointed look.

'Uh-huh.' No, she didn't know any of that. But she wasn't going to let it show. *Why hadn't Rav mentioned it?*

'With all the matches Rav's turned down over the years, I thought he was gay. I didn't think he was holding out for—' she managed to inject just enough of a question mark into her tone '—*you.*'

Before Nell could respond, Aanya called out to the group, 'Hey, everyone, this is Nell. Rav's girlfriend.'

Oh, perfect.

Nell's mouth went dry. Somehow, she answered avidly curious questions while Aanya said hurried goodbyes. On the pretext of getting a drink, Nell tailgated her back into the house.

'Social obligation fulfilled, Mum. And now I have to go or I'll be late.' The front door slammed and Aanya's footsteps crunched over the gravel.

Neeta shook her head. 'She is a stubborn one. Aravindan, you need to speak to her.'

Rav shrugged. 'She's working hard, Mum. Her studies are going well; she fits in a job. She just wants some freedom. All her uni friends live away from home. No curfew, no justification of what they're doing. You know, being adults. She just wants you to trust her. It's not that unreasonable.' Rav stole a pakora from the plate his mum was about to take outside and chewed it, grinning.

'We do trust her, Aravindan,' Rakesh said. 'We just don't trust everyone else.'

Chapter 6

Now, as she stared at Aanya's earrings on Jack's car's dashboard, Nell's phone beeped. She unlocked it without looking, her mind racing.

What the hell had Aanya been doing in Jack's car?

Glancing at her phone, she opened Rav's text:

> So sorry, not left yet. Aanya didn't come home last night. Never done this before. Everyone's panicking. She's not answering calls or messages. Please text when you get this.

Nell stared at Rav's text, then at the car, her stomach crawling with dread as an awful thought struck.

She grabbed James's arm, barrelling straight through his quiet discussion with Ashley as her words spilled out.

'Sorry, but . . . I think someone else could be in there. Aanya – Rav's sister. Those are her earrings on the dash and she didn't go home last night. Which isn't like her. Did the divers check all of the pond, in case she got out? Or check the rest of the car? The back seat? The footwells?'

James's face paled but he nodded. Ashley relayed the request to the divers, who slid back into the water, and a forensic officer, who ran straight to the car, water still leaking from its doors. He peered in through the windows as Nell, James and Ashley hurried over.

The officer turned and shook his head decisively at Ashley. 'There's still water in there but it's low enough to see the floor of the car. The windows and doors were shut so we can assume no one got out of the car, then drowned in the pond, and there's no one else in there.' Almost as an afterthought, he added, 'Unless they're in the boot.'

Nell blanched at his words, the suggestion conjuring an even worse scenario. 'Will you check. Please?'

With urgency, James reached into his pocket, took out his penknife and jimmied the boot's lock. After a few tries, it popped. He slid out the knife and the boot sprang open.

The four of them peered inside, each holding their breath.

A synchronised sigh exploded from them. The boot was empty.

'Why do you think she was in the car, Nell?' James asked.

Nell walked to the side of the car and pointed at the earrings. 'They're commissioned. Only Aanya and her sister Marla have a pair like it. And Marla's in India. Aanya was waitressing at a party Jack hosted at his house in Nye Valley last night. She's only eighteen.'

'And she never got home?' James clarified. 'Could she have stayed with a colleague? Or a friend?' They moved aside to let the white-suited pathologist get past as she pulled on latex gloves and opened the driver's door. James steered Nell up the bank, away from the medical examination, and they both stared at the occasional bubbles on the pond's surface.

'Apparently Aanya never stays out without letting her folks know,' Nell said. 'She lives with her parents. In Richmond. It's out of character for her to be away and she isn't answering her phone. They're a bit . . . protective. And they're panicking.'

Nell recalled Rakesh's words about trust. He and Neeta would be fearing the worst. She imagined Rav trying to keep the peace and do something constructive. Her heart lurched.

James's eyes narrowed at the word 'protective'. 'Could she be rebelling? Proving a point, perhaps?'

'Perhaps,' Nell said. 'But after seeing her earrings on the dash, I'm worried.'

The two divers surfaced at the other end of the pond. They both shook their heads. Nell's body sagged with her exhaled breath. But her relief was short-lived.

'Then . . . where is she?' She looked at James imploringly. 'I know it's early to start a search, but, under the circumstances, isn't searching sooner, rather than later, *better*?'

'You're thinking like that because you've just had a scare that she might have drowned or been abducted,' James said. 'If she's eighteen, it's far more likely she's got caught up with friends and just hasn't thought about her parents.' He checked his watch. 'It's only 7 a.m. If she *was* drinking with friends she probably isn't even awake yet. I'd suggest you and her family call everyone you can think of that she knows and keep at it until you get an answer.'

'Oh, come on, James! Would *your* parents know all your uni friends? Or even *any* of them? How can you expect them to have that contact information!' Nell shrugged impatiently. 'I expect Rav can try to find some through her social media. But even that's a long shot.' Nell folded her arms and pursed her lips as an idea struck her.

James groaned. 'I know that face. What? What are you going to get me to do now?'

'Aanya's very probably the last person who saw Jack alive, isn't she? Wouldn't she be able to shed some light on what happened here? To help wrap up your investigation?'

James nodded. 'I can't disagree with your logic.' He sighed. 'Fine. I'll go myself if you give me her home address. Email me a picture of Aanya and I'll get a search started.'

'Thank you.' Nell's relief avalanched over the adrenaline rolling in her stomach. She almost hugged him, but he strode over to Ashley to relay his plan.

Pulling out her phone, Nell relayed the update to Rav, asking for a picture of Aanya and his parents' address. Out of the corner of her eye, Nell spotted Ashley throw her hands up as James spoke to her. It looked like a disagreement. Nell frowned, but focused on Rav.

He texted the address and photos, but his voice was tight with worry. 'What the hell was Aanya doing with Jack? And how has he ended up dead?'

'The police think it was a road traffic accident. But finding Aanya will help shed some light. So they're as keen to find her as we are.'

'She's still not answering. And I don't know her friends' details to check with them.'

'Have you tried accessing her emails? Or looking at her social media?'

'No.' He groaned. 'I'm going to have to, aren't I? I can probably guess her passwords.' She heard him swallow. 'Feels so bloody horrible invading her privacy, especially when she fights so hard for it.'

'Yes, I know.' Nell squashed the same rising fear that was paralysing Rav. 'That's because you're a good brother. But let's just focus on finding her. Hopefully she can be mad at us for looking at her DMs soon enough.' In a gentler tone, she added, 'I love you.'

'I love you, too.'

They rang off and Nell texted Aanya's photo and address to James. Holding up his phone, he walked towards her. 'Got them, thanks. I've called in and Val's going to the hotel for statements now.'

'Thanks.' But Nell wasn't relieved at the update: if DCI Val Johnson was spurred into immediate action, then the detectives must be concerned.

'I'll head over to Aanya's parents with Hesha,' James continued, 'and Ashley's mobilising the search team, so she'll keep in touch with you.' He sent the details on as he spoke.

'Can I help?' Nell asked. 'Drive around and search?'

James shook his head. 'We'll have it covered. But if we haven't found her by this afternoon, we'll coordinate a wider search, and as many hands on deck from the local area as possible then will be very welcome. Just have your phone to hand and keep us posted with any updates.'

Nell glanced over at Mai. Her shoulders were slumped as she stared at the churned-up water, the ripped-up plants strewn haphazardly across the field, the bare mud smeared and rutted, graffitied with spray-paint markers. 'Now SOCO have finished, can we finish the pond work?' Nell asked.

'Sure. We've done all we can here.'

The fire engine had gone, and the Mustang was being loaded onto a recovery truck. A gurney with a black body bag on it was being steered across the grass to a waiting ambulance. As Nell watched it pass in silence, guilt squirmed. She'd spent all this time worrying more about the pond, about what would happen with the rest of the race team – and about Aanya . . .

As James and the team left, Nell answered Ashley's questions as best she could. But her worry only grew at how seriously the police were taking the search. They clearly thought Aanya could be in danger.

Chapter 7

Friday 19th April – 7.30 a.m.

Rav was losing the battle to keep his family calm.

'I will kill her when she gets home!' Rakesh paced the bay window like a caged lion, looking out at the street every few seconds. 'Bringing police to our door! Showing us up in front of the neighbours—'

'What is the *matter* with you?' Neeta's voice cracked with emotion. She jabbed Rakesh in the chest with her forefinger. 'After what I've been worrying about all night, those things are *nothing!* I've been imagining an accident . . . or worse. And you're worrying about what people *think?* You need to get your priorities straight!' She glared at Rakesh, simmering.

But Rakesh stabbed a finger at the morning paper on the coffee table. 'She's been off, getting herself involved with . . . with . . . *men* like *that!*'

The stark headline, '*Love Rat Rafferty Crashes Out*', sat above a picture of Jack at the Finchmere track, kicking the gullwing like a tantrumming toddler. Next to it was a picture of Jack kissing Svetlana, and an inset photo showed a smaller, grainy shot of him at a nightclub, in a clinch with a different woman.

'I'm sure she's not involved with him, Dad,' Rav said. 'He probably just gave her a lift to the nearest station. Let's not assume the worst, eh?'

'Tell your mother that! Look at how worried your sister has made her!'

Neeta had sagged onto the sofa, shivering. Sitting beside her, Rav passed her the cup of tea that had sat, untouched, on the coffee table, wrapping her icy hands around the warm mug.

'She always lets us know what she's doing, Aravindan.' Neeta's voice tremored. She stopped him as he leaned over to give her a hug. 'Keep trying. Please.' She nodded at Aanya's laptop.

Before Rav could resume his search of Aanya's social media, Rakesh's head snapped towards the window as a car pulled up. A man and a younger woman got out of the car and walked to the door, glancing up and down the street.

Neeta dashed across the room. 'There, see? An unmarked car, and they're not in uniform. And they will advise us what to do.' She stared at Rakesh until he bobbed his head in agreement.

At the knock on the door Neeta hurried to open it, ushering them in before they got their ID out. In the hall, James showed her his card and made introductions.

'Good morning. I'm DI James Clark; this is DC Hesha Patel.'

Hesha slipped her shoes off and nudged James, who immediately did the same, before following Neeta into the sitting room as she announced their names. 'This is my husband Rakesh and my son Aravindan.'

Rav looked up from the laptop. 'Hi, James.' *It would be James, wouldn't it.* They eyed each other like rival stags. When Nell and James had broken up last month, Nell had assured James that she hadn't cheated on him with Rav. But James had taken some convincing. And it hadn't helped that Rav couldn't claim that his thoughts had been as pure as his actions.

'Hi, Rav.'

Neeta gestured for everyone to sit down. Rakesh remained standing in the window, looking tense, his head snapping towards the street at the slightest sound.

'Right.' James leaned forward on the sofa and lightly clasped his hands in front of him. 'The first thing you should know is that it's early for us to start a search. Aanya's only eighteen. She may well be with friends and has just been unusually thoughtless . . . You know how teenagers are sometimes?' He paused. 'However, we may need to talk to your daughter in relation to our inquiries about Jack Rafferty's death—'

'What?' Rakesh gaped in horror. 'Are you saying she's somehow involved?'

James held up his hands. 'No. We aren't making any assumptions. Everyone's priority is to find Aanya and get her home safely. But her statement will help us. All I'm saying is, *that's* why we're starting the search this early, *not* because we have any specific concerns about Aanya herself.'

'*You* might not be concerned, but we are!' Neeta's eyes blazed. 'She never disappears without telling us. This is totally out of character. She's just a young girl . . .'

Hesha reached for Neeta's hand. 'We're covering all bases. Checking with hospitals, searching roads near Cookingdean, going door to door. But she's most probably with a friend.'

'I've contacted her manager,' Rav said. 'And I've got contact details of six friends from her social media. I've messaged them. When they wake up, I hope they'll reply.'

James nodded. 'Let's see what that yields over the next hour. And then next steps would be to increase the house-to-house, widen the search and begin a media campaign, radio, TV. It may not come to that, but if it does, we'll need your cooperation.'

Hesha shot a hopeful glance at Rav. 'Do you share locations with Aanya's phone?'

He shook his head. 'She has an iPhone but we don't share locations.'

'If she has an iCloud account and enabled "Find My Phone", we may be able to trace her,' Hesha said.

Rav passed his phone to his mum. 'Keep an eye out for texts.' As Neeta held Rav's mobile in cupped hands as if it were a sleeping scorpion, he angled the laptop towards Hesha. He followed the officer's directions, opening websites and logging in. 'I've been lucky guessing her passwords so far. First pet, last holiday, nickname and birthdays.'

Neeta jumped as Rav's phone vibrated into life. She handed it to Rav to open with face recognition, and he read the text.

Nah, didn't see A last nite. She borrowed my heels and I really need those back by Weds. Lol! She posted about Jack's party, but idk what else. Did they hook up?????? OMG!!!

He rolled his eyes at the string of aubergine emojis. *Nice.* As he shook his head at his parents, they visibly sagged.

Hesha nudged Rav's arm and he turned back. Having successfully logged in to 'Find My Phone,' a map jigsawed across the screen. The resolution sharpened. A hopeful blue dot blinked. He gasped.

'She's near Cookingdean!' Rav zoomed again, waiting while the streets filled in. 'Nye Valley! Jack's place or nearby?'

As Neeta and Rakesh froze, staring at each other, unsure if this was good news or bad, Hesha grabbed her mobile, walking out to the hall. A few seconds later, she returned. 'DS Ed Baker's almost there. He'll update us soon.'

As the expectant silence drew out, Neeta fidgeted, then stood. 'I'll make tea.'

When she came back, the beverages were ignored as the company waited.

Finally, Hesha's phone beeped. Reading the text, she frowned. 'Aanya's phone *is* at Jack's house. But *she* isn't.'

'What?' Rakesh barked as Neeta covered her face. 'What does that mean?'

'We'll check CCTV of the train stations on her route, increase house-to-house and start a campaign. Meanwhile, can you get back to her friends, Rav? And keep me posted.'

As the detectives left, Rav redialled the first number on his list. 'Millie? It's Rav. I left you a message earlier. Do you happen to know where Aanya is? Or someone who might?'

Noting the number she gave him, he rang off and dialled it. Another dead end but another number to try. Rav worked through the list, his hope dying with every unsuccessful attempt.

Slumping back in the sofa, he rubbed a hand over his face. His eyes felt as if they had been rolled around in grit. His head throbbed as he fought back dark thoughts.

No one had seen her, heard from her or knew where she was. *Where could she be? What if . . . ?*

Friday 19th April – 7.45 a.m.

Wondering how Rav was, and racking her brain for ideas of where Aanya could be, Nell kept her phone to hand as she helped Mai deal with the mess the pond had become. But the lack of messages, from anyone, was agony.

Trying to focus, she told herself to trust that the police were searching, and that Rav and his folks would be interviewed soon, so the only person she could be of use to at the moment was Mai.

Assessing the damage, Nell sniffed the air around the gouged bank. *No oil slicks, no discoloration in the water, no discernible fumes.*

'I can't smell any petrol or oil. That's something.' That would be a nightmare to fix. 'The only other liquids that I can think of that could leak from the car are brake fluid and coolant. We can check that using the water meters and compare the levels to your baseline data, thanks to your brilliant records!' She nudged Mai encouragingly.

Mai remained despondently unmoved.

'But our first priority is to release those poor newts before they boil in the bottle traps.'

'Oh, crap!' Mai sprang to her feet. 'Yes, of course.'

'We should exclude the newts from the pond while we remediate the water.' Nell picked up both buckets, filling them with leaves and grass and handing one to Mai. 'Let's go.'

Automatically, they started at the same point and worked their way around opposite sides of the bank. Traps were made from plastic litre bottles, the tops sliced off and inverted back into the bottle, making a funnel so newts could swim in, but not out. A bamboo cane pierced the bottle at an angle, so when the cane was speared into the pond bed, the bottle's neck pointed downwards, trapping an air bubble inside so the captured newts could breathe.

The first two traps yielded nothing. But, through the bulging lens of the next water-filled bottle, Nell saw the unmistakable orange belly and warty skin of a great crested newt – like a grumpy baby Godzilla. He glared at her, his elaborate frilled crest rippling down his speckled back, meeting his white-flashed tail, his feet splayed out like little stars. She transferred the newt into her bucket, drained the water from the bottle into the pond and chucked it, along with the cane, on the bank.

Finally, she met Mai at the other end, beside the scraped-bare bank. Walking back the way they'd come, they gathered up the traps.

'I got six. You?' Nell said.

'Three, and one smooth newt, also in the bucket.' Mai peeled back a leaf to show Nell the GCN's slinkier relative.

'Great.' Nell picked up the clipboard and recorded their findings. 'Anything else?'

Mai shook her head.

'Right, if you look up the averages for your water chemistry so far, I'll take readings.' Nell slipped the meters into the inside pouch of her waders and grabbed the clipboard. 'Do you take the readings at consistent locations?'

Mai nodded as she scrolled through her phone. 'Each mesohabitat, by macrophyte type.'

In trepidation, Nell pulled on her emptied but still soaked waders, feeling her nearly dry trousers cling wetly to legs that turned to jelly as she waded in. The water constricted the waders coldly around her damp calves as her feet sank deeply into the mud. Nausea roiled. But she forced herself to move carefully, methodically taking measurements.

Clambering out, Nell crawled up the bank, waves of relief crashing over her. Sitting beside Mai, she noted the averages Mai read out beside the numbers she'd just measured.

The dissolved oxygen near the site of the crash had plummeted. And that would kill everything in the pond. They'd have to act fast to reverse this – if they even could.

Sitting, Nell googled frantically. 'I've done a few pond remediations for clients. The last one made quite a good paper for *Nature*. I'm trying to recall the details. Here.' She showed her screen to Mai. 'The sudden drop in dissolved oxygen may be caused by glycol. From coolant or brake fluid, perhaps.'

Mai chewed her lip. 'It's happened so *fast*, though, hasn't it?'

Scanning the data, Nell searched for explanations. 'Yes, look, probably because your nitrogen and phosphorus levels are low. If those were higher, they'd maybe break this amount of glycol down in, what, a week or so?'

'That's way too long to save everything.' Mai shook her head miserably. 'And even if it works, the raised nitrogen and phosphorus will change the chemistry and kill the rare species.'

Nell tried to logic it through. 'If we *can* break down the glycol, it would become acetals and acids, so still toxic. And any surfactants in the liquids would be even more harmful.'

'So, whatever we do now, it's trashed.' Mai's shoulders slumped.

'No . . . no, I'm sure I've found an option before . . .' Nell searched again. 'Yes, look!' She turned her phone to Mai. 'Add phosphorus and nitrogen to break down the glycol, then add these remedial floating islands to absorb the toxins and restore the water chemistry. Swansea Uni helped develop them. Do any of your student volunteers have connections there?'

Mai shrugged, unconvinced. 'I dunno. Maybe. I could ask.'

'Yes! Do it now! The quicker we get on top of this, the less it will damage all the work you've done! If you have contacts there, they may be able to bring some over this afternoon!'

'Yeah, right. This afternoon . . .' Mai shook her head.

'Why not? You're the master persuader,' Nell persisted. 'You know how to sell it, Mai! This would be an ideal field test case for remediation, especially with all the baseline data you have. Could make someone a great dissertation.' Nell gave her an encouraging smile.

'OK, I'll go back to the office and send some emails,' Mai said. She looked at the buckets of newts. 'What are we going to do with these?'

'Do you happen to have any waterproof membrane and sandbags?'

When Mai nodded, Nell said, 'Great. I'll come back with you and grab them. And if I can use your volunteers while you're busy in the office, that would help.'

An hour later, Nell returned to the visitor centre with the only volunteers who'd turned up: two middle-aged men, who had helped her create a barrier separating the contaminated section of the pond from the unpolluted area. They'd held the membrane from both sides of the pond while she'd tucked its bottom edge under a row of sandbags, then stacked sandbags up each side to keep the membrane in position and taut along the bank. She was sweaty, achy and muddy. But the job was done. It wouldn't be perfect, but it would contain the damage, and gave them somewhere to put the species rescued from the polluted side.

Grabbing her kit bag from the car, she stripped off the soggy waders and hung them upside down in the shed to dry. While she ached to get out of her muddy clothes and into something that didn't smell of pond, she decided to wait until she could have a shower and change. But she pulled on dry socks and boots and, as she went to Mai's office, she scrolled on her phone for some contacts.

Inside the office, Mai was on the phone, but gave Nell a thumbs up. Joining the men who'd helped her, Nell showed her phone to them. 'Here's some good contractors who install amphibian and reptile fencing. Can you work through the list and see who can come out today?'

With a nod, the two men noted the numbers and began making calls.

'Great news!' Mai announced. 'One of my researchers knows someone in the environmental department at Swansea. They can't get here but if we can get *there*, they'll have three of those islands ready for collection.'

'Oh, fantastic.' Nell was delighted to see Mai's enthusiasm restored. She looked pointedly around the empty office. 'But where's your assistant and the rest of the volunteers?'

'Only these two showed up.' Mai nodded at the older men, who were already speaking on their phones. 'And my assistant is "running late".' Mai rolled her eyes, clearly unimpressed.

'Does he make a habit of that? Or is today a one-off?' Nell whispered.

'Not enough to make a big issue out of. But it's not the first time.' Mai squirmed, conflicted. 'I'm not good at the manager stuff. But I do need him to take things more seriously.' She raised her eyebrows. 'So Jonty'll have a shock when I send him to Swansea in a minute.'

'Jonty?' The familiar name stirred a sense of inevitability in Nell.

'Someone want me?' a loud, confident voice asked behind her. Nell turned.

A tall, golden-tanned man smiled at her. He wore long, baggy, khaki cargo shorts, loosely laced Timberland boots and an olive safari shirt. Two leather bands wrapped around each wrist and a shark tooth dangled from a leather thong around his neck. Wavy, sun-kissed, light brown hair shaggily met his shoulders. He looked quizzical as he regarded Nell, his sleeves pulling tight around his biceps as he folded his arms.

'Jonty, this is Nell. We worked together two years ago at EcoLogical Solutions.'

Nell looked at Jonty and waited for the awkward acknowledgement, knowing once he'd made the connection, he'd be less than discreet.

His puzzled expression cleared and he gaped. 'Nell? No *way!* Wow! There's something . . . different about you.' He spoke with a laconic Chelsea-meets-surfer-dude accent.

'Hair,' Nell said pointedly. 'I cut my hair.'

'*Clothes!*' Jonty said emphatically.

'Well, yes.' She looked at Mai, who fixed her with a piercing, inquisitive stare. 'Jonty and I met on a diving expedition. Wearing swimwear most of the time,' Nell explained.

'We *met* on a tropical island, diving with dolphins and drinking rum under the stars.' He gave a dazzling smile of very white teeth and winked. 'Yeah, that red bikini . . .'

'Uh-huh.' Nell frowned. 'Since we're at work, let's keep it professional, Jonty.'

'Oh, yeah, sure.' Jonty chuckled, apparently unaffected by Nell's unimpressed tone. He had an air of easy nonchalance, as if he'd never had any more weight on his shoulders than the amount he chose to bench-press.

Remembering how resistant Jonty was to taking any action, Nell tried the direct approach. 'We've had a crisis here this morning, Jonty. Since you're running late, you've got a lot to catch up with.'

Still Jonty seemed unmoved. 'Sure thing. Fill me in, ladies!' He perched on the edge of Mai's desk and smiled at them both.

After the morning's ordeal, the pressure to address the pollution quickly and the persistent worry about Aanya, Jonty's casual attitude made Nell more than a little irritated.

But, before she could say anything else to get him to take this seriously, her phone beeped with a text. She whipped it out of her pocket and stared at the screen. *Was it Rav? Was Aanya OK?*

Having a meeting with the teams at the hotel now. I'll keep you posted. Dad x

Nell stared at her dad's text as inspiration struck. *Of course!*

Chapter 8

Rav jumped out of his slouch on the sofa as his phone rang. It was Nell.

'Hi, what—?'

'I've found her,' Nell interrupted him. Her voice was bumpy and breathless.

He realised she was running and sat bolt upright. 'What? How? Is she OK?'

'She stayed at Finchmere Hotel last night. Jack has a room during the races. I had a hunch and called reception.'

After tracking Aanya's phone, Rav still couldn't trust the optimism unfolding in his stomach. 'How do you know for sure? Is she OK?'

'The night duty receptionist was still there when I called. She was busy showing everyone the selfie she'd taken with Jack last night. When I sent her Aanya's picture, she confirmed it.'

'And she's still there? And she's OK?' Rav held his hope in check.

'As far as I know. Aanya's not gone down for breakfast or been seen leaving via reception yet, so I thought I could head over to see her. It's a half-hour drive.' He heard Nell's smile in her words. 'So I can be there in fifteen.'

'I'll be there as quick as I can,' Rav said. 'She has to go to the police station to make a statement. Will you call me as soon as you see her? Please. And let the police know if she is all right?'

'Of course. See you soon,' Nell said. He heard her car door slam, the click of her seatbelt, the spray of gravel as she sped off.

Rav ended the call and pulled up the train times on his phone. He had ten minutes to get on the next one. He yelled the news out to his parents while he dashed upstairs and got his things together.

'Mum? Dad? She's OK. Nell's found her . . .'

Friday 19th April – 10.30 a.m.

'No. No way! I don't care what you say, you can't *make* me go to the police.' Aanya's defiant glare stared down Nell and Rav across the breakfast table in Finchmere Hotel's Orangery. The splendid surroundings – the timber-framed, vaulted-ceilinged glasshouse overlooking the rose gardens and downland beyond – were lost on them.

The hour that passed after Nell had knocked on Aanya's bedroom door, to ensure she was there and arrange to meet her for breakfast – giving Aanya the time she'd insisted on to get showered and dressed – matched the time Rav had taken to leap on the first train down and get to the hotel.

Nell had used the time to update Ashley about Aanya's whereabouts, grab a quick shower in the hotel's spa, change into black capri pants, black top and ballet flats, and catch up with Lucio and Max to find out what they'd decided to do about the race. They'd both been dazed and were waiting to take a steer from the police – and Colin. Nell could only agree, knowing her father would rearrange the racing schedules considerably.

When Rav had sprinted into reception to meet her and Aanya, Nell had felt a surge of relief and they'd joined his sister together. Rav persuaded Aanya to FaceTime their parents, to *show* them she was OK. They'd been keen to race down after Rav, but he'd pointed out that she'd need to speak to the police, and they'd barely get a chance to see her. And since they'd already planned to head down the next day anyway, there was no need to change their plans. Satisfied that their daughter was OK, Neeta and Rakesh had agreed.

Now, the restaurant was empty, with only a few staff bustling a discreet distance away, laying tables for lunch. And Rav was trying to convince Aanya to actually *give* that statement to the police. Despite Aanya's defiance, her hand shook slightly as she raised her cup to her lips.

'Please, Aans. You have to. It's not optional.' Rav's voice was strained.

He'd brought Aanya a change of clothes. Though she was pleased to be out of last night's heels and tight dress, she'd bemoaned Rav's sartorial choice of baggy jeans, T-shirt and hoodie. But Rav didn't seem amused. He leaned back shaking his head in defeat. Wrung out.

Nell pursed her lips and glanced at Aanya. 'It's OK if you don't want to make a statement. Just bear in mind that being arrested and held in a cell overnight isn't fun. Not saying that would happen, but the police have the option in some situations.' She shrugged and bit into her toast.

Aanya's eyes widened, and she held her coffee cup in front of her like a shield.

Nell chewed thoughtfully and swallowed. 'I get that it's intimidating. All the unfamiliar procedure and suspicion. But I'll have to give a statement, too. It doesn't take long.'

'How do you know so much about it?' Aanya interrupted, raising her chin. 'You a mastermind crim, or something?'

'Could be,' Nell deadpanned.

'She *was* arrested for murder,' Rav said.

Aanya stared at her brother, then at Nell, clearly not knowing what to make of the remark. 'You were *what*, now?'

Nell styled it out, trying to leverage Aanya's interest. 'It was nothing. But in *your* case, sure, you don't have to see the police. Although, that *will* mean you'll have to survive without your phone. I hear the police have it.'

Aanya choked on her coffee and stared at Nell.

'Anyway, I need to go and make my statement.' Nell stood. 'Shall we go together?'

Glancing at Nell, Aanya's vulnerability leaked through her teenage bravado. 'Yeah?'

'Yeah.'

Friday 19th April – 11.30 a.m.

Nell grimaced at Rav as they waited to cross the road to the police station. Nervy as a wild horse, Aanya was tense and looked ready to bolt. Rav slung an arm around her shoulders and steered her across the road.

But Aanya stopped dead at the station door. 'I can't tell them anything helpful.' Her raised, crumpled eyebrows appealed. 'It'll be a waste of their time. Can you just get my pho—'

'Argh!' Rav dropped his arm from her shoulders. 'For God's sake, Aanya, we're right here.' He stopped and took a deep breath, turning to his little sister. 'It'll be OK. All you need to do is go in, make a statement, go home, move on. If you don't, you *know* the police will follow up. They might even go to Mum and Dad's. They might arrest you. And imagine what life would be like then. And . . . you know, Nell and I *do* have other things to do today.' He jerked his head towards the police station. 'So . . . ?'

Aanya rolled her eyes, then waved a hand full of glittering nail art. 'Fine, bro. Chill!'

Inside, Nell spoke to the desk attendant, asking to see James or Val to make a statement about Jack Rafferty's death. She looked around the waiting room, the memory of the last time she'd been there rushing back. Rav squeezed her hand.

But when James walked in, Rav and Nell stopped holding hands and shifted apart.

James fixed Nell with that detective stare and she forced a smile. 'We've brought Aanya over, to make her statement. And I can make mine, too.'

'Nice to meet you, Aanya. Good to know you're OK.' James shook Aanya's hand and glanced at Rav. 'Relief all round, I imagine? Let's get your statements. Follow me.'

The interview room sparked another flashback for Nell. Memories of disbelief becoming suddenly, frighteningly real when her voluntary – *helpful* – interview about a murder had degenerated into unexpected arrest. Nell glanced back at Aanya being led by Ashley into the adjacent room. Nell's pulse sped up.

What does she know? And what happens if it's used against her, like it was with me?

She blotted clammy hands on her trousers and took a deep breath as James turned on the camera, opened his iPad and took her statement with ruthless efficiency. It was over before she knew it, and she read what he'd written and signed it.

Switching off the tape, he glanced at her. 'You and Rav look happy together. I always did think you'd make a great couple.'

That had been the crux of the problem, Nell realised. But she nodded as they walked to the door. 'Thanks, James.'

In the corridor, Nell was relieved to hear Ashley ending Aanya's interview. 'Thank you for your statement, Aanya. You're probably the last person who saw him alive, so even the smallest thing could be important.'

As Aanya joined them in the waiting room, holding her phone, her shoulders sagged. Rav took one look at her tense face and gathered her into a hug.

Before Aanya could squirm out of Rav's embrace, the main door swung open. The slice of noon sunlight dazzled in the dim room and Nell blinked at the striking silhouette. From the stance alone, Nell knew who it was. Sunglasses were removed with a flourish before the statuesque figure stalked over to the desk.

But not before the model shot pure daggers at Aanya.

In a husky Russian accent, the woman announced, 'I'm Svetlana Verenova-Rafferty. I'm here to confess. I killed my husband.'

Chapter 9

Friday 19th April – 12 p.m.

James tried to look like he wasn't completely out of his depth.

Svetlana's knack for striking a photogenic pose made even the cheap plastic chair look like a fashion accessory. Draped over it elegantly, she fixed the detectives with a gimlet stare. James noted her eyes weren't red: this grieving widow hadn't spent any time crying. Her flawless makeup even included a cat-eye flick to her eyeliner. It looked like she'd spent the morning being styled to within an inch of her life. Her platinum quiff was immaculately curled and, in skin-tight white jeans and a white silk camisole, Svetlana looked about as emotional as an ice queen.

Did she expect press to photograph her at the station? Or is this normal weekday attire for a model?

'I'm DS Ashley Hollis . . .'

'And I'm DI James Clark, with Svetlana Verenova-Rafferty.'

Svetlana confirmed her name for the recording and pushed her chair back so she could cross one long leg over the other.

'And I'm D . . . D . . . Duncan Featherstone, Legal Aid, representing Ms Verenova-Rafferty.' Duncan looked to be in his early thirties but old before his time, bilious in beige: cream shirt, brown tie with a tight, lopsided knot, tucked inside a taupe suit.

Svetlana bestowed on her appointed solicitor the briefest glance, barely concealing her scorn. 'I do not want solicitor. I only have *your* solicitor because *you* insist I need one. I'm here to speak the truth. I can handle consequences.'

James didn't doubt it, as he eyed Svetlana's determined stare and her muscular physique.

'You've already said that you're here to confess to the murder of

Jack Rafferty,' Ashley said in a matter-of-fact tone. 'Would you tell us exactly what happened?'

Svetlana tossed her head and leaned back. 'Jack and I had violent argument at the party last night. And after all the guests had left, I killed him.'

Ashley didn't react and James knew she was waiting for him to follow up. He cleared his throat. 'OK. Let's start at the beginning. Would you tell us what the argument was about?'

Svetlana looked him in the eye. 'I will not. You only need to know who killed him. I tell you answer. Since you know that, you don't need to know our private details.' She gave a curt nod, as if that were the end of that debate.

'But we'll need to corroborate the details, Svetlana,' James reasoned. 'And, fine, you say you're guilty, but there may be mitigating circumstances—'

Svetlana held up a steady hand. 'No. Any details I tell you will end up recorded in your courtrooms, and then all over your papers. Where journalists will make up even more details. So no. I give you the answer you need, you arrest me. I confess.'

James held in the sigh. 'I can understand that, Svetlana. It must be very difficult to keep seeing details of your private life in the press.' He wondered if that was the answer to his original question. It can't have been easy for Svetlana to read about her husband's transgressions, portrayed as moralising entertainment.

Holding his eyes, with a challenging tilt to her head, Svetlana seemed to realise his restraint. She gave a grudging, faint nod, and James knew he was on a better footing to ask at least one of his burning questions. But Ashley beat him to it.

'Would you tell us how you killed him, Svetlana?' she asked. 'It will save our pathologist a lot of time.' James knew Ashley was targeting facts Svetlana would be willing to share, given the pathologist would run her tests regardless.

Her one-shouldered shrug with downcast eyes looked like a photo shoot. 'I punched him.'

'You . . . you *punched* him?' James winced inwardly at his voice rising in pitch with incredulity.

'Yes, like this.' Svetlana swung a right hook over her half of the table. It was well clear of James, but he rocketed backwards in his chair.

Reflex. It's just reflex. He cleared his throat. 'You've ... got a great technique there.' He shot Ashley a quick glance. Her impassive face told him how unimpressed she was with his flight response. But Svetlana's knuckles were bruised. He believed her.

'Of course. I box and am black belt in three martial arts. Jack fell to ground. He lay there. He makes no response, so I know he is dead. And I leave him. I drive off to Finchmere Hotel, where I had my own suite. Separate to Jack's.'

James made a note, surprised at newly-weds needing separate rooms. He frowned. 'Did you check your husband's pulse, or see if he was breathing? Or think ...'

'I did nothing more. And all I think was, "*Good.*"'

'I ... er ... I *think* we should say "No comment" to questions like that,' Duncan suggested, weakly.

Svetlana told Duncan he was a fool using only her eyes. He looked down at his paperwork miserably, while she folded her gym-toned arms.

'Where did this happen, Svetlana?' Ashley asked.

'In our driveway. Outside front door.'

'But your husband wasn't found dead outside your house,' Ashley said. 'He was found at Little Smitington, drowned in his car.'

Svetlana frowned. 'No ... how ... ?'

'Could he have come round, got in his car and driven off? Perhaps lost consciousness again and veered off the road?' James asked.

'Th ... that's a leading question,' Duncan stuttered.

Ignoring him, Svetlana shrugged. 'Maybe. This is your job to find out, no?'

'But, now that the picture is more complicated,' Ashley urged, 'we'll need to know the full story, Svetlana. Or we'll have to arrest you for wasting police time.'

'I do not mind. You will have to arrest me anyway.'

'You realise there are no stylists. No en suites. Barely decent showers in prison,' James warned.

Svetlana swept him up and down with a look so fierce it burned, then laughed at him. 'You think that would be toughest thing I've faced?'

'But there *will* be plenty of curious cellmates,' Ashley said. 'Who may sell stories about what you're like behind bars.'

Svetlana shifted in her seat, revealing a rare flicker of discomfort.

'Whereas we can keep statements confidential,' Ashley asserted, as James mentally added, *up to a point.*

Svetlana stared at the desk, then met Ashley's eyes with raging defiance. 'He did it again. And then again. Worse than ever. And this time, I had enough.'

James and Ashley both waited. He made his expression understanding, sympathetic, and Svetlana continued.

'He drove off, with the staff, then return ninety minutes later. He *think* he can just come home. I say, "No! Not *again!*"' She thumped her closed fist on the table, making Duncan jump.

'Just to be clear, who do you mean by "the staff"?' James asked.

Svetlana shrugged. 'A waitress. Very pretty. He flirted with her all evening. When the guests had gone, he said he was driving her to the station.'

James nodded. 'And what time did he leave and return?'

'He left with her about ten o'clock. He got back at eleven thirty.' She shot a sidelong glance at James. 'The station is thirty minutes away. What you *think* he was doing for another thirty minutes?'

James decided to push the point and see how Svetlana reacted. He shrugged. 'Waiting for the train with her?'

'No. He took her to his room at Finchmere Hotel, also thirty minutes away. For sex. I killed him.' She shot James another ice-blast glare. 'Better arrest me before I kill her, too.'

As James had ushered Svetlana down the corridor to take her statement, Nell and Rav had scooped Aanya out of the police station and into the pub across the road. It had small, snug nooks off the main bar, perfect for the quiet conversation she needed to have.

Though she seemed to know this was coming, Aanya shot uncomfortable, furtive glances at Rav, which told Nell there was something she didn't particularly want her older brother to know.

Asking Rav to go to the bar and get some drinks, Nell settled Aanya onto a bench seat and then sat opposite her, leaning forward confidentially.

'I *was* going to ask if you took precautions, but after seeing the death glare you got from Svetlana, I think you've got more to worry about than contraception.'

Aanya looked like she might throw up.

'If you need the morning-after pill, there's the hospital pharmacy down the road,' Nell said gently.

Aanya nodded, then her face fell. As understanding dawned, Nell took a couple of notes from her wallet and passed them over.

Aanya visibly welled up, and her chin dimpled.

'Just go, buy it, take it. And call your GP and book an STI check. If you say you're staying with Rav, you may get one in Pendlebury. Just get it over with. Then we can game-plan.'

Aanya nodded gratefully, then slipped out. From the bar, Rav craned his neck to watch his sister dash outside, then frowned at Nell. She gave a slight shake of her head to indicate there was nothing to worry about, saved from further interrogation by Rav having to wait for their drinks.

But when he eventually brought the three lemonades over, he asked, 'What's going on with Aanya? Where's she gone?'

'Just popped out to get some painkillers, she's got a headache.' Nell sipped her drink. 'Thanks for this.' She eyed him over her glass. 'You do realise Aanya's night with Jack could be why Svetlana killed him, don't you?'

Rav shuddered. 'Nell, she's my little sister—'

'Yes, but she could be in trouble, Rav, so you're going to have to deal with uncomfortable truths, I'm afraid.'

He sobered. 'What do you mean?'

'Well, if Svetlana killed Jack over it . . . ?' Nell let the sentence hang.

Rav exhaled. 'But it wasn't Aanya who betrayed her. She wasn't married to Aanya.'

'No, but she was being publicly embarrassed by her. A one-night stand doesn't happen out of nowhere. Jack probably flirted with Aanya all night. In front of his wife and their guests.'

Nell stopped talking as Aanya returned and slipped into the seat opposite her brother. She gave a slight nod at Nell. She smiled back.

'Aanya, what happened last night? How did things with Jack . . . escalate?' Nell asked. 'Who propositioned who?'

'He did. Obvs.' Aanya flicked her hair defensively.

Rav grimaced.

'How . . . overtly?' Nell asked.

'The way it started was . . . kinda lame. Two of the guests were late. They were in a right mood, and making some kinda point by coming to this fancy dinner in dirty overalls. Before they even arrived, they were causing stress. We had to keep pushing the serving time back, and Chef was stressing out over how dry the main course would be. I had to keep wandering around, serving drinks and canapés in the meantime, 'til my feet were killing me. And we didn't have enough to keep doing that for hours, so the sous-chef had to keep making more blinis and we were out of caviar. Jack asked me how much longer I was going to make him wait. I thought he was making a point, like I'd forgotten to bring him a drink or something, so I said, "What? For dinner?" and started to go to the kitchen and check, but he blocked me and said, "If you like." And he gave me this *look*.'

'Uh-huh.' Nell arched an eyebrow.

Beside her, she felt Rav flinch. His jaw clenched, but thankfully he resisted saying what he thought of Jack's manoeuvres.

Nell looked at Aanya, who squirmed with uncertainty. She realised that, despite her outer confidence, Aanya didn't have a lot of experience to chalk this one up against. *Or any?* The pit of Nell's stomach sank.

'How did he suggest you go to the hotel? Did he ask you in front of anyone?' Nell asked. 'I'm wondering if Svetlana could have been humiliated by her husband propositioning you – or anyone else – publicly.'

Aanya shook her head. 'Everyone except Svetlana, her friend and our crew of four had left. We were packing up. I had a return train ticket home and the furthest to travel. If I'd gone with the others, I would've been expected to go back to the depot kitchen to help unload the van. That would have meant getting an Uber to another train station on a slower line with fewer connections home. So they all agreed I could just get an Uber to Cookingdean station and go straight to Richmond. Jack overheard the chat. He'd just come in from the terrace and looked pretty annoyed, like he was itching for a reason to get out of the place. He said he could give me a lift to the station.'

'That was it?' Nell asked.

'Yeah. I mean, the way he asked was . . . *flirty*. He had all the swagger. Probably because he's famous and loaded. And he gave me this intense look and I just *felt* something would happen if I said yes. I didn't even remember to pick up my phone. I mean, *nightmare*.'

Aanya rolled her eyes, beautifully understating the worry and anxiety she'd put her family through by being uncontactable.

'*Aanya!* Come on! Mum and Dad were out of their minds wondering where you were and if you were OK,' said Rav. 'It was a nightmare for *them*.'

'Yes, but I *was* fine. And I *am* an adult. Remember?'

'I think they'd expect an adult to just pay them the courtesy of letting them know they weren't coming home, but that they were fine. Which is pretty reasonable.'

'Oh yeah! I can imagine that would have gone down well!'

Nell interrupted the sibling spat. 'So, what happened next?'

'When we were in the car, he asked what would happen if I missed my train. Then he made a move. I flirted back. And things got . . . carried away.'

Nell asked, 'Did he film anything? Or take any pictures?'

'Nell!' Rav looked horrified.

'Better to ask, and know, and be able to act. And fast,' Nell said. She'd been burned with a revenge porn incident; she'd hate the same thing to happen to Aanya. So she breathed in relief when Aanya shook her head firmly.

'Any possibility he could have, without you knowing?' Nell checked.

'No. I was totally sober. He couldn't've done anything sneaky without it being obvious to me.'

'Good.' Nell frowned. 'You said Jack looked annoyed when he came in from the terrace. Do you know why? And was that where Svetlana and her friend were?'

Aanya's groomed brows drew together. 'Yeah. Svetlana's friend – Dani – is her trainer, apparently. Chef told me that's why Dani had made a big deal out of overseeing the menu for Svetlana. They're pretty hardcore about what she eats. Jack told me later it was because Svetlana was trying to put him on a diet and she'd said if everyone ate the same thing, he couldn't moan.' Aanya frowned again. 'Thinking about it, all three of them – Svetlana, Dani and Jack – looked upset when they came in from the terrace.'

'Oh, do you know why?' Nell leaned forward.

Aanya shook her head. 'It looked like they'd had a row. But I wasn't paying much attention. We were clearing up.'

As Nell turned to Rav, the view through the restaurant's windows of the police station car park caught her eye. Two officers strode with purpose towards an unmarked car and drove off, while James and Ashley talked across the roof of another car before they got in and followed. *They were heading towards Finchmere and Nye Valley.*

'Nell?' Rav nudged her after a minute of her staring out of the window. 'I was saying that we should get back to our folks, but Aanya says she has to go into Pendlebury town.'

Nell nodded, relieved Aanya was going to at least try to see a doctor, though Aanya did shoot Nell a sharp, don't-say-anything look.

'I can get the bus. I don't need company,' Aanya groaned. 'But I'm not looking forward to going home.' She appealed to her brother. 'Will you come and stay for a couple of nights? Keep them off my back? Let this all die down?'

Rav reached across the table for Aanya's hand. 'I don't think this *is* going to die down. Not for a while, sis.'

'I don't either.' Nell nodded towards the window. 'The police have just leapt into action over something.' She met Aanya's worried eyes. 'Better brace yourself for more questions.'

With a groan, Aanya leaned over, head on the table. 'No! I don't need this in my life!'

As Rav shot a worried frown at Nell, Aanya sat up and appealed to him again. 'I *can't* have an interrogation at home! Mum and Dad will make sure they're right within earshot. How can I talk about . . . *stuff*? And if they take me to the station . . . Can you imagine? *Nightmare.*'

Nell glanced at Rav. 'There could be an argument for staying close at hand, on neutral territory . . . for a few days?' At his nod, she continued, 'Your parents are already staying with us for the Classics at Finchmere. They might change their minds after all this. But – how about . . . rather than hosting them at my parents' place, I move them into the hotel? They might prefer to be on neutral territory if they want to speak to you about anything . . . sensitive. Then you and Aanya can stay with me at my folks'.'

'Could work,' Rav said. 'They might want to cancel, but they'd feel more on top of any police interest here. And that might actually give you more privacy, Aans. What do you reckon?'

'Yes! Definitely yes!' Aanya looked like she wanted to hug Nell.

'Before you get carried away,' Nell warned, 'because of the Classics, the hotel's fully booked, and so are all the others in the area. The only room available will likely be Jack's . . .'

'Oh . . .' Aanya looked unsettled, then rallied. 'OK. As long as they don't find out, I don't care. And I don't mind bunking up at your place if it gives me some space.'

'There'll be plenty of space – remember that I won't be around much because I'm helping to run the Classics,' Nell told her. 'I'll get you a VIP ticket, too, so you can enjoy the event, but if it's not your thing, you can just make yourself at home or explore the area.'

'I want to know what's got the police back on the trail, though,' Rav said.

'Me too,' Nell said. 'Because if Jack's wife has just confessed, *why* are they still investigating? And *who* are they questioning?'

Chapter 10

Before they'd all headed off to Finchmere, the police incident room had *buzzed*. As officers had speculated about Svetlana's confession, James had studied the incident board with renewed concentration, seeing new significance in details from statements and the movements of the evening.

DS Ed Baker pinned the photos of chez Verenova-Rafferty on the board that he'd taken during his morning's search, next to maps and notes, the picture of the Mustang in the centre. He stood back, regarding the board and scratched his thinning hair.

James whistled at Jack and Svetlana's gated, landscaped, glass-and-white-render *Grand Designs* mansion. 'What time did you get to the house?' he asked. 'Anything seem odd?'

'I arrived at seven forty, just had a quick look around, left about eight so I didn't keep Val waiting.' Ed pointed at his pictures. 'Massive gates – still open. Horseshoe driveway, empty, totally private with trees down each side, around a huge fountain at the house. Nothing looked awry. The triple garage connected to the house through the utility room. Around the back, a large terrace, hot tub, heaters, rattan furniture. Huge immaculate landscaped garden, ornamental lake, fancy topiary. The front door was unlocked. I found the phone in the kitchen and nothing seemed amiss, so I didn't stay long because I was on my way to take statements of the team at Finchmere and others who were guests at Jack's party, with Val.' He glanced towards Val's office, the door open as she worked at her desk.

'How did you get on?' Hesha asked.

'We didn't find Svetlana or her friend, Danielle Marshall,' Ed said. 'I gather Svetlana heard about Jack's death and came straight here to confess. But we got statements from all of the team members.'

Ed pointed at their photos as he went through them. 'Cassie Sullivan, team mechanic, works with Mark Reynolds. He's the engineer and, it's worth noting, the disenchanted second racer to Jack. Maxine Armstrong is their team manager. Lucio Moretti owns the car they've done up to race and Maxine works for him sourcing classic cars at Moretti's Classic Car Dealership.'

'Anyone else who might be able to give statements?' James asked. He noticed that Val was leaning against the door frame to her office, listening, as avidly observant as ever.

'Jack's father, Colin Rafferty, was at Jack's party, and he was at Finchmere this morning,' Ed said. 'But he was in no state to speak to me. I agreed I'd go back for his statement in due course. The only other people present at the party were the catering team producing the food and serving guests. We'll get to them today.' He nodded at James. 'At least you've managed to speak to the girl Jack drove off with. Anything enlightening?'

James shook his head. 'None of this information contradicts Svetlana's account.'

'Do you think she really killed him? Over a one-night stand?' Ed asked.

'Over *several affairs*,' Ashley corrected. 'Maybe this was the last straw.'

'Sure, but knocking him out with one punch?' Ed shook his head.

'Doesn't necessarily need that much strength, if you get the right spot,' James said.

'Ha! She's plenty strong enough.' Hesha rummaged in her rucksack and pulled out a dog-eared magazine, finding the full-page ad of Svetlana in black Lycra shorts and orange crop top sprinting towards the reader, a swirling azure cloud behind her. She could have been carved from marble: taut quads and calves, chiselled six-pack, the fingers and hand of her leading arm straight as a blade. Determination lasered from her violet eyes as she raced to the acid-yellow lightning bolt striking the energy drink at the front of the frame, emblazoned, *CHARGE!*

'Uh-huh.' Ed patted his stomach. 'We can all look like that with a bit of Photoshop.'

Hesha laughed. 'No such luck. She doesn't go in for that. Doesn't even use filters on her selfies. Her blog describes her moving from modelling to being a sports ambassador, doing a few ad campaigns like this.' She swivelled her phone towards Ed and James as a page of thumbnail photos loaded of Svetlana, mostly in the gym with a female trainer, doing impressive routines.

Ed blinked. 'Bloody hell. I'll have what she's having.'

Hesha pointedly looked him up and down. 'What, about six hours of training every day and only grilled chicken for the rest of your life? No beers after work, no doughnuts during work and—' she tweaked the cigarette out from behind Ed's ear '—no sneaky ciggie breaks?'

'All right, all right. But how did her husband end up drowned in a pond?' Ed deflected.

'Jack must have come round,' James said. 'Got in the car and drove off. With a likely head injury he could have lost consciousness, lost control of the car, crashed and drowned.'

'Is this backed up with the pathologist's report?' Ed asked.

'I imagine it will be,' James said.

'Early lunch, then!' Ed brightened and shoved his cigarette back behind his ear.

'Hold on.' DCI Val Johnson's warning tone made everyone pause. The epitome of steely, she turned to James, her grey bob swaying as she passed her phone to him.

He read the internal police memo aloud: 'There's a major international fraud investigation at Finchmere this weekend. Over valuable classic cars with falsified provenance.' He handed back the phone, hoping for more information.

'That's all I know,' Val said. 'I'll tap up a contact. But what do you think? Coincidence?'

'Well, I guess it depends which car.'

'Presumably Fraud know that. The question is, who's behind it?' Val peered at the photo of the gullwing: the picture from the morning's paper, with Jack kicking the ruined wing.

'I suppose it's the same as forging an old master,' James mused. 'Or passing off a painting as some lost famous painter's work. The fake doesn't only achieve an unfair price, it devalues every other piece.'

He'd had reason to become interested in art lately. His days off were increasingly spent at galleries with Shannon – where he found himself soaking up all her art history knowledge, learning what made a good investment, developing his own opinions on good art.

After Percy's wedding a few weeks ago, he'd had a flash of insight into Shannon's resentment towards Percy and Nell – enough to show him there was more to Shannon than most people realised. He'd seen how the scorn Shannon had been forced to bear in her entitled circles from having – hushed tones – 'working parents' had cut deep; and knowing her parents had voluntarily created that situation by giving up what Percy would now inherit, had only deepened that wound. It made Nell's earnest approach to working to earn her privilege seem perverse to Shannon – as if Nell had the lifestyle Shannon *should* have, but didn't know how to live it. He didn't always agree with her, but he had to admit it, Shannon intrigued him.

He wasn't so sure what *she* saw in *him*. Novelty, perhaps. He wasn't Shannon's usual type and he didn't have anything like the money needed to keep up with her. Insecurity had gnawed while the effort to see each other had been one-way, and he wondered when she'd get bored with him and move on.

But, amazingly, this weekend Shannon had actually made the effort to come to *his* neck of the woods instead of him going up to London.

So now, a twinge of sharp frustration made him resent Val's curious mind. Any minute now she was going to declare this an investigation and ask him to cancel the rest of his leave. She probably wouldn't even ask the question directly; it would be an unspoken expectation.

Which meant that now, when Shannon had finally come down here, booked a suite at Nye Hall Hotel (deliberately *not* Finchmere Hotel) for the weekend, no less, he was going to stand her up.

Bloody perfect.

'Hmm.' Val's scrutiny moved from the gullwing to the racing team. 'Motive?'

'We've got an explanation of what happened, and why, haven't we?' Ed pleaded.

For a brief, blessed moment it looked like Val was about to agree, when an officer barrelled through the door.

Without any preamble, the officer said, 'Forensic report on the Shelby Mustang. Thought you'd like to know straightaway. The brake lines were scored. Definitely deliberate, done with a blade of some kind. Enough for the brake fluid to leak gradually.'

'So he would have been able to drive for a short while?' Val clarified. 'Until all the fluid had drained, and then he'd find that the brakes wouldn't work?'

'Yes. And the handbrake was loose, not unusual on a car like that, but it wouldn't have been any help.'

James groaned inwardly, noting Val's pursed lips: a sign of deep thought. About all these facts pointing them towards an investigation. 'Anything else?'

'Nothing else as yet – we're finishing up. Report'll be with you as soon as we're done.'

As the officer dashed off, Ed sighed and sat down while Val turned to the team. 'Well. Looks like we have a case. James, Ashley, can you get back out and do some more digging with the team?'

Walking into the corridor, James pulled his phone out of his pocket, and tapped Shannon's number to explain that he had to work. He knew she wouldn't be impressed. At her silence, he promised, 'I'll see you as soon as I can. I'll make the reception dinner for sure.'

'Oh, no hurry,' Shannon purred. 'You do what you need to do. I'll keep myself entertained.' He wondered if it was deliberate that she hadn't hung up, if he was supposed to hear her call out, 'Lorenzo! *Ciao!* Great race! You *must* let me help you celebra—'

And his heart sank.

Nell pulled up at Moretti's team garage. She checked her phone for the meetings Hugo had been able to rearrange and saw she had to speak to the auctioneers later that afternoon. But her first meeting was now, with Moretti's team, to hear their decision. *Would they still race the gullwing?*

As Nell approached the garage door, James and Ashley pulled up beside her. They walked inside to the sound of the team's heated discussion.

'You've heard our thoughts on this, Mark.' Maxine threw

her arms up in exasperation. 'Jack has died. We have to show our respect . . .'

'For God's sake! We can't get this far and not race her!' Mark boiled with incredulity.

'Lucio's feelings are clear,' Maxine said, her eyes straying to the office. 'He feels he owes it to Colin and the rest of Jack's family to cancel the race. Out of decency.'

'We've got so much riding on this! *Not* racing won't help Jack. What *good* will it do?'

'Sure, but when your driver's been . . .'

'*One!* One of our drivers!' Mark stopped short of shouting but he exhaled forcefully. 'I'm *more* than capable of taking the wheel . . .'

'We'll give it some thought, luv,' Maxine cut Mark off as she noticed they had company.

Nell nodded at Maxine. 'I'm just here to confirm what you'd like to do about your race,' she said. 'But if you need more time to discuss it, I can come back later?'

Maxine's gaze met Mark's levelly, then she nodded at Nell. 'If you don't mind waiting, you can stay here. But give us five, would you, luv?'

Nell wandered over to the restoration pictures, discreetly out of the way. Maxine began to talk again, then stopped as the detectives stepped forward and introduced themselves.

Hearing the word 'detective', Mark swore, making Cassie, who was hunkered on her creeper board and sliding to and fro, stop moving and stand.

Lucio darted out from the office as Maxine greeted Ashley and James, saying, 'Hello, detectives, can we help with anything?'

'Thank you all for your earlier statements,' James said. 'But we have a few more questions.' He turned to Maxine and Lucio. 'We'll be as unobtrusive as possible. We have a room at the hotel, or we could use your office or a corner of the workshop? Whichever is easier.'

Nell frowned. *James hadn't mentioned Svetlana's confession. Why would they have more questions if she'd confessed? Was Svetlana mistaken? How could you think you'd killed someone but hadn't?*

As she scanned the team, and James and Ashley preparing to ask more questions, dread squirmed in Nell's stomach: *they're not just checking out Svetlana's story. There's more to this.*

Watching Mark fold his arms tightly across his chest, James guessed he was about early forties and he seemed impatient. Determined. *Ruthless?* Mark's eyes bored into Ashley, then him.

'Have we really got to do this now? I've already given a statement to another officer this morning.' Mark darted a desperate glance over Ashley's shoulder, across the garage. He was clearly annoyed at being the first person singled out for questions.

James turned and saw that Mark was watching Maxine talking rapidly with Lucio, their heads close together, bodies tense, faces worried. Nell approached them and, after a few words, went into Max's office, presumably to wait for them to join her.

'Yes, Mark. We're gathering more information now that we have evidence that Jack was murdered.'

James and Ashley studied their interviewee. Usually, the revelation of murder made suspects react in some way. It could be a useful steer for their questioning. But Mark didn't even seem to be listening. He still gazed intently at Max, like a starving lion tracking prey. His lips moved and James realised Mark was trying to lip-read Max's conversation with Lucio. Mark's body moved almost involuntarily towards them.

James put a hand up, bringing Mark's attention back to the detectives.

'Really? This really can't wait?' Mark begged.

'Sorry. But I'm afraid our questions need to take priority today—'

Mark cut James off. 'Here.' He threw a chamois leather he'd balled up in his fist onto the immaculate workbench and pulled out the two stools underneath it, gesturing elaborately.

'Please. Sit. Interrogate me more about that total . . . *waste of space*. Now that I've risked *everything* and worked for *months* to create a perfect racing machine, and I have this *minusculely* finite chance . . .' Mark pinched his thumb and index finger together, wincing. '. . . This *golden* moment of probably *literally* a matter of minutes – *these* minutes, *right now* – to persuade my team to let me actually race her, and show what she can do – *and* give my company a small glimmer of hope that it won't go down the sodding pan today along with everything else I've put on the line to get it up and running. Then, yes, I assure you, I have absolutely nothing better to do than sit around and talk endlessly about that poxy . . . good-for-nothing . . . bloody, bastarding . . . *twunt.*' He wiped spittle off his mouth with the back of his hand, then put both hands on his hips, breathing heavily.

Ashley and James were momentarily silenced.

'Don't go quiet on me now! Come on. What do you want to know?' Mark demanded.

Across the garage, Maxine and Lucio walked towards Maxine's office. Mark watched them, and a small whimper escaped him.

Ashley relented. 'We can give you five minutes, sir.'

Mark bounded across the garage, calling to Max and Lucio. They turned and invited him into Max's office. Through the open door, they saw Nell give up her chair for Mr Moretti and shuffle to the side, making room for the gathering in the small space.

'Way to undermine our authority,' James griped.

'We barely had his attention. We weren't going to get anything out of him. Besides—' she tilted her head '—he couldn't have spelled out his motive any more clearly, could he?'

James shrugged, opting to check his phone rather than snipe. 'The preliminary search at Jack and Svetlana's house has gone well.' He noted the time. 'Very efficient.'

'Right, well, let's speak to Cassie, then,' Ashley suggested.

Cassie was perched on a stool, an *Evo* magazine open on her lap. But she wasn't reading. She picked at her short nails, peeling off already chipped red varnish. She looked up guiltily as the detectives approached.

'Cassie, we have a few more questions,' Ashley said. 'May we take a moment?'

Val had warned them that Cassie was prickly when she'd given her statement. They'd since found out why, and James knew they'd have to address it in their questioning. Now, though, Cassie nodded. Her hunted gaze flicked between the detectives. She had a watchful air, as if she expected to always be the outsider and had to weigh people up carefully before she would trust them.

'I've already given you a statement about Jack's party and . . .'

'Yes, thank you for that,' Ashley said. 'But we're revisiting everyone to ask a few more questions, now that we know Jack Rafferty was murdered.'

Cassie's body stiffened. But she said nothing. Her eyes now didn't meet theirs. Instead, her gaze constantly moved around the garage as if scanning the horizon for danger.

'We're aware from your records that you're familiar with the police procedure.' Ashley's pointed words received a sullen glare from Cassie.

James fought to keep his expression neutral. Behind the defiance, he saw a fearful young woman. He'd need to carefully, gradually, earn Cassie's trust. He leaned forward, hoping to draw her out. 'We know that you're the mechanic here, on Maxine Armstrong's race team.'

Cassie nodded.

But Ashley didn't seem to be on his wavelength. She leaned forward. 'Quite the opportunity?'

At Cassie's enthusiastic nod, Ashley landed the blow. 'So tell us how you felt when Jack's actions ruined this project. And the gamble Maxine had taken on you.'

Her face draining of colour, Cassie frowned. 'W . . . what?'

Ashley casually fished a file out of her bag. 'Given how high-profile this work is, it was very civic-minded of Maxine to entrust someone with such an . . . *extensive* record.' She flicked through the pages.

Cassie's mouth opened and closed until defiance made her close it and raise her chin. 'What's this got to do with my work? Or Jack's driving accident?'

'Well, that's the thing, isn't it? Why *would* a racing driver have a driving accident?' Ashley's eyes bored into Cassie's. But instead of mentioning Jack's head injury or the sabotaged brakes, she said, 'Looks like you could have outdriven Jack or perhaps Mark, too, based on the account of your joyriding. Then car theft. Several cautions with, I note, the cars getting more and more expensive.'

She looked up at Cassie, narrowing her eyes. 'You must have been popular with the contact who sold them on. Until you got that custodial prison sentence.'

Chapter 11

In the small garage office, Nell tried to keep her frustration in check. 'I can understand the need for respect. And I know that Colin is a dear friend. But Colin, more than anyone, would do everything possible to keep a car on the track. Look at what he endured to win the twenty-four-hour race at Le Mans!'

The way Lucio's chest heaved, she knew this was an uphill battle. Maxine was uncommonly silent. Mark was a mercurial blend of sullen and hopeful, which wasn't helping to restore faith in a calm, masterful drive on the track. Now, at Nell's coaxing, he nodded optimistically at Lucio.

'I can do it. You know I can. Even with that awful starting position.'

'But this is the point, no? We have such ground to make up that an embarrassing appearance is worse than no appearance.'

Nell shook her head. 'Oh, come on, Lucio. You're not telling me that you'd have prevented Jack from driving today?'

Lucio scowled, but didn't reply. *Maybe he would have . . . ?*

'I can tell you this, Lucio,' Mark persisted, '*Jack* wouldn't have come back from this rubbish start. But *I* can. We have everything riding on this. So it's up to you. Don't take a chance on me, and we'll definitely lose. But take that gamble, and maybe . . . *probably* . . . everything we've done will pay off.'

As Lucio and Maxine fixed their shrewd gazes on Mark, Nell glanced at Mark's hands in his lap, curled into fists, knuckles whitened – and wondered what 'everything' might include.

Cassie recoiled like a kicked puppy. She pushed her stool back, physically distancing herself from Ashley, folding her arms like a barrier.

James regretted Ashley's blunt approach. He had to assume she had a reason. But he would've liked to have been clued in. And now he was left to rebuild any remnants of rapport . . . He leaned forward, made his tone warm. 'We can't ignore your record, Cassie, so let's address it. OK?'

'Sure.' But Cassie's defiant pose remained steadfast. 'Yeah, Max gave me this chance. She knew I'd done time, and she took me on anyway. I felt . . . *lucky.* I wanted to justify the faith she had in me. Where I grew up, that doesn't happen . . . *ever.*' She clamped her lips together.

'And Maxine believed you'd put your past behind you?' James clarified.

'I had!' Cassie looked earnest. She leaned forward. 'I was only in prison for four months. But while I was inside, I learned basic car mechanics. And I found a garage doing an outreach scheme, and they gave me an apprenticeship. Turned out Maxine sponsored the garage and she turned up once a year to meet the team, give some motivational team-talk. She encouraged me in the skills I was learning. Worked alongside me on the engine I was tuning for a bit. I didn't expect that. She was cool. We kept in touch as I moved jobs.

'I went on to an independent dealership and then to a specialised garage restoring classics. I was good at it. I had the patience. I liked taking time and care over the individual pieces to put something broken back together, the way it should be. My boss kept giving me trickier things to work on.' Cassie unfolded her arms. 'I liked that. I liked the challenge and feeling like I was trusted with something precious and difficult to fix. I started getting a bit of a rep, actually.' She shifted on the stool. 'And then, all this time later, Max said she was putting a team together and needed a specialist mechanic.' Cassie shrugged. 'And that was it. I was on the team.'

'Can you tell us about your specific role?' James asked.

'I helped Mark with the restoration.' She nodded at the picture boards.

James stared at the photos. '*This* is how the car looked before all your work? That's amazing!'

Cassie flushed. 'Yeah, she was in a right state. We took her apart, cleaned her up, then put her back together. With a few key changes.' She grinned, then leaned forward. 'Mark had to retool some parts himself. When we needed an obsolete part, he just made it from scratch. His work is *amazing* . . .' Her eyes lit up. 'So my job is to make sure the car is race-ready. Monitor everything. Check how she is after each race, talk to Jack about the limits he can push her to.'

'That's great technical expertise,' James said. 'Jack must have appreciated your advice.'

A sarcastic laugh exploded from Cassie at James's question. 'Advice? Jack? He *never* took my advice! Are you *kidding*?'

James sat back, waiting. Cassie looked away, chewing her lip as if replaying past grievances in her head. James pushed his advantage. 'Is that why Jack crashed out in your qualifying lap? Because he didn't take your advice?'

'Pff.' Cassie stood up and paced. She stared at her feet, scuffing one boot into the concrete floor. 'That was a bloody embarrassment. But we should have seen it coming. Jack knew best about *everything*. You can't talk to a man like that. Every poor lap time was my fault for not tuning her properly, or the steering was off. He'd get out of the car and throw a tantrum, saying stuff like, "My dad didn't have to put up with a team of amateurs." *Amateurs!*' Her lip curled, then she nodded towards the office. 'Max has been in the business for *decades*. She's *awesome*. And Mark's the most talented engineer I've ever worked with.'

'But Jack didn't respect the team?'

'Not a bit!' Cassie turned to face James and leaned against the wall. 'But it was even more embarrassing because when Mark drove, his times were usually better than Jack's.'

'If Mark's times were better, why wasn't he the primary driver?' Ashley asked.

Cassie threw up her hands. 'Wish I knew. You'll have to ask Max. Mark drove every alternate trial while we were tuning her. But not since we got to the track. No idea why. But if Mark had driven the qualifier, we'd have got pole and the car wouldn't have been damaged.'

'Yes,' Ashley said. 'Repairing the damage made you and Mark late for Jack's party. Maxine said in her statement that you both turned up in your overalls, like you were making a point.'

Cassie's flush crept up to her headscarf. 'Yeah, well. Look what he did to our car! D'you think we wanted to go to his sodding party? He was showing off, reminding us that we're the little guys. His bloomin' minions. We don't live like that. With poncy art on the walls. Or a garage full of cars. Well.' She gave a small laugh. 'Not in one piece.' She tugged at her overalls. 'These were clean. We were late. I could have changed but I couldn't be arsed. We would have been even later. Me and Mark just wanted to get the bloody thing over and done with.'

James made a pointed note. '"*Just wanted to get the bloody thing over and done with*".' He looked up at Cassie. 'Still talking about the party?'

Cassie glowered at James. He stared back until Cassie broke eye contact.

'OK. Tell us more about the evening. Had you been to the house before?' James asked.

'No. He and Svetlana had just bought it and only just moved in. But the place was lit up like Blackpool. Couldn't miss it. Lights in the trees, in the driveway paving, along the path, blazing through all the windows. Inside, everything was open-plan, so you could see the two chefs in the kitchen and drinks lined up on the bar, with a couple of waiting staff taking things around. Everyone had gathered in the lounge. It had these folding floor-to-ceiling glass doors, which were open, leading out to the terrace, which was also lit up.

'Everyone was already in little cliques, talking. Maxine was talking to Mr Moretti. He didn't look very happy. It was pretty obvious they didn't want to be interrupted.

'Svetlana was all done up in a silver gown and huge heels even though she's already over six foot. She wasn't really doing much to make anyone feel welcome. Proper ice queen.' Cassie shrugged. 'She had a friend there that I didn't recognise. Dani . . . something. She looked like an athlete, too. A waiter kept offering them drinks, but they only had water.

'But then I saw Colin. I could *not* believe it – he came straight over to say hello. He knew my name and everything.' Cassie's delighted smile faded into a frown at the lack of recognition from the detectives. 'Jack's dad? Colin Rafferty?'

'Oh, yes!' James recalled Hesha's research. 'Racing driver.'

'Racing *hero*. Unbeatable on the track, in any car, for most of his career. Amazing talent. He asked me all these questions about how I'd tuned the car for the race, questioned me on lap times, asked *me* for *my* ideas on how to improve them. When I told him what I'd tried, he said I'd done a great job. I was blown a-*way*.' Cassie hugged her arms around herself.

'Do you see Colin at the track? Does he get involved in what your team does?' Ashley asked.

Cassie shook her head. 'No. He leaves Jack to get on with it. He's retired now. He comes to meet up with his old teammates and enjoy the cars.'

Making a note, James asked, 'What happened next?'

'We went through for dinner, sat at this huge glass table on uncomfortable wrought-iron chairs while the chefs served the food in the kitchen and one waiter brought it over while the other one topped up our drinks. Fully awkward, seeing people working for us. And the conversation was uncomfortable. Jack tried to kick things off with a speech. He stood up at the head of the table, dinging his glass with his fork. Talk about *cringe*. Said it was *so nice* to welcome us to his *new* home with his *new* wife and how he hoped that our *new* team would have success on the track tomorrow.'

Cassie rolled her eyes. 'That went down like a lead balloon, I can tell you. Dead silence. No one raised their glass. Then, Mr Moretti said, "Yes, let's toast. To keeping on track and ahead of the competition." Then he *glared* at Jack. We all got the point.' Cassie puffed out a long breath. 'Awk-*ward*. Colin and Jack looked furious. Svetlana gave Mr Moretti a death stare. But that's how she looks at most people. Mark hoped Mr Moretti would let him drive instead. But he didn't.

'Then the starters arrived. Ugh.' She shuddered. 'Awful. Plates piled with crushed ice and three oysters on top. I just couldn't . . .' Cassie looked like she was going to gag. 'Jack went on about how fresh and expensive they were. Everyone seemed to think they were amazing.

But there was no way I was touching them . . . Across the table, Dani said she had an allergy. *Genius.* I said I did, too. Svetlana looked put out – maybe she hadn't thought about that. I slid my plate to Mark and he polished them off.

'The small talk was pretty forced and we couldn't even say how the food was nice, it was so dull. Chicken and a "medley" of roasted baby vegetables. I guess when the hostess is a model and a gym bunny, meals are about counting calories. Mr Moretti quizzed me, almost the same questions as Colin. I was surprised – I thought he just owned the car showroom; I didn't realise he knew so much about racing and mechanics. He didn't say much when I answered. It felt like a weird interview.

'Then we had dessert. Blueberry sorbet. And that was it! I'm not even *kidding!* You can get fancier meals from Marks and Sparks' ready-meal section. Then Jack made this big point of taking everyone all over his gaff. Like I say, showing off. He said to me and Mark, "Since you're dressed for it, let me show you the car collection. Maybe you could do an oil change while you're there." Goady sod. Then he said something about showing us his Yamaha Niken. I haven't seen any of those bikes in the UK yet, so I went out to see. But he didn't have one. Probably blagging. As usual. He tried to lead us into the garden, but I said I'd had enough, and Mark and me went back in.

'Jack ended up walking around the garden with Max,' Cassie continued. 'I hoped she was bollocking him. Next thing I knew, Max was back inside and Mark was practically begging her to let him race instead of Jack. Jack was too busy chatting up the waitress to notice.

'I don't remember much else, really, until Svetlana argued with Dani on the terrace. Jack joined them and then they were all going at it. I couldn't hear what Dani and Jack said but Svetlana was yelling, "How could you? How dare you?" to both of them over and over again.

'The rest of the guests were inside, watching through the glass. It was like watching badly dubbed *Big Brother.* Horrible. Mr Moretti put his glass down, thanked the staff and left. Max followed him, so me and Mark were out of there like a shot. Who wants to hang around to watch a domestic? I drove Mark back to Finchmere.'

'The hotel? You went straight there?' James asked.

Cassie shifted uncomfortably. 'Not exactly.'

Looking at her sharply, he asked, 'What do you mean?'

'We . . . um . . . we . . . Look, it was a really weird dinner. You can't blame us . . .'

James waited.

'We went to Cookingdean. For fish and chips.'

James bit back the laugh, keeping his face straight. 'And then?'

'Then we went to the hotel. I was there for the rest of the night.'

'With Mark?' James asked.

'Yes, we both went back to the hotel.'

'Did you and Mark . . . stay together all night?'

'Mark's married! Of course not!' Cassie's eyes were wide with indignation.

'Uh-huh.' James made a note.

Cassie looked incensed. Her mouth twitched with the effort of keeping silent.

'But you and Mark seemed to be thick as thieves at the party,' James said, 'according to some statements we took. Apparently, you were both notable by your absence at one point.'

Cassie shrugged defiantly. 'Dunno what you mean. Everyone was wandering about. Jack had made a big thing about wanting everyone to admire the place. I couldn't tell you where every single guest was for every single minute.'

James made another note.

'You say the party was awkward because of Jack's performance,' Ashley said. 'What, *exactly*, did the rest of the team think of his drive in the qualifying lap?'

'Mark was . . .' Cassie pressed her lips shut. 'Well, he wasn't impressed. And Max was furious. Let's just say tempers were high.'

'Wasn't that a bit of an overreaction?' James asked, deliberately disingenuous. 'To a place in a race?'

Cassie stared at James. Her brow creased in incomprehension. She opened her mouth to speak, then closed it. She looked at James, narrow-eyed, assessing him, then sat back. 'Nah, you're playing me, mate. You can't be that thick. But, to spell it out, the qualifier's outcome *only* decides our entire racing outcome. Which Mark's banking on to get a return on what he put in. Oh, and *all* our reputations in the industry, and *any* work we'd get afterwards, all depend on it. That's all.' She glared at James. 'Would any of that matter to you?'

James nodded. 'A lot at stake, then. And a lot of pressure. I can understand that would cause some tension. Is it unusual for that pressure to show, for arguments to occur?'

'Mark and Jack did bicker. But I'd never seen Mark get angry before. And Max had her own way of managing Jack. She's tough. She doesn't take any crap.'

'How *did* Max handle Jack?' James asked.

'She's very no-nonsense. Doesn't pander to egos.' Cassie shrugged.

'Did Jack have an ego?' James again affected innocence.

Cassie laughed. 'Have you met him?'

James spread his hands. 'Well, no. We didn't meet him.'

'No. Well. But you must have known of his reputation?'

Nodding, James recalled the tabloid stories and clickbait surrounding Jack: swanking around the track like a racing champion, winking at female racing fans, stumbling out of nightclubs with women who weren't his then-girlfriend, fiancée or wife.

'One of those blokes who thought he was God's bloody gift.'

James sat back, waiting for Ashley to pick up the questioning.

She did, asking, 'Did you have problems with Jack in other ways?'

Cassie glanced up, her eyes wide. 'What do you mean?'

'You're an attractive young woman. Just his type, probably,' Ashley said.

'I didn't have anything to do with him!' Cassie's hands balled into fists in her lap.

'Did he try it on, though?' Ashley asked, her tone level.

Cassie looked away with a cynical laugh. 'He tried with everyone. All the time.'

'Yes, that makes life difficult when you're being professional. When your work matters.'

'Difficult? It was revolting. Bloody gropey hands, endless insinuations, being told I didn't have a sense of humour for not laughing at his sexist jokes, daily threats that he knew all the big names and I had to play nice if I wanted to get on.' Her face contorted with disgust. 'He pestered me every bloody day.' Her chest rose and fell rapidly.

'Even worse when this is your big opportunity,' Ashley pressed. 'Did you report the behaviour? To Max? Or Mr Moretti?'

'Now you *are* having a laugh.' Cassie's words seethed with venomous resentment. 'Who, out of the two of us, do *you* think they'd see as disposable? They didn't even want to replace Jack with a better driver. I'd have been out on my ear if I'd rocked the boat.'

Cassie glared accusingly at the iPad James typed on. 'Look at you!' She stabbed a finger at him. 'You're making notes that now I have a motive for doing him in! Yeah, fine, OK? I'd have happily ripped his puny balls off.'

'Well, you had more than one reason to want him off the team,' Ashley reasoned. 'Sure you wouldn't have done more than that?'

Chapter 12

Friday 19th April – 2 p.m.

James knew their key moment would be broken as he spotted Mark sauntering over, his step jaunty, blundering straight into Cassie's simmering rage and Ashley's accusation. 'Hey! We're on!'

But Cassie had sprung up from her seat, glaring at Ashley. 'I don't have to put up with this!' She kicked the stool over and stormed out of the garage.

Mark looked dumbfounded. 'What happened? Is Cassie OK?' He hesitated, then jogged over to Cassie, catching up with her stride and getting her to slow down, then stop as they spoke. The discussion looked intense. Mark held up his hand for a high five. Cassie eventually obliged.

Glancing at Ashley, James said, 'Thanks for picking up the questions about Jack's behaviour towards Cassie. I'd been . . . concerned until then. I didn't think we were very in step at the start of that interview. We should have agreed a game plan.'

'Yeah, I thought you started off a bit soft with Cassie.' Ashley met his gaze with a hint of challenge. 'I didn't think that was the right approach. Police interviews aren't exactly novel for her. I didn't want it to feel too easy. I just had to wait for you to catch up.' She nodded towards Mark. 'Speaking of which, are we just waiting here for the good of our health?'

James decided striding over to retrieve Mark was better than saying something he'd regret to Ashley.

Soft? As if! He knew Ashley was peeved at his promotion but he'd hoped they'd get back on their familiar, in-tune track. *Looks like that's going to be more of a challenge than I thought.*

As he cogitated, he nearly collided with Nell as she walked out of the office. 'Oops! OK?' James put out a steadying arm.

'Yes, thanks.' Nell scanned the empty garage. 'Have your questions scared them off?'

'Yeah,' James sighed. 'Just another standard day of police intimidation.'

'Thought so,' Nell said. She hesitated, then whispered, 'Why are you questioning everyone when Svetlana confessed?'

James hissed, 'Jesus, Nell! I can't discuss it. And don't mention that. To anyone.' Over Nell's shoulder, he caught Ashley's annoyed eye-roll. But the familiar gleam lighting up Nell's eyes at the hint of suspicion was even more problematic – her gaze on him was as riveted as a cat with a mouse in its sights. He immediately tried to emphasise their respective roles. 'Kindly remember that *we're* the ones who get to ask the questions.'

'Fine, I'll leave you to it.' Nell waved James goodbye – too cheerfully – as she got in her car.

As he escorted Mark back, Ashley stopped reading the email on her phone and looked up.

Mark hovered by the workbench, his hands on his hips, as if, with nothing to work on, he didn't know what to do with them.

'Thanks. For that.' He jerked his head towards the office.

'Sounds like your powers of persuasion were successful?' Ashley said.

'Yeah! Yes. I can race her. The race has been bumped to Monday, and we can't redo the qualifier, but I'll live with that.' His face cracked into a wide beam and he shook his head in delighted disbelief. 'Nell's even added a parade lap before the race! It gives the car more exposure *and* means I get the chance to feel out the track in the gullwing beforehand.'

'Good old Nell,' Ashley said, a hint of acid in her tone. 'Right, if you're ready, let's finish our questions?'

Mark righted Cassie's stool, and sat. 'Yes. I'm ready. Thanks.'

'We understand there wasn't much love lost between you and Jack,' Ashley said. 'And thank you—' she mirrored Mark's nod at Maxine's office '—for reminding us that you've had a lot to gain by his death. That's especially interesting now that we're investigating his murder.'

'His . . . *what?*' Mark's stunned face stared at Ashley, then James. 'How?'

Finally, a reaction. James tried to assess if Mark really had been too preoccupied with the race to notice murder being mentioned before, or if he'd had to steel himself to project enough convincing shock.

'We can't disclose any details at the moment,' Ashley said. 'We just need to talk again to everyone at his party. Especially those who argued with him.'

Mark flushed. 'Right.'

Ashley let the pause draw out, but Mark seemed too lost in thought to volunteer details so she pressed: 'We know you argued with Jack. You're going to have to talk to us about it.'

Mark's shoulders rose as his breathing became shallow. 'Yeah, I'll tell you. After he crashed that lovely machine, and left Cass and me to put it right, he lorded it up at his place, showing me his car collection. And I'm not too proud to admit that it was bloody galling. He had a Lancia Stratos, one of Colin's classic rally cars, worth a fair bit with her racing provenance, and a mid-Eighties Porsche 930 Turbo cabriolet. *That* betrays that he's more into posing than driving, but she's still a nice runaround. More than I've got in my garage, that's for sure. He'd parked the Mustang in the third space in the garage, so Svetlana's Range Rover Velar was on the drive. And he enjoyed ramming it down my throat, playing the big man, showing me all his expensive toys.'

'And that's what you argued about, was it?' Ashley said evenly. 'Your toys?'

'No! Good God! I didn't want him to *know* that his showing off was bothering me.'

'So, what *did* you argue about?' Ashley remained solidly insistent.

Mark's face hardened. His gaze pulled away to the wall across the workbench. He rested his elbows on the bench and leaned his head against both hands. His breath escaped in a groan and he took a long inhalation, then looked up at the detectives.

'I can't bloody keep up with today. I feel like I'm on some sodding emotional roller coaster.' He shook his head. 'Look, I don't want this to get out. I need you to keep this confidential.'

With the briefest exchange of eye contact, James understood that Ashley had tagged him in. She'd observe, letting him draw out why Mark needed their discretion. It was the first reminder he'd had in ages of how well they used to work together.

Mark glanced around the empty garage. Through the open door they saw Maxine on the phone in her corner office, and Mark sighed deeply again.

'I think it's pretty clear that I've put a lot on the line for this team, for this . . .' Mark winced '. . . this *experiment*.'

James nodded, giving a sympathetic smile.

Mark continued, 'I had a small restoration company. Not like one of the big trendy resto mods . . . um, you know, a restoration and modernisation company, like Singer or Eagle. But still a solid company, built up over a decade or so. Good rep, reasonable profits. But now . . .' He gave a long exhalation. 'To support this team, I've pivoted into converting classics. It's obviously a niche market, in a new area. The turnover and margins aren't easy to predict. So I've used all my stake from my solid business to start up one with much higher, unknown risks. Like a new supply chain.' He splayed his hands. 'It's more interesting, more of a challenge. I feel excited about my career again for the first time since . . . I don't know when.' A small smile cracked through his tight expression for a fleeting moment. 'But I had to finance everything. New tools, new kit, new workshop.' He sighed.

'You? Not Mr Moretti?' Ashley clarified.

Mark gave a grimace as he nodded. 'Yeah, he would probably have helped financially, but then he would have wanted a stake. And *then* driven a hard bargain. It was already all in for me. I'd still have had the same risks and I didn't want to have to give up shares in the company and diminish my return.' He shrugged. 'That might be a bit bloody-minded, but there we are.'

'So, how *did* you finance it?' James asked.

Mark leaned his head on his hand again. 'The house. I remortgaged the house.' He rubbed his face with one large hand. 'I haven't exactly hocked it up to the eyeballs, but it's not far off.'

'Is the loan serviceable?' James asked, with just the right note of empathy.

Mark nodded. 'If everything goes to plan.'

Ashley cleared her throat. 'Interesting choice of words.' She tapped her iPad.

Mark's head whipped round. 'Making sure you can quote me in court, are you?'

'Just noting points of interest,' James said easily. 'What *was* your plan?'

'That she comes first in the race!' Mark waggled his hands at Ashley. 'That *nefarious* enough for you?' He sighed heavily. 'Look, the electric engine gives her far more power. We tune her to match her classic contemporaries but then, if she doesn't come in first, well, it's a bit of a bloody poor show, isn't it? We need her to *win*, even *with* her full power dialled back. We need to create a *buzz*.'

'Is that so you'll gain some business after this race?' James asked.

'Exactly! I need to spark a bit of imagination here. Classic collectors who want something different. Or want new tech to modernise their prized machines. Or want to give their classic car some longevity. Then there's the crowd who want those vintage looks without compromising reliability or comfort or tech – the type who want all their gadgets while they drive and don't want to get stuck having to invent a fix with cable ties and wire on a motorway hard shoulder, at night, in the rain. *And* we'd love to make the racing aficionados consider a new racing class, as a way to keep classics on the track. *That's* what will give me some security. Make the risk worthwhile.'

James almost wondered if Mark would end his pitch with: 'and I'm here today to ask for all your money for ten per cent.' Except he didn't want to share a stake in his high-risk company.

Ashley leaned back, observing Mark's impassioned speech. *What had she picked up?*

'Have you got family supporting you through this venture, Mark?' she asked casually.

'I . . . yeah . . . Well.' Another sigh. 'I *did*.'

Ashley nodded. James had a feeling she already knew what was coming.

But he could only offer a sympathetic smile and ask, 'What happened?'

Mark looked over his shoulder to see the garage was still empty. 'My wife . . . we're going through . . . through a divorce.' His voice cracked. His large hand slid across his forehead, as if trying to smooth away the misery. A defeated sob made his shoulders heave and he held his breath for a moment. After a pause, he drew a long breath and looked up at the detectives. 'No one here knows. And I want to keep it that way, OK? That's why I asked for your discretion.'

'Of course,' Ashley said. 'It must be a stressful time. But wouldn't it help for your team to know what you're going through?'

Mark gave a bitter laugh. 'What, and have to admit that my own wife didn't have enough faith in me? In my venture? And *so* little that she left me? That would be a great message to share with your team, wouldn't it!' The false laugh faded, his lips tugging downwards miserably.

Ashley nodded. 'Thanks for your candour.'

Mark shook his head slowly. 'I don't know how that bastard found out. I only took a couple of calls at work about all this, and I always made damn sure I went somewhere private. But somehow he was always in the wrong place at the wrong time. I think he had a way of finding out the chinks in people's armour. And then he'd pick away at them, like a schoolboy with a scab. And that's what he needled me about at his poxy party. When Cass left the garage to go back inside, Jack asked me about the state of my marriage. Said he heard me fighting with my wife on the phone. Said the only time he could remember fighting with women was when he was fighting them off. Said he pitied me.' Mark stared at the wall again.

The detectives waited. After a pause, Ashley asked, 'And then what?'

'And then, nothing.' Mark sighed. 'Not like I could start a fight at his own house, at his own party.'

'That's what you wanted?' James asked. 'A fight?'

'No!' Mark shook his head. 'Well, yeah, honestly I'd have liked to have punched his lights out. But you can't go around doing that, can you. Not exactly dinner party behaviour.'

'Unless you find another outlet for that frustration?' Ashley mused.

Mark stared at her.

'After all, there's more than one way to harm someone.'

Mark gaped. 'No!'

With a nod, Ashley stood up. 'Thank you, that'll be all for now.'

Mark walked away briskly, muttering under his breath. He leaned into the gullwing's open bonnet, just outside the garage door. The detectives watched him, then looked across the garage. Through the door, James saw Maxine was still in the office, on the phone, pacing and rubbing her neck as she spoke. They walked towards her office and Maxine held up three fingers, indicating she'd be free in a few minutes.

Cassie walked back into the garage, clearly bristling. Seeing Mark looking upset, she went over, and they muttered together as Cassie shot shocked, then wary glances at the detectives. Then she made a beeline for Ashley.

'Excuse me, but how do you know Jack was murdered? Wasn't it an accident?'

Despite the question being addressed to Ashley, James assumed the authority to answer. 'His car was tampered with.'

Cassie's face drained of colour and she returned to Mark. James watched as she shared the news with him, and how he mirrored her shock.

James's flicker of optimism that he and Ashley were finding their rhythm again was immediately dashed when she leaned in, her tone barbed. 'While we're waiting, if you want to get *in step* with our next line of inquiry, here's the background.' She passed her phone with the email she'd received earlier still open on the screen – from the forensic team examining Jack's computer.

Trying to keep his focus professional, James read the message, which outlined a complaint of sexual harassment involving Jack. He passed the phone back. 'What do you make of that?'

'Well, we won't know, will we? Until we talk to Maxine.'

Chapter 13

Maxine opened the door and Ashley and James squeezed into her compact office. James looked around. Two bookcases, which had an appearance of hastily constructed flat-packs, contained files, old car magazines and classic car auction catalogues. A world map was stuck to the wall, with handwritten notes posted over Dubai, New York and Monaco. On the wide desk was an open laptop, a stationery tray holding a couple of thumb drives and pens, the printed booklet of the Classics at Finchmere programme and, incongruously, a copy of *Vogue*. Out of the corner of his eye, he noticed a security camera, above the bookcase, in a very discreet position.

'Thank you for making time for this,' James said. 'We appreciate this is a difficult time.'

'That's all right, luv.' Maxine leaned back in her ergonomic chair with an understanding smile, making her heavy foundation crease. 'Not a bundle of fun for you lot, is it?'

Ignoring the ingratiating remark, Ashley cocked her head towards the garage. 'Why was it so difficult to let your second driver step up? Surely that's the point of having one?'

James surreptitiously glanced at Maxine, wondering again about Ashley's blunt technique.

Irritation flashed across Maxine's face. She tilted her chair to an upright position slowly. 'It's a matter of decency, isn't it? Using the second driver for certain races, that's one thing. But when a man's died . . .' Her voice trailed off and she interlaced her fingers.

'Yes, I can appreciate it's delicate. But Jack didn't die on the racetrack,' Ashley said.

Maxine pushed herself back in her chair again, folding her arms across her chest. Her nose wrinkled, showing clear distaste for Ashley's words.

But Ashley continued, apparently unaware. 'If he had, I could understand not racing, or perhaps even cancelling the whole event. But an accident off-track? A moment of respectful silence, perhaps? But then back to business. With the second driver getting on with things. Maybe an interview expressing condolences for the family, continuing with the race in his name, et cetera, et cetera.' Ashley shrugged. 'Wasn't that the obvious course of action?'

'Well, it's complicated . . .' Maxine looked at Ashley. 'Think about it, luv—'

James wondered if the endearment would make Ashley bristle, though he read Maxine's tone as an attempt at being conspiratorial rather than patronising.

'This is a big event, run every year . . .' Maxine lowered her voice. 'Jack's *father*, Colin, used to race here and still attends as a guest. And Colin's good friends with the lord of the manor over yonder, and with our Lucio. I had to be sure we weren't going to cause any upset, or look insensitive.'

Ashley's silence conveyed scepticism.

Maxine shifted on her seat. 'And I couldn't assume Mark wanted to do it . . .'

'Oh, come on!' Ashley protested. '*I* can see how desperate he is to get behind the wheel after five minutes! You couldn't possibly be in doubt. With your sensitivity.'

Under her heavy makeup, Maxine blushed.

'And,' Ashley continued, 'considering the huge investment Mark had made in this conversion and in his new company, you'd at least offer him the opportunity, surely? That would be reasonable.'

'Aye, pet, and we were having those discussions when you arrived.' Maxine folded her arms.

Ashley looked Maxine in the eye. 'Hmm.' Maxine looked away.

Leaning forward, as if an idea had just struck her, Ashley then asked, 'I suppose if Mark had raced here more, like in the test runs and qualifying lap, you'd have a clearer idea of how keen he was. Perhaps trust his ability with the car more. Would you agree?'

'Well, it's not that straightforward,' Maxine said. 'You have to remember that Mark would be fulfilling two roles if he raced. That's a lot to ask . . .'

'Mark seemed OK with that ask,' Ashley pressed. 'Preferable – in his view – to the car being raced by someone who didn't have the talent to win. Who couldn't even keep her on the track. Sorting out the damage Jack caused created more work for Mark. Work he *didn't* want, rather than work, like racing, that he *did*. So, let's try again. *Why* didn't Mark race more often?'

'Ugh,' Maxine groaned, pushing her chair back, the foot of her crossed leg tapping in agitation. 'That wasn't the only thing I needed to deal with in managing this team,' she said. 'I have to balance press interest. Winning here would be very nice. The paper isn't going to print stories of an earnest mechanic driving brilliantly and winning. But they will give us a front page of "Love Rat Jack" crashing out.' She shrugged. 'Just the way it is, luv.'

'Is that one of Jack's interviews?' James pointed at a thumb drive labelled '*Press*.'

Maxine glanced at it, frowning. 'Yes.'

James pointed at Maxine's laptop. 'May we take a look?'

With an irritated tut, Maxine plugged the drive in. As the file loaded and opened, she turned the screen towards the detectives. The recording of Nell, Mark, Maxine, Cassie and Lucio describing the gullwing played.

'Oh, yeah, he's *really* good at these interviews,' Ashley said, watching all the team except Jack represent the project. 'I can see why he's your big press bet.'

Maxine sighed at the sarcasm. 'He does appear. In a second.'

The sound of a growling engine muffled Lucio's last word. At the word 'Cut!' irritation bristled across the team. The camera kept rolling, catching the calls of the crowd. And the press.

Maxine arched an eyebrow. 'Mark's a great guy. But that doesn't happen when he arrives.' She reached for the thumb drive. 'Seen enough? Have I proved my point?'

'Wait.' Ashley held up a hand. 'Let's see to the end.'

They watched Jack's attempt at humour, and Maxine's interruption as she controlled the narrative.

'Loose cannon, though, isn't he?' Ashley observed. 'Quite a burden for you.'

'Yes, well. Again, that's life.' Maxine flushed. 'And getting the Rafferty name attached to our project is a big deal in these circles.'

'Yeah, if it was *Colin* racing,' James said. 'Has Jack really earned his stripes?'

Maxine threw the thumb drive into the tray with a huff. 'You're right. He rests on the family reputation, he's lazy, he's more interested in creating scandal off the track. But what can I do? He still brings what we need. Unfortunately *because* of that promise of scandal.'

'So what did his father make of all that?' James asked. 'He spent years building the reputation that Jack leans on. What's his reaction to his son's performance?'

A silence hung as Maxine regarded them steadily.

Finally, Maxine pursed her lips. 'I suppose that's a question for Colin. I can't speak for him, can I?'

But James had picked up enough. He made a note. *CR unhappy re JR's performance?*

'It suggests to me,' Ashley mused, 'that there was another reason to keep Jack in the driving seat. A reason that overlooked his many obvious . . . inadequacies.'

Maxine tilted her head. 'What's that?'

'Blackmail.'

As she held Ashley's searching eye contact, Maxine's expression hardened. But a pallor leached down her face to her neck. 'You think Jack was blackmailing Lucio?'

'Oh no,' Ashley said conversationally. 'Not Lucio. You.'

James watched closely as a shocked laugh erupted from Maxine, her eyes wide and startled. '*Me?* You think *our Jacko* was blackmailing *me!*'

Ashley remained silent.

'Go on, *tell* me. What was he blackmailing *me* about?' Maxine said, shaking her head.

'We have evidence of a complaint Jack made of sexual harassment. Against you.' Ashley pulled her phone from her pocket and showed Maxine the screen.

Maxine's laughter stopped abruptly. Her face flushed. 'What the . . . ?'

'Shall I read his email?' Ashley asked. 'With his accusation of what you did?'

'No, I've . . . I've got the gist.' Maxine pushed Ashley's phone away. 'Anyone can make that stuff up. Or fake an email.'

'Our forensic team found these emails in Jack's draft folder on his laptop,' Ashley said. 'Unsent. But he could have shown you without sending them. And used them as leverage.'

'And how do you make *that* out?' Maxine spluttered.

'If he threatened to send the emails to Lucio, or any one of his contacts in the press, or anyone on the team, that would be embarrassing. Might harm a carefully built career. *Definitely* might buy him a guaranteed seat behind the wheel at a groundbreaking race.'

'Oh, *do* give over.' Maxine was rapidly regaining her composure. 'Me? Embarrassed by a bloody little scrote like him? If he went to the press, or the team, or Lucio, who do *you* think they'd see as the sex pest?'

'Well, that's an interesting point, isn't it,' Ashley agreed. 'It doesn't have to be true. It doesn't even have to be embarrassing. But it could well stick. And with the marvels of social media and the internet, once it's there, it's there forever. You were just on the phone to a sheikh, I believe, if my lip-reading is still what it used to be. How well would your high-end clients react to such a scandal?'

Maxine frowned. Then shrugged. 'If he tried anything like that, I could sue him.'

'But you'd need proof,' Ashley reasoned.

Maxine raised a finger and pointed to the wall to her left, while looking straight at Ashley. 'Yeah, lady. This is not my first rodeo.'

Ashley studied it. 'Is that your only security camera?'

'Yeah.' Maxine shrugged. 'It covers some of the garage if the door's open.'

'But not all,' Ashley said, a note of finality in her voice.

'No.'

'And it would be a pretty obvious rebuttal that if you knew where the camera was, you wouldn't exactly make your advances right in front of it.'

Maxine opened her mouth. Hesitated. 'No.' She sank back in her seat.

Ashley looked at James. 'Remind me, what did Maxine just call her team's driver?'

Making a point of reading from his notes, James confirmed, '"A bloody little scrote".'

'Hmm. Not *exactly* on the friendly terms you'd have us believe, were you?'

Friday 19th April – 5 p.m.

Rav sat at an outside table of the Foresters' Arms and enjoyed the fresh spring evening and the downland view, waiting for Nell to meet him and Aanya. He tapped his foot impatiently against the leg of his wooden seat, only half listening to his sister. He watched the car park like a meerkat, rising slightly in his seat each time a car approached.

'. . . so it took me ages to find some clothes,' Aanya was saying.

'Looks like you managed.' Rav nodded at her collection of shopping bags.

A sharp tut. 'Get off my case. I can't live in your choice of hoodies and jeans. I got some bargains. Plus, I really love that luxury of clean knickers, if that's not too fussy of me.'

He couldn't disagree. When he'd hastily packed for her, Rav hadn't been able to bring himself to root around in his sister's underwear drawer. But he was saved by another car turning in, and he craned his head, hoping to see her – then beaming at the welcome sight of the Taycan.

'Oh, you got it so bad, bro,' Aanya teased as Nell parked and walked over.

Ignoring her, Rav stood and wrapped Nell in a huge hug. As he kissed her, Aanya said, 'Jeez, get a room.'

'God, it's so lovely to sneak away from the track for an hour.' Nell sank onto the seat. 'Everyone expects me to have all the answers about the race schedules. And Jack. Word's getting out that it wasn't an accident, and that's making everyone worried. I'm honestly not sure what's going to happen with all the plans for this weekend, though. Dad's muddling through. Tonight's welcome dinner was cancelled because, well, it seems a bit in poor taste and Dad needs a chance to rearrange everything.'

Rav knew Nell was making light of it. Before Jack's death, after all the incidents at Percy's wedding last month, her family had needed to talk event participants into still coming. But she sank into the seat beside him, mustering a smile, and tugged his clean T-shirt. 'You look like you feel better.'

'Tons better after getting some shut-eye and a shower at your folks'. Thanks for that. I needed to catch up after the sleepless night.' He shot a fake glare at Aanya, who just tutted in reply. 'And I went to your place to feed Jezebel. But, then, um, actually, I brought her back with me. She's camping out in your – our – room. Just for the weekend.'

'Oh—'

'I can see how the next couple of days are going to go – you'll never have time to keep running back to feed her. And no one should go that long without a cuddle. And Sylvia's not free to look after her again, even though I know our hero of a colleague would take her home in a heartbeat if she could.'

'I was going to say, "What a cute idea", Nell said. 'Thanks, you're right.'

'Oh!' Rav beamed. But he spotted her eyebrow-flash at Aanya, as if asking a silent question. Aanya seemed to give a slight nod back. *Have I missed something?* Before he could ask, Aanya leaned forward.

'Man, I'm starving. Fancy buying me dinner, Rav?'

'Good idea.' Nell took the menu with a smile. 'But let me get this.'

As the waiter brought out the drinks Rav had asked for, they ordered food, then Nell turned to Aanya. 'I'm looking forward to your folks visiting tomorrow . . .'

Aanya, mid-sip of her Jägerbomb, spluttered. 'Yeah, sure – you know they're going to be a nightmare, right?'

With a grin, Nell agreed. 'They're worried. It's natural. But I'm sure they'll be reassured pretty quickly.' She glanced at Rav. 'I mean, it's all OK now. You're only really staying so you're on hand in case the police want to talk to you. You're hardly a prime suspect.' She looked searchingly at both of them. 'Or am I missing something?'

Rav nodded. 'Yeah, Aanya, they'll just be pleased you're OK.'

'Maybe in your world, Number One Son.' Aanya rolled her eyes. 'They'll be giving me grief about this for the rest of my life.' She sighed theatrically.

'Hey, Nell? Twice in one day?' A loud, languid male voice interrupted their conversation.

Rav saw Nell's shoulders drop as she adopted a bright, fake smile and turned, standing, to exchange air kisses with a tanned, wavy-haired man. 'Hi, Jonty. If you're here, does that mean you and Mai have had a good day at the pond?'

'Nell!' Mai squealed. 'And Rav! No *way!*' She barrelled into a hug with him.

Laughing, he hugged her back. 'It's great to see you!'

'Rav, this is Jonty, Mai's new assistant at Little Smitington Reserve. Jonty, this is Rav, also an ecologist. And my partner.'

Mai squealed again and punched Rav's arm, saying, 'Finally,' in a stage whisper.

At the same time, Jonty grasped Rav's hand and twisted the grip into a hand clasp. Rav's bemused look became a wince as Jonty pulled Rav forward to slam their shoulders together. The one he'd almost torn out of its socket, rescuing Nell last month. 'This is my sister, Aanya.'

Aanya said hello but didn't move from her seat. She regarded Jonty over her drink and smiled at Mai. Rav noted that Mai must have had a rough day. Messy hair, grubby leggings, mud streaked across her top and her cheek. She looked shattered as she sat heavily at the next table and a waiter approached to take their order.

Passing Jonty a menu, Mai warned, 'As nice as it is to catch up, we're just here for a quick bite before we need to get back to the ranch. The rescue mission continues.'

'What would you like, Mai?' Jonty asked. 'Have anything! Have everything! Lady Nell will pay!' He bestowed on Nell what he obviously imagined was a winning smile.

Rav and Aanya gaped at him, clearly shocked by Jonty's presumption. Nell shrugged easily. 'Don't tell me you've drunk your way through your trust fund, Jonty? I'm sure you can manage to cover your own dinner.' She smiled innocently.

As Mai and Jonty ordered food, Rav tried to make eye contact with Nell. When she finally looked at him, their gazes locked. She leaned towards him, and he wrapped an arm around her. Nell took the opportunity to whisper, 'You should know, Jonty is kind of an ex. Don't judge me. I didn't know any better.'

'No *way*, dude!' Rav whispered comedically into Nell's hair.

'Yes, way. Unfortunately,' Nell replied.

Rav kissed her and released her, but saw that Mai was muttering crossly at Jonty.

'Yeah, Nell's done more than her fair share today, Jonty.' Mai was on the defensive. 'And don't be a knob about her paying and throwing her title about.'

'Oh. My bad.' Jonty raised unrepentant hands. His grin flashed teeth that were toothpaste-ad-ready.

'Yes, I can see how a little discretion might be an intellectual stretch,' Nell muttered.

'Yah, yah,' Jonty agreed, unruffled. In fact, Rav realised, everything about him was unruffled. Unlike Mai, his khaki shorts were pristine. Knowing the likely state of the pond, and the scale of the work, Rav wondered if Mai had been doing at least two people's work today. And he knew that would be needling Nell.

As the waiter brought out a coffee for Mai, she took a thankful gulp, then turned to Rav. 'So *you* already knew about Nell's background, then? That was news to me today.'

Rav hid a grimace. It had felt awful when he'd found out. Like a barrier he'd never known about was stacked between them. But he just nodded.

'Really?' Jonty shot Mai a surprised look, then turned to Nell. 'You should tell us, then, Nell, how much of the land on which we stand is yours?'

'The racetrack, the hotel, some farmland.'

Jonty whistled. 'That's what, ten thousand acres?'

Rav re-evaluated the feckless-looking guy: his guess was pinpoint accurate.

'Nice work, Rav.' Aanya swigged her drink. 'Scored a tycoon. No wonder Mum's matches didn't make the grade.'

'Oh, classy,' said Rav, rolling his eyes. Knowing Nell would be keen to deflect the conversation, he asked Mai, 'How's the pond restoration going?'

Mai huffed a long exhalation, shaking her head as she recollected the day. 'I suppose we've made some progress today.' She nudged Nell. 'The membrane and sandbag divider you and the volunteers put in is holding up well. The pollutants aren't spreading. The fencing contractor you recommended turned up, so I fingertip-searched the ground while he dug the trench and installed the amphibian fence around the pond. So nothing can get into the polluted half now. And I've been trapping frantically all day with bottle traps and nets to translocate everything from the contaminated side to the unpolluted side. I don't know if it'll take, but I've tried to reseed the grassy banks, too. It's a quagmire over there now.'

'Slow day, then,' Rav teased, trying to make her look less worried, maybe even smile.

The tension fell away from Mai's shoulders and she managed a small grin. 'Sorry. It's just such a lot to keep track of.' She had another gulp of coffee. 'I still don't know if I should postpone the assessor's visit, or risk it, to be honest.' Mai thanked the waiter when her steak sandwich was set in front of her. She looked across to Jonty, who was checking his phone, ignoring his food, totally unhurried.

Mai leaned in to whisper, 'You'd think the end of the world had come when I asked him to drive to Swansea. And, sure, it's a long way. But he took *so* long.' She mimicked his accent. 'Because I, like, needed to have, like, twenty million *breaks*.' She huffed. 'Meanwhile, *I'm* rolling around in mud single-handedly!'

Nell nodded gravely. 'Yeah, I can see that's really annoying when you'd rather be rolling around in the mud double-handedly.'

Mai shoved her, pulling a comedy grimace, mouthing, 'He's too *hot* to get upset with.'

Nell shook her head, and Rav could see that she disagreed with Mai: Nell was more interested in substance than style.

'So what's your schedule?' Nell asked. 'Traps out and torching tonight? Emptying traps tomorrow at six?' When Mai nodded, Nell added, 'Want a hand? Or even delegate and have a lie-in? I can spare a couple of hours.'

Rav froze. Nell was already too busy – *crazy* busy – to spend much time with his folks. He hadn't realised that, when he'd invited his parents to the event. He knew Nell was doing everything she could to free up her schedule, but she didn't really need an extra layer of work.

Then he caught sight of Mai's face and realised why. Relief and delight were palpable. 'Some *help*—' Mai shot a glare at Jonty '—would be *amazing*.'

And even Rav had to admit that his parents were unlikely to be free for quality bonding time before 7 a.m.

Nell's phone beeped and she answered the email hurriedly. Over her shoulder, Rav recognised the event manager's name – Astrid – and a series of bullets:

8 a.m.–8.30 a.m. – Lucio's team meeting
8.30 a.m.–9 a.m. – hotel staff meeting
9 a.m.–9.30 a.m. – review / sign off filmed footage for TV release
9.30 a.m.–10 a.m. – free (circulate)
10 a.m.–11 a.m. – Montague's auction house meeting
11 a.m.–12 p.m. – free (circulate)
12 p.m.–1 p.m. – lunch
1 p.m.–2 p.m. – Montague's auction
2 p.m.–4 p.m. – prize-giving
4 p.m.–5 p.m. – end of day meeting

Nell nodded firmly at Mai. 'It's fine. I'd love to help.'

Chapter 14

Friday 19th April – 5 p.m.

'I'm just saying, it's all been a bit one-note, too *blunt* in today's interviews,' James criticised, trying to keep up with Ashley as she stormed down the hallway of Finchmere Hotel.

'Blunt?' Ashley gaped. '*Seriously?* I'm just trying to provoke responses. You know the score. Don't make this something it isn't. And I'd say the questioning is going well. We've already got several leads, uncovered plenty of issues. So what's your problem, exactly?'

'I'm just recommending that we'd get further by building a rapport.'

'Oh, well, thanks for your recommendation, *DI* Clark. I'll be sure to keep my gauche DS ways in check.'

James bit back the retaliation, but he glared at Ashley.

'Shame you can't say it, isn't it?' Ashley said, as she turned towards the spa.

'Say what?' James didn't want to extend the argument. He'd only wanted the two of them to get back into their solid working rhythm. When they knew what the other would say, supported the line of questioning. Transitioned between techniques. And *trusted* each other. He'd wanted those small moments they'd had this morning to be the norm again, not the exception.

'Shame you can't say that you're passing on a valuable recommendation because your interview skills – or *any* skills for that matter – earned you those DI stripes.'

Ashley shoved open the door to the gym, leaving James unable to answer. But he felt stabbed in the gut. He knew Ashley had taken issue with his promotion. But he wouldn't have been promoted if his work wasn't up to it. And fine, Chief Constable Trent may have only been a supporter once James had started dating Nell. But networking was a skill, too. And Ashley was losing at that. *Why is she making such a big deal about it? We already had that argument – and resolved it. So what's still bothering her?*

Spotting Dani Marshall doing pull-ups while wearing a weighted belt, James felt even more uncomfortable and distinctly out of place in his suit amongst these Lycra-clad women. He hastily looked away from one doing a post-workout stretch in downward dog, only to be confronted with the same view in the mirrored wall. He was relieved when Ashley finally attracted Dani's attention and she agreed to join them in the meeting room that Nell had set aside for questions.

Passing the gym café, Dani asked, 'Can I pop in and get something for dinner, before it closes, so I can eat once we're finished? I'm running late today. My morning was . . . a bit of a mess.'

'Sure,' Ashley said. She and James waited while Dani made a quick selection from the fridge. Despite the menu being exclusively healthy, James found himself looking at the options almost longingly. Their hastily grabbed afternoon tea in the hotel's Orangery had seemed to be the quickest way to eat. But the dainty micro-herb-garnished sandwiches hadn't exactly been hearty fare. He couldn't eat while he had to take notes, though, so he ignored his growling stomach and followed Ashley and Dani to the meeting room.

The three of them clustered around the end of a long conference table and Dani, who'd looked so strong and capable in the gym, suddenly seemed vulnerable and overwhelmed. She took a tissue from the packet that James passed to her. She blew her nose and dabbed her eyes. Her face tremored with emotion and James felt a pang of sympathy.

'Sorry. I feel all over the place with all . . . all this going on.' Dani had a sip of water and took a deep breath. She looked at the detectives. 'I don't know what I can tell you that could help.' Her shoulders rounded, adding even more definition to her muscles, as she sat forward in her workout vest over an acid-yellow sports bra, clutching a bottle of what looked like a protein shake, beside her prawn salad.

James was determined to begin the questions this time, to set the tone of the questioning. 'You were at Jack's party last night? You're a friend of Svetlana's?'

'Yes.' Dani mouthed the word but no sound came out. She tried again. 'Yes. I left soon after dinner. The catering staff were still there. I came back here. Lana . . . Svetlana . . . had got me a room in case she stayed here with Jack, so we'd still be able to train while he was racing. That way she'd be on hand for all the press and sponsorship appearances, but she wouldn't miss any workouts.'

'Is that how you and Svetlana met?' James continued, tapping his iPad. 'As her trainer?'

'Yes. I'd worked with another client of her agent's, so he referred me. Lana's a sports ambassador now. We produce workouts for vlogs and social media. Generates publicity for her brand and the products she sells. But we have to keep getting more and more hardcore.'

'Here.' Pulling her iPhone out from her armband, Dani searched, then passed the phone to James. To a pounding soundtrack, Dani and Svetlana's fearsome montage showed impressive gymnastics, powerful sparring, kickboxing and racing each other up salmon ladders.

'Wow. That really *is* hardcore.' James considered himself pretty fit, but even so, he held in his already lean stomach. He regarded Dani. 'If you're doing all the same things as Svetlana, how come she's the ambassador and you're the trainer?'

With a disdainful smile, Dani screwed up her used tissue. 'Profile. Lana's a model, going out with, then marrying, a racing driver. She has the platform. Us mere mortals need real jobs.'

James couldn't mistake her stung tone. 'How was it, working with her, when you're just a mere mortal?' He gave Dani a smile he hoped indicated solidarity, to invite her confidence.

'Honestly, working with Lana was great. She was tough, never complained, nothing diva-ish about her.' Dani's lower lip trembled, and she bit it.

'Was?' James said.

'Yeah, I think it's all over now.'

'Why's that?' James asked.

'Because of Jack . . .' Dani dabbed at her running nose with the balled-up tissue.

James wondered what that meant. *Because Jack had died? Was*

Svetlana moving? Retiring? Had something happened between the women? He waited for Dani to compose herself and explain. As the pause drew out, he followed Val's example of using the power of the silence. Let the interviewee feel the need to fill it. He sat still, ignoring the immediate itch on his face.

But Ashley had other ideas. 'Well? What about Jack?' she demanded.

Dani winced and finally answered, 'Lana will leave here. There's nothing here for her now. The house was convenient for Jack – commutable to London but somewhere he could enjoy a bit of space, especially for his garage, near his family. But now . . . ?' She wiped her nose again.

'If Svetlana moves, would you move with her?' James asked.

Dani shook her head.

'Why not?' James pushed. 'You've followed her here.'

'It's all different now,' Dani said.

Ashley interrupted his questions to ask, 'Because you argued with them at the party?'

Dani's face drained of colour but she rallied. 'Yes, there was a minor disagreement. But that wasn't . . .' Her voice trailed off. 'Look, I think Lana wants to carve a different path for herself now that Jack . . .'

'Is out of the picture?' Ashley interrupted again, to James's increasing irritation. 'Doesn't that sound a bit convenient?'

'No! Well, maybe, but not like *that!*'

'Then enlighten us,' Ashley invited. 'Like what, exactly?'

'Oh, for God's sake.' Dani was visibly rattled and James hid a groan. 'Lana and Jack's agents worked for the same company, so they're linked on a few endorsements. It's how they met, actually, at some product launch. But now Lana will have more freedom, she doesn't have to go along with things that would also suit Jack's profile. I think she'll be pleased . . .'

Ashley narrowed her eyes.

'No! Oh for . . . *No!*' Dani looked exasperated. 'Stop twisting my words!'

Ashley folded her arms and sat back in her chair, silently pointing out she wasn't talking.

Shaking her head, Dani's lips set in a trembling line. James saw her fighting back tears.

'You're understandably upset.' He tried to get the conversation back on a positive footing. 'Is that because you argued with them both? Right before Jack died?'

Dani bit her lip and her head turned sharply. She gazed at the wall, her brimming eyes unfocused. James and Ashley waited until she spoke again. 'It's all such a mess.'

'Look, you can talk openly with us,' James said. 'We know what you argued about.' He at least knew Ashley wouldn't give away his lie.

But Dani's features stretched with incredulity, making her reddened eyes bulge. 'I *cannot* believe Lana told you.'

'We need to understand the full picture,' Ashley said. 'And we need everyone's cooperation.' To Dani's uncomprehending expression, she added, 'This *is* a murder inquiry.'

Dani looked shocked. 'It's . . . *What?* It's . . . ? I thought he had an accident in his car?'

Ashley and James watched her reaction, saying nothing.

'I see.' Dani stared at them both. 'And Lana's thrown me under the sodding bus, has she?' She propped an elbow on the table and leaned her forehead into her hand, closing her eyes.

'So, you know Jack and I were having an affair.' Dani's voice was flat. James and Ashley didn't react.

'Lana told me she knew at the party. I'd got there early, we'd got ready together, and she waited until after dinner to say anything.' Dani groaned. 'She yelled at me, then Jack. In front of everyone.' She looked up sharply. '*Did* Lana tell you? Or someone else?' Her chin shook.

James saw her unguarded reaction, and how much it mattered. 'It was someone else.'

Dani let out a breath. 'OK, OK.' She rubbed her forehead. 'I'm not sure if that's worse. That people overheard and knew what she was so upset about. But . . .' She bit her lip.

'*She* didn't throw you under the bus,' James reiterated, hoping to encourage details.

'But this is why you think she wants to terminate your working relationship?' Ashley clarified. At Dani's nod, she asked, 'Has she said so?'

'No. But I know.' Dani looked at her lap.

'Do you think Svetlana would have "terminated" anything – any*one* – else, as a result?'

Dani's head jerked up. 'That some kind of sick joke? No! *Definitely* not!'

'No?' Ashley pursed her lips, as if this was a new theory.

'How long had the affair been going on?' James asked.

Dani's face flushed. 'Six months, or thereabouts.'

'So it started before they were married?' James clarified. 'How did Svetlana find out?'

Dani squirmed on her seat but she nodded. 'She'd overheard us talking the day before.' She swallowed hard. 'It would have been obvious.'

'Bit careless,' Ashley observed.

'Jack liked to take risks. He liked to say things or do things at parties, or when people were around. I'm not sure if it gave him a thrill or if he genuinely wanted to be found out.'

Ashley arched an eyebrow. 'Did it give you a thrill, too?'

'No! I hated it. I didn't want to . . . to . . .' she searched for words, and said, 'create a scene,' just as Ashley offered helpfully, 'get caught?' and scored a scowl from Dani.

'Did you want to end it?' James asked. 'Or did you want a relationship?'

Dani shook her head. Then shrugged. 'Oh, I don't know. I didn't set out to hurt anyone. Least of all Lana. But it just happened. And then it was too late to do anything.'

'If Jack took risks,' Ashley pressed, 'of *course* you'd be caught. And hurt your friend.'

Dani studied her lap.

'I'd hate Jack for that,' Ashley said. 'Taking risks, outing the affair, ruining a friendship.'

Dani's head jerked up and she stared at Ashley.

'Not only ruining a friendship,' Ashley pushed, 'but your career? Your high-profile role in celebrity circles – your star was certainly rising. How's it doing now?'

Dani looked stunned. She tried to protest but Ashley continued.

'Instead, you have a scandal on your hands, blurring professional and friendship boundaries, making it hard to be employed again in such rarefied circles.' Ashley nodded at Dani. 'Especially when getting posts through referrals is how it tends to work at this level.'

Dani stood, grabbing her food. 'Fine. Why should I care what you think?'

'You're right. You shouldn't care about what we think, Dani,' Ashley agreed. 'But you *should* care about what we *deduce*.'

Storming out, Dani slammed the door forcefully behind her.

James sighed at Ashley. 'So that's what Svetlana didn't want to tell us? That her husband was sleeping with her best friend?'

Ashley frowned. 'I don't know. I don't think that can be all there is to it. Not given Jack's reputation.' She tilted her head, as if in challenge. 'Any ideas?'

James hated the hint of game-playing. That wasn't how they worked. Or how they *should* work. He was relieved at the beep from his phone, until he read the message.

'Great. Fraud want to brief us on what we can and can't do in our investigation.'

'Oh, this'll be fun.' Ashley stood up. 'You can take all your constructive critique to them and remind them that murder trumps fraud. I'll take notes on how to handle this, DI Clark.'

Great. Just what I need.

Chapter 15

Saturday 20th April – 6 a.m.

Nell emptied the final bottle trap in her section and looked around. Rav was pulling up his last trap. He was sweet to come along with her and help. Mai was clambering up the bank, having finished, looking knackered. Jonty was still grappling with his first trap. Nell prickled with irritation. *Get a bloody move on, Jonty.*

Checking the sandbagged membrane, Nell was pleased to see how well it was holding up, and released the newts into the uncontaminated section of the pond.

Nell collected Rav's and Mai's buckets and liberated their newts. She picked up the meters and recorded the readings in the contaminated section, then looked to see how far Jonty had got. He was only on his third trap out of ten.

Trying not to roll her eyes, Nell turned to Mai. 'By the look of your readings, I reckon we can get those floating islands in today. We have time now, if you'd like?'

Mai nodded. 'Thanks, I'd appreciate that.'

Nell turned and called out, 'Jonty? Would you finish that trap, then get the truck and bring the floating islands down? I'll finish your section.'

Rav stood up. 'I'll give you a hand, Jonty.'

As Nell emptied Jonty's traps, she studied Mai, who sat on the grassy half of the bank. She looked wan, fed up, like she'd aged a hundred years. With a groan, Mai flopped on her back.

'God, everything aches. I feel like a zombie.'

'I'm not surprised,' Nell said, as she transferred the captured newts to the unpolluted side. 'Did you get much sleep last night?'

'Sleep? What's that!' Mai said. 'Here before dawn, working all day, a break for dinner, then back at night.' She let out a long, cathartic sigh. 'It's not just these past two days, it's that it's on top of all the long days and nights preparing for the SSSI assessment. I had such high hopes. But look at it.'

Mai nodded towards end of the pond, once grassed and fringed with reeds and sedges, now naked mud slides, police activity still apparent. The membrane across the middle marked the extent of the pollution. The contaminated section was ringed with smooth, white amphibian fencing dug into an ugly trench that tore through the grassland, with bucket pitfall traps sunk into the ground on the pond side of the fence for unsuspecting newts to fall into. Mai was doing everything to maximise her chances of moving the sensitive species – and any others she caught along with them – away from the harmful chemical spill.

'I may as well admit it,' Mai groaned. 'It's a disaster.'

'I don't think so,' Nell said. She scissored her wader-clad legs over the thigh-high fencing and crouched to check the pitfall traps. 'Your levels are getting back to normal; we can start to absorb the remaining pollutants from today – which is *brilliant*. The populations are still thriving thanks to your rapid rescue.' She stretched her back, glancing at the bank. 'And the vegetation will grow again. Quicker than you think.'

'But it won't make the grade,' Mai said. Her voice sounded hollow.

Nell's head jerked up from the last pitfall trap and studied her friend. Mai sounded utterly defeated. It was so unlike her. 'I think any assessor would be impressed, Mai. Look at how you've tackled this. You're turning around a pollution event in record time. You're making sure impacts are minimal, recovering everything you can. This is *exceptional* management, Mai.'

As she delivered more trapped newts to the clean side of the pond, Nell turned, hesitating, but decided to say something. 'I'm just slightly worried that you're looking after the newts better than you look after yourself.'

Mai shook her head.

'I mean, you *do* have an assistant. And volunteers . . .'

'None of whom are reliable,' Mai said. 'My fault. I didn't build the right team for the job. *Jobs*. So of course it's all ruined.'

'It's not ruined, Mai. But you do need some reinforcements. Can I make a few calls? We've got a couple of terrific interns, both really keen to get their newt licences. This work will help them qualify and might give you a break. Or even a day or two off?'

'Ha! I'd put money on you not managing it.' Mai sighed again. 'Although anyone would be less useless than me right now.'

Nell looked up as Jonty and Rav pulled up in the truck. Rav leapt out, his sleeves rolled up, ready to unload. Jonty got out slowly and leaned against the door, looking at his phone.

'Hey, Jonty,' Nell called out. 'Give Rav a hand to unload, then we can all have a break.'

Rav lugged an island to the side of the pond and went back for the second. As he hefted it to the far side, Jonty managed to pull the last one from the truck and carried it to the nearest point.

'Thanks,' Nell directed her appreciation at Rav but Jonty answered. 'Hey, no problem!'

Using a net, Nell pushed the islands to space them out around the polluted area. 'You happy with this, Mai?'

Mai looked over wearily and nodded.

Beckoning Jonty over, Nell did her best to rein in her annoyance. 'Jonty, seriously, you have to up your game. Haven't you noticed that Mai is exhausted?'

'Really?' Jonty asked. He looked towards Mai. She was heaving herself to her feet as if her body was made of lead.

'I think it's worse than exhaustion, actually,' Nell said. 'I think this all meant so much to her that she feels like a failure, like she can't put it right. She can't seem to see that she's making it better, and impressively so. I think . . .'

'She could be depressed?' Rav asked.

Nell nodded. 'Maybe a bit? This has certainly hit her hard. I'm worried about her. We *have* to help her get this fixed, and in the best shape possible for her assessment.'

'Sure.' Jonty nodded emphatically. Uncertainty flickered over his usual confident expression. 'But, like, *how?*'

Chapter 16

Rav hurried back to Nell's handsome Porsche Taycan clutching two bacon sarnies and strong coffee. Around him, the racetrack's themed food trucks were stirring the circuit into life as vendors got their early breakfasts. Aromas of bacon and onions made Rav's stomach growl as the pale sunlight crept across the sky.

Opening the door, he heard Nell speaking as she changed from site gear into her snug black jumper. 'Thanks, Astrid,' Nell said to the event manager. 'I can make those extra meetings today, but I do need to keep lunch free. Yes.' She looked at Rav, wincing.

He couldn't help the bite of disappointment that he and his folks wouldn't be spending an hour or so looking round with her today. But lunch was better than nothing, and even that seemed under threat. So he mouthed 'thank you' back, as she squirmed and tucked her top into her capri pants. She jumped out and they sat at a picnic table, watching vendors open their tented stalls, share jokes over steaming cups of coffee as they passed each other, and stamped feeling into cold feet.

'I'm sorry about abandoning you,' Nell said between bites. 'Astrid's just snapped up my free windows with two extra meetings, which I can't postpone, under the circumstances.'

'I'll survive,' Rav said. 'It's nice to wander about while it's quiet.'

'Dad will probably show you around. The cars for today's races will assemble in the East Field.' She nodded towards it. 'His Alfa's out today. It's his pride and joy. If you want to impress him, believe me, saying something nice about the Alfa is the way to his heart. And you look the part. Sexy outfit.' Her eyes gleamed through the steam of her coffee and she reached out and tugged the collar of his jacket.

Rav felt a shiver of delight. He hadn't exactly been overrun with options: jeans, white T-shirt, well-worn leather jacket and his thick wavy hair styled into something like a quiff was his low-budget option that would have to work all weekend. He leaned closer and teased a kiss out of her – until her phone beeped and she groaned.

After she'd raced off, Rav wandered over to the East Field. Black and chrome vintage bikes were lined up opposite a pastel rainbow of Vespas, with stylised information boards. Working his way along the rows, he drank in the details, jumping when a hand clapped his shoulder.

'Rav! Good to see you out and about so early!' Hugo Ward-Beaumont was ramrod straight beside him, grey hair combed smartly.

Rav grinned at Nell's dad, who'd been nothing but welcoming ever since he'd saved Nell from drowning and they'd shared hospital vigils. He shook Hugo's hand warmly. 'Morning! Nell's already in her meetings, so I can admire these without the crowds.'

'You more of a bike man than a car man?' Hugo asked, taking in his outfit and the line of bikes Rav was admiring. 'You want to ask Nell to let you take her fancy electric superbike for a spin on the track. You should also ask her about the courses she took, if you're interested.'

'Oh, I'm interested!' Rav said. 'Not sure she'd let me loose on her machine, though. And anyway, it's nice to find things to appreciate in both,' he added, remembering the Alfa.

Hugo's face lit up. 'Too true! Bikes are where I started out. I had a lot of fun with one like this. But . . .' he sighed wistfully '. . . I had a crash, just after Nell was born. Imelda told me to pack in the bikes. I got a car for rallies, instead. Still fun, but a bit safer.' He beckoned Rav to a dainty, Italian-red car, gleaming in the soft morning light. Polishing an imaginary mark off the front wing with the sleeve of his tweed jacket, he beamed. 'She gave me the car bug, all right. Stylish, feisty, and won almost every race she's been in.'

'What a beautiful Alfa,' he gambled out loud.

'Aha! More of a buff than you'd led me to believe!' Hugo looked delighted. 'Alfa Romeo Giulia Sprint GTA.'

'Is she going out today?' Rav asked. When Hugo nodded, he added, 'Then she'll be the star of her show. Such lovely lines. She's gorgeous.'

He looked at Hugo, who seemed to be expecting more. But Rav was out of compliments. 'How does she drive?' he asked.

Hugo looked around at the empty field, the silent circuit. The only activity was from vendors setting up and getting food. He grinned at Rav. 'Why don't I show you!' Heading to the driver's door, he called across the roof, 'Come on, son! Let me show you what she's made of!'

Inside the car, beside Rav, Hugo pulled a walkie-talkie from his belt and radioed a marshal. 'Can you give me the all-clear to take the Alfa for a quick spin on the track?' He gave Rav a gleeful nod. 'Good-oh. Thanks!' The Alfa's engine barked into life with the sharp smell of petrol. Hugo revved the engine.

'She needs a bit of firm handling to start with!' Hugo called above the engine as he expertly encouraged the temperamental car across the uneven field towards the racetrack. Hugo pulled up, unlocked the gate to the track, got back in the car and checked the temperature gauge. 'Ah, she's nicely warmed up,' he enthused as they drove to the starting line. 'We'll do a sighting lap so I can show you the landmarks and get the tyres warm.'

Rav listened as Hugo showed him the features he used to brake and accelerate, how to take a racing corner and the key turns. He approached the starting line for the second time.

'Righto. This is our flying lap!' Hugo changed down a gear, slamming the accelerator to the floor. Lurching forward, Rav gripped his seat as they shot forward like a bullet. It was the most exhilarating feeling! His senses sharpened and blood rushed into his cheeks. 'Woohoo!'

Handling the car with fearless skill, Hugo swerved through the chicane, accelerated smoothly, hugged a wide, arcing bend, then hurtled down the home straight. At the finish line, Rav and Hugo looked at one another in breathless elation. As the car drew to a stop, Hugo got out and gestured to Rav to do the same. 'Your turn, son. Let's see what you're made of.'

Rav scrambled eagerly out of his seat, walked around the car and sat reverently in the driver's seat. The controls and dials were neat, contained. He familiarised himself with mirrors, gearbox range, pedals. The engine snarled at the lightest touch to the accelerator.

'Careful you don't flood the engine,' Hugo warned.

Rav nodded, slipped the car into first gear and pulled away. Moving off was jerky and he needed to change up to second immediately. He found third, used the long gear to accelerate more confidently and slipped into fourth, then fifth. He tested the brakes, which weren't as responsive as he expected. He braked harder and jerked nearly to a standstill, having to change to second to match the speed and avoid stalling.

Hugo nodded at Rav's reaction. 'Good!' he called out over the engine's roar. 'Listen to the engine. Experiment a bit on this slalom, get a feel for her. Watch this camber. Now the chicane. You've got it! Keep on the inside of this corner, now open her up on the home straight.'

As Rav became more familiar with the car, the racetrack straightened out ahead of him.

'Let it rip!' Hugo cried gleefully.

Rav obeyed, squeezing the accelerator to the floor. The speedometer's needle turned purposefully around the dial. The small car shook and Rav braced his arms and shoulders to maintain control inside the rattling cockpit. He kept the wheel straight and the pedal on the floor. His face was taut as he crossed the finish line at a respectable speed.

After easing off the accelerator, Rav brought the car to a stop. He turned to Hugo with an enormous beam on his face. 'That was amazing! Thank you so much!'

'Drive us back then!' Hugo suggested. He grinned at Rav's reaction as he radioed the marshal to confirm they'd left the track.

As Rav turned towards the field, Hugo leaned in. In a confidential manner, much like Nell's, he said, 'Not bad at all. Bit of practice and you could be a decent racer.'

Rav pulled up in the Alfa's original spot and saw Nell walking towards them. As she approached, she laughed when she saw Rav in the driving seat.

'How was it?' she asked, opening Rav's door so he could get out.

'In-*cred*-ible.' Rav beamed. He suddenly realised how much his arms were aching and rolled his shoulders, then bent down and rubbed his injured foot.

Nell gave a knowing nod. 'Speeding down the home straight?' she teased. She glanced at her father, and Rav saw him flash her a grin as he closed the passenger door.

'I'm running into my next meeting, over at the hotel,' Nell said. 'But I'll be free for lunch. Your parents are getting here for twelve, right?'

'Yes.'

Nell winced but nodded. 'I'll do my best to be on time. It'll be tight, though.'

'Turn up when you can,' Rav said. 'I'll explain that you're busy. I'm sure they'll understand.'

Saturday 20th April – 12.15 p.m.

Nell tried not to let her impatience show as she, Rav and Aanya waited at the table in Finchmere Hotel's Orangery. Waiters cleared the tables, set into nooks created by screens of fragrant citrus trees around them, replacing the snowy table linen and making sure the scented freesias on the laid tables were fresh and watered.

Rav checked the time and sighed. 'God, they're going to be so stressed out when they arrive. They hate being late.'

'Can't you call them?' Nell asked.

Aanya and Rav both gave a short laugh. 'Yeah, right!' Aanya explained, 'Mum and Dad only switch their mobiles on when *they* want to make a call. *So* annoying!'

Nell kept a diplomatic silence. She'd curtailed her main morning meeting, which had threatened to overrun, and, on being asked to 'just go over one more thing', had firmly said it had to wait until after lunch, which meant shoehorning it in before the afternoon's auction. All so that she'd be punctual for Rav's parents. And every minute that ticked by made it harder for her to be able to keep to that amended schedule. She picked up her phone and sent yet another apologetic email asking to move the discussion again. She was not going to be popular.

Rav glanced around. 'Is it going to cause problems? If they're here when they've finished serving lunch.'

'Not today,' Nell tried to reassure him. 'When we have events going on, Chef serves all day. And I've let him know that our guests are late.' She looked at Rav, then Aanya. 'Shall I go out to wait in the car park, in case they're not sure where to go?'

Aanya sighed and stood up. 'I'll go. I'll have to face the music eventually.' Like Rav, she'd sourced an outfit, finding a bargain at a stall: an emerald pencil dress that made her look like a Fifties movie star.

As Aanya walked towards the restaurant's door, two figures rushed in. Neeta looked disconcerted, wisps of hair escaping her bun. Behind her, Rakesh followed, his brows gathered low in a deep frown.

They stopped short just inside the doorway, scanning the mostly empty room, then spotted Aanya as she reached out her arms in greeting.

Neeta hurried to her daughter, cupping her face in both hands, gazing at her, then gathering her into a tight hug.

'Terrible journey,' Rakesh grunted. 'Traffic was awful.'

Neeta squeezed Aanya fiercely. 'We were so worried, *Beta*. It's good to see you.'

Released from the hug, Aanya led her parents to the table. As a waiter brought a large tray of tea accoutrements, Neeta asked, 'Are we too late for lunch?'

'Not at all,' the waiter said, deftly handing out leather-bound menus. 'And here's the wine list. *Do* let me know if you have any questions.'

After murmured thanks, the menus were ignored as Aanya was the subject of her parents' laser focus. 'Your mother has been beside herself,' Rakesh scolded.

Nell noticed sunken black smudges below Rakesh's eyes. His eyelids had puffed up like Rav's did when they'd had an especially gruelling week of nocturnal and diurnal surveys with reports to write in between. His anxiety and sleep deprivation was practically carved in his face, but Rakesh wouldn't admit it.

'I'm sorry you were worried.' Aanya managed to look contrite, even if Nell did believe it was artful acting. 'I should have told you I was fine. Just that I'd made other plans.'

'I'm not sure what must have occupied you so much that you managed to be separated from your phone,' Neeta said, side-eyeing her daughter knowingly.

Aanya had the grace to look sheepish.

Nell wasn't sure if Rakesh had picked up Neeta's subtext, but while Aanya was looking apologetic, he laid on the guilt trip. 'Yes, you should have kept your phone at hand so you could have called us, *Beta*. And you should give more thought to your family. Can you imagine what we were thinking? When we found out that the man you worked for died in an accident? Just after he'd driven you somewhere?'

Aanya looked dangerously like she was going to roll her eyes. 'I've said I'm sorry. I don't know what more I can say.'

'Oh, I do,' Neeta said. 'There is a lot more we need to say.'

Neeta and Nell reached out simultaneously for the tea and then both drew their hands back quickly. With pursed lips, Neeta regarded Nell and she sensed herself being weighed up again. This time, Neeta gave her a tight smile and Nell deferred to her, sensing her need to reassert the matriarchal role.

As Neeta poured cups of tea, she surreptitiously watched Aanya. 'You *are* going to have to tell me what happened.'

'Fine.'

Nell was quite impressed with Aanya's well-honed knack for emphasising the details of the party, padding out her talking time with totally inconsequential information, skimming over the ending: '. . . So Jack offered to bring me here, this being the closest hotel, and to cover the cost for my room.'

Neeta's eyes narrowed shrewdly as she regarded her daughter. 'How *kind*.' Her tone was distinctly sceptical.

Aanya didn't flinch. 'Yeah, wasn't it. He's a millionaire. It was peanuts to him.'

Neeta said nothing, continuing to stare at Aanya with the diagnostic stare of a doctor who'd heard a hundred excuses before. Aanya stared back, unblinking, giving away her lie by omission with her refusal to break eye contact first.

Nell glanced at Rakesh, who was either oblivious to the silent sparring or used to it. Then she saw that the waiter was approaching. 'Shall we order food?' she suggested.

As the silent interrogation between Aanya and her mother was broken with a flurry of passing and scanning menus, Neeta heaved a deep, annoyed sigh and shot an irate glare at Nell. After the waiter had taken their food orders and disappeared, Neeta continued to shoot her daughter dismayed glances, looking more and more desperate to speak to Aanya alone: frankly and privately.

'Rakesh, may I show you the view of the racing circuit?' Nell stood, nudging Rav's arm, who looked puzzled, but followed. Bemused, Rakesh joined them at the French windows. 'Ah! There's a race going on at the moment,' Nell said. 'Let's see who it is.' Leading them outside, she pointed across the formal garden at the cars whizzing past in the distance, within the downland valley.

Rakesh nodded at the scene, unmoved, then returned to the door. As he opened it, Nell heard Neeta's defensive tone. 'Well, no, I can't disagree with Nell's advice, Aanya.'

'So what's the problem, then?' Aanya hissed back, hurriedly, glancing at her approaching father.

'Nothing. It's . . . it's nothing.' Neeta's shoulders slumped an inch. 'I just . . . I suppose I should be glad . . . *someone* was there for you to talk to.' She squeezed Aanya's hand, but the glance she gave her daughter was pained.

Hanging back, Nell finally joined them at the table. Neeta took a moment to meet Nell's eyes, her expression conflicted, until she forced a smile and a nod.

Beside her, Aanya slouched in her seat, arms folded. But, as the waiter served their lunch, polite smiles and appreciative comments glossed over the tense mood.

'Why are you so intent to stay here?' Neeta asked Aanya, when they'd eaten a little.

'Just to be close at hand. If the police need to follow anything up.' Aanya shrugged.

'Why should they?' Rakesh looked up. 'You've made your statement, yes?'

'Yes, well, it is a murder inquiry, Dad,' Aanya muttered, shifting in her seat.

Rakesh dropped his cutlery. 'What!' He looked at Neeta in horror. 'We thought it was an accident! We thought the worst of it was you being implicated in causing it. But *murder!* How?'

'I don't know exactly,' Aanya said, flustered now. 'But we . . .' Nell's heart sank as Aanya glanced in her direction and Neeta's annoyance crackled again '. . . *I* thought it would be better to be on hand. Just in case. I don't want it to look like I have anything to hide.'

Rakesh and Neeta exchanged their heated concern across the table in taut, silent glances.

'Anyway, Mum, you should be getting to know Nell.' Aanya nodded at Nell, her eyes pleading for her to take the baton of scrutiny.

Nell tried not to squirm as she searched for something to say. So Rav nobly filled in. 'You'll love the event. The VIP tickets Nell's got you for the weekend means you can go anywhere you like. And there's loads to see, not just racing. Plus, she's got you a gorgeous suite to stay in, here in the hotel. She wants to make you as comfortable as possible, give you a chance to relax, after all the worry.'

'Thank you.' Neeta still sounded a little starchy, but her gaze flitted around the room and she took in the view through the window. 'This must have been a lovely place to grow up, Nell.'

'Yes, it was. I think it's beautiful here.' Nell, hopeful for a thaw, tried to pull the conversation back to ecology, and her common ground with Rav. 'I'm finding ways to make it sustainable—'

'For future generations?' Neeta cut in. 'That you'd raise here?' She shot a nakedly pained look at Rav, then averted her gaze quickly to her lap. 'I see,' she said quietly.

Nell's heart sank. Neeta only saw distance. And, since Rav lived nearby in Pendlebury, it wasn't in the geographical sense. Rav's parents feared her seducing him away from his honest, hard-working roots into a world that they believed – mostly from the tabloid accounts of immorality, marital discord and murder – was one of style over substance at best, corruption and danger at worst. As Neeta's rueful, analytical gaze moved – from Nell, to Rav, then Aanya – Nell saw her fear that it would be Nell who would lead the Kashyap siblings astray. She felt a gulf crack open, and didn't know how to bridge it.

But, the second she understood Neeta's misgivings, irritation flared. Rav's parents didn't know her, but they'd already judged her. She tried to quash her annoyance by rationalising: Aanya's parents had been worried, hadn't slept well, and all that would bleed into everything right now.

Rakesh watched his wife as they ate in silence. The waiter appeared just as the last piece of cutlery was set down and cleared the plates. Neeta asked for the bill.

'Oh, please don't worry about that,' Nell said. 'I'll—'

'I might not be an earl, like your father with a huge estate,' Neeta interrupted, 'but my family can still pay our way.'

Nell felt like she'd been slapped in the face. But she nodded.

As Rakesh settled up, Rav tugged his mother's arm. 'Let me take up your luggage and show you your room, settle you in?'

Nell understood she was dismissed. She stood back, smiling tightly, until the family left the restaurant, then deflated onto a chair with a long sigh. She anxiously checked her phone, saw the meeting change she'd requested had been accommodated and emailed a heartfelt thanks. She only had five minutes before she had to dash off again.

After pouring a cup of tea from the dregs in the pot, she walked outside and took a deep, steadying breath. With Neeta and Rakesh's room being over the Orangery, she didn't venture far into the garden, where she might be seen from their window. Instead, she sat on the nearest bench. Above her, she heard the balcony doors burst open.

'I told you that this would lead to trouble, Aravindan.' Neeta's voice brimmed with regret. 'I beg you to see sense, son. She's a bad influence on you. And now on Aanya. She would *never* have gone off like that if she wasn't showing off in front of your new girlfriend—'

Nell heard Aanya make a muffled protest, which was ignored as Neeta continued.

'When would you ever imagine your little sister *fornicating* with a married man? It's no coincidence it's happened straight after seeing you in your new relationship—'

'I seriously doubt Aanya is that impressionable, Mum. And she *is* an adult; she's free to make her own choices—'

'Yes, but not *good* ones, Aravindan, that is the *point!* What if she got herself in trouble from a one-night stand? We raised you to have opportunities, and for those to be easier for you than they were for us. We're proud of you, getting your degrees so you can have the careers you choose. We don't want either of you to throw away your potential because of one stupid mistake.'

Nell could only imagine the trail that Neeta, now a doctor, and Rakesh, an engineer had blazed when they'd come over to study at uni in England, then met, married and stayed.

'I don't think Aanya was doing that, Mum.'

'Huh!' Neeta's scorn scorched. '*Don't* you.' A pause was filled with muffled words. 'Your sister not only took stupid risks, she also colluded with that *woman*.'

Oh, nice! Neeta barely knows *me! Hasn't even* tried *to get to know me! All she actually knows is that I tried to help Aanya.*

'For God's sake, Mum!' Aanya must have joined them on the balcony. 'No, Nell did *not* collude with me, she just pointed me in the right direction for help. And you're a doctor – you can't exactly have a go at her for that. And everything is *fine.* Now can you please stop discussing my *private* business like it is up for general discussion. It is nothing to do with you, Mum, or you, Rav. So *back off.*' From the footsteps Nell could hear, it sounded like Aanya had flounced off.

'You see?' Neeta said. 'Your sister is like a different person. Can you imagine her talking to us like that a week ago?'

'Yes,' Rav said. 'Yes, that's pretty normal, as far as I remember.'

'See? Now you all collude!'

'Oh, Mum! Come on! *No* one's colluding. Nell just tried to help.'

'No. Aanya will move out now,' Neeta said. 'I have lost Marla. I will lose Aanya. And soon I will lose you.' Her voice cracked.

'Don't be daft! Why do you think Nell wanted to invite you here? To meet her family and get to know them—'

'You should ask yourself why *you* want to know *them* so badly. I knew that Nell's circle would be bad news, after reading about so many deaths – murders – here last month. And as soon as she's introduced to our family, what happens? Aanya loses all her good judgement and now *she's* involved in a murder inquiry! You cannot tell me I'm wrong about this. About *her.*'

Nell gripped her cup, her face flushed and her stomach churning.

She couldn't exactly disagree. And that made it worse. Wandering inside, she left the cup on the table. It was obvious she wasn't going to be able to do anything right.

A few moments later, a harassed-looking Rav was beside her. 'Mum's a bit . . . upset.'

'Yeah, I gathered,' Nell said. She noticed his jaw clenching. 'What are you going to do about it?'

Rav looked surprised at the question. 'Just . . . wait for things to calm down, I guess. They're shocked at Aanya being involved in a murder inquiry. But if the case is resolved quickly then, hopefully, that won't last long.'

'Right.' Nell bit back the words she wanted to say. After all, she'd thought the same a few minutes ago. But she somehow hoped Rav would at least say something in her defence, to try to change his parents' minds before they set against her entirely.

'I'd just like them to make an attempt to get to know me. Before they write me off.'

When Rav nodded, but made no offer to say anything, she handed him the envelope that had been left on their table. 'If they still want their VIP tickets, maybe you could pass them on?'

'I will, thanks.' Rav moved closer and stroked Nell's cheek. 'Are *we* OK?'

Nell fought down her frustrations. She knew Rav was trying to keep the peace. It couldn't be fun, being in his position. 'I hope so.'

She meant it – because the alternative was a family war that might last well beyond this weekend.

Chapter 17

Saturday 20th April – 1.50 p.m.

The auctioneer rapped his gavel on the shining mahogany lectern. In clipped, well-projected tones, he announced, 'Sold, at two hundred and eighty thousand pounds. Congratulations!'

He adjusted his burgundy cravat as an assistant drove the purchased car from the staging area. A second car entered, its driver revving the sleek sage-green classic Aston, which was stylish enough to turn heads if it were amongst Monaco's glitterati.

'Here we have the star of today's show,' the auctioneer declared. 'One very fine Aston Martin DB4 GT Zagato. Your last chance to make a purchase here today is a once-in-a-lifetime opportunity to own a legend of motor-racing history. One of only two in the world bearing the VEV registration, and one of the Aston Works cars with impeccable racing pedigree. So!' The auctioneer beamed at the gathering in the packed marquee. 'Who'll start us off at six million pounds?' He pointed to someone at the back. 'Thank you, ma'am. Do I have six and a half?'

From her seat at the side of the white tent, Nell scanned the bidders. A telephone operator raised his hand from the row of officials along the front. The bidding moved along swiftly, with light-hearted repartee as the participants relished their involvement in the historical sale.

Nell spotted Colin Rafferty in the front row. He'd withdrawn from interviews, retreating to spend time at home with his wife. But he'd originally been commissioned as the auctioneer and, while he'd told Hugo he wouldn't be up to auctioneering, he *had* promised he'd turn up for press photos. He was bearing up extraordinarily well, responding to the witty commentary. A solicitous Lucio Moretti sat beside him, not laughing at jokes until Colin did. On Lucio's other side, Maxine followed the auction with intense attention, craning her neck to track the bidders.

Shannon sat behind Colin, speaking occasionally to him or to Lucio, alert as a cat as she studied the bidding – no, the bidd*ers*. *Typical. Sniffing out the money.* As Nell scanned the rest of the audience, she caught sight of James and Val, standing with some latecomers at the back. Val ignored the repartee as her eyes flicked around. James scanned the crowd, but his gaze always fell back on Shannon, who used the excuse of turning to see a new bidder to shoot a half-smile at James. He seemed to melt on the spot, until Val cleared her throat and he attentively looked around the company again.

Why are they watching an auction, in the middle of an inquiry? Is it relevant?

Nell was so lost in thought that she missed the bidding reaching its end and jumped when the gavel was struck.

'Sold, at fourteen million pounds! Congratulations to the new owner of this magnificent machine!' The auctioneer applauded a well-preserved woman of senior years, unapologetically wearing an elaborate, peacock-feathered turban while sitting in the front row. Standing, she held up her paddle so her number could be recorded. She adjusted her draping dress as the rays of sunlight streaming in from the marquee sides glinted off her beringed fingers, then she bowed.

'This concludes our exciting auction. With thanks to Montague's Auction House and Finchmere Estate.' The auctioneer – and Shannon – went to shake the hand of the woman in the front row as the attendees filtered outside. Nell slipped out quickly, heading for the historical showpiece car. The stunning Aston gleamed behind its red-velvet ropes, now parked at the marquee entrance. When the auctioneer, new owner and Colin joined her, Nell congratulated the buyer and smiled for the press photos.

As everyone dispersed, Nell noticed James and Val talking to a man wearing a mismatched tweed jacket and trilby, and an air of authority. Watching the stranger, Nell wondered if she recognised him. She couldn't place him.

Beside her, Colin looked suddenly distraught. Nell gave him a small smile. 'Thank you for coming today, Colin. We didn't really expect you to—'

Shaking his head, Colin cut Nell's words off. 'Nothing helps. Not being at home, not being busy.' He looked so desolate, Nell's heart lurched. 'Of course, Angie blames me. Says if he hadn't been so keen to follow in my footsteps and prove himself, that our son would still be alive. We were both looking forward to grandchildren. He and Lana were trying. So I'm responsible for killing off two generations.' He looked broken.

Nell couldn't fill the silence with well-intentioned banalities. She reached out and clasped Colin's arm. He moved minutely towards her and Nell found herself hugging him. Leaning heavily on her shoulder, he wept openly. Surprised and concerned at his unguarded actions, Nell felt oddly protective. She didn't know Colin that well, but she wanted to offer some comfort. Over his shoulder, she scanned the crowd for press, to ensure the private moment wouldn't be insensitively captured. Instead, she saw Rav and his parents staring at her. Rav waved discreetly but his parents looked askance.

Sighing inwardly, Nell ignored their questioning glances at what must look like a fairly intimate and lengthy hug of a man they didn't know, resigned to the reality that everything she did would probably be misinterpreted by Neeta and Rakesh in their current frame of mind. Spotting James and Val hovering nearby, she patted Colin's back, releasing him, as they came over.

Colin dabbed his eyes with his fingers. 'Sorry, Nell.'

'Don't be.'

'Afternoon,' James nodded at them both. 'Colin, we understand this is difficult, but we would like to speak to you at some point. Would you be ready to make a statement today?'

He nodded. 'Yes. You've been very patient. I appreciate it.' He took a deep breath. 'Would you let me clean myself up and get a decent cuppa first?'

'The hotel meeting room's still free,' Nell said. 'I can send in refreshments for all of you.'

'Thanks,' Colin said. He looked at James. 'Give me a few minutes to wash up?'

James nodded. As Colin left, James nodded at the car.

'Amazing machine. But *fourteen million!*' He shook his head. 'More money than sense!'

Nell shrugged. 'Depends on your point of view. I guess it's like any investment. More interesting than shares, though.' She leaned in conspiratorially. 'You should see the *real* showstopper. Lucio has an amazing car, a Ferrari 250 GTO, going for private sale. Which is how the *really* interesting machines change hands. Most bidders in those circles don't want press attention or publicity. Lucio said the Ferrari is going for thirty-six million.'

Behind her, a man cleared his throat pointedly. 'This is *precisely* why the sale was confidential, Nell.'

Blushing, Nell spun round. Lucio and Maxine now stood in front of her, arms folded, faces stern.

'I'm sorry for the indiscretion,' Nell said. 'But I think it's safe to let an officer of the law have some information.'

'It's not relevant to your investigation, is it, though?' Maxine said curtly.

'We don't always know. Sometimes surprising details turn out to be vital.' James looked unruffled by their prickly reactions. His eyes met Nell's. She knew her embarrassment was palpable, and felt some relief when he added kindly, 'But I appreciate it's confidential information, and it will be treated as such.'

Lucio and Maxine nodded, shot Nell an unimpressed glare and swept off.

As Nell and James watched them go, James nodded at the Aston again. 'What gets them up to those sorts of figures? The provenance?'

She nodded. 'Races they've been in, wins, drivers, owners. All part of the story that makes the car unique.'

James studied the car, his eyes darting around, clearly thinking quickly.

'Why so interested?' she asked. 'Thinking of investing? Or is something else going on?'

James shook his head. His eyes slid sideways towards her: a warning glance. The look he always gave her when he wanted her to stop asking questions.

Adrenaline lanced through Nell's stomach. She immediately *did* ask questions. '*What?* What's going on?'

James shook his head again. He held up one hand.

Nell felt suddenly sick, realising something was wrong. 'James, I know you're investigating, and I won't interfere. But this isn't just my family *business*, it's my *home*. If something is going on, I think I should know.'

James gave her a level look. 'I'm sure you do.'

Nell's stomach lurched. 'Am I . . . Are *we* under suspicion for something else?'

'I'm just learning about the racing and auction world. It's new to me.'

'Well, I'm always happy to help.' Nell felt an urgent need to assist, hoping it would invite confidences and information. It might at least show her what he was interested in, where the investigation was heading. 'If you want, I can give you all the auction back catalogues. We store them at the office in the garage. Let me know if they'd be useful for research.'

'That could be helpful, thanks,' James said. 'I'll let you know. I'd better head to the hotel to see Colin now.'

'I'll let you walk me over, James.' Shannon appeared from the tent, her offer making James's face brighten – until she added, 'I have a hot date for high tea and champagne.'

Glancing at her uncertainly, he said, 'Oh? Didn't think you liked—'

'Why don't you stop detecting for five minutes?' Shannon interrupted gently. 'And just walk with me?' Slipping her arm through his, she steered him away.

Once Nell was left on her own, Rav and Aanya approached with their parents. Rav gave Nell an enthusiastic kiss. 'Did it go well?'

'Very well, thanks,' Nell said, turning to greet his parents and sister. 'Have you had a good afternoon?' She noticed Aanya had added a veiled emerald hat to her outfit, at an elegant angle.

'Oh yeah! Rav made us watch the bike race—'

'Yeah, those racers have got some serious skill,' Rav gushed.

'Then we went round the funfair.' She side-eyed her father who, despite his unimpressed expression, clutched a large pink teddy bear complete with racing helmet and goggles. 'He's been in heaven with all the car workshops. Then I showed Mum the vintage shops—' she touched her new hat '—and we had a milkshake at the rock 'n' roll diner.'

While Aanya chattered on a little nervously, neither Neeta nor Rakesh said anything: no comment on anything they'd seen, let alone enjoyed. And their stern faces suggested they'd not enjoyed much.

'How much did this one go for in the end?' Rav valiantly kept up the small talk.

'Fourteen million,' Nell said.

Rav's jaw dropped, and Neeta gasped. 'That's . . . Goodness. Think of all the things you could actually *do* with that amount of money.'

Nell saw that all this excess was only cementing their view of her as a hedonist. *Perfect.*

Looking embarrassed, Rav glanced down, then held out to Nell the paper bag he was carrying. 'I got something for you.'

With a smile, she pulled out a black T-shirt and held it up against herself, reading it upside down: a sleek suggestion of a classic car's outline, swerving tyre tracks, and the caption, '*Drive it like you stole it*'. Nell rolled her eyes and laughed, just as a press photographer snapped a photo. Nell groaned, then made sure her face was neutral as she bundled the T-shirt into the bag.

Glancing at the photographer, Nell's worry about the photo being used was drowned out when she saw James reach the distant hotel, and she wondered what turn his case was about to take now.

Saturday 20th April – 4 p.m.

James had been trying to build bridges with Ashley as they added the team's latest updates to the incident board. When Val joined them, he felt her shrewd eyes flicking across the notes, absorbing every detail osmotically.

'We're still missing the autopsy report?' Val asked.

'Yes, but it's due any time now,' James said.

'Let's pop over and see if we can collect it,' Val suggested.

As they crossed the car park to the pathology lab, Val grilled them. 'What do you two make of motives so far? How about Maxine? What background do we have on her?'

'Grew up in Newcastle,' Ashley reeled off the facts. 'Quite a tough upbringing, by all accounts. Lost both parents when she was in her twenties, sole carer for her brother who has advanced MS. He lives with her in Pendlebury. She got involved in the prison outreach programme in her early thirties. Possibly because her brother was a bit of a delinquent when he was a young teen. Low-level shoplifting, things like that.'

'How is she financially?' Val asked.

'Good. Not suspiciously so, given everything we're looking at, but more than comfortable.'

'Well, if Jack had intended to blackmail her, he might have threatened her with it, or she might not have known,' Val said. 'But she *was* frustrated by his lack of talent and her inability to replace him due to Lucio's friendship with Colin. Could that have led to some drastic action on her part to get Jack out of the picture and the more capable Mark in the driving seat?'

James shrugged. 'Maybe. Because she obviously felt she couldn't push that harder with Colin and Lucio, despite having data to show his poor performance.'

'No, something doesn't add up there,' Val said. 'What's the background on Lucio?'

'His family live in Sicily,' Ashley said. 'He visits them frequently. Never married. No kids. He's *very* well off. Lives comfortably here while also sending large amounts to relatives in Europe.'

'And he and Colin both quizzed Cassie on her technical input. Perhaps to confirm in their own minds that Cassie and Mark were doing a good job and it was Jack letting the side down? Or to see if any blame could be shifted in their direction?'

'Mark said that "Jack was good at finding chinks in people's armour",' Ashley said. 'Maybe he knew something that gave him some sort of influence over Colin, Lucio or Maxine? Or any combination of them.'

'Plausible,' Val agreed. 'And we know Mark wanted to keep his divorce private. If Jack did blackmail Maxine with those emails claiming sexual harassment, or even if he only planned to do so, he could easily have done the same to Mark. Who was already under pressure for the car to succeed, having gambled everything – his reputation, financial security—'

'The financial forensic team confirmed he still has the full loan on the house while only having half the asset's value,' James said as he held open the door to the mortuary. 'Poor guy. What a *disaster*.'

Val's eyes narrowed. 'He – and Cassie for that matter – are the obvious suspects to have tampered with Jack's car.'

James nodded. 'He must be pretty ruthless to proceed with a high-risk business idea at the cost of his marriage. He clearly doesn't want anything to stand in his way.'

The words hung in the air, until he added, 'And Cassie's loyalty to Mark, *and* Jack's behaviour, give her plenty of motive.'

'Yes,' Val agreed. 'And she has form. We can't hold it against her, but we can't discount it. Not difficult to imagine her sabotaging Jack's car.'

'True, but we also shouldn't write off Svetlana, either.' James ploughed on before Val disagreed. 'Her confession didn't mention the brakes, but that could be a double bluff.'

As they walked along the corridor, Val replied, 'Possibly. Did you get any information from Colin today about their relationship?'

'Oh, yes, interesting,' James said, having to hold in a smile at the reminder of their meeting – and walking to it with Shannon's arm through his, her fluid chatter, their easy closeness . . . 'Yes. The tabloids paint Jack and Svetlana as having a tempestuous relationship – she's the tolerant girlfriend, now wife, while he's the perpetual love rat. But Colin said they were a good match. He said he found their dynamic a bit odd, but he also saw that fame, as they courted it, was very different than in his day. Their sponsorship deals demanded near-constant publicity; they had to maintain a following on social media with never-ending new stories. Colin said just watching them made him feel exhausted! But he thought they relished the drama and, underneath all that chaos, they were closer than you'd think.'

'Any opinion on their relationship?'

'Well, he said they'd only been married a month but they'd been trying for a baby since they'd got engaged ten months ago. Colin and his wife, Angie, had been pleased about that. They loved Svetlana, thought she'd make a wonderful mother. They said she only wanted two things in life: a child and financial security. They wished Jack had half her work ethic.'

Val raised her eyebrows. 'How telling.'

'Yes,' James said. 'But Colin sidestepped the question about Jack's performance on the track. He just said he kept hoping it would all come together for him, and he'd be able to acquit himself with an outstanding drive. Especially if Svetlana had any influence over him.'

Val frowned. 'So why do you still think Svetlana's in the frame?'

'Because of Dani,' Ashley said.

James nodded. 'If Svetlana thought the marriage was sound, or even if they had an open arrangement, she could have been devastated by Jack's affair with her closest friend.'

'Especially one that predates the wedding. Possibly the engagement.' Val's eyes focused on the middle distance again.

'No, it's more than that.' Ashley's pointed look at James had the same impatient air she'd adopted after Dani's interview. '*Shellfish.*'

James was irritated to see a half-smile escape Val's inscrutable expression. *What the hell does shellfish mean?* 'You've got me.' He tried to sound magnanimous. 'Go on, explain.'

'How can someone with a shellfish allergy eat a prawn salad for lunch?' Ashley asked.

'Well, they couldn't,' James reasoned, frantically trying to follow their train of thought.

'Right. And couple that oddity with the fact that Jack and Svetlana were trying to have a child for the last ten months, since they got engaged.'

'OK.' James still didn't see the connection.

'And *that'll* tell you what Svetlana, Dani and Jack were *really* arguing about at the party.'

'Right. Um, can you—?' James's faltering question was cut off as Dr Saunders came through the double doors in front of them.

'Ah! I was coming over to see you!' she said. 'Come in, I'll talk you through my report.'

As they walked into the autopsy lab, the chemical smell hit James like a punch on an empty stomach. He'd always hated the smell and the associations it instantly conjured.

Jack Rafferty's body lay on the stainless-steel gurney, the Y-shaped scar of the pathologist's intrusion neatly stitched. He'd been cleaned of the mud from the pond, but his face was still bloated.

Dr Saunders pointed to the marbled bruising around Jack's jaw. 'He's sustained a fractured mandible, suggestive of a punch, which possibly floored him and stunned him but wouldn't have knocked him unconscious.'

Her finger moved to his nose. 'See the fine froth in his mouth and nostrils? That, along with the water in the stomach and his ballooned lungs, are conclusive signs Mr Rafferty died by drowning. And here—' she pointed at the side of his buttocks and thighs '—these purple marks of lividity show he'd been seated when, or soon after, he died.'

'So, nothing untoward? Straightforward drowning?' Val reached for the report.

But Dr Saunders held on to the folder. 'I was coming to show you this, but I can't leave it with you without signing it off.'

'So, sign it off, then?' James said.

Dr Saunders hesitated. 'I can't. I need to get a couple of tests done first.'

'What tests?' Val asked.

'I want to match the diatom samples in his tissue to those in the pond. Just to be sure.'

'OK. How long will that take?' Val asked.

'Usually not long, but my specialist is in Scotland, giving evidence in another trial. I'm not expecting her back for about three weeks. And the only other expert I can find with these skills is off sick. I'll keep you posted. Hopefully we'll get these processed in about a month.'

'Great.' Val disguised her impatience with a smile. 'I appreciate your thoroughness.'

As James and Val returned to the incident room, James checked his phone. He groaned and glanced at Val. 'Fraud want us to come in tomorrow for *another* meeting. Do we really need to be told for a second time that they're active and our investigation can't trample on any toes? If I *have* to work over scheduled leave, I'd rather be making progress on our case.'

'We'll be here anyway,' Val pointed out. 'And an hour is a sound investment for good working relations.'

James sighed and looked at his notes. 'Hesha's overseeing the forensic team at Jack and Svetlana's house. They're going through everything in detail. Ed's seeing Lucio – he's the only one from the party we haven't got a statement from yet. He's a bit of a slippery fish. Hard to pin down.'

Val gave a quirky smile. 'You don't fish with pins. Try a hook.'

Chapter 18

Saturday 20th April – 6 p.m.

Nell read the text, her heart sinking. Rav, his parents and Aanya had returned to the hotel after an afternoon at the track. She knew without him telling her that he wouldn't have dinner with her. She was clearly *persona non grata* with his family. She didn't begrudge their time together. But she *wished* the weekend had worked out differently. The Classics was her favourite estate event, and now she had more responsibility, it mattered to her that guests enjoyed it. She'd imagined showing Rav's folks her favourite spots, giving them great seats to watch the races, getting to know them and tailoring the weekend around the bits they'd enjoy most – and taking Rav to tomorrow's reception dinner. *Will Rav even be able to go with me now? Or want to?*

She was also still unsettled by her conversation with James. *What the hell's going on there?* Was there a separate investigation? Her thoughts wandered to the auction and, as she started up the Land Rover, she found herself driving towards her parents' house and garage. She pulled up inside the courtyard of the former stable block, now an immaculate quadrant garage, and stepped through the small door leading to the workroom. Her eyes adjusted to the dim sunlight filtering through the high windows. Beyond the makeshift office, the hazy beams alighted on the intriguing shapes tucked up in protective car covers. But Nell went straight to the desk at the back and opened a cupboard. Inside were rows of auction catalogues, ordered by year.

She scanned last year's catalogue, then the previous one, then the catalogue from the year before, flicking through each one quickly, taking photos of each year's showpiece car, its value and the supplier with her phone. She jumped when her phone rang. It was James.

'Hi, James,' Nell said. She dropped the catalogue like a hot coal, as if she'd been caught reading something she shouldn't.

'Hi, Nell,' James said. 'Can I take you up on that favour? May I come and have a look at those auction catalogues?'

James flicked through the pages. He didn't really know what he was looking for, but he knew something wasn't right, and hoped that inspiration might be kindled. He put down last year's auction catalogue then picked up the previous year's, scanned quickly, then looked at the next.

Beside him, Nell fidgeted. He knew she was worried. They'd done well to keep things on a friendly footing after their break-up. He'd been an idiot over that. *And me and Shannon . . . ?* His mind wandered to tomorrow evening's glittering reception dinner. He imagined them sitting at the table, him enveloped in her seductive heady scent as they talked and laughed. Her spiky social observations were unerringly accurate – but once he'd understood that her intention to sting was only a long-ingrained defence mechanism, he'd enjoyed her sharp wit. It would be the first time he'd wear his newly ranked dress uniform, and he couldn't wait to join Shannon at such a glamorous event. With effort, he made himself concentrate, and flicked through another catalogue.

'These are all the catalogues we have,' Nell said. Her clasped hands twisted. 'One every year for the past twenty-two years. Before that, we didn't have the arrangement with Montague's Auction House to host an auction. But, as the Classics increased in popularity, Montague's saw it was a great way to attract bidders and some mutually beneficial publicity for them and us.'

James scanned around. 'Have you got anything I can put them all in? An old box or something?'

Nell cast her eye about the garage. 'Sure, let me see . . .'

'If not, I'll just pile them on the passenger seat.'

As Nell searched, James glanced at his beeping phone. He laughed. 'Ah, it's OK. Hesha asked Montague's directly. They've couriered their copies straight to the station.'

'Oh?' Nell's head snapped round, the amber lights in her eyes flashing.

James groaned inwardly, at revealing that this wasn't just idle curiosity but a key part of their investigation. 'I . . . er . . . I better get back.'

'OK.' Nell nodded. But she started to gabble. 'Let me know if I can do anything else to help. I can provide any information you might need. We keep really thorough records. And I'll be pleased to help. You know that, James. Don't you?'

Her expression entreated, like she was calling on all their prior experiences to influence his treatment of her now. He couldn't accuse her of holding a grudge. The only thing he could level against her was that she was a bit too keen to interfere. But, even then, he couldn't deny that her interference yielded insights. No, *evidence*. Hesitating in the doorway, he turned.

'There is something you may be able to help with. Do you happen to know any forensic botanists?'

'I appreciate what you're saying.' James had to bite down hard on his impatience. 'But you *cannot* disagree that this has potential to give our case an important steer, just when we need it.'

'Oh, I *can* disagree!' Ashley countered comfortably. 'For all we know, Nell's family may well be implicated in this fraud. Which might be linked to Jack's murder. So giving Nell key evidence, showing *her* this "important steer" of our investigation – in fact, giving *her* the chance to steer it – it's *clearly* a conflict of interest.'

James rolled his eyes. 'Nell isn't a stranger to our processes now. She'll know she has to keep this confidential. If she doesn't, she'd be guilty of obstructing a police investigation. She's not stupid.'

'No, she isn't, is she, James? In fact, we could possibly credit her for your recent cases. Even the one you were unofficially helping.'

'Oh, for God's—'

'And that *doesn't* change the fact that we'd be disclosing information to her that she *shouldn't have*. Not to mention relying on her interpretation of it.' Ashley's breathing heaved with her exasperation.

Hesha and Ed stood at the incident board, doing their best to pretend they couldn't hear the argument.

'Fine, then! Let's wait at least three weeks for Doc's expert to come back, shall we? Let's all sit on our hands for almost a month! God knows, Fraud are doing everything they can to make this investigation difficult. So let's do nothing, then!' James wanted to slam something, to channel his frustration into action. The best he could do was to shove his chair against his desk.

Val glared out from behind the glass pane of her office, into the incident room. With a jerk of her head, she summoned them inside.

'Shut the door.' She walked around to the front of her desk and perched on it, making a point of putting her pen down. 'I can't have my two lead officers arguing like this. It's not fair on the case, on the team *or* on the victim's family. So let's have a frank, off-the-record chat.'

Ashley folded her arms. James turned his palms up. But both remained silent.

'One of you will have to tell me what's going on.' Val moved her cuff to check her watch and sighed. 'I don't have anything better to do right now, so please do take your time.'

'I'm just trying to expedite the case,' James said. 'Nell – *Dr* Ward – happens to have the right skills to process our samples. She's remediated ponds, using diatom and microinvertebrate species lists to assess water quality, and written scientific papers on the results. She'd stand up well as an expert witness. But it seems Ashley has a problem with that—'

'No.' Ashley turned to face him. 'No, that's not what I have a problem with – as you well know.'

Val pursed her lips and James knew she was already a step ahead of them. His stomach dropped. In his heart, he knew that Ashley had a point. Chief Constable Trent's investment in his career – once Nell was on the scene – was an extension of Trent's own agenda, since Nell's MP mother supported Trent's reform ambitions. James knew Trent was strengthening ties when, with him and Ashley both in line for promotion, he was the one who landed it. And Ashley could easily curtail his career trajectory by telling Val, on the record, that he'd accessed police files during their last case, when he wasn't officially working. The disciplinary would cost him about two years' progress. Nausea churned.

Ashley turned to Val. 'What I have a *problem* with is this team's over-reliance on a civilian. Who may be implicated in this case. And may be given sensitive, revealing intel about our investigation. I'm concerned about that knowledge being outside of our team, beyond our control and affecting the outcome.'

With a nod, Val agreed. 'Fair points.' She tilted her head. 'James?'

'I think you heard my position. Nell can identify those samples to get Doc's report signed off. And it will clarify where our investigation should turn.' He sighed and turned to Ashley. 'Yes, I can understand your concerns. But Nell is too straight to falsify results, even—'

'Even if her family – or her – are involved in this massive fraud case. Worth *multimillion* pounds?' Ashley looked at him in disbelief.

'OK,' Val interjected. 'So if we don't follow this line of inquiry with Nell, what do you suggest we look into, Ashley?'

'I'd put pressure on Dani. For obvious reasons. And Mark. Have we spoken to his wife? Can we get Finance to dig around and find out exactly how much debt he was in? And see if Tech can uncover if Jack was blackmailing anyone else?'

'Excellent. Go ahead and lead those investigations with the team, Ashley—'

As Ashley gave a tight smile at the endorsement, James complained, 'None of those investigations prevent Nell checking out the samples, though.'

'True. So go ahead and ask her to,' Val said. At Ashley's protest, Val held up her hand. 'But book in Doc's expert, too. We might get a steer from Nell's results, and we should certainly impress upon her the responsibility of being a potential expert witness. But she couldn't realistically act as one, not in her position. So we'd need her IDs to be verified by someone who could.'

As James nodded, relieved at the outcome, Val cautioned, 'And, that way, James, if Nell *does* have any reason to . . . *misguide* us, then, in about three weeks, we'll know. And wouldn't *that* be one hell of a steer?'

Chapter 19

Sunday 21st April – 6 a.m.

Nell's feet felt like lead as she walked down the long corridor with James. She'd never admit it, but she was worn out. The small suitcase she tugged behind her, heavy even on wheels, kept slamming her ankles as she lacked the coordination to pull it at the right speed for her stride. The visitor pass on the lanyard around her neck flapped against her chest each time the case whacked her heels and jolted her body.

Ever since she'd had to drag herself out of bed this morning, that headache had returned: a persistent dull thump behind her eyes. From lack of sleep and worry. Until the early hours, Nell had scrutinised the photos she'd taken of the auction catalogues for all of the twenty-two years the auction had run, wondering what James was looking for.

Moretti's had supplied the prestigious showpiece car for the past eight years. All rare specimens or racing legends. Before that, a showroom in London had supplied rare classic cars for four years and, for the first decade, local dealerships had provided interesting but not unusual classics. The auction prices had steadily increased over that decade, but had rocketed in the last ten years, particularly under Moretti's tenure.

Nell had always thought that Moretti's renowned reputation for being one of very few dealerships who handled such cars was the main reason her father had such a good relationship with Lucio. Now . . . ? Well, even Nell had to admit that if the fraud investigation was triggered by an ability to reliably source rare machines, this impressive record looked utterly damning.

And if Moretti's record was dubious, then did that mean . . .

collusion? With someone who worked for the Finchmere event? Or even – but surely *not* – her own *father . . .* ?

After that, sleep had been impossible. In the darkness, the swimmy fear had settled in, and still hadn't left her. Stifling a yawn now, Nell wished she'd been allowed to bring coffee into the lab, and shook herself. If nothing else, this was a chance to speak to James and perhaps find out what was going on. *And a favour never hurts . . .*

So she smiled when James opened the door to the agency forensic lab, even as her nostrils were assaulted by the familiar chemical smells of formalin and aldehydes: pear drops. And corpses.

The apricot sunrise streamed through the windows, glinting off the sterile white lab benches, arranged in rows like bleached ribs towards the back of the room, leaving a wide corridor down the centre.

The waiting technician had set up a phase-contrast microscope, sorting trays and latex gloves beside a taped-closed box. He passed her a packet containing a lab coat. As Nell pulled it on, she noted the stark difference between this crisp, pristine coat and the oversized, dubiously stained ones she'd worn in her university labs.

Like hers, the technician's lab coat was immaculate. Unsheathing a scalpel from his top pocket, he sliced one smooth straight line through the tape on the box of evidence. As the lid sprang open, Nell saw orderly lines of labelled slides, stacked against separators to ensure the samples weren't compressed.

The technician signed the tape to show the chain of custody – who had opened the packet of forensic evidence, when and why – then passed the pen to Nell. She signed where he pointed.

Buttoning the lab coat, Nell instantly felt ready to start, her muscle memory locking in to her many days and nights of painstaking lab work, and getting into the methodical mindset needed.

Crouching, she unzipped the suitcase, pulling out the folders and books it contained, stacking them neatly on the bench: dichotomous keys for diatoms and a selection of printed research papers on their distribution. She reached into the case pocket and placed her dissection kit and pencils with a new, unused notepad beside them.

The technician nodded towards the box of slides. 'These are all labelled dry samples, and grouped according to their origin.' He pointed to the first section. 'These are from the pond, on Little Smitington Nature Reserve.' His finger moved to the next section. 'These are from the bone marrow of the deceased, then the kidney, liver, lung and brain.'

Nell nodded. She had known what this would involve. It was gruesome, if you thought too much about it. But now she was in a professional frame of mind, she simply nodded.

The technician tapped the scalpel on the bench in impatience, and Nell realised a time estimate was required. 'I guess, in all, this could take me maybe . . . four hours?'

'Righto.' The thin line of the technician's lips conveyed how unimpressed he was.

'I'll be as quick as I can. But I'm a bit rusty and I'm not sure how many diatoms species each slide will contain, or if they'll be common or rarer species,' Nell said. 'But I asked for the early start so I'd have time to get it all done. I'm sure I will. I expected more samples, to be honest . . .'

He stared at her. 'Oh. That's just as well. You're going to take long enough as it is.'

Nell pressed her lips together to prevent herself from retorting that this was a precious Sunday morning for her too, when she was already somewhat busy, yet here she was, delivering a promised favour by spending hours in a smelly lab, staring down a microscope at bodily samples. She realised that, while James had agreed to allow her access to the lab at six in the morning so she could fit the lab work in and get back to Finchmere, it was the poor technician who'd had his schedule disrupted to accommodate hers. She felt a stab of sympathy.

'Sorry. I guess my visit has messed up your plans. Thanks for coming in early. I'll be as efficient as possible.' She hesitated. 'I'm Nell, by the way.'

'I know.' The technician walked away, pressing his earbuds in. A hectic, tinny soundtrack exploded into the uncomfortable silence, fading out as he reached the end of the lab.

As James pulled out a stool to perch on, Nell shot him a grimace. In tactful silence, he checked his emails while Nell sat and pulled the microscope, notepad and pen and box of slides towards her. She drew a sketch of the box so she could mark off her progress without having to set the slides aside, then pulled on the latex gloves and took out the first sample. She slid it under the metal arms of the microscope and rotated the magnification to 100x.

To avoid crushing the slide, Nell focused tight into it, then peered through the eyepiece as she dialled the focus back. Microscopic algal specimens sharpened under the lens. Being between two and five hundred microns, a diatom on the slide was invisible to the naked eye. But, on the stage and perfectly lit, the modest alga became a dazzling star. Its glassy silica frustule, which enclosed the cellular structure, shimmered with an unexpectedly glamorous iridescence.

Nell homed in on the key features to identify the species, initially differentiating between peridot sunbursts and elegant emerald ellipses. Their delicate, kaleidoscopic structures were like glittering Art Deco jewels under the microscope's beam.

Looking up from the microscope, Nell searched through her books for the key she needed, flipping over the well-thumbed pages to the starting point for pennate species. She compared the specimen under the microscope to the key, turning pages and flicking back occasionally to check a detail. She recorded the slide label, then sketched the slide, marking the position of the diatoms, numbered them and labelled the first. She continued methodically until she'd identified each diatom, then returned the slide, ticked it off her main sketch and took the next one.

She got into a rhythm and within two hours, she'd completed the samples from Little Smitington Pond. She drew a line under her list, relieved to be making good progress. The species list was short, but she knew these species were indicators of high-quality waterbodies. She couldn't help thinking that Mai would be pleased.

About the same number of samples remained, taken from the body parts of the deceased. She set the first slide on the microscope and stretched, realising her shoulders were stiff, and she rubbed her eyes, dry and stinging from the heat of the microscope. She glanced over at the technician, who was engrossed in distilling something from a flask into a bottle, then at James, who was typing rapidly.

Nell wrote the next label in her notebook. *Sample 1. Left femur bone marrow.* She blanched, then took a deep breath and resumed the position, staring down the eyepiece. The sample looked no different from having been cut out of the victim's tissue and processed through nitric acids a few times, until the human tissue had melted away and only the tough, glass-encased algae remained.

The next species was new to her. Nell had to double-check it before she was certain of her identification. She rubbed her eyes. It felt like her already dry, sleepless eyeballs were being gently cooked by the backlight as she stared down the lens. Finally, she made an ID.

But the second one was different again. She doubted the identification and checked it several times before recording it, making sure of her accuracy. She shot a guilty glance at James and the technician. *God, the sleep deprivation is making me slow . . .*

About ninety minutes later, she'd worked through all the slides and was still frowning. But not only from tiredness. A tingle of unease had settled at the back of her mind. She returned the last slide to the box and ticked it off her main sketch, then turned to the men.

'I've finished.'

James nodded and began to stand, but didn't tear his eyes away from his phone. The technician, mid-titration, concentrated until he could turn the tap on the long tube, then make a record in his notebook.

Still plagued by that nagging feeling, Nell compared her lists. With both men engrossed, she surreptitiously photographed them. Searching through her stack of scientific papers, she found one, and scanned it avidly. She compared it to another paper and rechecked her lists, making notes.

'I thought you said you'd finished?' James was suddenly beside her as the technician joined them and closed the box of specimens.

Nell jumped. 'Yes, I'm done. Sorry it took a while. But I'm sure the IDs are accurate.'

The technician retaped the box and held out the pen for James to note the chain of custody, then passed the pen to Nell, who signed the tape distractedly. She turned back to the paper, scanning the last few paragraphs, confirming her hypothesis.

'If you've finished, you have to go!' The technician sounded exasperated. 'You can't sit here all day. I can't lock up the lab until you go.'

'Sorry.' Hopping off the stool, Nell hastily stacked her books back in her case with her notepad and the paper she'd been reading. She took off her lab coat and, as directed, put it in the laundry bin by the door. James took the handle of her case as the technician escorted them to the corridor, pointedly locking the lab behind them.

'Thanks, Nell. I think it would be best if you hand over the list under interview conditions,' James said. 'Then we'll have a formal record of your input.'

Nell nodded. 'I think that would be a good idea under the circumstances.'

'Oh?' James looked at her, frowning. 'Something wrong?'

Nell nodded. 'Yes. Something's very wrong.'

Chapter 20

Sunday 21st April – 10.30 a.m.

In the small interview room, James started the recording. He asked Nell for details about her methodical approach to the identification process, the keys she'd used and any previous experience and training that made her a credible expert to fulfil the work accurately.

When he asked for her results, she opened her notepad on the desk and read out the species recorded and the abundance they'd occurred in, in the two different sample sets.

With a frown, she asked, 'Is there any chance these samples could have got mixed up?'

'Absolutely not.' For the sake of the tape, James explained how the samples were taken and labelled, the slides processed and numbered, and all samples kept securely throughout.

'I assumed that would be the case.' Nell nodded. 'In which case, my findings are either going to make your life much easier . . .' She raised her eyebrows. 'Or much harder.'

'Oh?' James leaned forward. 'Go on.'

Nell turned her page of notes towards him. 'Here's the species list of diatoms from Little Smitington Pond, and I've added a count of how abundant the species are in the overall sample.' She pointed to the tally chart she'd drawn against the list. 'Here.'

James didn't know what he was supposed to be looking at. 'You're going to need to explain—'

'OK, if you compare *this* list to the species list and abundance from the . . . human sample, you'll see a notable difference.'

James glanced between the pages, hoping for something to leap out.

'Certain species are used as indicators of the environment,' Nell explained. 'The science is more accurate for rivers but the principle

144

also applies to ponds. And I'd say it definitely applies when it's this marked.'

She pointed at the list of species again. 'See? Hardly any species in both lists. The species found in high numbers in Little Smitington Pond are *Cymbella delicata*, *Hannaea arcus* and *Epithemia sorex*. These are indicators of low-nutrient and high-quality habitats. Nutrients come from road or farm run-off, so high nutrient levels reduce the habitat quality in ecological terms. So the presence of these species indicates that the habitat they're found in is pristine.' Nell winced. 'Which Little Smitington Pond *was*.'

'I see.' James scanned the species names.

'But, look, *those* species aren't even *present* in the tissue samples. Instead, it has high numbers of *Nitzschia sigmoidea*, *Ellerbeckia arenaria* and *Rhoicosphenia abbreviata*. Those are species that would be used as biological indicators for a moderately nutrient-rich river. Specifically, one with relatively high nitrogen or phosphorus levels in the water. Yet – *again* – those species were *not* found in the pond.'

James checked, seeing the difference for himself. Their heads were close as they leaned over the lists. He caught her orange blossom scent, which had so briefly been so familiar. He forced himself to remember Nell's family were on the edge of this investigation. He had to question her records, of her giving him such a stark steer onto a different track.

Does Ashley have a point?

'So he didn't drown where he was found.' James cut through the technicalities.

'Exactly.' Nell nodded. 'I'll see if I can think of a suitable place in the area where he could have been drowned. I guess you'd be looking for a freshwater habitat nearer a road, or a farm, or with fish or ducks, like in a park, perhaps?' She shook her head. 'Nowhere leaps to mind. There's the river in town, but I'm not sure if there are any private stretches where someone could be conveniently drowned and driven about in a conspicuous car.'

'Well, your new evidence is a start.' James picked up the list and turned off the recorder. 'I'll need to let the team know.' He eyed Nell knowingly, needing to impress the gravity of this onto her, even if he knew he was stretching the truth. 'You'll need to keep this confidential.

It's important you follow procedure, Nell. You could be called as an expert witness in a murder case. You can't play sleuth now.'

Sunday 21st April – 11 a.m.

As Nell packed her books into the boot of the car, her phone beeped. Her heart leapt – *Rav?* But the number shown was unidentified. She answered the call.

'Hi, Nell speaking.'

'Nell? Oh, thank *God!*' Jonty sounded stressed.

Nell felt a tingle of apprehension. 'What's going on, Jonty?'

'It's . . . it's Mai. She . . . she collapsed. At the pond.'

Nell's stomach dropped. 'What?' Mai shouldn't even have *been* there this morning. Nell's two interns were helping, with a full list of instructions so not even Jonty could confuse them. 'Call an ambu—'

'Oh, yeah, I did. We're at the hospital. And you don't need to worry, your interns are still working at the pond. They're, like, amazing. They know what to do and they're just getting on with it.'

'Never mind the work, Jonty, how's Mai?'

'"Never mind the work", Jonty scoffed, 'That's, like, *all* you care about! You're always on my case if I'm not doing enough but, now I'm on it, it doesn't matter! Make your mind up.'

Nell bristled. 'The clue, Jonty, is if someone's in bloody *hospital* or not. How *is* she?'

'I don't know exactly. She's on a drip. They're doing tests but the doctors said it looked like exhaustion. They asked me about next of kin but I don't know anyone.'

Nell tried to recall what Mai had told her about her family, but it wasn't much, definitely no contact numbers. 'No, I don't either.'

'She's all pale. And *so* quiet. I've never seen her be, well, *quiet*.' Jonty's voice sounded so desolate that Nell was taken aback for a moment. 'I don't think she needs anything. But . . . would you come? I don't really know what to do.'

She checked the time. 'I can be there in about half an hour. Which ward?'

As Nell drove to the hospital, she called Rav. His voice boomed through the car stereo. 'Oh my God, I'm *so* pleased to hear from you! I've had the *worst* morning. Aanya must have said something that made Mum realise you put them up in . . . *the* room where . . . *Jack's* room . . .'

Nell's heart sank – and kept sinking – as Rav continued.

'. . . I've never seen my parents so incensed,' he said. 'Aanya and I have tried to explain that you've worked miracles to get them checked in at all. But they won't listen. Aanya's stormed off in a strop because she's sick of how they talk about her. I mean, it doesn't take much from Mum and Dad to put Aanya in a strop, but they've decided it's your fault. They're insulted – they think you're making some kind of point. They're saying it's unreasonable to expect them stay—'

'Well, then, please invite them to move out,' Nell said crisply.

'You . . . *what?*' Rav asked.

'I think you heard,' Nell said. 'I had no intention of making them feel like that. I'm sorry they do but I can't change that. Tell them they're free to leave; it's a hotel, not a prison.'

'I can't say that!' Rav protested.

'Why not?' Nell asked. 'They're fixated on the idea that I'm upsetting them on purpose. When I'm not. I wouldn't even dream of it! I *like* them! I sympathise with what they've been dealing with. But honestly, I've no idea why I've been so firmly put on the back foot here without any allowances for any misunderstandings. I've only tried to help. If my help's not welcome, I don't want to force it on anyone. Including your folks.'

'Nell?'

'I'm serious, Rav. I know this hasn't worked out the way we wanted. I thought I could give them more time. I didn't factor in a bloody *murder* to throw everything off track. But I've still tried, really hard, to make time for them. Even when these past few days have been . . . pretty challenging. But what can I do if your parents are this desperate to take everything I do the wrong way?'

'Right, well, if that's how you feel—'

'It is,' Nell said. 'And I have to go now. I'm at the hospital. Mai collapsed this morning. So I'm seeing her and then I'll check in with the interns. And *then* I'll go to work.' She hung up.

Despite her exasperation that Rav was tiptoeing around his parents, Nell instantly regretted her snippy words, which rattled around her head as she speed-walked the sterile corridors to Mai's ward. When she got there, a curtain was drawn around Mai's bed and Jonty loitered awkwardly. He looked lost.

'Hi, how's she doing?' Nell whispered.

'Better. Much better.' A brief smile. 'They're doing some tests. Said it would take a few minutes. They're sure it's exhaustion.'

Nell nodded, looking at him. 'And how are you?' His face was grey.

Jonty shook his head. 'I'm fine. I just want to make sure she's OK.' He rubbed his face miserably. 'It's my fault. I've not been pulling my weight. Mai's been doing everything, *and* she's been carrying me.' He dug his hands into his pockets and stared at his feet.

Unable to disagree, Nell kept a tactful silence and Jonty continued, 'Those interns have put me to shame, really. It was . . . a wake-up call, if I'm honest. I've been so useless. Mai deserves better.' He took a deep breath. 'I'm going to do everything I can to sort out the pond – *and* get that designation.'

'Have you got a plan?'

'Yes. I tracked down the plant supplier and reordered all the plug plants for the bare banks. They'll arrive tomorrow morning and the interns have agreed to help me get them planted by tomorrow lunch. Just in time for the visit by the assessor.' He gave Nell a mock grimace as if half exhilarated by his boldness, half worried his risk wouldn't pay off.

'Wow!' Nell was stunned. 'That sounds . . . *great*. Do you need any reinforcements?'

Jonty shook his head. 'I'm determined to do it. But thanks.'

Nell didn't have a chance to voice any concern at Jonty's new overconfidence. The curtain was whisked open and the doctor nodded at the two of them.

'Can either of you persuade this woman to rest? She needs to rehydrate—' he checked Mai's drip '—and sleep and eat well. But my advice is falling on deaf ears.'

'It's fine, Doc,' Jonty said. 'I'll take care of everything.'

Sunday 21st April – 12.15 p.m.

As Nell hurried towards Finchmere Hotel's entrance, she checked her phone. Several messages from Rav asking about Mai had stacked up. She stopped walking and typed a brief reply. But it sounded too curt. Groaning, she rewrote it and, finally, sent it. She felt the estrangement between them in how carefully she selected her words.

When she finally walked into Finchmere Hotel's reception, she saw a vast bouquet of mixed country blooms and a silver bucket of the estate's sparkling wine being taken to the lift. The romantic gesture underlined her own heartache. She hated being at odds with Rav.

'What's the occasion?' Nell asked the receptionist.

The receptionist beamed in delight. 'An engagement! The man is a-*dor*-able. He's colluded with us for *months* to make this the perfect weekend to pop the question. He's going to ask her over dinner tonight! Booked in at seven, so I'll still be here to see if she says yes! They're in the Spindle Room, with a private garden terrace so they can have a moment alone in the moonlight. Aww!' She fanned herself. 'So romantic!'

'Have we done anything for them?' Nell asked.

'Only flowers and sparkling wine, which he ordered in advance. We won't charge him, but he doesn't know that yet.' The receptionist raised her hands in regret. 'We couldn't upgrade because when he booked, I knew all the suites would fill up for the Classics.' She shrugged. 'We could cover their dinner. What do you think?'

'I might have a better idea,' Nell mused. 'Let me check and get back to you.' She hurried on to the Orangery, not wanting to keep her father waiting for their meeting over lunch.

As she walked in, she saw a large table was taken up with Moretti's racing team. Lucio, Maxine, Cassie, Mark and Colin were obviously having a team talk about the race and the police investigation.

Hugo sat at his preferred table, by the window, with the distant view of the racetrack nestled in the downs. As Nell joined him, he flicked the napkin adroitly across his lap to protect his three-piece suit and got straight down to business. 'With the gullwing's postponed race scheduled for tomorrow, we now have a revised, and fixed, programme of races and parade laps.' He flashed a relieved smile at Nell.

'Good.'

Nell knew the teams had tried to be accommodating, but updating them, shuffling the programme and constantly updating the updates, had kept Hugo busy and disrupted his own schedule.

Even so, the rest of the event depended upon whatever James was looking into.

'I've got some catching up to do with the press,' Hugo continued. 'And whatever else has been happening across the event while I've been schedule-juggling.'

'Well, I can tell you that the auction's press coverage was good.' Nell anticipated his question and showed him articles on her phone with photos taken outside the auction marquee, headlined, *'Private Collector Races Away with Historical Car.'*

Hugo nodded. 'Very nice. She got it for a good price, too.' He sat back as a waiter set their pre-ordered lunch on the table then departed discreetly. 'Have you had the follow-up meeting with Montague's about next year?'

Nell hesitated, then leaned forward to whisper. 'No. I cancelled, actually.' She glanced over her shoulder, unnecessarily, since the tables were well spaced out and screened with citrus trees. 'Do you know about anything ... *dodgy* ... going on with the auction?'

'What do you mean?'

The way her father's eyes snapped up, his fierce, guarded expression, made Nell's stomach drop. 'The police are investigating it. They watched the whole thing yesterday ...'

'Well, they're quite entitled to,' Hugo said. 'It was an open auction. And, with a murder inquiry in progress, they could have been waiting to speak to someone.'

Nell shook her head. 'James asked for all our auction back catalogues.'

'Did he say why?' Hugo frowned.

'No.' Nell stared at her father for any sign that he might know something. But he just chewed in an unnerving silence. She couldn't bring herself to eat and just picked at her salad.

Catching sight of the man she'd seen at the auction, in his tweed jacket and trilby, his assertive body language dialled up to eleven, caught Nell's attention. He and his female companion paused as he cast his eye around like a hawk scanning for prey. His gaze fixed on the large table where the gullwing's team were gathered, and he made a beeline for them. The engrossed team didn't notice his approach, until he was standing beside Lucio, holding out his police ID.

Hugo turned in his seat to see what had gripped Nell's attention. 'What the . . . ?'

'Lucio Moretti, I'm here to arrest you for the sale of a Ferrari 250 GTO, which constituted fraud by false representation under Section 2 of the Fraud Act 2006. You do not have to say anything. But it may harm your defence if you do not mention when questioned something which you later rely on in court. Anything you do say may be given in evidence.'

'Fraud?' Hugo repeated. He sounded as shocked as Nell felt.

Leaping to his feet, Lucio stared, open-mouthed, at the tweed-clad officer, who took advantage of Lucio's surprise by deftly handcuffing his hands behind his back.

Hugo hurried over, with Nell quick behind him.

'What's going on, officer?' Hugo demanded, blocking his way.

'This is private police business.'

'Forgive me, officer, but I rather consider anything happening on my property to *be* my business.'

The man appraised Hugo. 'Sorry, Lord Beaumont. I can't disclose anything. I hope you understand. We're in the middle of an investigation.'

Hugo looked at Lucio's face, then back at the officer. 'There's a lot of press about. I'd consider it a personal favour if you'd use the side door and don't make it obvious Mr Moretti is in handcuffs.'

He nodded, and Lucio gave Hugo a grateful look. As the officer steered Lucio from the room, followed by his silent colleague, Lucio shot a desperate glance at Colin.

A babble broke out as Colin jumped to his feet, hauled back by

Mark with cries of, 'No, you'll only make it worse!' and, 'The police need to follow their process.'

But Colin yanked his arm out of Mark's grasp and strode towards the door. He nearly collided with Dani, standing with Svetlana in the doorway. The women turned to watch him catch up with a handcuffed Lucio.

As Dani turned back to the team at the table, Nell saw her face drain to a Halloweenish white as she clamped a hand over her mouth and dashed towards the bathroom.

Hugo hissed at Nell, his face stern, 'Is James behind this?'

Nell was lost for words. She remembered how unimpressed Lucio had been about her telling James about the sale of the Ferrari. She bit her lip.

'I simply can't imagine Lucio committing fraud.' Hugo shook his head.

Nell wished she had her father's faith.

Gazing around the shell-shocked company, Hugo muttered, 'Let's hope it doesn't get picked up by the press. If they get wind of this, it'll be bad news for Moretti's. And the team. And your gullwing project.'

Nell swallowed. *Did he really not get it? If Lucio was guilty of fraud and he'd supplied their auctions, it wasn't the gullwing's race on the line. It was Finchmere.*

It was their home.

Chapter 21

Sunday 21st April – 1.30 p.m.

'For the benefit of the tape, I am DI James Clark.'

'And I am DS Walsh, Fraud Division.'

'I am Signor Lucio Moretti.'

'And I am Ms Mortimer, Signor Moretti's legal counsel.'

Lucio's body screamed tension. He sat stiffly, his face grim as he regarded Walsh. James had only been allowed to attend Walsh's questioning as a courtesy for Fraud Squad's use of Pendlebury Police Station. He sat back, listening and observing.

'Do you confirm that your company, Moretti's, recently sold a Ferrari 250 GTO for thirty-six million pounds to an overseas collector, one Mr Brooks Bryant IV of New York?'

'No comment,' Ms Mortimer answered for Lucio before he could speak.

'Can you tell us how the record of provenance for said car was produced?' Walsh asked.

'No comment.'

'Do you agree that the record of provenance for said car was falsified?'

'No comment.' Lucio's eyes bored into Walsh's as if he was staring him down. But, as he held their continuous, challenging eye contact, Lucio's brow sheened with sweat.

'Do you admit that, by creating a fictious record of provenance for said car, it inflated the sale price by several million pounds?'

'No comment.' Lucio folded his arms, maintaining his steely glare.

Walsh closed his folder. 'Fine. Interview terminated at . . .' he checked the clock '. . . thirteen thirty-two.'

Walsh stood, and James followed him out. From the next room,

James watched Lucio muttering to Ms Mortimer on the screen, showing the live footage from the camera that he hadn't switched off.

Beside James, Walsh paced. 'He's going to be a brick wall. We won't get anywhere like this.'

James considered Val's suggestion. 'We need to reel him in. We could start with what he *will* talk about, and work our way into the more . . . dubious activity.'

Walsh sat at the desk and opened his folder. 'Care to help me formulate a plan?'

Sunday 21st April – 1.45 p.m.

Nell frowned, trying to force herself to focus on the press meeting, despite the clamouring worries. She felt her face flush as she nodded along with others in the room, having not listened to the question or remarks.

'Sorry, could you repeat that?' she asked.

The speaker gaped at Nell. 'I *said* that at this juncture, it would be appropriate to observe a minute's silence for Jack Rafferty.'

Nell blushed. Around her, disapproval bristled. She couldn't blame them: these were individuals whose schedules she'd chopped and changed frequently over the past two days.

She was just about treading water with her meetings, but she knew she had to be more attentive. But it was impossible not to be distracted: her mother was detached from the event, and Nell somehow felt she was protecting her by making her stay that way, and not sharing her worries. *Is Dad implicated? If so, hopefully – surely – without knowing . . . ?* Nell didn't dare ask, not wanting to voice the fear, and more than slightly scared of the answer. And worried any conversation they might have would somehow incriminate him if he *was* questioned.

And her father had enough to do. He, like Nell, was still catching up with all his meetings and the changes to the schedule, as well as fulfilling the usual expectations of the event's host: speeches, prize giving, race launches, greeting groups and teams. His eyes were bloodshot, his face grey. Exhausted and fraught. She couldn't add to his burden.

Rav had enough to handle with his parents. And she wasn't even helping there, despite her best efforts. Everything she did was viewed in the worst possible light. It wasn't just wildly unfair, it was draining. And she hated the misunderstandings between her and Rav. She wished he'd just occasionally stick up for her a bit. But him failing to even notice made her feel lonely in a way she never had before she'd begun seeing Rav. She closed her eyes, gritty and dry from lack of sleep and microscope work.

As people shifted around her, she realised the minute was up and she forced herself to look up brightly, ready to give her full attention to whatever was next on the agenda. She pulled her meeting notes towards her and smiled at the next speaker.

In the meeting break, Nell poured herself a large coffee, grateful for steaming caffeine, and walked to the garden door for some fresh air. She ached to talk to Rav, but she doubted he would want to hear from her after their conversation this morning. Even so, somehow, her fingers found her phone, tapped Rav's number . . .

'Nell!' Rav sounded pleased to hear from her. 'I'm so glad you called. I've been worried.'

Her heart lifted at his voice and his kind nature. 'How's it going over there? Any better?'

'I hope so.' Rav let out a huge sigh. 'Aanya came back, so Mum and Dad have relaxed. And I was all ready to have a word with them about . . . well, the things *you* said, when Aanya basically went to battle about you. She told them how supportive you were with the police interview and the fallout with Jack.'

'Oh?' Nell was momentarily stunned. 'That's so nice of her. I didn't expect . . .'

'No, well, it *is* nice. I'm pleased she likes you so much. And then, um, well, *I* took that moment to say that I also thought they'd treated you unfairly.' She heard him swallow.

'Really?' Her heart lifted a little. Guardedly, she asked, 'What did they say?'

'They were pretty surprised. I don't usually disagree *forcefully* with them. But I pointed out that they hadn't really tried to get to know you. That they'd come here with a heap of preconceptions – which were wrong – and that they were missing out on the opportunity to really get the measure of you.'

'Oh, great!' Nell laughed, surprised at her rapid thaw as she joked, 'Please do invite more judgement.'

'Yeah, well, that's what would pique Mum's interest more than anything.'

'Well, I guess we'll see.' She hesitated. 'I *do* have an option about your parents being in Jack's suite. A couple are getting engaged. We could swap rooms and tell the couple it's a free upgrade. It means your folks will be in a smaller room, but it's still lovely. If your folks have dinner at seven, the same time as the other couple, I can organise the room swap and arrange housekeeping. What do you think?'

'Oh, that would be . . . They'd appreciate it. That's really kind. Thank you.'

'And I'll be at the reception dinner at Finchmere tonight,' Nell said. 'Any chance you can make it?'

'Yes, please. I'm looking forward to some time with you.'

'And what's Aanya doing tonight?' Nell asked, impulsively. 'We're one down on the guest list, so I can fit her in. Would she want to come? Might be nice for your folks to have some time to themselves, now things are calmer? Think about it and let me know.'

'Aanya would bite your hand off if you asked her, but she hasn't got anything to wear.'

'Then send her over to get ready with me. I'm getting dressed at about six. Reception starts at seven but I like to make sure I'm there early. I'm sure I can find her something.'

Sunday 21st April – 2 p.m.

James studied his notes, feeling the pressure of Walsh's suggestion to lead the next round of questions, along with Val's invisible gaze beyond the camera. He took a deep breath and smiled at Lucio.

'Signor Moretti, we're just here to establish what happened with this sale. We accept that you might not be involved, but you may have information that can help.' He leaned forward, allowed his forehead to crease with a concerned frown. 'And I know one thing for certain, if you're *not* involved in this fraudulent activity, it's definitely hurting your business. And your team. So I'm confident that, on those bases, you'd want to help with our inquiries.'

Lucio's eyes fixed on Ms Mortimer; his face clouded with confusion.

'In which case, release my client from arrest,' Ms Mortimer instructed.

'We're happy to do that,' James said.

Ms Mortimer looked deflated. Her eyes darted from James to Lucio. Lucio's face had brightened with a triumphant smile.

'But,' James warned her, 'since we're sure that Signor Moretti's statement will form part of our body of evidence – and how can it not?' he asked reasonably. 'Given the sale of the vehicle in question was through his own dealership – we advise that we question him under caution, with you remaining present as his counsel.'

Ms Mortimer frowned as if detecting an unseen trap. She squinted at Lucio. 'That . . . *sounds* reasonable . . . ?'

'Excellent,' James said. 'Thank you both. Now, Signor Moretti, can you tell us your recollection of the discovery of this car?'

Unfolding his arms, Lucio glanced at Ms Mortimer. '*Sì*, this is easy to explain. There is a gentleman who values cars for Montague's. Richard Tyler. He verifies the reserve price for vehicles for their sales. Let us say you inherit a property and find something in a locked-up outbuilding, Richard is the one who would go out to tell the new owner if it is worth anything. More often than not, it is a rusty Morris Minor. And they are nice little cars! But, for those little cars, the restoration costs more than the restored car's value.' He shrugged. 'Of course, the people, they want to be told that they have uncovered a gold mine. And for some, very – *very* – occasionally, this is true.'

James nodded, hoping Lucio would continue on his own but he stopped, so James asked, 'And this Ferrari, was this one such *occasional* find?'

'*Sì*,' Lucio confirmed. 'Richard has a reputation for being fair. He tells people what their cars are worth and what the restoration would cost them. If the car interests him, he makes a good offer to buy it, then finds a team to do the restoration at cost for a percentage return on the sale price.'

'And everyone does well out of a deal like that,' James agreed.

'Exactly so. And everyone's keen to do a job that is both efficient and . . .' he kissed his fingers '. . . *bellissima!*'

'OK, so for our Ferrari, here,' James asked, 'who did Mr Tyler entrust with the restoration?'

'Mark and Cassie, of course!' Lucio frowned at James as if he'd not been paying attention.

'Why them? Why "of course"?' James asked.

'Because Richard passed the information on to Maxine and gave her first refusal to be the second verifier and to recommend a team for the restoration. Mark and Cassie were the obvious choice: already, they were under commission for the gullwing, with all the right expertise. Mark in particular has restored classics for years. Not for nothing does he have a reputation for his eye for detail. And Cassie, she is very skilled, very capable.'

'Yes, you make a good point – your gullwing. After all the work to restore it to such high standards, why were you satisfied with poor performance from your driver?'

Lucio looked surprised at the unexpected tangent. He studied James for a moment and then leaned forward. 'Allow me to be frank. I adore the racing world. It is fun. But the honour of the racetrack was not my pressing issue. I am a businessman. I want to sell my gullwing for the highest price possible. It matters not to me if she wins on the track, because her performance has been reduced anyway. So this is not a true indication. If Jack wins or loses—' he shrugged '—I care not one fig. What I *do* care for, is the new kind of buyer we are trying to attract: a *wealthy* buyer, happy to pay a premium for a car that has something of a following. And by launching her in a trailblazing race at a high-profile event – driven by a *Rafferty!* – this gives her a little history. A little stardust. Where value becomes invaluable.' Lucio wagged his finger. 'And, so. It is Jack who we need.'

'Even though Jack disrupted the rest of the team?' James pressed. 'Who thought they were playing their part by showing the gullwing to her best advantage on the track . . . ?'

Lucio gave an elaborate shrug. 'It was for Maxine to manage Jack.'

Disappointed that Lucio's answer downplayed any hint of motive resulting from Jack's poor driving, James made notes, then changed tack. 'Right. So at the point of purchase, then, what did Maxine do, as second verifier?' he asked.

'She verifies the provenance. This is to corroborate every detail to determine if the car is genuine. She must examine the car, the bodywork, the chassis number and engine number, match the Vehicle Identification Number, check the logbook. This is detailed, specialist work.'

'Was Maxine an obvious choice? Or was that unusual?' James asked.

'Of course this is not unusual! This is Maxine's job. She sources rare cars, lovingly gives them a new lease of life! She is well connected to restorers and buyers all over the world. It means she can tailor a restoration for any particular taste or requirements. And *this*—' he turned his palm up with a flourish '—guarantees the top price for all involved.'

'Sounds like you've got this business pretty well sewn up,' James mused. 'But, with a tight working group like yours, you'll all benefit from the fraudulent activity of conjuring up an extremely rare Ferrari, with supposedly unique provenance, from a much more common donor car.' He raised his eyebrows. 'So you'd probably all keep quiet about it.'

Lucio's face surged with purple. Behind his goatee, his jowls trembled. 'How dare you! I'd swear on my life that my team are above reproach!'

'Well, swear all you like,' James said calmly. 'But *someone* isn't.'

Chapter 22

Nell leaned over the reception desk and pointed to the rooms on the plan. 'These two are the rooms to swap, please: Mr and Dr Kashyap from the Oak Suite to the Spindle Room, and *its* occupants to the suite.'

The receptionist updated the details. 'I'll let housekeeping and the porters know. They'll be ready to do the changeover at seven.'

'Perfect, thank you.' As Nell walked from the desk, her phone beeped with a text from Jonty:

> Mai's home! Looks better, finally agreed she needs rest. Watching Netflix with your chocolates ☺ I'm replanting at the pond – all good. Planning to surprise her with a finished job!

Nell smiled at the news, but then looked up sharply as the wail of an emergency vehicle grew louder until it was deafening. The receptionist stood and joined Nell at the glass-fronted double open door as blue light flooded in and swirled around the marble reception hall.

In the maelstrom, Nell heard the faint chime of the lift and someone stagger out. She turned to see Dani, looking like death, propped up on each side by Maxine and Svetlana.

Two paramedics jogged in, pushing a gurney, and gently helped Dani onto it, while a third asked Maxine questions.

Nell crept closer to hear.

'Miscarriage,' Maxine murmured. 'Poor love. I didn't know if 999 was right or not ...'

Beside Nell, Svetlana looked shell-shocked, concern carved into her pained frown. But a sob from Dani made Svetlana dash to her friend's side. The paramedic hunkered beside Dani for more information and Maxine squeezed Dani's hand as she forced words out through broken sobs.

Nell backed off from listening to Dani's private medical details. But she did hear an anguished: 'It's all . . . my fault.'

And Maxine's murmur: 'No, pet, it doesn't work like that. You can't blame yourself.'

With a look of pure anguish, Svetlana shushed Dani, smoothing her hair back from her sweaty forehead.

The paramedics wheeled Dani away, but she reached out to her friend as the distance between them grew. 'Lana?' Dani's face trembled. 'I'm sorry. I'm so, *so* sorry.'

Striding to keep up with her, Svetlana brushed her hand across her cheek and raised her chin. 'No, I am sorry that you are going through this. I would not wish it on anyone.'

As the paramedics pushed Dani slowly through the door, she asked, 'Will you come . . . ?'

Svetlana nodded as she stopped in the doorway. 'I will drive. Then I hope I can bring you back.' Her smile was kind and Dani managed a small nod as she was whisked away.

But as the ambulance bore her friend away, Svetlana turned to Maxine, her rage boiling. '*Svoloch*,' she spat out. 'That *bastard*. Look at what he leaves behind him. I heard him at the party. He told Dani to just get rid of it in secret.' Her face hardened. 'That should not be his decision to make. It showed him to be coward, who'd bully someone he was supposed to care about into making difficult choice, and to bear it alone, just to make sure *he* had no consequences to face. How *weak*. I could not love a man like that. I could not *live* with a man like that.'

Maxine stared at her. 'What . . . what are you saying, Lana, luv?'

'Pff. I have already told police I killed him. They don't arrest me. I don't know why. I punched him; he was unconscious. I left him in driveway and drove here.'

'Bloody Nora, Lana!' Maxine's jittery gaze swung around reception, resting on Nell.

'Pff. She was with police when I confessed. With the other girl Jack slept with.'

'But they can't believe you,' Maxine reasoned, 'if they haven't arrested you.'

'This is not my fault. I tried to help, but it seems they do not want it. But Dani needs my help now.' Svetlana called the lift. 'I will take her a change of clothes.'

Once the lift doors had closed behind Svetlana, Maxine turned to Nell with wide eyes, blowing out a long exhalation.

'Is there anything else we can do?' Nell asked. 'To help in any way?'

Maxine threw an arm around Nell, squeezing her in a bearlike grip, which was blessedly brief. 'You're like me, luv – you're a fixer, aren't you? But sometimes people don't *want* fixing. Sometimes they just want to be understood, have a friend to talk to, cry with. Dani's got Lana, now. I've a feeling they'll both get through this.'

As Nell chewed her lip, Maxine nudged her. 'You don't need to fret, luv. Don't go looking for tragedy. God knows, it finds you easily enough on its own.'

James watched Lucio's reaction to their interview on the screen. His last words had riled Lucio and now he was speaking rapidly to Ms Mortimer, his gestures emphasising his words. He spoke in staccato sentences, as if every phrase was a final pronouncement. Indignation radiated from him. Ms Mortimer tried to keep up, making rapid notes.

Val had only given him a brief nod when he walked into the room with Walsh. But James felt a flash of encouragement at her understated approval.

'Now we're getting somewhere!' Walsh sat down, watching Lucio's agitation in delight. 'Let him stew on who might be undermining their lucrative arrangement. Then, I'm sure, he'll talk.'

James noticed that Val, who stood behind Walsh's seat, narrowed her eyes. He agreed with her silent assessment: Lucio would still need more incentive to point the finger at his colleagues. For him, business was personal.

'It's the reception dinner at Finchmere tonight,' James said. 'Might be interesting to release Signor Moretti, especially since we don't have grounds to hold him, and give him the chance to speak to his circle. See what that shakes up?'

And with any luck that'll ensure I should attend, and definitely keep one promised date with Shannon . . .

Val's eyebrow rose in thoughtful approval. Walsh looked pained, clearly hoping that Lucio was ready to crack, and a full confession would pour out in time for his team to wrap up by the end of his shift. He turned to Val for her reaction.

'If you continue with his interview now,' Val replied to the unasked question, 'he'll direct all that outrage and indignation at you, and it will manifest as resistance to your questions and your inquiry. But if you let him go, he'll direct it at his colleagues.' She glanced at James. 'And that may, indeed, shake things up.'

Walsh nodded, with a deep sigh, and returned to the interview room. Val and James watched the screen as Walsh told Lucio he was free to go. Lucio looked almost crestfallen at not being able to extend his tirade to Walsh.

'Nice work in there,' Val said as she and James walked to their incident room. 'Especially getting insight on how the purchase of a car like that works. Very defensive of his team, wasn't he?'

As James updated the board's motive section with question marks and data from the fraud investigation, Val stood beside him. 'Just a suggestion, but in your shoes, I'd cancel your night off and show a bit of support to Ashley and her ideas for the investigation. She's got the suggestions she'd already made underway. And tonight she's planning to speak to Richard Tyler. Plus, Fraud have tipped us off that we might want to be on hand this evening.'

James held in the sigh at his ring-fenced reception dinner with Shannon being hijacked.

As if sensing reluctance, Val said, 'I know it's a pain. But we all have to do things sometimes to pull together. *You* might think Ashley's being unfair, but not everyone will agree with you.'

James's head jerked up. *Does she agree with Ashley?* He couldn't bring himself to ask.

'And you're a DI now, James. You have to show your team support. And situations like this show *them* what kind of a leader you are.'

Holding in another groan, James nodded. 'Sure. I'll just make a call.' In the corridor, he leaned against the wall and phoned Shannon.

'I'm so sorry—'

'Don't tell me. You're bailing.' Her voice, as ever, was totally neutral. He couldn't tell if she was disappointed, upset, or just didn't care at all.

'It's the nature of the job—'

'So *draining*. Look, don't worry . . .' The phone muffled for a moment as Shannon called out, 'Raffers? Did you say your wife isn't coming tonight? Fancy pairing up?' Her voice became clearer as she spoke into the phone again. 'Don't you worry about me one bit. I'll go with Colin. And, silver cloud, darling, I'll get plenty of coverage being photographed on *his* arm.'

'Colin?'

'Rafferty. I'll be in good hands. You have fun cracking your case!'

James tried not to drag his feet as he walked back into the incident room. He managed a smile and nodded at Val. 'All sorted.'

Before Val could ask for any more favours, an officer burst in, nearly whacking him with the door as he breathlessly called out, 'Ma'am?'

'Yes?' Val walked over.

'We've had an update from the forensic team at Jack and Lana's house. Another two cars in the garage have also been tampered with.'

Val's eyes widened. 'Go on.'

'Inside the triple garage were two cars, with space for the absent Mustang. The other two cars were a Lancia Stratos and a Porsche 930 Turbo cabriolet. The cars looked perfectly normal but, for both cars, the rotor arm inside the distributor cap had been removed.'

'Oh!' Val said. 'So not quite the same type of sabotage as tampering with the brakes.'

'No,' the officer agreed. 'Without a rotor arm, the car wouldn't start. Unlike the brakes, where you could drive the car but lose control and not be able to stop.'

'But . . .' Val smiled at the officer, guessing what he had been going to say. 'If you can't start the other two cars, you'd *have* to drive the sabotaged car.'

The officer nodded. 'We've got someone going down to take

fingerprints. We don't know if we'll get anything conclusive but we can try.'

Sunday 21st April – 6 p.m.

'Whaaaaat!' Aanya shrieked as she stepped into Nell's closet. 'Holy *what* now?!'

She ran her fingers through the small but exquisite selection of dresses and came to the end, where an Art Deco cocktail dress, shimmering with intricate beadwork, was hung. A large antique Cartier box sat on the dressing table.

'Is this what you're wearing?' Aanya asked. She lifted the edge of the fine black tulle over the forest-green silk, admiring the flapper-style fringing. 'It's proper vintage!'

Nell nodded. 'Amazing, isn't it? So lucky my great-grandmother had good taste! But what about you?' Nell walked back to the dresses and pondered over their different shapes. 'What do you think . . . hang on . . . about this?'

She pulled out a scarlet, corseted gown with a full skirt. 'What about this? The shape's a bit Fifties, so it fits with the vintage theme.'

'Oh, I love it!' Without needing further encouragement, Aanya tried on the dress, holding her breath in as Nell fastened it.

Nell poked her – 'You have to breathe, Aanya!' – making her release the breath and giggle. She stepped back to take a look. 'Oh, wow! It's quite a different animal on you!'

Aanya turned, her eyes fixed on the mirror. 'It's amazing!'

'Right, give me half an hour and I'll be ready,' Nell said.

Sunday 21st April – 6.30 p.m.

Thirty minutes later, Rav heard Nell and Aanya approach from the upstairs hallway as he waited for them in the huge hall of Finchmere House. He hoped this time, wearing his Savile Row tux, that the night wouldn't end in disaster, like it had every other time before: the last time, the night had ended in murder; the time before that – even worse – he'd been about to ask Nell out but was beaten to it by James. He fiddled with his cufflinks and smoothed his jacket. The jazz band was warming up in the ballroom, beyond the great room, off the hall to his left. As Nell appeared, he felt that familiar, irrepressible grin spread across his face.

Aanya ran down the stairs to meet him and twirled, her skirt flaring out. 'What do you think!'

'I think you look lovely, sis,' Rav said.

He turned to Nell. She took his breath away. Under the chandeliers, her dress, like her, was alive with sparkle. Her eyes shone as she looked at him and he felt like his heart would burst. 'You're so beautiful.' He smiled at the Art Deco diamond headband and her kiss-curls. 'That's stunning. Very *Great Gatsby*.'

She leaned in and kissed him thoroughly. 'You look incredibly sexy in a tux!' Her eyes gleamed and Rav instantly melted.

'Where do we go?' Aanya interrupted their moment, looking around the hall. Nell had shown her around when she'd stayed on Friday but, with the preparations underway over the weekend for tonight's dinner, Aanya had kept out of the way, either at the racetrack or the hotel.

'Guests will arrive here,' Nell said, 'but we'll wait through there . . .' She led them through the great room and into the ballroom. The vast room had been zoned, with round tables covered with gold cloths clustered at one end. The middle of each table was a puddle of light with candles around a centrepiece sapling English oak. Nell would plant the centrepieces afterwards as part of the event's carbon offsetting.

The jazz band were tuning up at the far end, below – rather than in – the minstrels' gallery so they could easily take requests and fill the vast marble floor between them and the tables with dancing. Just inside the door to the great room, the Art Deco bar bustled with staff putting the final touches to cocktail garnishes. Beyond the bar, the great room was zoned with sofas and inviting chairs creating alcoves to chat in.

Nell's parents arrived, Hugo in black tie and Imelda in a long beaded gown with black evening gloves. As early guests arrived, introductions were made, drinks provided and – before Rav knew it – the room was filling.

Taking his cue from Nell, he stuck to water. She managed to seem relaxed while treating it very much like a work event. With an apparently effortless ease, she greeted everyone by name, recalled their latest news, asked them about named relations, connected guests with mutual interests and shared anecdotes from the track. She radiated confidence.

Rav bit back a smile when he noticed Aanya staring at her to begin with, remembering that her first impression of Nell was nervous and self-conscious at their parents' barbecue. But Aanya clearly enjoyed the halo effect of meeting everyone alongside the host.

So, when Nell stiffened slightly beside him and brushed her shoulder, the prearranged, subtle signal to summon a security guard, Rav fixed his eyes on her, wondering what was wrong.

Chapter 23

Nell recognised the press photographer instantly. He wasn't as unobtrusive as he thought he was, taking photos with his phone. The security guard tapped the photographer on the shoulder and held his hand out for the phone.

Her mind raced to think of his name. She'd studied the party guest list like cramming for an exam, to ensure she wouldn't be lost for words or make some awful *faux pas*. But this man evaded her. She racked her memory for his name as she approached him.

'Hi . . . Joel?' Nell was relieved that his name came to her in the nick of time. She extended her hand with a smile. The security guard backed off and waited a step away.

Joel shook Nell's hand, looking at her warily. 'I've blown it now, haven't I?' he whispered. Nell saw he was aiming for conspiratorial and trying to save face.

'Very probably,' she agreed, but with a smile. Better to resolve this cordially than create a scene and an enemy in the press. 'At least you got a drink out of it.'

Emboldened, Joel shook his head. 'Yeah, but what we're after is a *scoop*.'

'Shocking news. Who's "we"?'

'Only Greg.' He jerked his head towards a man, already being escorted out by another security officer.

Joel was usually this candid, Nell remembered. It made him easier to compromise with than most on where the line between publicity and privacy could be drawn. He leaned in and whispered, 'Did you hear that Jack Rafferty had it away with some mystery girl the night he died? More than a little suspicious! Any idea who?'

Nell's heartbeat pounded. She hadn't known the press had got hold of that information. Or that Aanya's identity was being hounded out. 'No idea!' she said smoothly. 'But if you find out, don't tell me! I don't want to get on the wrong side of Svetlana.'

'Too true!' He grinned.

Nell felt a wave of relief. Hopefully she'd put him off.

'But that's just an occupational hazard for me. Always bound to upset someone.'

Nell smiled tightly. 'Well, I hope you're not going to upset anyone tonight, Joel. You know I have to ask you to leave.'

'Yeah, I know. Don't blame me for trying, though.'

'And I have to ask you to delete any pictures you've taken. We won't be able to hold events like this if guests get papped.' Nell didn't give herself away by glancing at their security guard. She knew he'd have been busily removing any pictures from Joel's phone, and any backup storage he might use, while they'd been talking.

At Joel's reluctant nod, Nell smiled. 'Thank you. And if you want a scoop,' she offered, 'how would you like a lap in the converted gullwing after the races finish tomorrow?'

Joel winced as the heavy hand of the security guard clapped his shoulder. 'Love it! It's a deal!' he called as he was steered outside.

Rav turned to Nell. 'What was all that about?'

Nell looked at Rav and Aanya. 'We need to be very circumspect about the press.' In the crowd of people, she didn't dare elaborate about Aanya in case she was overheard.

As everyone took their seats for dinner, Nell noticed the dancers from the Fifties diner take their seats. Each year, a different team from the event was invited to the dinner as a thank you for their contribution. Nell scanned the room and her eyes were drawn to Lucio's table. She frowned.

'Everything OK?' Rav asked.

Nell leaned in to whisper, 'Lucio was arrested for fraud over that Ferrari earlier today. He's obviously been released, but I don't know what's going on. The police have been investigating the auction history.'

Rav's eyes widened. 'Sounds serious.' He gave Nell a questioning look. 'Do the police think your family are implicated?'

'James has been pointedly professional. I guess he's at the "can't rule it out" stage. Which is . . . pretty unpleasant. To have your integrity called into question.'

'But if they've made an arrest, they must have some idea who's behind it?'

Nell sighed. 'But I hope to God it isn't Lucio.' She leaned in even closer. 'With him supplying cars for the auctions, if he's involved, then . . .' She let the words hang, knowing Rav would make the connection.

His eyes widened. 'Jeez. Was all this going on while my folks were being difficult?'

'Well, only since last night,' Nell said.

'It was still a load of grief you didn't need to deal with. I'm sorry.'

'It's fine. I *do* get why your parents have been so worried. And maybe now you've said something, we might actually have a nice day tomorrow. And maybe they'll even go home not totally hating me.' She shot him a comic grimace, so he'd know she was joking.

But he shook his head, taking her hand. 'I shouldn't have left you to deal with all their issues mostly on your own.' For a brief second, he leaned towards her and she caught the scent of his faint woodsy cologne, felt the heat of his body near hers.

A waiter coughed, making them move apart by setting down Nell's plate. As the person to Nell's left began a conversation, Nell gave Rav a reluctant parting smile and turned to the guest.

After dinner, tables were cleared with invisible efficiency and guests moved towards the dance area in front of the band.

Nell couldn't help observing Lucio's team, wondering who amongst them was a murderer and perhaps also a fraudster. Or if they were two separate people who just happened to overlap – *this* weekend, of all weekends! She'd had such high hopes for the event and felt a real affinity for the team and the project: the exciting prospect of transforming and racing the gullwing and the potential it would herald in a new dawn for racing events at Finchmere. But now, the mood was totally different. She didn't even know who on the team she could trust . . .

Lucio, dapper in black tie, danced with Shannon. No doubt, she was mining his connections. A hot lance of fear made Nell worry that if he was dodgy, it might affect Shannon too. But a glance at Shannon's calculating cat eyes reminded Nell that Shannon was more streetwise than she was, and could probably more than handle it. *She may even have some useful insights* . . . But Lucio didn't look as charmed by Shannon as most men; his stern gimlet eyes scanned his team over her shoulder as if he expected something to happen, and she quickly excused herself.

Nell assumed that the reason Shannon didn't dance with Lucio for long was because she wasn't used to *not* being the centre of attention, and she'd pulled out all the stops tonight. Her unique take on the dress code was head-turning – a scarlet general's ceremonial jacket, tailored as a minidress that buttoned at her navel, gold brocade gathered over her right shoulder, a striking emerald bar brooch, in lieu of medals, on her left.

As Shannon leaned in to air-kiss Nell, she said, 'Bless you, sweetie, for dusting the mothballs off Great-Aunt Edna's ancient number. Don't really have the legs for this, though, do you?' Before Nell had a chance to simmer at the remark, Shannon winked. 'I am putting the distraction technique to good use, though. Hope James will be pleased.'

Invited to dance by Colin, Shannon whisked off, leaving Nell wondering if Shannon really was – *genuinely* – into James. *More to the point, what has she found out . . . ?*

Nell scanned the company, now hungrier than ever for clues. Maxine, in her mulberry sheath dress and long gloves, danced with a man Nell recognised from Montague's Auction House. As she watched them dance, his name popped into Nell's mind: *Richard Tyler*. They didn't look like they were having much fun, but Nell couldn't blame them under the circumstances.

Nell was surprised to see Dani, who'd come as Svetlana's plus-one. She wore a plain navy dress, sitting on the sidelines, understandably pale yet with a new determined attitude. By contrast, Svetlana, in a daringly short dress that dazzled in the candlelight, looked like she was wearing molten silver. Nell was intrigued at how the two women appeared to be repairing their rift, and wondered how their friendship would evolve after this experience.

Maxine brought a glass of water over to Dani, squeezed her hand and chatted for a few minutes. Dani drank the water as if she was parched and smiled as Maxine chatted, colour gradually returning to her cheeks.

Mark and Cassie talked at their table. They darted looks around the room like rabbits at the edge of a clearing, too fearful of predators to venture into the open. Cassie didn't only look anxious, she seemed uncomfortable. She wore a 1950s navy-blue-and-white polka-dot dress over a red petticoat. She looked fabulous in it, yet also distinctly uncomfortable. And judging by the slightly too-short trousers and long sleeves of his jacket, Mark's tux was obviously hired. Maybe they felt underdressed, or just didn't enjoy parties. But somehow, they'd isolated themselves as misfits.

Hoping to make them feel more welcome, Nell went over, knowing she'd have to get the obvious question out of the way. 'Hi. How are you both? Especially after Lucio was . . . apprehended today.'

'Not great,' Cassie said.

'Isn't he happier that he's been released?' Nell asked. Although, she knew from bitter experience, that didn't mean the police had finished with you.

Cassie gave a short laugh. 'He's been like a bear with a sore head ever since he came back. Frankly, I wish the police had kept him.'

Mark nodded in agreement. 'He's been provoking everyone into arguments. Making accusations. Asking leading questions.' He shook his head. 'It's not good, Nell.'

'No, I can imagine. But has anyone reacted?' Nell asked.

'Oh yeah,' Cassie said.

'Who?' Nell leaned in, her face intent.

'All of us!' Cassie snorted. 'You think we're bleeding well made of stone? After everything that's been going on?'

'Yes. Sorry.' Nell grimaced in contrition. 'How are you feeling about the race?'

'I'm just gritting my teeth to get through it.' Cassie knocked back the last of her pint.

'That's the way to think of our moment of glory!' Mark tried to raise a smile.

As Cassie side-eyed him wryly, Nell nudged her. 'I love your dress . . .'

'Oh.' Cassie pulled at the cotton skirt, about to say something self-deprecating, but Nell interrupted before she had a chance to, gambling, '. . . And I wondered if you jive?'

Cassie blushed. 'Yeah, I do a bit. Swing, Lindy Hop. Love it!'

'You *don't?*' Mark exclaimed. 'So do I!'

They looked at each other in delighted amazement.

'Well, you have a jazz band on hand – they take requests, you know!' Nell said.

'Oh, I couldn't!' Cassie protested, though her sparkling eyes contradicted her words.

'Well, I might make a request. Then it's up to you,' Nell said, leaving them with a grin. She darted to the band leader, asking for a rousing rendition of Louis Prima's 'Sing, Sing, Sing'.

As the irresistible drumbeat began, Nell looked back to find Cassie and Mark heading to the dance floor, looking a bit tentative. But their feet were already dancing. As they locked into a sequence, Mark caught Cassie in a running kick step, their feet flying in time. Without his tight jacket, Mark's shirt and trousers looked like a Fifties outfit, and Cassie became the most vivacious woman in the room, twirling in the middle of the floor.

As their moves became more certain, Mark led Cassie in another rapid sequence of kicks and twirls, their dancing unexpectedly exuberant, huge smiles across both their faces. He spun Cassie away from him, lifting her by the waist as she kicked her legs in the air, her skirts foaming.

The dancers from the Fifties diner whooped and clapped around the edge of the dance floor, and Mark and Cassie split up to partner them. A man from the dance group swung Cassie around his waist and over one shoulder, to cheers, while Mark made a beeline for Nell.

'You got us into this!' he challenged.

Nell laughed, trying to follow Mark's steps. Meanwhile, Cassie had moved on to another dancer, who spun Cassie in a standing backflip.

'Your mother looks like she's up for a dance,' Mark yelled in Nell's ear. 'Shall I ask?'

'Oh yes!' Nell grinned. 'She'd love that!' She turned to see Rav holding out his hand for her, and instantly melted at his invitingly raised eyebrow and sexy smile.

Whirling her into his arms, he whispered, 'About time you got to try out my moves.'

The floor filled as all the guests joined in, to varying degrees. And the contagious fun transformed the mood. Despite basically dancing on spikes, Svetlana attempted fancy footwork with Colin, while Dani sat, clapping along with Maxine, both laughing and pointing out the more daring moves. Even Lucio and Shannon looked like they were enjoying themselves. Aanya was whirled this way and that by a dancer with a hipster pencil moustache. And Nell bit back a laugh at the sight of her parents shimmying around each other doing jazz hands.

But, as Cassie turned for a new partner, she came face to face with Richard Tyler. She froze, then backed away, shaking her head. Out of the fray of the dancing, she rushed from the ballroom.

Chapter 24

Sunday 21st April – 7 p.m.

James sat in silence in the car. Watching Richard Tyler's unlit detached Victorian house near Clapham Common. *Perfect.* He'd given up a precious night off, for this.

Checking his silenced phone for the thousandth time, he saw yet another photo of Shannon on yet another social media account. She'd not wasted any time at the Classics, tapping up wealthy contacts to attend her upcoming gallery opening, creating a buzz ahead of the event. Maybe that was the only reason she was here this weekend. Maybe it was just coincidental that he happened to be local. And she didn't exactly look heartbroken that he'd missed the event, as she posed in tonight's typically provocative outfit with a racing driver legend.

Beside him, in high surveillance mode, Ashley twitched at every movement outside the car. And being in a busy part of a major city, there was a lot of movement. And a lot of bloody twitching. When a car pulled up and a group of teenagers ran past, Ashley skittered like a frightened deer.

A sigh of irritation escaped him before he could stop it.

Ashley glared at him. 'At least I'm paying attention. Not transfixed by my bloody phone.'

'Yeah, well, I should have been somewhere else tonight.' James sighed, but he shoved his phone back in his pocket.

'Oh yeah, don't remind me, *this* week's fancy bit of glad-handing. It's astounding you can fit any time in for work.'

'Oh, come on, Ash, that's hardly fair—'

'Fair? Bloody hell, James, you've got some nerve.'

'Look, I know you're upset about the promotion. I know you think

175

you've been, I don't know . . .' James waved his hands, struggling to think of the right words '. . . passed over. But do you really think you're building any bridges? It's not like strengthening your network is a bad thing to do.'

Ashley swivelled in her seat, her glare red-hot but her voice calm. 'James, I do *not* need lessons in how to do my job from you. I'm not the one who's put my colleagues at risk of a disciplinary out of misplaced loyalty, am I?'

'What the—?'

'Yes, I didn't think you'd even given that a second thought. *You're* fine, with Nell helping you to solve your cases and getting promoted. But you don't give much consideration to the position you put everyone else in, do you?'

'You're going to have to explain, Ash.'

'You know what, Detective Inspector? You have all the same facts as me. You really should be able to work it out.'

James's mind raced. *What the hell is she talking about?* Then he saw her sharp disappointment. The same crushed expression he'd seen when she and Ed had told him about Nell's accident, with obvious and heartfelt sympathy – until Shannon had slinked in to say her alibi for the time of the accident was James, leaving Ashley in no doubt what they'd been up to. Ashley's dawning understanding had been awful. And it had been right after Ed had given him the police files about the investigation that he shouldn't have had access to. Ashley *had* protested, but Ed had argued that James deserved access, given Nell was his girlfriend at the time. *Supposedly.* At Shannon's revelation, Ashley knew that James had broken up with Nell, but had omitted saying that, when Ed had used James's relationship with Nell as a justification to share the files – with both men risking disciplinary action for themselves . . . and Ashley.

'I didn't ask Ed to give me those files, Ash.'

'No.' She turned to face him. 'And neither did I. He made the choice to give them to you, and you made the choice to take them. But neither of you cared very much about putting me in a compromising position, did you? I didn't have any choice in the matter, yet you've both managed to make me complicit.'

'Ed was only doing what he thought anyone would want under the circumstances—'

'Well, yes, of course, because we all thought you were in a relationship with Nell, and that you'd be out of your mind with worry. But you weren't, were you.'

It was an accusation, not a question, and the judgement stung. All the more because he couldn't deny it. But even though he'd broken up with Nell, he still cared about her. He still wanted to help – and the files were his shortcut to doing that. 'Things had happened fast, Ashley. And you're too experienced from your psychology insights and FLO work to leap to quick conclusions. And I *do* care about Nell.'

'I just wished you cared about your *colleagues*. But you're too busy scaling the greasy pole and convincing yourself it's all on your own merits.'

James couldn't speak. Shock fizzed in the pit of his stomach. *Is that how the whole team see me? Does Ed share Ashley's resentment?* 'Fine. Val's invited you to talk to her about it. If you want to make a formal complaint, you're perfectly within your rights to do so.'

'Except I can't, can I? Because that will screw Ed over. And myself. For the split second I failed to back my instincts and be firmer about disagreeing with Ed.' She heaved a long sigh. 'And look at the rest of your track record: you get suspects to help with cases. You share intel with civilians. You've slept with at least two suspects—'

'One,' James interrupted. 'Shannon is the only person who's been a suspect that I've—'

'Well, give the guy a medal. *None* is the aim, James. It compromises the whole team. Yet, even though you skate all over thin ice, you still manage to come up smelling of roses. But I play everything with a straight bat – and even *then* my record could be at risk from *your* actions – and who gets promoted out of the two of us? And *you* ask *me* to be fair?' She gave a hollow laugh. 'You should try it sometime.'

'Jesus, Ash, if these are the most grievous issues you can level at me, then they're pretty minor transgressions. I *was* worried about Nell. And Ed – and *you* – all thought we'd get further by working together. And we did! We got the right result, and we got it fast.

Maybe you should remember how quickly we've been able to solve our cases. And that makes all the difference.'

'Don't be so naive, James. You know as well as I do that carefully built cases can crumble to nothing if we don't follow procedure. It might not have made a difference last time. But it might next time, if this is how you work.'

'So make a complaint then.' He turned to face her. 'Own your mistake as much as you want me to own mine, and we'll all deal with it.' He remembered Val's advice. 'Because we *have* to put this behind us one way or another. Every second we spend banging on about this is a second we're not focusing on the case. And you're better than that, Ash.'

She turned away, staring out of the window again, wedging her elbow against the glass and leaning her chin on her hand.

They shared a few minutes of sullen silence until the persistent vibration of his muted phone made him take it out of his pocket. *Shannon.* His mood lifted. *Is she missing me?*

Shannon's voice through the phone was breathy. 'Can't speak long, gorgeous. Just a couple of bits of hot goss. Might lead to something. Thought it was worth letting you know.'

James sat up straighter. 'Great. Anything helps. Honestly. Anything. However innocuous it might seem.'

'Lucio's furious after today. I softened him up—'

'Uh-huh.'

'Got him to confide in me a bit. He was devastated at Jack's performance on the track. He'd wanted the car to give a stellar performance. But he felt tied by his loyalty to Colin. The *tragedy* is . . . Colin felt exactly the same. He'd *known* Jack wasn't up to it. But he couldn't say anything – he said he'd feel like he was stabbing his own son in the back.'

'So Lucio and Colin were both unhappy with Jack racing the gullwing.' James spoke for Ashley's benefit – if grudgingly.

'So, if Maxine *wouldn't* fire Jack and put Mark behind the wheel,' Ashley murmured, 'then Jack *had* to have something over Maxine, or Lucio. Or both. Surely?'

James half nodded while he listened to what else Shannon was saying. But Ashley's frown as she took out her phone and read her emails made him tilt his head at her, asking what she'd read.

'Fraud have intercepted a shipment of car parts. Addressed to Lucio's dealership.' Ashley hesitated. 'Do you think those parts might make a standard car look a bit more unique—?'

Not knowing the answer, James shrugged.

'So you might want to look into that, too,' Shannon concluded through the phone.

'Sorry, say that again?' James asked.

Shannon huffed down the phone. 'Please pay attention. I do have to complete the social circuit here before the champagne runs out. I *said* that Cassie is upset over something. Some fellow seems to be bothering her. Not sure if that might be relevant. I'm told his name is Tyler. Richard Tyler.'

'What?' James jolted into high alert. 'Richard Tyler's *there*?'

'Yes. Anyway, I hope that helps your inquiry. I need to get back to the party.' She hesitated. 'Have I helped?'

'More than you know.' He hung up, checked the time – eight thirty – and thumped the steering wheel.

'Bloody perfect. We've missed him.' *And I've missed an evening with Shannon.*

'Let's get over there, then,' Ashley said.

But James shook his head. 'It's not worth it now. By the time we get to Finchmere, even if Richard's still there, he'll have probably had a couple of drinks. So we're unlikely to get anything useful out of him tonight.'

'Fine. Let's try tomorrow.' Ashley started the car. 'We can give this up as a bad job.'

As she drove them back in silence, James wondered if she was talking about more than their unsuccessful stakeout.

Sunday 21st April – 8.30 p.m.

Rav had seen Cassie run off, and Nell, noticing, murmured, 'I'll be back in a minute.'

'Sure,' he said. But he watched Nell leave and, a few seconds later, he followed her through the great room to the hall.

There, Nell loitered outside the bathroom. As she backed into the shadows, under the stairs, he squeezed in beside her. Nell tutted, but her fingers found his and laced between them.

As they waited, Mark strode into the hall from the great room and stomped outside, his phone pressed against his ear, his face grim. Aanya was a few paces behind, heading towards the bathroom. But she hesitated. Rav felt Nell lean forward, about to walk over, when Mark came back in, shoving his phone in his pocket, nearly colliding with Aanya.

'Oh! It's you,' he said in surprise. 'From Jack's party . . .'

'Yes. Um . . . Excuse me,' Aanya said, darting into the powder room next to Cassie's.

As Mark wandered back to the ballroom, Cassie came out into the hall.

Rav let go of Nell's hand so he could remain out of sight while she dashed out. 'Cassie? Are you OK?'

Cassie nodded. 'Yeah? Why do you ask?'

'You left in a bit of a hurry, when it looked like you were having fun,' Nell said.

'Yes, I'm fine. Just . . . I had a bit of a surprise. I'm OK. Thanks.'

'You *looked* like you had a massive shock,' Nell said.

Cassie looked at her sharply. 'Oh.'

'Can I help? Do you need anything?'

Cassie shook her head uncertainly. Rav realised he was clenching his jaw in frustration at Nell's slim opportunity to prise out any information.

'Sure, I don't want to interfere. I just wanted to make sure you're OK. I'll give you some space.' She started to walk away.

No!

'No . . . no. I appreciate the company.' Cassie reached out to stop Nell leaving.

Rav's body sagged in relief. He felt a bit foolish – there was no guarantee that whatever had surprised Cassie was relevant to the investigation – and, maybe, Nell's family – but clearly he, and Nell, thought it must be related.

'I . . . I just saw someone I haven't seen for ages. Someone I'd never in a million years expect to see *here*.'

'Oh?'

Cassie turned to face Nell, and her already low voice became a whisper. Rav strained to hear. 'Do you know you have a criminal on the guest list?'

What, as well as a murderer and a fraudster? Rav nearly said aloud. Nell didn't say it either. She opted for a more neutral 'Who?'

'The guy on the dance floor. Who danced with Maxine earlier. *Tricky Dicky*.'

Nell nearly choked in surprise at the unexpected nickname. 'Richard Tyler?'

'If you like,' Cassie said.

'How is he a criminal?' Nell asked. 'And how do you know?'

From the gloom, Rav saw Cassie turn as red as her lipstick.

Nell nudged her. 'Don't be coy. Just spit it out.'

Cassie looked at her in surprise. 'Well, let's just say I had a . . . wayward youth.'

'Uh-huh.' Nell managed to make her tone encouraging, conspiratorial.

'Bit of joyriding. Bit of car theft.' Cassie looked at her feet. 'Tricky Dicky was my contact. I passed on the cars to him.'

Nell frowned. 'What kind of cars?'

'Anything he asked for. I started out with right old bangers just for joyriding. But I got quicker and more ambitious. The cars got more fancy, more of a challenge . . . more *valuable*. Then he asked me for specific models that he could sell. He singled me out, and paid me well.'

'How . . . enviable,' Nell said wryly.

'Yeah, well, *my* type of *estate* is a bit different to yours, shall we say?'

Oh! Rav managed to hold in a chuckle at Cassie's neat rebuke.

'Fair point. But it seems that despite a difficult start in life, you've been pretty enterprising and now have a solid career. Right?'

Cassie pursed her lips.

'Is that why you were worried about seeing him? Do you think he'll say something?'

After frowning for a moment, Cassie shook her head. 'Nah, I don't think so. Max knows about my past. Her outreach scheme helped me get my first job, put me on the straight and narrow. And I guess if he's Richard Tyler these days, he must have put all that behind him, too. If I can change, why can't he?'

'In that case, won't *Richard* worry about *you* saying something to out his shady past?'

Cassie shrugged. 'Shouldn't think so. If I tried that, it would be his word against mine, and he looks like he's done all right for himself. He's tight with Lucio. So he'd be believed over me, wouldn't he? And I'd only be able to grass on him by outing my own past. He wouldn't know that Maxine knows and is cool with it. So I reckon he feels pretty safe.'

'Then let's get back to the party,' Nell suggested.

Rav waited while the women went in ahead of him, then followed. The music had changed, the dancing had thinned out, but the mood was still merry.

Nell exchanged a pointed look with Rav as she leaned in to ask him to keep an eye on Richard, so she wouldn't be tempted to stare at him all night.

'He's talking to your father now,' Rav whispered.

'Oh no!' Nell's dismay was obvious as she turned to see him and Hugo in deep discussion – and laughing.

'Lucio's giving him a wide berth,' Rav commentated. 'He smiled in Lucio's direction a few times, but Lucio is firmly ignoring him.'

'Oh. Avoidance seems as damning as socialising, doesn't it?'

'He's chatting with Svetlana now, but she's ignored him and is speaking to Mark.'

'OK, OK!' Nell pleaded. 'I don't need a report for every second. I've got the picture.' She looked up as a loud crash interrupted the music.

The racing driver who'd won the Nye Cup earlier that day immediately leapt to his feet holding one hand aloft. 'I'm fine!' He looked around like he expected a cheer, but none came.

A security guard took him gently by the arm towards the door. 'Breath of fresh air, sir?'

Nell followed the action, so Rav followed. On the way, he noticed

Aanya sitting at a table, alone, her fingers twisting a napkin like she was strangling it.

Walking over to her, Rav asked, 'You OK, sis?'

Aanya shook her head. 'Can we . . .' she looked around the room nervously '. . . *talk?*'

'Yes, of course!' Rav jerked his head towards the hall and Aanya got up.

The drunk racer was arguing with the security guard by the front door, a throng of guests following. 'But I'm a prof-*vessinal* driver! I can drive *myself!* It's just to the hotel!'

'Sir, it would be an honour to arrange a driver for you. Please allow me.' With a disarming smile, the security guard removed the bunch of keys – suggesting his car was a classic – from the driver's hand. 'I'll keep your keys safe, and you can pick them up tomorrow. In the meantime, I'll arrange a car.' He put the keys in the drawer of the desk by the door and took his phone from his pocket, pacing as he spoke.

Aanya pulled Rav past him, so he was pushed back into the shadows under the stairs. This time, Nell followed him. They looked at Aanya expectantly.

Aanya's breathing was rapid. 'I think . . .' She paused, swallowed and took a deep breath. 'I think I know . . .' she mouthed the last three words: '*who killed Jack.*'

Chapter 25

Nell's heart raced as she and Rav stared at Aanya. He hissed, 'What?' as Nell whispered, '*Who?*'

Aanya shook her head. 'I . . . I don't want to say here. I don't . . . *feel safe.*' Her brown eyes were as huge as a deer's who'd just caught the scent of a stalker.

'Right.' Nell felt the familiar prickle of fearful anticipation. She'd felt it enough in recent months to trust her instincts. 'We're going straight to the police. *Now.*'

She pushed them both through the front door, grabbed her car key from the desk drawer, hurried past the busy security guard and, as they ran towards the garage, dodged the car that had come to take the drunk racer to the hotel.

Her Taycan automatically unlocked as they approached. Aanya scrambled into the back seat and Rav jumped in the front as Nell slammed on her seatbelt. Her headlights washed eerily over the copper beeches lining the drive as she shot towards town.

'Call DI Clark as we head over,' Nell said. Rav passed Nell's phone to Aanya, knowing James's number was listed, and Nell called out her PIN so Aanya could unlock it.

'No signal,' she said. 'And it's nearly out of juice.'

'Plug it in.' Nell gestured at the cable. As she met the road to the village, she put her foot down. 'I should be able to get us there in about half an hour. If you can call ahead, at least James will be ready and waiting.'

The country road to Pendlebury was narrow, an earth bank rising up on the far side of the road, the embankment plunging away on their nearside. Each side was flanked with wood and scrub with trees arching overhead, only illuminated when Nell swung around the tight bends. She drove with confidence; these roads surrounding her family estate, marked with its tall flint boundary walls, were familiar friends and she knew them like the back of her hand.

'Who do you think it was, Aanya?' Rav asked. 'And how do you know?'

'I . . . I overheard someone say something. It reminded me of something Jack said.'

'Which was?' Rav demanded.

'Jack said something to me about coming into some money soon. He was laughing, in the hotel suite, saying he got all this stuff for free, and that he didn't really need it. But he said that wasn't his *problem*. And he stressed the word in a really weird way. I didn't know what he was talking about, but I wasn't that interested; I just thought it was another deal or a sponsorship or something.' She bit her lip.

'So?' Nell urged.

'Well, just now, I overheard someone talking and saying that no, they wouldn't have to pay up now. That the *problem* was . . . *sorted.*' Aanya shivered. 'It was the way that same word was emphasised that reminded me. And it sounded . . . calculated. Like someone had sorted the problem by . . . you know. *Killing Jack.*'

'But who was it?' Rav insisted.

'What the—' Nell interrupted. She stared into the rear-view mirror.

'What?' Aanya asked, gazing back at Nell in the mirror.

'You're OK – I'm not looking at you. There's a car behind us, sitting on my tail with his headlights on full beam. And it's not like I can go any faster along these roads.'

Rav leaned over and noted how much Nell was exceeding the speed limit by. 'No.'

The car dropped back and Nell was distracted as the headlights hit her wing mirrors. Even auto-dimmed, the lights were bright. With her eyes dazzled, her sleeping headache had awoken. She held one hand up over the glare and put her foot down. The car behind sped up.

'There's some serious funny business going on,' Nell said.

'Is there anywhere you can pull in, let him get past?' Rav suggested.

Nell shook her head, and instantly regretted it as her head pounded.

'No, and it's not the easiest road to overtake on if I just stop.' She winced again as the car dropped back and she got another blinding glare from the wing mirror.

Aanya turned to see the car, squinting her eyes at the beams. 'I can't see anything. It's pitch-black. All I can see are those damn headlights.' She turned back, blinking. 'And now I may not have any retinas left.'

Suddenly the car jolted forward with a sickening crunch. Aanya, thrown forward against Nell's seat, gave an ear-splitting scream that ripped through Nell's skull.

'Aanya . . . ?' Rav asked, turning in his seat. 'What happened? Everyone OK?'

Aanya was shaking as she stared at Rav. With another thud from behind, the car lurched forward again.

'He's *ramming* us! He's bloody *ramming* my *Taycan!*'

'Yes, your Taycan and, perhaps more importantly, the three people *in* it,' Rav said.

Nell flicked the drive mode to Sport Plus. 'Fine. Let's play.' She floored the accelerator and tried to relax her arms as she treated the road like a racetrack and ignored her throbbing head. Able to see that no cars approached from the opposite direction, she used both sides of the road, taking racing corners, inching ahead of the pursuing car. It put on a spurt of speed, and Nell swerved right to miss the anticipated impact. She veered towards the earth bank and turned away sharply, nearly oversteering.

'Nell! What are you doing?' Aanya screamed. She'd scrunched into a ball, her arms over her head, adopting the brace position of a passenger in a crashing plane.

'It's OK, Aans,' Rav said. The conviction and reassurance in his tone quietened Aanya's panic and sent a flash of pure love through Nell's heart.

Nell felt like she was pushing the pedal through the floor, her leg taut, as she strove to get ahead. The pursuing car kept pace surprisingly well, having the advantage of copying Nell's road position and braking points. With an oncoming car approaching, Nell couldn't slice off the next corner, and had to stay in her own lane. Clearly irritated at the pursuing car's full-beam lights, the oncoming car put theirs on full beam in retaliation. Nell was blinded from both directions. The searing pain slicing through her forehead made her gasp. Aanya, who'd just sat up, shrieked again and recoiled into brace position.

As the oncoming car sped past them, the pursuing car surged outwards, then diagonally forward. It clipped Nell's rear off-side wing, sending the Taycan off balance, towards the left kerb where the earth bank fell away. The mud and grit grabbed Nell's front wheel, acting like a pivot point, pulling the car around and forcing it down the bank. The steering wheel snapped left and Nell fought for control, hauling the wheel hard right. She resisted the urge to brake and decelerate, letting speed force the car through the skid as her tensed arms wrestled with the shuddering steering. As she expected, the car lurched to the right, and Nell controlled the sideways slide. Various lights on the dash blinked as the car stabilised, and she floored the accelerator again.

'They're trying to ram us off the road!' Rav said in disbelief. 'They're trying to . . .'

'Kill us?' Nell finished. She glanced in her mirror at Aanya, the eye movement painful. 'Aanya, can you try and take a photo? Or film it with your phone while Rav calls James on mine? I'm damned if my car's getting wrecked for a message we don't manage to deliver.'

Aanya whimpered from her brace position, her breathing ragged. She tried to pass Rav Nell's phone but Nell heard the thud as she dropped it in the footwell and then dived to scrabble for it.

'Bend coming up, Aanya,' Nell warned her but had to take the tight turn at hair-raising speed, adrenaline coursing through her veins as she focused on the near white line and followed the outline of the road with instinctive hands.

Aanya's muffled 'Ow!' as she hit the back of the driver's seat threatened to shatter Nell's focus, but she couldn't afford to brake or ease off the accelerator through the twists. Determinedly, she kept the pedal on the floor, thanking the car's all-wheel drive for keeping them planted on the road, and not skidding around the corners.

But the car behind kept up. Beads of sweat trickled down Nell's face.

The car dropped back, then a huge surge forward made a hideous crunch as the Taycan jolted forward again. A loud *clunk* echoed through the car. Aanya covered her face, screaming and sobbing. Nell stared in her rear-view mirror, realising a chunk of bodywork had fallen off the back of the Porsche and saw it bounce off the bonnet of the pursuing car.

'Great,' Nell muttered. 'Another hit will damage the subframe now it's exposed.'

'Isn't there anywhere we can turn off?' Rav asked.

Nell shook her head, grimly watching the warning lights turn on, one by one, across the dash. 'No roads off this one.' She thought for a moment. 'Except . . .' She rounded a corner that wound up a hill, keeping her foot down. 'At the top of this hill, there's that huge veteran oak by the corner of the flint wall?'

'I know it,' Rav said.

'Keep your eyes peeled for that tree. About a metre past it, there's a small gap where the wall's crumbled in. I don't want to slow down and warn our friend. I'm going to hard-turn into that gap. So brace yourselves.'

'But . . . but it's scrub and woodland. It's not a road—'

'Just tell me.'

Nodding, Rav peered out into the inky, endless blackness beyond the beam of the headlights. She knew he was wondering how the hell he was supposed to see a tree. But if he really focused, watched out for the ghostly movement of branches, she could hope . . .

Nell crested the hill.

Rav's nose was practically pressed against the windscreen. 'Now!'

Like a rally driver trusting her navigator, Nell swung right, then hard-locked left into the blind turn – hoping, hoping, *hoping* she wasn't about to slam them straight into a wall.

With a blood-curdling shriek, Aanya threw herself prone on the back seat.

Nell was blinded: the headlights of the pursuing car were now side on, unavoidably burning into her eyes, making her head pound like a bass drum. But the Taycan had responded perfectly, turning the car forty-five degrees with tight control. With her foot stamped down on the gas and fully committed, Nell saw, with stomach-dropping relief, that she was lined up with the black gap in the wall and speeding towards it, out of the path of the chasing car.

She turned off the headlights. Once through the wall, she didn't want their pursuer to see them.

Now, unable to see where they were going, Nell and Rav jumped as both wing mirrors smashed inwards violently and the Taycan plunged through the narrow gap, the broken mirrors thumping against the wings as they bounced on their wires. Nell felt the sickening sensation of being unexpectedly airborne. The jagged flint of the collapsed wall's edges gouged screeching scratches along the bodywork as they flew down the bank.

The Taycan crunched as it landed on all four tyres, plummeting down the steep slope. Rav's side of the car crashed heavily into the earth and the flints of the collapsed wall, smashing the front wing and spraying mud and rocks over the car and windows like a meteor shower. Nell and Rav flinched as stones crazed, then cracked, the windscreen and dented the bodywork. The impact threw Rav and Nell forward, against the bruising impact of locked seatbelts, whiplashed them back against their seats, then forward again into the unexpected eruption of airbags.

Nell thought she'd throw up. The pain in her head blazed white.

Rebounding, the car leapt again, before bumping over the rocky ground, making shocked gasps explode from all three of them.

The dash flickered with emergency lights and the steering tugged to the left, jolting. Nell realised one of the tyres was shredded, the wheel probably damaged. She willed her wrecked car on, over the scrub and through the brambles that scraped the car with shrill metallic shrieks.

Heading for the estate's service track, Nell urged the Taycan to get as far as possible before its electronic sensors automatically shut it down. The car beeped ignored notifications, which only frayed their already rattled nerves.

'Jesus, Nell. What are we going to do now?' Rav squinted through the cracked windscreen, into darkness.

Nell struggled to keep the shuddering car on course, then stared into the rear-view mirror. 'I don't think they followed us.'

'Well, no, they're probably not freaking crazy!' Aanya sat up, her hair dishevelled. 'What were you *thinking*?'

Rav glanced sideways at Nell, then turned in his seat to look at his sister. 'I think she just killed her car to save our lives, Aans. So play nice.'

Aanya folded her arms. 'Well, OK, it was quite a move.' Her tone was contrite.

'Yeah.' Rav's eyes slid back to Nell. 'But we're not going to get much further, are we?'

To a chorus of insistent beeps, like chicks in a bird's nest, her car died. Lights flickered across the controls, then went out, plunging them into total darkness. Nell sank back in her seat with a heavy sigh. She rubbed the steering wheel. 'She's got us as far as we needed her to.'

Nell wanted to sag in her seat, to sleep off the pounding pain. But they weren't safe. And she was probably the only one who knew where they were. She took a few deep breaths, gathered herself, let the throbbing in her skull settle. She looked at Rav. 'Let's go.'

As Nell shut the car door, she was glad the deep blackness of the dense woodland prevented her from seeing the extent of the damage. She patted the dented roof and walked purposefully towards the nearest estate barn. Rav used the torch on his phone to help them see where to walk along the muddy, rutted track.

The overload of adrenaline pooling in Nell's stomach, her aching head and the cold night air hit her stomach like a punch of nausea. Her beaded dress didn't offer much in the way of warmth. She glanced at Aanya, imagining she felt the same. As she walked, Nell turned and looked over her shoulder, scanning the road beyond the wall for lights, glancing around the shadowy forest. Unease sat heavily on her shoulders, making her jerk round at the slightest creak of a tree bough, rustle of a leaf, snap of a twig.

'Are we walking all the flipping way to Cookingdean?' Aanya asked, as she tripped, landing a satin stiletto in a puddle. 'Oh *balls*.'

'No.' Nell bit back a sympathetic laugh at Aanya's unhappy misstep. 'Only to the barn. Here.'

Aanya huffed. 'I'm not hiding out in a spider-infested, damp old hut all night. I'll walk to the station if I have to.'

'If you like,' Nell said, heaving open the wooden door. Rav's phone shone around the space and fixed on the Land Rover. 'But this might be quicker.'

Nell slipped her hand under the wheel arch to feel on top of the back wheel for the key. 'Oh bollocks. The estate team usually just leave the keys here.' She went to the other side as Aanya and Rav each checked a front tyre.

Aanya tried the driver's door. It opened. She raised her eyebrows hopefully at Nell.

Nell hitched her beaded dress up to climb into the seat. She felt in the ignition, then on top of the sun visors, then along the front pocket for the key and frowned. She leaned forward and put her hands behind the steering column, rummaging for a moment, and got out of the car so she could get a better look.

'Rav, would you shine your light here so I can see what I'm doing?'

Rav held his phone higher.

'Perfect, thanks.' Nell scrunched her nose in concentration as she disconnected a bundle of wires and examined the two she wanted. 'Dad showed me how to do this—' she leaned in and bit a couple of centimetres of plastic off the end of each one, exposing the wires '—when we'd been working on the estate one day and I lost the keys in a ditch.'

She twisted the naked ends of the wires together, then looked at the starter. It had a small tip of exposed wire and Nell didn't want to risk stripping its insulation with her teeth, so she struck it against the twisted wires – and hoped. The engine turned and she reached out to press the accelerator with her hand but wasn't quick enough. She jumped in the driver's seat, put her foot on the pedal, struck the wires again and revved the engine – once, twice. As she eased her foot off the pedal, she sensed the engine would keep ticking over.

'Phew!' Nell grinned.

'Thank God!' Aanya said. She slid into the middle seat and kicked off her shoes. 'I really thought we'd have to walk for a minute there.'

Nell and Rav exchanged a glance at Aanya's teenage self-absorption as Rav got in and slammed the door.

As Nell negotiated the bumpy track across the edge of the estate to the road, she noticed Aanya, just in her dress, was shivering. 'There might be a blanket behind your seat.'

Aanya leaned forward and Rav rummaged and pulled out a soft tartan picnic blanket, tucking it gently around Aanya's shoulders. She snuggled into the warmth like a cat.

'Oh, that's better.' She glanced at Nell. 'Thank you.'

Nell shrugged. 'That's down to the site team. They usually have the essentials packed.'

'Not the blanket.' Aanya jerked her head back towards the road. 'All . . . that.' She bit her words off quickly, betraying how shaken she felt.

Suddenly too choked up to speak, Nell gave a single nod, glancing at Aanya, then Rav. He didn't meet her eyes. He stared out of the window, but his voice shook a little when he spoke. 'No one's coming. I think we're clear.'

With no one in pursuit, Nell finally breathed easier. 'If you think you know who killed Jack, it looks like you're really on to something, Aanya.'

Aanya bit her lip and stared at her hands. 'Looks like it.'

'Who was it?' Nell asked.

Aanya tugged the blanket tight around her and shrank into it. 'It was Mark.'

Chapter 26

Nell's head whirled. Her mind went back over every conversation she'd had with Mark, looking for signs of guilt. It was obvious how angry he'd been about Jack driving. She felt a frisson of fear as she realised keeping up with her on a country road would hardly be a challenge for him.

As the service track opened out to the luxury of a real road with a proper surface, Nell felt wary again. She wondered if their pursuer would be lying in wait. Her eyes darted between windscreen, rear-view mirror and both wing mirrors in anxious rotation. Rav and Aanya were equally watchful, turning to stare at every car. The drive into Pendlebury was tense and, when Nell parked opposite the police station, they all heaved a sigh of relief.

'We made it!' Aanya sang as if she'd never acted like a quaking wreck or a grumpy teen.

Rav and Aanya leapt out and dashed across the road. Nell followed, running round from the far side of the Landy. As she crossed the road, the leonine growl of a hard-revved straight-six engine roared towards her. Nell froze in horror, dazed by the full-beam headlights of the oncoming speeding car, her headache pounding through blackened vision. Then, bolting for the kerb, eyes blinded but arms outstretched, she shoved Aanya towards Rav, who yanked her onto the pavement then reached for Nell.

The car clipped the backs of Nell's legs, sending her flying forward. Her breath erupted from her lungs as she fell against the kerb. Rav tried to break her fall but the sharp sting of tarmac scraped her hands and arms and made her head throb. Hauling Nell to her feet, Rav pushed Aanya ahead of them, herding them all into the police station.

Inside, Rav turned to Nell, staring into her eyes. 'Are you OK?'

Nell nodded, gasping. 'Just . . . just a bit winded.'

Pulling her tightly against him, Rav gave her a fierce hug.

Aanya stared out of the window, apoplectic. 'I cannot believe this! He just literally tried again! To mow us down on the street!'

The sound of feet running along the corridor made them turn to see James dash towards them. 'What's going on?'

'Aanya needs to speak to you urgently,' Nell said. 'She's got new information.' She shot James a grim glance. 'And someone just tried very hard to make sure we didn't tell you.'

Sunday 21st April – 10 p.m.

A short while later, while Aanya was still giving a statement to James, Hesha had taken Nell and Rav's account and administered first aid and sweet tea. 'Any other injuries?' she asked after she'd helped Nell clean and dress the grazes on her forearms and palms.

'No, I'm fine, thanks. Just these few scrapes. It was shock, more than anything.'

'It was terrifying,' Rav said. His tone was matter-of-fact, but his hand holding the mug of tea shook.

'Did you see anything?' Hesha asked.

'It happened so fast,' Rav said. 'The car was a blur.'

'It was a BMW,' Nell said. 'I know that much from the shape of the headlights. Nothing else. The petrol smell might indicate a classic. And it had no trouble keeping up with me at high speed, so something a bit special . . . But then for teams like . . . Ohhh.' She groaned, leaning her head on her hands, then wincing at the sting in her palm. 'Of course. It was the car that security took the key for. Because Tony was too drunk to drive home from the party. The officer put the keys in the desk in the hall. Anyone could have taken them. And any of the team could have kept up with me. So it's a CLS. A BMW CLS.'

'I'll put a call out,' Hesha said. 'And I'll see if I can trace any CCTV footage.'

'There won't be much,' Nell warned. 'We took the country route.'

As Hesha left to start the checks, Nell shuddered, and Rav took his jacket off and placed it around her shoulders. She shivered again as her bare skin touched the cold satin lining, only warming up when Rav put his arm around her.

'I think we've just been very bloody lucky,' he said conversationally. 'I couldn't have driven like that, got us out of that situation.'

Nell hugged her teacup and gazed at Rav. 'See the lengths I'll go to, to get in your parents' good books?' She was relieved he cracked a smile at the weak joke.

'You should get points for flair, at least.'

'I won't argue.' She nudged his shoulder with hers and settled against him, leaning her head on his shoulder. But she sat up again when Val walked in with James. Aanya shuffled behind them, looking worn out, a police hoodie over her dress, sleeves tugged over her hands.

'How are you?' Val asked them both.

'Fine, thanks,' Nell said. 'Hesha's checking CCTV.'

'Yes, thanks, I know,' Val said. 'But you can't think who this could be?'

'Well.' Nell took a deep breath. 'Aanya believes Mark killed Jack.' She watched Val for her reaction, but she remained admirably neutral. 'Anyone could have taken the key to the BMW. And I assume it's someone from the race team. Don't you?' She frowned and muttered to herself, 'Or Richard Tyler. The valuer for Montague's.'

James nodded at the name.

'I gather he had quite a different name, and quite a different life,' Nell said. 'Selling on stolen cars.'

'Ah,' James said. 'Been talking to Cassie, have you?'

Nell nodded. 'She was shocked, maybe even scared to see him at first. But she reasoned that she's changed, so perhaps he has, too.'

'Well, if we're talking about people who used to steal cars and joyride for a living,' Val pointed out, 'they'd be quite happy to purloin one now, wouldn't they?'

'Where did you have to abandon your car?' James asked.

Nell walked to the large local map on the wall and pointed out the position.

'OK. Given we've already had one accident amongst this group of people caused by a car being tampered with, we'll need to get this car transported to the lab, along with any crash debris, for forensics. Tonight, ideally. Before anyone can interfere with it and before the roads get busy.'

'I'll call Astrid, our event manager,' Nell said, already unlocking her phone. 'She'll be able to sort out access for your team.'

As Nell phoned, James sent orders for the retrieval, and an officer walked into the waiting room and drew Val aside, handing her a piece of paper. She read it, then passed it to James.

As he scanned the page, his eyebrows disappeared into his hairline. His hand strayed to the handcuffs in the police belt under his jacket, then he nodded at Val. 'Let's go.'

With a spike of certainty, Nell knew. *An arrest. Mark? Or someone else?*

Within seconds, Nell had loaded Rav and Aanya back into the Land Rover and she was pushing the poor engine as fast as it would carry them, back along the country lanes, but failing to keep on the heels of Val's S8.

'I just want my bed,' Aanya moaned.

'How can you have such little curiosity?' Nell marvelled. 'Don't you want to *know?*'

'No! I do *not* want to retrace our steps where someone just tried to kill us, and then followed us to have a second go, no.' Aanya folded her arms.

'Well, then . . . that's unfortunate.'

Since she was the one driving, Nell motored along the road, heading to Finchmere Hotel.

As Nell parked in an unloading space, next to Val's Audi, Aanya's protests resumed. 'There's no *way* I'm going in. Mark'll know it was me who told the police!'

'I'm pretty sure he'll be under arrest. You'll be safe,' Nell said. Rav heard her impatience to get inside and see what was happening. 'Or, you can stay here. You don't have to come in.'

Nell began to close the door, but Aanya followed with a grumpy: '*Fine.*'

Rushing ahead of them, Nell dashed inside, headlong into furious arguments. Protests from the team bounced around the marble reception, the soft cream sofas barely muffling the sound as Val and James tried to calm the crowd.

'You are ruining *everything* for us!' Lucio's face turned purple with outrage. 'First, you decide Jack's accident is murder. Then I am fraudster, and my Ferrari sale – she is void! My reputation in tatters! And now, *again*, you want to disrupt our race!' He spotted Nell. 'Lady Beaumont will tell you where to *stick* your rights.' He hooked a finger in his shirt collar.

Beside Lucio, Maxine stared at Cassie and Mark in horror, her arms folded. As Aanya sat on the nearest sofa, watching the tableau with wide, worried eyes, Rav inched towards her, obviously protective about his little sister. And, for once, Aanya didn't complain about it.

'We can't control the timing of these events,' James reasoned with Lucio. 'And we have a duty to arrest people on evidence. And that is why we're arresting Mark and Cassie on counts of murder and attempted murder.'

Cassie and Mark gaped. As James stepped forward to handcuff Mark, he backed away. 'No . . . no!'

Cassie stared at Val so fiercely it was amazing Val didn't burst into flames.

'Lady Beaumont!' Lucio entreated her, expressive hands outstretched.

'I don't know what you think I can do, Lucio,' Nell said. 'I'm not above the law. I was arrested not that long ago . . .' Nell looked directly at Cassie, who gave a tight smile back.

'*You?*' Lucio shrieked. He glared at Val and James. 'Then you two . . . are *stupido!*'

'. . . But they released me when evidence showed I was innocent.' Nell finished her sentence. Next to Rav, Aanya hugged her body, shrinking back into the sofa.

'Yeah, good point.' Mark folded his arms. 'Where's your *evidence?*'

Cassie closed her eyes, a grimace flickering across her features. Nell frowned. *Was it her?* Uncertainty squirmed. *Would Cassie or Mark really try to run them off the road . . . ? Especially after I've been working with them so closely?* As she watched them, recalling the pressures of all that work, she found herself justifying the arrest. *Depends what's at stake . . . ?* There had only been a brief reprieve from that simmering tension: when they'd been dancing earlier. That bright, fleeting moment suddenly felt sinister. Nell shuddered.

'The evidence will become clear at the station, Mark.' Val turned to James. 'Shall we?'

As they escorted Mark and Cassie outside, Lucio slumped onto the sofa opposite Aanya, his head in his hands. 'Ruined. All ruined. My business. *Everything*. Gone.' He pulled the handkerchief from his top pocket and blotted his face.

Taking the armchair opposite, Maxine sat, as brittle as an autumn leaf. 'It'll come good, luv. You're well known in these circles. In a year's time, this'll just be a blip. In five years, it might even be an anecdote.'

But Lucio was inconsolable. He blew his nose loudly.

Maxine winced, then smiled encouragingly again. 'Come on, you know as well as I do there's always another good find, always another race.' She shrugged. 'So, we've had a hiccup. We'll get over it.'

Fidgeting in her seat, Aanya frowned. 'Ow!' She rummaged near her thigh and pulled out a magazine that had been tucked between the side of the sofa and the cushion. She threw the offending magazine on the floor.

'Hey!' Nell's annoyance was clear in her voice. She picked up the magazine, to put it on the coffee table. But Svetlana's face stared out from the *Vogue* cover: a stark reminder that Svetlana and Dani and, for that matter, the mysterious Richard Tyler, weren't here.

Flicking to the article, Nell saw pictures of, as the magazine put it: 'Jack and Lana's Honeymoon Phase' as they kissed on an arching wooden bridge in their landscaped garden.

The bridge spanned an ornamental lake. In the dark water, amongst the couple's artfully caught reflection, were the curving, shimmering bodies of expensive koi carp: orange backs blotched with black, like reverse great crested newts.

Peering at the picture, the seed of an idea blossomed in Nell's brain.

Sunday 21st April – 10.45 p.m.

James waited for Cassie's answer. She looked so vulnerable, sitting across the table from him in the small interview room, her lips tight, saying nothing. She sat on her hands, as if she needed to clamp down all her physical reactions, her full skirt frothing over the seat.

Duncan Featherstone, the Legal Aid solicitor, looked just as nervous, chewing his pen.

'Look—' James aimed for an inviting tone '—we know that you and Mark tampered with his other two cars. Your fingerprints were all over the bonnets of both cars. *And* on the distributor caps, which had their rotor arms removed.'

Duncan cleared his throat. 'Cassie's a mechanic, and Mark's an engineer, correct?'

'Yes,' James said.

'Both working regularly with Jack Rafferty, yes?'

'Yes,' James confirmed.

'So why on earth would it be unusual for their fingerprints to be on the car bonnet or various parts of the engine?' Duncan reasoned. 'It's entirely plausible and possible that this happened as a normal part of their work.' He sat back, a little straighter in his seat than before, glancing at Cassie with an almost-confident smile.

Ashley leaned forward, without glancing at James. After last night, their relationship had become glacial. 'The point is, Cassie, that yours and Mark's fingerprints – and *only* your two prints – are on the parts of the car that were tampered with. Which, yes, does suggest that Cassie and Mark are entrusted with the cars' maintenance. However, in the absence of any other prints, and – *crucially* – with your prints being very clear, not smudged like someone else has opened the cap wearing gloves, it *also* suggests that Cassie and Mark are responsible for sabotaging two of Jack's cars.'

She paused, watching Cassie for a moment before continuing. 'And the logical inference is that, if you tampered with two cars out of three, then you could easily have tampered with the third car, too.' She shot a hard stare at Cassie. 'Forcing Jack to drive the Mustang, and causing his accident.'

'No!' Cassie blurted. 'No! We only removed the rotor arms so he couldn't start his sodding cars. That wouldn't cause an *accident*. It was a *prank*.' She glanced at James as if he was the easier to convince. James nodded encouragingly, and Cassie explained.

'Jack thought he was such a star driver, and so full of himself with his car collection. Mark and I thought, if he was so hot with cars, he'd know how to look after them. If we took out his rotor arm, most car aficionados would be able to work out what had happened and be able to replace the missing part. No big deal. But we *knew* Jack wouldn't. *That* was the . . . the joke.' Her voice trailed off.

'Hilarious,' Ashley said. Her pause, James knew, was long enough to let the confession sink in with Duncan.

'But we didn't touch the Mustang.' Cassie folded her arms and glared at Ashley.

'You expect me to believe that, do you?' Ashley said. James noted that Ashley was talking about herself in the singular, rather than them as a team.

'Yes!' Cassie said. 'We couldn't if we wanted to – the engine was still hot from Jack driving it to the party!'

'You were late, you could have tampered with the car at any point during the party. Plenty of time for it to cool off,' Ashley pointed out.

'Not a huge hunk of engine like that, especially the way Jack has it tuned,' Cassie said. 'Cools quite slowly.'

'Ah, so you know it very well,' Ashley noted. 'Maybe that's why you'd tamper with the brakes instead of sabotaging the engine?'

'No!' Cassie looked at Ashley, wide-eyed and shocked. 'No! You have to believe me!'

'So, are you saying that it was Mark? He could have slipped out of the party later?'

'No!' Cassie said. 'I'd have noticed if Mark left to do something like that!'

Ashley pulled a page from Cassie's file. 'Hmmm. Yes. This is what you said. "You couldn't keep track of everyone at the party for every minute."' Ashley fixed Cassie with a pointed gaze. 'Were you lying then? Or now?'

At Duncan's 'No comment', the interview was terminated.

'Thanks. Let's hope Mark reciprocates your loyalty, eh?' Ashley dismissed Cassie and Duncan and, as the door swung shut and James stated the time and stopped the tape, she made rapid notes, as if avoiding looking at James or making conversation.

Before he could speak, the door opened and Mark and Duncan sat. Before questions even began, Mark's fury was plain on his mottled-red face. His hands shook. He looked like he wanted to pace and had to corral himself to stay seated.

Taking the lead, James asked, 'Look, Mark, Cassie's already told us what happened. But we'd like to hear your side of things, in your own words, please.'

Mark glanced from James to Duncan. 'Fine. I want this over with.' He took a deep breath. 'I'm not proud of it. It was a petty-minded thing to do. We just thought Jack should know the basics of looking after his *fleet*. And if he *didn't* know after all his bragging, well, then, he *deserved* to be a bit inconvenienced by his ignorance.' Mark glanced at James. 'And, let's be honest, he'd've just asked me or Cass to fix it.'

Mark sat back, folding his arms. 'Like I say, I'm not proud of it.' He unfolded his arms restlessly and shrugged. 'I'd been putting in long days, what with Maxine's restoration of the Ferrari and the parts I needed to engineer for it, on top of all the work for the gullwing. And what with the divorce, and financial worries *and* all the crap about the race, well . . .' He flexed his hands. 'Jack needling me was the final straw.'

As if sympathising, James summarised. 'So when that – very heavily laden – straw *did* snap, all you did was harmlessly immobilise Jack's cars? Nothing else? When you had the chance to get rid of the person behind all your problems?'

Chapter 27

Monday 22nd April – 4.30 a.m.

Nell stared up at a ceiling she couldn't see. Rav snored gently beside her, his arm slung over her shoulders. The temptation to snuggle into his warmth was irresistible . . . *Almost*. If her mind hadn't been racing. Jezebel sensed the lack of sleep, and stirred at Nell's feet.

'Are you awake?' Nell whispered to Rav. He answered with another snore so she paused, then repeated it a little louder.

'Mmm?'

Nell leaned over and kissed his neck. 'Are you awake?' she whispered again.

Rav moved sleepily, yawned, then his eyes flew open. He jerked up, as if he was lying on a bed of hot coals and turned to the side table. 'What? Jesus! Have I overslept?' He snatched his phone up, checking the time as he voiced the typical ecologist's fear of not waking up at the odd time they'd set their alarm for.

He rubbed his eyes and checked the time again. 'It's four-sodding-thirty!' He sank against the pillows, pulling Nell against his chest, his biceps tensing. 'Don't you ever sleep?'

Nell curled up against him, in much the same way as Jezebel. 'I *knew* you were awake.'

His fingers trailed down her back, leaving a delicious shiver in their wake. 'Oh, yeah?'

With effort, she pulled away. 'Yes. I need to talk to you. I think I have a theory about the murder. I've been chewing it over all night.'

'Yep. That'll do it.' Rav pulled his arm away and sat up. 'Gold-plated mood-killer.' He flicked on a bedside lamp, the bright light making them both squint until their eyes adjusted. He plumped up the pillows, looked at Nell and gave a resigned sigh. 'This better be good.'

'Jack didn't drown in Little Smitington Pond . . .'

Rav's eyebrows flashed up in surprise. 'OK, good opener, I'll give you that,' he deadpanned. 'Why do you think that?' Jezebel stealthed up the bed a few inches, hunting a hug, then paused.

'The diatom samples from Jack's tissue and from Little Smitington Pond didn't match. Radically so. The species in the sample from the nature reserve were from an S1 profile, so low nutrient levels, good water quality, whereas the diatoms in Jack's tissue were more like an S3 or 4 profile, so we're looking for a more nutrient-rich environment . . .'

'Like a duck pond?' Rav pushed himself to sit straighter with his elbows as he thought.

'Fish pond,' Nell said with certainty.

'You know where?' Rav asked, apparently not noticing Jezebel curl up against his thigh.

Nell nodded. 'The ornamental koi carp lake. At Jack's home.'

'Oh? Right . . .' Unconsciously, he fussed Jezebel's cheek.

'He must've drowned there, and the murderer moved him and set the crash up. I think the murderer wanted it to look like someone had sabotaged his brakes and that caused the crash . . .'

Rav started to protest but Nell shook her head. 'Just go with me for a minute. It's a working hypothesis, but I think it pans out. The murderer would've wanted it to *look* like the Mustang had skidded out of control, but they'd have needed the brakes to be usable at that point. Then, once the crash was staged and the Mustang was lined up, near the pond edge, the murderer could move Jack into the driving seat, nip out, slice the brake lines and push the car into the pond. The engine would have dragged the car deeper into the water. And the brake fluid would have drained into the pond.' She stabbed the air with her finger. 'And *that* explains why the chemistry levels of Mai's pond shot through the roof and the effect was so toxic. *All* the brake fluid was dumped in, in one go.'

Rav frowned. 'Let's think about this. Jack was at home, somehow he was outside . . .'

'Svetlana punched him, remember? And left him in the driveway while she came back to the hotel for the night.'

Rav blinked. 'Right, yes. So, what, someone happened to find him and drown him in his lake? Or maybe he got up and wandered about and fell in? Do you reckon Svetlana found him and decided to move him?'

'Unlikely, since she confessed. Why do that if you tell them the wrong reason?'

'Double bluff. Obviously. And gamble you'll get away with it?'

'Maybe,' Nell conceded. 'OK, so anyone could have put Jack's body in his car and driven him to Little Smitington . . .'

Rav frowned. 'Which is what? A ten- or fifteen-minute drive down the road?'

'Roughly, yes,' Nell agreed. 'Stage the crash, brakes, move Jack . . .'

'Yeah, hold it there,' Rav said. 'It's not an easy thing to lug a body about like that.'

Nell eyed Rav's torso. 'How much strength would it take?' she wondered aloud. She jumped up and prodded him. 'Get up, let me see how far I can move you.'

Rav got up and pulled his boxer shorts on. Nell tried to drag him across the carpet, with Jezebel as a moving obstacle and Rav complaining of carpet burn. So she tried to lift him in various ungainly ways. Despite her best attempts, she couldn't move him far. Rav illustrated the contrast in their relative size and strength by throwing her easily over his shoulder, running around the bedroom and flomping her onto the marshmallowy piled-up duvet on the bed, where Jezebel playfully pounced.

'Fine! Truce!' Nell giggled, flat on her back, sinking into the bedding like it was a snowdrift. 'But you're taller than Jack and far more muscular. He might have been easier to move.'

Rav comically flexed his muscles until she swatted his tensed arm. 'Come on, this is serious. Help me here.'

'OK, on the serious "who could move Jack" question,' Rav said, counting off on his fingers, 'I reckon: Mark, Svetlana, Dani – for sure. Cassie, Max, Lucio – maybe.' He glanced at Nell. 'Is that everyone?'

'Possibly Richard Tyler. He wasn't at Jack's party, but that doesn't mean he didn't go there afterwards.'

'And how *does* the fraud fit in with all this?' Rav asked.

'I'm not sure,' Nell said. 'But it doesn't seem too outlandish to assume that it's connected. If Jack found out about the fraud and was going to jeopardise the sale somehow?'

'Blackmail?' Rav asked. 'Or surely he'd want in? Get a piece of that profit margin?'

Nell paced as she thought. 'Richard was a fence in a former life, remember. So it doesn't take much imagination to think how he could either find or offload cars. He could be a useful part of the team. And whether he was or not, you could still be on to something with blackmail.'

'OK. But over who? Presumably Lucio, then?' Rav said.

'Do you think the whole race team was involved?' Nell asked. 'I'm amazed that if the car wasn't genuine that they didn't all know. Take Max, for example. She'd have to verify the car for Lucio. That would mean examining the entire vehicle and the paperwork. To sell it on, at those prices, she'd have to be pretty bloody convinced . . .'

'. . . Or in on it?' Rav concluded.

Nell nodded. 'Unless she's not as good at her job as she suggests. Or just didn't spot something. Or was distracted? But even then, that kind of failure would be leverage to someone like Jack.'

'What about the others? Would Mark and Cassie have done the restoration?'

'I'd've thought so. It would be odd to buy a car that needs specialist attention and not use your conveniently assembled specialist team, wouldn't it? They'd do the work at cost and then you'd split the profit between Richard, Max, Lucio, Mark and Cassie. That's a *lot* of money.'

'You reckon it was a one-off?' Rav asked.

Nell stared at him. 'Jesus. You think this could be an organised . . . ongoing *thing*?'

Rav shrugged. 'Why not?'

Nell thought back to the Finchmere Classics auction catalogues. The annual sales at her family's estate. She sank onto the bed. 'Moretti's has supplied the showpiece car for the auction for the past eight years. I guess it's not entirely unfeasible that . . . some of those could have been fakes? And then they gradually got more ambitious with these private sales?' Nell's face drained of colour. 'Organised fraud being sold through our event. Which devalues other people's collections. Jesus . . .' She held her head in her hands. '*That's* why James wanted the auction back catalogues.'

'In which case, they could be in it together. So who's responsible is immaterial.'

Nell shook her head. 'That's too convenient, isn't it? *Someone* still had to do it.'

The first hint of sunrise broke through the clouds. Nell nodded at the window. 'Good. Now it's morning, I want to drive the route between Jack's place and Little Smitington.'

'What? *Now?*' Rav asked.

'Well, I'll shower, dress, feed Jezebel and have breakfast first,' Nell said, reasonably.

'I promised Aanya I'd have breakfast with her and the folks at the hotel this morning,' Rav said. 'And I was going to see how the pond work is coming on.'

'I can take a look when I get there,' Nell said. 'Then I'll go to the team's garage, to see what's happening *now* about racing the gullwing.'

'Oh no, of *course!*' Rav said. He shoved his hand through his thick hair, leaving it sexily dishevelled. 'I guess the race is off, now?'

'Not necessarily.' Nell couldn't resist kissing him. 'I have an idea about that.'

Monday 22nd April – 6.30 a.m.

Blue-and-white police tape fluttered against Jack's gates. The privacy his exclusive property benefitted from was *total*. Even with the height advantage from last night's borrowed Land Rover, which usually guaranteed an investigation over most hedges, Nell could see precisely *nothing*. Treelines defended all boundaries, reinforcing high walls and fences, while all the hedges comprised the landscaper's weapon of choice: thorny shrubs.

Not that the thorns would deter Nell; most ecologists had to find a way through those just to get on site to begin their job. But James's warning after she'd identified the diatoms rang in her ears. She didn't *need* to take a closer look, and she wouldn't risk the investigation by trying.

Turning back, it only took a few minutes to drive the straight road to Little Smitington. There were no side roads, driveways, lay-bys – nowhere on the narrow lane to park. The two driveways to country houses were gated, with no room to pull off to the side of the road. If the murderer hid their car while they moved Jack's dead body, they must have parked at his house – which would have been risky, unless Svetlana really was the culprit *or* – Nell turned onto the track to the visitor centre – *here*. This was the only place the murderer could have parked. It wouldn't be out of the question to walk back, or even run.

Nell scanned for tyre prints but the stone-strewn earth was too rutted and criss-crossed with several types of vehicle tracks. She drove on through the open gate and saw Jonty, sleeves rolled up, lugging the pond islands from the truck and stacking them in the shed. He heaved the last one to the pile then dusted off his hands. He turned and waved at Nell as she approached.

'Hey, Nell!'

'Hi! Need any help?' she asked. 'I've got an hour.'

Jonty shook his head. 'It's all in hand!' He beamed proudly. 'Want to come and see?'

Nell nodded and as they walked to the pond, Jonty reeled off the progress he'd made with the interns. 'The islands have done their work; the water chemistry was perfect this morning. The amphibian fencing is up and stacked in the shed for reuse with the pitfall traps; the trenches are filled in and seeded over. Even some of the plug plants are in.' He nodded towards the trailer crammed with seedlings. 'The rest go in once the interns have had their breakfast. Then we can take out the membrane, disinfect it and put it away. We'll be done in a couple of hours.'

'This is amazing, Jonty.' Nell admired the work. It wasn't quite the tranquil habitat it once was, but it would be – when the new plants grew, it would buzz with wildlife again. As if to encourage them, a lazy dragonfly floated past, hovering over the water.

'I'm really impressed,' Nell said. She drew out her phone and sent an email. 'That's the diatom list for the pond. The species show it is – *was* – a pond with pristine water quality.'

Jonty checked his phone. 'Got it, thanks. Great timing – I'll include it in the site data for the assessor's visit this afternoon.'

'I'll do a post-restoration comparison to that baseline, if she wants,' Nell offered.

'Oh, she'll want,' Jonty said drily as they turned back. 'One thing I know for sure is that she always wants everything.'

Nell laughed. 'Yup, that's Mai. How's she doing today?'

'Resisting house arrest. So, she's coming out this afternoon, just for a walk.' His wry look at Nell told her he was fully aware Mai was checking up on him. 'She'll arrive just as the assessor finishes his survey.' He made a comic grimace.

Nell returned the wince. 'Really? Isn't that a bit of a gamble?'

Jonty shrugged, impenetrable as ever. 'Guess we'll see.'

Monday 22nd April – 7 a.m.

Arriving at Moretti's team garage, Nell found Maxine and Lucio sitting beside the gullwing, seemingly in a state of shock. They didn't look up when Nell walked over.

'Morning,' she said. 'Anyone else around?'

'No,' Maxine said. 'Cassie and Mark are still being held at the station. God knows what this does for the race today. Looks like all bets are off.'

Lucio looked heartbroken. 'I cannot believe . . .' he repeated under his breath. He gazed at Nell. 'The one good thing I thought we would salvage from all this was our gullwing's moment on the track today. But it isn't to be. And whoever has done all this, and the fraud, and damaged my business, has also hurt you. I have brought this to you. I have let you down.'

In the stranglehold of suspicion, Nell couldn't quite accept the heartfelt words as she might have. But she nodded at Lucio's despair. 'I agree with you about the car having her moment,' she said. 'I wondered about asking Colin to drive her. I know he's retired, but he might. And Svetlana might even like to join him in the parade lap before the race. Might be a nice way to pay tribute . . . ?'

'And good publicity, too.' Maxine's shrewd eyes narrowed. '*You* should ask him, Lucio. He'll most likely say yes to you. And we already know he and Svetlana are coming today to watch the last day of racing.'

'I cannot put him under more pressure.' Lucio flourished his hands. 'The poor man has lost his son.' He shook his head. 'What will we say if he says no?'

'OK, so, if Colin says no . . .' Nell hesitated. 'Perhaps I could drive her in the parade lap? I wouldn't dream of racing her – those other drivers are ferociously competitive! But I *could* give her a good showcase in a parade, and that would at least get her out there. *If* that would suit you, and *if* the other teams are OK with that? Then, at least, Colin needn't feel under pressure to race her.' She shrugged, unable to gauge their reactions. 'But I do think it would be courteous to give Colin first refusal. He might be pleased to do it.'

Lucio started to nod. 'Yes, yes I think that's a good plan.' His face gradually brightened. He looked at Max for her agreement. She was nodding enthusiastically.

'Just . . .' Nell said hesitantly. 'Who'll get her prepped for the laps without Cassie or Mark here?'

'Oh, leave that with me, luv.' Maxine stood, practically rolling up the sleeves of her Armani jacket. She prodded Lucio. 'Get on the *blower*, Lucio! What're you waiting for!'

As Lucio dialled Colin's number and paced away from them, Maxine eyed up Nell's vintage racing driver outfit of boiler suit, racing hat and racing goggles.

'Nice outfit. Perfect for, ooh, driving a classic car.' She pursed her lips. 'It's as if you expected us to agree.' She folded her arms, but her voice was conspiratorial. 'You're a smart cookie. Always a move ahead, aren't you?'

Nell smiled uncertainly. 'Oh, this? I always wear this for the last day!' She echoed Maxine's tone. 'Easy to put on when you've got a hangover from the reception dinner!'

'*Magnifico!*' Lucio nodded emphatically at Nell and Maxine as he spoke into the phone. 'You are hero of the hour, my friend. Thank you.' He ended the call and punched the air. 'He will do it! And he said he would like Svetlana to ride with him in the parade.'

'That's great news, Lucio!' Nell glanced at him, then Maxine. 'I'll let the race coordinators know and leave you to get on.'

Walking off, Nell sent an email to the race coordinators, confirming that Colin would drive. Nell was pleased Colin would race her – that the epic work wouldn't be wasted. Three days ago, that was her main focus, keeping her on tenterhooks. But now the mood wasn't only flat, it was almost sinister. With a shiver of distrust, Nell glanced over her shoulder. Maxine and Lucio had turned to watch her. *Coincidental timing . . . ?*

A slice of unease iced Nell's blood. Her gaze swung over Lucio's neat Ferrari Dino and Maxine's bullish Lamborghini Gallardo. She froze as ideas crystallised.

But her thoughts were interrupted by the beep of a text from Astrid, the event manager:

You OK after last night? Police took the Taycan but it was crashed to bits and caked in mud. Are you OK? What happened?

Nell immediately called her back, but struggled to get a word in edgewise as Astrid bombarded her with questions. 'Hi . . . yes . . . yes. Fine. Yes, I'm really fine. Sorry to have worried you. I should've left a message—'

'But what the hell *happened?*' Astrid asked. 'It looked like a serious accident.'

'Can I tell you later?' Nell asked. She had time, but she didn't want to relive it right now.

'Sure. But . . . There is one other thing. We've found another crashed car this morning. Further along the lane from the collapsed wall. And well down the bank, hidden from the road. A dog walker found it.'

'What?' Nell's mind reeled. 'Was it a classic BMW?'

'Er . . . yes—'

'Where? Exactly?' Nell headed for the Land Rover.

'Just before the junction.'

'Have you called the police?'

'Yes, apparently they're on their way.'

'Good. I am, too.'

'But . . . it's not just a car, Nell,' Astrid said, her voice shaky. 'Someone's *in* it. You know. *Dead.*'

Chapter 28

Monday 22nd April – 7.15 a.m.

Having responded to Nell's breathless call, Rav then *hared* through the woodland, as the crow flies, from Finchmere House to where she was heading. Undergrowth whipped at his face, and stumbling on uneven ground reminded him that his ankle was still healing. But he ran.

Confronted with the rising bank, topped with the flint wall that had sheltered them from pursuit last night, he scrambled up, then clambered over the wall. Landing in the narrow lane, opposite the K-shaped junction before him, he saw Nell.

He sprinted, sweaty and panting, to join her approach towards the car. Well, the *crash*. Astrid, the event manager, was on the phone, pacing a respectable distance from the accident like a guardian, and gave an unhappy wave. She paused only to point at her phone and mouth, '*Your dad*,' to Nell.

While Astrid was occupied, Rav and Nell stopped short of the car, staring at it.

The verge between the road and the wall was wider here, on the steep slope of the bank. The trees had thinned out, leaving only two nearby – one of which was outside the boundary wall, with a car smashed into its trunk. The car had first ploughed down the bank and into the sparse bramble scrub before crashing. With its bonnet staved in, the car was much worse off than the stout oak.

A figure in the driving seat was slumped forward, over the wheel.

Nell reached for Rav's hand and whispered, 'Do you think this crash could have been staged, too?'

He didn't need to answer to realise that Nell, like him, was scanning the ground. Too much leaf litter for prints – of tyres or feet. Next, the bramble, for fibres or hairs from someone who might have squeezed out of the car. If the car door had been opened post-crash, the vigorous spring green growth would resist tearing, so there were no helpful signs of broken stems. Now, they examined the car door, looking for scratches matching it opening. But the spiderweb of scratches from landing in brambles made that impossible to detect, too.

Nell gasped.

Rav crept closer beside her and saw the face of the man in the driving seat, and the same shock of recognition jolted through him.

But then he saw it. *Proof.* 'Look! It *was* staged. The airbag didn't go off!'

'Classic car.'

'So . . . ?'

'No airbags. Rarely seatbelts, to be fair.'

Deflated, he stood back, to take in the wider scene. And his gaze fixed on the second nearby oak, inside Finchmere's boundary wall.

But Nell was still peering in the driver's window. He tugged her arm.

'Look!'

Strapped to that second tree was a small, camouflaged box.

Before Nell could say anything, and presumably before the police could arrive to intercept the box, Rav scrambled up onto the wall to reach the tree branch, Nell watching him anxiously, willing him on. Having hauled himself up onto the branch, Rav paused astride a stout bough and rotated his recently injured shoulder. Guilt stabbed at Nell, but she covertly checked the road, praying that Astrid wouldn't turn around, and that he'd be back down on solid ground before the team arrived.

He reached for a high branch and pulled himself up, but the way his feet flailed, Nell knew it was painful. He had one more bough to climb up to. The height, the thinning branches and how much his shoulder hurt made her hold her breath. She couldn't see far along the winding road, but she could hear a distant Land Rover Discovery. Like the one James drove . . .

With a grimace, Rav hauled up to the next branch and caught his breath. He fiddled with the strap that secured the box to the trunk.

It took a while, and Nell's eyes darted between him and the road. *Come on . . . Come on!*

Finally, he released the box and strapped it round his waist, then eased himself gingerly from the highest branch, grunting as he dangled, feet grappling to feel the bough below. Finding his footing, he steadied himself, let go, and carefully crouched.

James's Land Rover Discovery came into distant view. 'Nell grimaced at Rav. *Hurry . . . Please hurry!*

Rav gripped the branch, lowered himself, but slipped. He held on, feet floundering for purchase. He slipped again and then fell, making Nell swallow a scream and bolt forward, just as James pulled up.

Nell scrambled over the wall, but Rav was nowhere to be seen. Part running, part stumbling down the bank, she nearly collided with him at the base of the oak. He was dusting his jeans off, and mouthed, 'Fine,' as Nell mouthed, 'James.' With a nod, Rav unstrapped the box from his waist. Nell took it from him as they climbed back up the slope to the wall. As Rav climbed over, saying a loud, 'Hello!' to James, she slipped the box into her Land Rover.

'Hi, James, we were just checking out the scene . . .' Nell knew she sounded guilty, but she knew James would attribute that to nosiness.

'So I see. Hope you haven't compromised any evidence.'

As Ashley joined James from the other side of the parked Discovery, Nell saw her roll her eyes.

'Of course not!' Nell assured them both. 'But I can help. I know that the car belongs to a racing driver. I'll give you his contact details so you can inform him. Because the person in there isn't the owner. It's Richard Tyler.'

James sagged, grabbing the tailgate of Nell's Land Rover. 'Richard . . . Richard Tyler?'

He noticed Ashley turn sharply away, looking like she could easily be sick, and he knew she shared his gut-wrenching guilt.

His frustrations over last night's failed stakeout had been drowned out by the buzz of Nell's close call – twice over – and the arrest. But, if he and Ashley hadn't argued, he might have had the sense to inquire whether the reason Richard wasn't at home was because he'd been invited to the dinner at Finchmere, given his connections. Hell – even if they'd set off after Shannon had told him, they might have been able to question him. He'd been prepared to give up because he was angry. They might have gleaned valuable intel, which was now certainly lost. *And we might have saved his life . . .*

Nausea burned. He could only imagine what Val would make of his leadership so far. But Nell was still speaking. He forced himself to focus.

'. . . But this is definitely the car that pursued us last night. The right headlights, right shape, speedy enough for the chase.'

'Yes, OK, that makes sense . . .' James tried to get his brain into gear. 'If Richard was a key part of the fraud, and thought you knew and were about to blow his scam wide open . . . ?'

Nell didn't look convinced. 'Maybe Richard was only part of the fraud?' Glancing at the arriving SOCO team, she tugged James's sleeve. 'Can I talk to you,' she suggested the word '*privately*' with a jerk of her head.

With another sinking feeling, James followed her a few steps away from the busy team and the event manager, who was still on her phone. Leaving room for the SOCO team to do their work, Ashley stared at the crashed car, at Richard, her face stricken.

'I think this was staged. Just like Jack's murder. We know Jack didn't drown in Little Smitington Pond. I *think* he was drowned in his lake at home and moved into the car and the crash faked so it looked like he died at the pond. I bet if you sample the diatoms in his lake, they'll match the species found in his tissue.'

James rubbed his face and nodded. 'OK, I'll ask the SOCO team to take some samples – if they haven't already. I'll check.' He made a move towards them.

'That's not all,' Nell said. '*Think* about the logistics. If the murderer found Jack outside his house, then everyone, except Svetlana, would need to hide their car somewhere. And there's nowhere along that road except the turn-in for the visitor centre. So, if they'd met Jack at the house, when he was coming round, maybe staggering about in the garden, then the murderer could have drowned him, put him in the Mustang in the garage, taken *their* car to Little Smitington

Visitor Centre, dashed back, then driven *Jack* there in the Mustang to fake the crash and left in their own car.'

'Right,' James considered the scenario. 'Yes, OK, that makes sense.' He dredged his memory for alibis at that time after Jack's party. Most people had said they'd been alone, in their rooms at the hotel or their home if they were local. Only Mark and Cassie had been together.

'*But*,' Nell urged, '*think* about it. Mai's worked hard to create a species-rich habitat. With *rare* flora and fauna. So, *if* someone *had* parked there, there's a chance they left tyre prints at the reserve, although the track is hardcore, and has had some traffic over the past few days, so that's not going to be easy to check. *But* the microscopic soil particles, or seeds or pollen, that could have got under the car's wheel arches or in the tyre treads—'

'—Would be unique to that site,' James finished. Nell looked relieved he'd grasped her point, and headed off. He made a note and turned back to Ashley.

She'd already started walking towards him, and he met her halfway, as she extended one hand with a handshake. 'Truce?' she asked. 'We can't carry on being at odds like this, can we? If we hadn't argued, the ... outcome ... might be very different. Richard might still be ...'

James swallowed, clamped his lips and gave a brisk nod. But as he looked at Ashley, he could see that the reasons she was upset wouldn't just disappear because she was offering not to let them interfere in their working relationship.

'A truce isn't a resolution, though, Ash. What do you want, as an outcome?'

Sighing, Ashley admitted, 'Honestly, I don't know. I know it's petty, which makes this ... even worse.' She raised a hand in the direction of the car. 'But you keep bending the rules and getting rewarded for it. And things I could forgive in you as my colleague are very hard to accept in you as my boss – when your role means you set an example to me.' She glanced at him, then stared at her feet. 'And having my peer as my boss doesn't just feel like I've missed a promotion, it feels like a demotion.'

James didn't contradict her with meaningless platitudes. He'd probably feel the same, in her shoes.

She shook herself. 'But none of this should impact our work. Not when there's so much at stake.' Meeting his eyes, she took a breath. 'I don't know what outcome would make me feel better. But, for now, let's get back to working like usual. No one else can get hurt because we're squabbling.'

Monday 22nd April – 8.30 a.m.

Rav hurried into Finchmere House and bolted up the stairs for his laptop, to begin the painstaking work of checking the sound file from the bat detector.

'Why couldn't this have been a camera?' he huffed. 'You have wildlife cameras everywhere. But no, it has to be a detector that'll only record ultrasonic sound.'

'Well, for someone who thinks this is a lost cause, you're in a hell of a hurry.' Nell poked him. 'And you went to a fair amount of trouble to make sure the police didn't nab it.'

Rav ignored her as he retrieved the memory card. 'It was nine thirty, wasn't it, when we arrived at the police station last night?'

'Thereabouts.' Nell peered over his shoulder as he opened the file.

'Right, so the BMW tried to hit you then, and would have taken about thirty minutes to get back to the location of the crash, at the earliest.' He searched for the timestamp and played the file. 'What did you tell James?'

Nell relayed her theory. As she spoke, they heard muffled noises from the recording – ambient sounds, but distorted from their usual frequency so impossible to discern what they were with any accuracy.

'Oh . . . nice. Do you think he'll get a SOCO team over there today?'

'Yes, I hope they'll check during the race. Lucio and Maxine will be at the track.' She stared out of the window.

'I know you need to go. I'll check—' A clinking sound on the recording made them freeze. It was fainter than usual, but instantly recognisable. The sound every bat ecologist made at the start of every survey to check a recorder was working.

It was the jangle of keys.

Nell stared at Rav. 'Play it again.' It was unmistakable. 'When the security officer took the driver's keys off him, it was a bunch of keys. If they were in the ignition—'

'And someone knocked against them—'

'When, say, someone was moving a body into the driving seat—'

'What time?' Nell asked.

'Ten thirty-two,' Rav confirmed.

They stared at each other. 'No other reason to hear keys in that location, at that time.' Nell nudged Rav with a smile. '*There's* your proof.'

'Are you going to tell James?'

Nell bit her lip. 'He'll be cross that we purloined this without telling him. I've told him I think it was staged, like Jack's. And the pathologists will prove that pretty quickly, I'd imagine. The killer must have whacked him on the head, I guess. And the chances of the blow that killed him perfectly matching the crash is pretty unlikely. So they'll know soon enough that this was set up. But by *who?*'

Chapter 29

Monday 22nd April – 10 a.m.

An hour and a half later, Nell was heading over to the team's garage. Though she wasn't keen on going there alone, she had to at least wish them all good luck.

Her heart lifted when she spotted Rav and Aanya walking briskly towards her with Rakesh and Neeta – and when they all waved cheerily at her, Nell did a double take.

Wearing a fantastic fuchsia vintage gown, hair styled underneath a jewelled headscarf, Neeta greeted her with a sunny, 'Morning, Nell!'

'Morning!' Nell wanted to smile in delight at this change, but . . . what had happened?

In a badged boiler suit, with an artful smudge on his cheek, Rakesh clasped Nell's hand. 'Look at us! We're twins!' He pointed at Nell's boiler suit, driving goggles resting on her vintage leather racing helmet, and the same artful smudge on her cheek. He leaned in. 'Aanya told us what happened last night. Quite some manoeuvres. You saved our babies!'

'Oh, for God's sake, Dad!' Aanya looked disgusted at being called a baby.

Rav laughed, nudging his sister's offended, rigid frame with his shoulder.

'I just happened to be driving,' Nell said. 'That's all.' She gave an awkward shrug.

Rakesh looked at her intently, the corners of his eyes crinkling. 'Yes, that's all it was.' The good-humoured tone made Nell smile back.

Neeta fell in step with Nell. 'And thank you, for moving us to such a lovely room,' she mumbled. Nell noticed her cheeks trembling. 'We appreciate what you did about . . . all that.'

'That's . . . of course. The least I could do,' Nell muttered. She felt her face flush. She took a deep breath and turned to face Neeta. 'And I'm sorry. I know our meeting hasn't been ideal. But I hope you know how much I care about Rav.' She glanced at Rav, who was teasing a grin out of Aanya, and couldn't stop the smile spreading across her face.

Neeta pulled her into a hug. 'Ah, *Beta!*'

Neeta moved to walk with Rakesh, Rav caught up with Nell and shot her a tender smile.

'Knew you'd be a hit with my folks. *Eventually,*' he said.

Nell prodded him in the ribs. 'Well, before I get too comfortable, I need to wish the team good luck.'

Approaching the garage, Nell knew from the Range Rover Velar and the classic streamlined silver BMW 507, parked next to Lucio and Maxine's cars, that Svetlana and Colin had arrived, along with someone else in a sturdy-looking Nissan Juke. Dani, maybe?

Rakesh needed no encouragement. He poked his head inside the garage. 'Hello?'

'Engineers,' Rav said with a grin. 'Never can resist a workshop.'

Nell hurried in after him, to make introductions with Lucio and Maxine, who soon relaxed when Rakesh admired the car and their restoration pictures.

Colin, already in his racing suit, talked him through the work. Fascinated, Rakesh asked ever more interrogative questions. Neeta absorbed the same details with detached tolerance. But her gaze travelled to the gullwing, her head tilting as she noted its fine lines and sheer presence.

The race verifier watched Maxine plug a laptop into the portal in the glove compartment and scroll through the performance statistics. He nodded, then walked to the bonnet and saw that two battery packs had been disconnected, giving the car parity with her racing contemporaries.

'We'll check the batteries at the start and end of the race,' he said to Maxine, 'so there can be no claims of unfair advantage. But it's an honourable group, and this all looks fine to me.'

Lucio shook the verifier's hand enthusiastically and glanced hopefully at Maxine.

Amidst the distraction, Aanya tried to take a surreptitious selfie with Svetlana in the background. But Svetlana walked over, leaving Dani sitting at the workbench.

'You want picture? Just ask. But I check before you upload.'

Aanya tried to copy Svetlana's effortless posing. After a few tries, they apparently both agreed on a picture. 'Shall I delete the others?' Aanya asked with self-conscious politeness.

'No need. I look phenomenal in all.' Svetlana's assessment was matter-of-fact.

Aanya checked. 'It's true.' She looked deflated as she compared herself to the model.

'It is my job, darling.' Taking the phone from her, Svetlana scrolled through Aanya's pictures and pointed at one. 'You are beautiful when you don't pose. Here, when you are laughing? Gorgeous. I cannot take such pictures. My face does not relax like that, even when my guard is down.'

Nell wondered if Svetlana's guard was ever down. She certainly hadn't given any impression of mourning her dead husband.

'All right, team!' Maxine announced. 'Let's get going! Our moment is finally here!'

Colin held open the passenger door for Svetlana, who sank into the seat elegantly. He dashed to the driver's door, where Lucio shook his hand with vigour.

'Good luck, luv!' Maxine waved, spurring everyone else in the garage to chorus good wishes as the car stirred into life and glided silently away, interrupted only by the distinctive 'pip' of the gullwing's horn, politely asking the unsuspecting crowds to move aside.

Nell looked around the gathering. 'Let's head to the grandstand to watch!'

'We'll follow in a bit. You go on with your folks,' Maxine said.

In their VIP seats, Nell supplied Rav's parents with Finchmere sparkling wine mimosas. With heady excitement, they watched the starting grid and finish line, with a view of the dramatic last chicane before the final straight. This stand had filled up, being the best on the track, and these seats were favourites that Nell had reserved. She was pleased to see they were looking forward to the race. Even if Aanya was fixated by her phone, texting rapidly and taking more selfies after Svetlana's compliment. On her other side, Rakesh and Neeta were more engaged, firing off questions about the race and the cars.

But Aanya suddenly looked horrified. Nell nudged her, and mouthed, 'What?'

She passed her phone to Nell, and she looked at the loaded webpage. A tabloid article announced: '*Love Rat Rafferty beds mystery woman hours before death*.' The speculative piece listed several potential women, including Nell – and Aanya – at last night's reception dinner.

'Ugh.' Nell's lip curled in disgust at the misogynistic overtones. 'Sorry, Aanya. I thought security cleared out all of that hack's photos. He must have sent some in before we got to him. Just ignore it.' She sighed unhappily. 'And I'll have to issue apologies to our guests.'

'Svetlana's just been so nice to me.' Aanya bit her lip, her gaze dropping to her lap, then over to her parents, her face distraught.

'Show them, and Rav, the article. Now,' Nell said. 'If you don't, they'll hear it from someone else, and that will be a million times worse.'

'No *way!*'

Nell held her gaze and Aanya sighed. But she stood up and moved to her mum's seat and showed her the phone.

'What's this?' Neeta asked with a smile. As she stared at the screen, her face visibly registered the change from the expectation that Aanya was sharing something lovely – to the brutal fact that a national newspaper had just made their daughter the subject of scandal. And a sex scandal, at that. Which was only the more unfortunate because it was true. Confusion became disbelief, then fury.

She pushed Aanya's hand down, as if trying to hide the story from the world. 'Who's written this?' Neeta hissed. 'We must . . . we must . . .' She looked lost for what action she could take. 'Sue!'

'It's best to ignore it,' Nell said. 'Hopefully it will just be forgotten.' But she pulled out her phone and looked up the number for her family's press team. 'Hi, can you call in some favours and request an online article to be taken down? I don't know if it's in print or not.'

As Nell answered a flurry of questions about the publication, the editor, writer and photographer, Rakesh took the phone, eyes narrowing and chest heaving as he read. The look he exchanged with his wife was laden – as if they were telling each other, *this is exactly what I was afraid of* . . .

Meanwhile, Nell tried to think of any leverage she could offer her PR team to encourage the desired result. 'I'd offered Joel a lap in the gullwing if he didn't publish speculative gossip about our guests, so you can ask if that's still of interest – on condition he removes the piece. And you can volunteer anything else if it will get the article removed.' She didn't like rewarding slippery players like Joel with future cooperation, but she liked the look on Aanya's face even less.

Rav scanned the article, then shot a concerned look at his sister.

Ending the call, Nell leaned over to Neeta. 'I've asked our team if they can do anything to restrict its circulation. I don't know what they can do if it's already out, but at least if it doesn't get sold to several papers or websites, that will help limit the exposure.'

Rakesh shot Nell a pained glance, matched by Neeta's. *Great,* Nell thought. *I've been on their good side for all of ten minutes.*

Squeezing Nell's hand, Neeta said, 'Thank you for trying to help.'

Nell felt pleasantly astonished.

Aanya's phone lit up with messages. She read them and started to giggle. She glanced up. 'So far, I'm just getting a lot of compliments about the picture and the dress and the fancy digs.'

'Yeah, don't look at the comments,' Nell said. 'Quit while you're ahead.'

Aanya couldn't resist another look. Her face fell into a disappointed, then disgusted expression. Then she cried, 'Ugh!' and shut her phone down with an angry snap. She looked so unhappy that Nell nudged her. 'Let me guess. Something about airbags?'

Aanya nodded, looking outraged.

'Yup. Highly unoriginal bunch.' Nell sighed. 'If only they knew that one day you could be in charge of their medication.' She gave Aanya a sidelong smile and Aanya returned it, shaking her head.

'They're driving out from the paddock!' Rav said, looking over at the track.

The parade lap was led by the gullwing, so its silence could be appreciated. Its dramatic doors open like a suspended silver bird, seeming to float past in eerie, attention-demanding silence. Without a growling engine to drown out their noise, the crowd stopped talking. An almost reverent hush fell over the audience. Colin and Svetlana waved at the press and the first few grandstands. Then, they pulled the doors shut, and the Mercedes shot forward like a glinting bullet, as other cars joined the parade in a cacophony of growling revs.

'Now, that's how a seasoned pro gets our parade off to a stylish start,' the commentator crackled through the silence. 'Paying tribute to his son Jack's tragic death just three days ago, Colin Rafferty has come out of retirement today in his honour, to take the driving seat with Jack's wife, Svetlana, for this parade. After this, Colin will race the gullwing, that's been specifically tuned to match her contemporaries and, it is hoped, will blaze a new trail for converted classic car racing here at Finchmere next year. It's an exciting new move . . .'

'She looks great!' Rav leaned in, sounding excited.

'Yes, she does,' Nell agreed. 'And I feel a whole lot more confident with her being in Colin's hands than I ever did about Jack.'

'You're probably not alone,' Rav said.

'Trying again, Nell?' Shannon wafted past. 'What a brave little spirit your team has! Especially in light of this.' She showed Nell her phone, with the headline, 'Finchmere's Classic Car Race on the Wrong Track: major crime puts the brakes on the Classics at Finchmere.' Between the article's paragraphs was the photo of Nell holding up Rav's T-shirt, its unfortunate caption – '*Drive it like you stole it*' – all too visible.

Nell's heart dropped, but she couldn't let it show. Even if the threat seemed to be closing in. She managed a shrug, relieved when Shannon wiggled her fingers at a cluster of men who Nell – and Shannon – knew owned the fine classic Bentleys and Mercedes on the track. Shannon joined the wealthy owners, as Lucio, Maxine, Dani and Hugo found their front-row seats. When Hugo turned, looking for Nell, she beckoned, and he excused himself from the team and headed over.

Forcing a smile, Nell said, 'Can I introduce you to Rav's parents, Neeta and Rakesh?'

'Yes! How lovely to meet you!' In turn, Hugo shook both of their hands warmly and then sat beside Rakesh, pointing out things on the track and sharing anecdotes about the cars.

As they chatted, Nell surreptitiously checked her phone. She'd already seen the articles about the murder and fraud, but no others featured her as the face of the crime, at least.

But her social media had blown up – prominent amongst the messages were Shannon's stylish shots, of her alongside some of this event's wealthiest car owners to attend her art gallery's upcoming opening. No doubt in the hope they'd be persuaded into buying an original piece of art – or two. Nell narrowed her eyes at Shannon, watching her weaponise her charm on her wealthy prey. Shannon could have secured similar clientele from a couple of nights out in Chelsea. She didn't really need to stay here all weekend. Nell recalled Shannon's intel-gathering at the dinner. *Is she really here for James? Does she genuinely like someone, for once?*

Interrupting her thoughts, Hugo called out to Rav, 'How do you fancy driving the Alfa in the closing parade lap?'

A huge grin spread across Rav's face. 'I would *love* to! Thank you!'

'Wow. You *must* have impressed Dad on the track!'

'Ah, action stations!' Hugo announced, and Nell turned to watch the cars line up on the grid, passengers offloaded and ready to race.

The gullwing trailed right at the back, in the position Jack had earned. Despite everything, Nell's pulse sped up. This still mattered. Some good could still come out of this weekend.

The flag dropped – and the race for the Finchmere Cup began.

Chapter 30

Nell watched as the cars jostled, surging ahead. Colin forged forward from his place at the back with immediate confident aggression. After fourteen laps, he'd pulled ahead of eleven cars with almost no effort.

'Oh my God, he's made it into the top half!' Nell whispered.

'How many cars are there?' Rav asked. 'I can't keep count!'

'Twenty,' Nell said, her eyes fixed on the track. 'And soak it up, this is a two-hundred-million-pound race you're looking at!'

Rav whistled. 'That's the combined price of the cars? Jeez . . . Oh! He's trying to overtake again!'

Colin swung out, moving to the other side of a far Jaguar. He cut in assertively at the first corner, forcing the Jaguar wide, which pushed a Ferrari out even wider. Slicing through, Colin accelerated hard out of the bend and through the chicane. He held his advantage over the Jaguar and the Ferrari, and snapped at the heels of an Aston. The Aston held the lead but Colin gained gradually, steadily. The drivers sped towards a corner, a test of nerve.

Nell waited, jittery with excitement, until the cars came around from the far side of the track and into view again. She leaned forward from the edge of her bench as the first ten classic cars thundered around the chicane of the racetrack. The front three clustered together, terrifyingly close as they pressed into the racing line around the corner.

As the next three flashed by, Nell saw the gullwing overtaking another Aston. The two drivers were side by side, the Aston benefitting from the racing line. The Aston's brake lights flickered, but Colin's didn't. Colin glided around the corner on the outside line, and still overtook the Aston.

Nell's heart hammered. 'He's in fifth place and he's got one more lap. Do you think . . . ? God, he might just *do* this!' Her voice had a note of wonder in it and Rav laughed, pulling her in tightly to his side.

They had to wait while the cars took the far side of the track, out of sight. Nell twitched, having to force herself to not rip her father's binoculars from his hands. Since her job meant she was rarely parted from her top-quality binoculars, it was beyond annoying that she didn't have them to hand.

The first three drivers tore around the final chicane. They jockeyed for position, apparently unconscious of the rarity and value of the machines they drove, fighting for first place: the Aston Martin DB4 GT Zagato sliced close to the lead Low-Drag Jaguar E-Type, cutting in with a daringly sharp overtake. The Jaguar was forced to brake and the Ferrari 250 GTO swerved sharply to miss the Aston's unexpected manoeuvre, avoiding a crash but oversteering, fishtailing, then righting itself.

'Christ! They're not playing, are they?' Rav had tensed in his seat.

The gullwing shot around the corner, swooping past the halted Ferrari, taking a tight line through the bends and overtaking the Jaguar. Finally, Colin surged forward, bearing down on the Aston as they both sped hard along the home straight.

Nell held her breath, gripping Rav's hand.

With only feet to spare, Colin inched ahead . . . And – *finally* – it was the gullwing's nose that the chequered flag fluttered over.

'*Unbelievable!*' Nell leapt to her feet along with Rav, Hugo and most of the VIP guests, as a cheer swept around the entire grandstand and roared along the side of the track.

But Nell's cry caught in her throat as she realised, probably like everyone else, that she wasn't cheering for a race won, or the gullwing's victory, or their project – but for a father honouring his son, in the best way he knew.

Approaching the team's garage, Nell froze, staring at Val's imposing Audi S8 and the two police cars. *They've come. With a team. Have they done the forensic tests?*

Her heart sped up and she reached for Rav's hand, making him pause his discussion with his family. Hugo was a step behind, with Lucio, Maxine and Dani, and their conversation also broke off. The silence after their cheerful chatter was as eerie as the silence of birds during an eclipse. But Nell knew that once she walked into the garage, there would be a confrontation. She stepped inside with rising trepidation.

James and Val stood in silent expectation. Nell did a double take at the sight of Cassie and Mark standing beside them.

Nell's heart pounded as she pressed her clammy hands against her overalls.

She jumped as an excitable *pip-pip!* of a horn broke the tension, and Colin pulled up in the gullwing with Svetlana.

'The man of the moment! Congratulations, Colin!' Maxine proclaimed. 'Get in here – I've got some champers. The good stuff.'

But the bonhomie evaporated as Maxine, Colin and Svetlana entered, like they'd walked into an atmospheric black hole.

Cassie and Mark both looked bewildered, sleep-deprived and anxious. Nell sympathised; she knew the feeling of a night in the cells. Val and James radiated professional detachment.

'You're not here to congratulate us, are you?' Maxine challenged the detectives. 'What do you want now, then?'

When they made no attempt to explain their presence, Maxine turned to Cassie and Mark. 'Nice to see you two back where you should be, though.'

Mark gave her an exhausted smile. 'Thanks.' But when Colin walked in, he reanimated. '*You* raced her! And she won!'

Colin charged over and shook Mark's hand, then Cassie's. 'Terrific work. She's tuned like a charm. *What a drive!* When the event's wrapped today, can I take her out on full power? And Mark, give me your card. I've got a little motor I'd like you and Cassie to look at converting.'

Beside Mark, Cassie gaped, then beamed. She thumped Mark's arm, her face flushed in delight.

'I'll make vlog,' Svetlana offered with an elegant shrug. 'Montage the process, the skill, the driving. Could be very cool.' She appraised Colin. 'With your profile, would be very lucrative.'

Lucio held up his phone. 'And I have inquiries! Asking if I have any motors in stock suitable for conversion!' He clapped Mark on the shoulder. 'You're going to be a busy man, Mark!'

'He's going to be a *rich* man,' Maxine said with a knowing nod.

Hugo surveyed the officers with tense interest. His eyes continually flicked towards Nell, as if monitoring her reaction, as he anticipated the detectives beginning more questions.

'Before you get into your celebrations,' Val cut in, 'may we take a moment of your time?' She continued as if she'd had a resounding 'yes!' from all concerned. 'We are here to request your permission to allow us to forensically examine your cars.'

'Our . . . *cars?*' Maxine asked.

'Yes,' James said. 'In your case, Maxine, that would be the white Lamborghini Gallardo?'

Maxine nodded, and James turned to Lucio. 'In your case, sir, it's the red Ferrari Dino?'

Lucio nodded.

Colin spoke up. 'Mine's the BMW 507, with Svetlana's Velar and Dani's Nissan Juke.' He hesitated. 'I . . . I take it this is related to Jack?'

Nell thought she detected James trying not to wince at the question, presumably not wanting that to affect everyone's cooperation.

'Yes,' he said. 'And thank you for making this as easy as possible.'

'I want answers as much as you do. Believe me,' Colin said. His quiet understatement conveyed so much dignity that the garage fell into an awkward silence.

As if hopeful that Colin's comment might have made refusal impossible, James pressed on, looking at Cassie. 'An officer is ready to inspect your VW Beetle over at Finchmere House, if you agree? You drove Mark to the dinner reception last night, I gather?'

Mark and Cassie both nodded. 'But we both walked back to the hotel afterwards.'

'And you also drove the both of you to Jack's party?'

Again, they nodded. Cassie shot Mark a pained glance.

'My car is . . . unavailable at the moment,' Mark said tensely.

Cassie shot a worried glance to the detectives, but Val nodded. 'Understood,' was all she said. Cassie frowned at Mark.

Nell noticed movement in one of the unknown cars just outside the garage. A team of four got out. Through the open door, Nell saw them pull on Tyvek suits and boots and take cases from the car boot. They stood in a row, an anonymous, homogenous army, awaiting deployment.

'Thank you for your cooperation,' Val said. 'We usually process vehicles at our labs, under controlled conditions. However, we have decided to take a preliminary look *in situ* first, in case this helps us narrow things down. But please be aware that if we need to continue the examination, we will take the car concerned back to our compound.'

The car owners all looked shocked. Although they seemed desperate to, they didn't protest.

'Car keys, please,' James said, holding out his hands.

Lucio whipped his keys from his pocket and threw them across the room. Despite the rapid fire, James's hand shot into the air and caught them reflexively. Maxine separated her key from her key ring, and thumped it belligerently into James's hand. Svetlana drew her key elegantly from her Everlane tote, as if in a handbag commercial, and Dani fumbled for hers in her pocket.

'Thank you,' James said. He walked outside and gave the keys, along with some directions, to the team.

Two officers left for Finchmere House, to locate Cassie's Beetle. The other three each approached a car to start work: one to Maxine's Gallardo, one to Dani's Nissan and one to Colin's BMW. The keys to Svetlana's Velar and Lucio's Dino were left on the wings of their respective cars, ready to be taken by whoever finished their work first. They began with photographs of the car's bodywork and tyres, then underneath the floorpan and mudguards.

James and Val stood by the doorway, like centurions.

'How long is this going to take?' Maxine raised her hands in frustration.

'It could take all afternoon, depending on what we find,' James said.

'Oh, for . . .' Maxine turned to Lucio, shaking her head in total exasperation. She huffed, standing with her hands on her hips.

'There's plenty we can do in the meantime, though,' Nell said, trying to distract the rising dissent. 'If we go back to the house, you can do your press interviews, capitalise on the interest, or even take the gullwing to East Field for the public to have a closer look.'

Colin nodded. 'Yeah, let's do that.'

Mark and Cassie nodded. Lucio looked to Maxine, trying to encourage her to join them. She seemed resistant all the time she could see someone scrutinising her car, hunkering by the side and gazing at the tyres, under the wheel arch and the floorpan.

Her eyes jerked towards James and Val, who were watching her response, and she huffed, 'Just make sure your guys don't scratch my paintwork. Costs a fortune, that pearlescent white.'

'Of course,' Val said evenly.

'Can I ask,' James stepped forward, addressing Lucio, 'if you put the gullwing out for the public to appreciate, do you think you'd get interest from customers?'

'Oh, yes,' Lucio said. 'Maybe not many for a car like that but certainly for a little classic runaround. Like a Healey or a Sprite, say. Ideal cars for your country roads on a fine spring day like today! Maybe a picnic hamper on the back. A silent engine so you can hear the birdsong. Or woo your sweetheart.' He spoke with the evocative artfulness of a born salesman.

'Yes, around here, I can imagine it's ideal,' James said. 'Leafy country roads.' He glanced at Lucio. 'Do you know them well?'

'Fairly.' Lucio nodded, tilting his hand to show he had a little knowledge.

James scanned the gathering, inviting everyone to answer. Colin, Svetlana and Dani nodded firmly, while Mark shook his head. Cassie shrugged uncertainly.

'A bit.' Maxine pursed her lips.

'You don't tend to take anyone out on these roads for test drives?' James said artlessly. 'To some of your ideal picnic spots? Like Little Smitington?'

Nell's heart thudded as she guessed where James was pushing the questioning. She studied the team.

Lucio frowned. He hesitated. 'No,' he said. 'I don't know it.'

James again scanned the company. Nell held her breath, her eyes flicking over faces for reactions. Everyone shook their heads. No one seemed to react, as far as Nell could tell. The faces were collectively growing dour, probably increasingly unamused at the investigation, questions and suggestion of guilt.

'We don't bring people out here for test drives,' Lucio said. 'We stay nearer the showroom unless it's a serious customer, and then we loan the car for a day.'

'Wow, that's remarkably trusting.' James gave a sceptical tilt of his head.

Lucio just shrugged, and although Nell knew he spoke the truth, she shared James's disappointment that his subtle line of inquiry had yielded no results.

In the lull, general attention was again seized by the activity outside the garage door. The forensic officers were brushing or scraping microscopic particles into clear sample bottles or plastic bags.

At a beep from his phone, James checked it, then added conversationally, 'That's Fraud Division. They found a burner phone inside a panel of Richard Tyler's car.'

At the name, Nell's head snapped up, meeting James's gaze as he scanned the company. Her alert eyes roved around the team hungrily, hoping for something. *Anything*. Even the smallest reaction. But still everyone was poker-faced.

James continued, 'So now we know for *certain* that Richard was working with someone on this team to make this sale. It's just a question of who.' He looked around with an amiable smile.

This time, a frisson of shock rippled through everyone at the inference of guilt being shared by one of their number. But still no guilty body language, no expression of recognition at Richard's crime. *Nothing*.

And no acknowledgement of his death, either.

Nell guessed James must be waiting for the pathology results, so he could use the information in formal questioning.

As the implications of the fraud sank in, Lucio dug his hands into his pockets, his mouth downturned. Maxine shot dour glances like arrows around the team. Mark and Cassie looked furious. 'Was our work all for nothing, then? It really was a *fake*?' Mark demanded.

'Apparently so,' Lucio said, his voice slow and heavy. He sat shakily on a stool and mopped his brow with his pocket square.

Maxine folded her arms, her lips taut.

'So, are we getting paid for that, or what?' Mark said.

'The time and parts, yes, of course,' Lucio said. 'But not the share of profit, since now—' he flourished his hands '—there is none.'

'Oh, for . . .' Mark turned away sharply. But he'd turned towards the gullwing, and as his gaze met it, his raised shoulders relaxed. He took a long, deep breath. 'Sure. You win some, you lose some, I guess.'

Another uneasy silence fell over them. Outside, one by one, the forensic officers opened the car doors, leaving the key on the driver's seat, checked the inside seals and footwells, then stood up and walked to the passenger side of the car they were working on.

'We can't do anything here, so let's leave them to it,' Colin said. 'Let's make the most of the attention our car has had today.' He headed towards the gullwing.

Svetlana nudged Dani towards the passenger seat. 'You ride, I'll walk.'

'I can give as many of you as will fit a lift in the open pickup back of the Landy,' Nell offered, walking towards the door, glancing back at the group, hoping to encourage them away from the garage so the investigation wouldn't be interrupted. She was relieved when everyone else – Lucio, Cassie, Mark, Maxine, Svetlana and Rav's folks – joined her.

As her passengers climbed into the Land Rover, and Nell walked to the driver's side, she noticed the SOCO team were compiling samples and regrouping.

A plastic evidence bag sat on top of a case, and James had wandered over to pick it up.

'Where's this from?' he asked.

'Under a wheel arch,' the SOCO officer said.

Squinting at it, Nell recognised a long green stem and indigo bloom. Her heart thumped.

If the murderer had parked at Little Smitington, there was one way to tell for sure.

Dashing over, she asked to see it.

James held his hand out to block her. 'No, Nell, this is evidence. I can't—'

'I don't want to touch it,' Nell clasped her hands behind her back, desperate to convince him. 'But can I just take a closer look? It might be significant.'

With a sigh, James held it up, close to his body, but enough for Nell to see the contents.

Through the clear plastic, the flower head was squashed, but the elongated, indigo bell's petals curled back tightly, revealing anthers – bearing creamy white pollen. There was a chance it was a hybrid – but a hybrid was unlikely to bear every single characteristic of a native bluebell. Like this one.

It was enough to make Nell gasp.

'Which car?' she demanded.

Automatically, the SOCO pointed at the car. The white Gallardo.

Gasping again, Nell turned to Maxine, whose horrified gaze flicked from Nell to James.

Following Nell's eyeline, James reached for his handcuffs, striding towards the killer.

With unexpected agility, Maxine leapt over the side of the Land Rover, landing unsteadily then bolting towards her car. The SOCO threw himself in her path and she shoved him hard enough to send him flying. Jumping into the driving seat, ignoring the key, she pressed the ignition button. The Gallardo throbbed into life with a hollow growl as Maxine stamped on the gas. The cold rear tyres squirmed on the concrete, and the car lurched forward, swerving as Maxine sped away.

Chapter 31

James's adrenaline pumped. He hadn't needed to check what Val would do, they'd both sprinted to her S8; he'd flicked on the blue lights to laser their warning from the grill, as Val had pursued.

Ahead of them, Maxine was doing the hard work of splitting the crowd. Keeping up, Val tried to force her to stop. But Maxine kept going.

Hoping to sound calm, while frantically trying to work out what road they'd emerge on, James called for backup from Pendlebury station, giving their rough location.

Through the crackling radio, Hesha confirmed she'd redeploy officers on traffic duty for the Classics at Finchmere to close the roads leading to the dual carriageway.

James braced himself with both hands as Val bumped over the last few metres of field and onto a country road, immediately accelerating around a tight bend. Maxine was well ahead, but within sight – in the rare seconds the lane was straight enough to see that far.

'Doing well to keep up with a supercar in your saloon.' James attempted humour.

Val's concentration didn't crack. 'Same engine,' she said.

James's surprise nearly made him miss bracing in time as Val took a wide curve at speed.

Over their heads, a rhythmic whoomping made James squint up through his window. He gave a shocked laugh. 'Well, we really do have backup. They've sent a chopper.'

The helicopter hovered low overhead, making the tree branches along the sides of the narrow road lurch to one side, as if the landscape was leaning into the bends like James's body. The movement made the chase feel even more dramatic as they continued. All James could do was hang on. The twisting lane seemed never-ending.

Ahead, Maxine began to turn right, onto the road leading towards the dual carriageway. The Gallardo's screech of brakes and shuddering swerve made James grin. 'Hesha's got the road blocked!'

Forced to continue, Maxine drove on, but the false turn and correction had closed the gap. Now Val was hard on Maxine's tail. When Maxine approached the next crossroads, she made an unexpected, last-minute hard right turn, losing control and fishtailing in the road before righting herself and speeding away.

James did a silent check for oncoming cars as Val followed. She wasn't as fast, but she didn't lose control, and they surged forward as she slammed the accelerator.

As they approached Little Smitington, the twists lengthened into a wide arcing bend and Val *flew*. James gripped his seat as, inch by inch, they gained on Maxine.

Without warning, Maxine violently swerved right, spraying gravel as the Gallardo made a four-wheel drift into the track leading to the visitor centre. Val missed the tight turn into the narrow track and slammed on the brakes.

'The track's a dead end!' James leapt out, leaving Val to reverse and drive in, as he sprinted ahead, flinching under the thundering helicopter and its tornado downdraught.

Ahead of him, Maxine forced the Gallardo's low suspension over the bumpy ground – slowing her progress towards the open gate. As he ran, James noted there were three civilians by the visitor entrance, beside a red, muddy Hilux and two other cars.

In his bobbing vision, James recognised Mai but not the two men with her. They were shaking hands, very businesslike. Until Mai and the man with blond wavy hair high-fived.

The potential of a hostage situation flashed through James's mind. *Who knows what Maxine would do, in desperation.* He forced his legs to sprint like pistons, propelling himself up the uneven lane towards them.

As Maxine reached the gate, the three people looked up. Their faces, first happy, then curious, dropped into dismay as the car forced its way through the narrow gate towards them, then veered off towards the grassland, as purposeful and unstoppable as a tank.

The blond man leapt forward, his arms outstretched towards the car. 'No!' he shouted. 'No *way*, man! Not again!'

He ran like a berserker into battle, impervious to the danger. He held his hands up with such forceful belief, as if they were a superhero shield, that he didn't baulk from running straight into the path of the car, staring the driver down.

Maxine swerved and her car landed in a pothole with a crunch. The man looked momentarily euphoric to have stopped the car, then stared skywards at the low helicopter, his mouth dropping open.

Hearing Val's car behind him, James continued running along the side of the road, slowing to a jog as he approached the Gallardo. But Maxine rolled out of the low car, kicked her heels off, hitched up her dress and dashed across the grass.

What the . . . ? James dug deep for another burst of speed. But then the car drew alongside him, and he did a double take. Not Val. But a van. With *Dog Unit* emblazoned on the side. He laughed and slowed to a jog, then a walk. *These guys will beat me any day.* He paused, hands on his hips as he watched the scene unfold.

Still running, Maxine was ungainly but unexpectedly fast, and had already reached the far corner of the field. The wavy-haired man watched her, equally astonished.

As James's breathing steadied, he smiled as the vehicle doors opened. To a single command, the German shepherd dog leapt from the back of the van, sniffed the air and shot up the track.

James was close enough to see Mai's reaction as the dog barrelled towards her. She yelped and hit the deck.

The dog sped past Mai, across the field, out of sight. Moments later, a terrified wail echoed across the meadow.

The wavy-haired man helped Mai to her feet and pulled her into a tight hug.

James's stride picked up pace as he fell into step with the dog handler. When he climbed over the stile in the corner of the field, a terrified Maxine was standing, stock-still, in front of the growling dog. Her slightest move elicited the dog's low snarl through bared teeth, making Maxine recoil, whimpering.

As James made the arrest, the handler gave the dog a treat. 'Good dog, Hercules! You gorgeous little poppet.'

Maxine side-eyed the handler, but James pushed Maxine ahead of them, with Hercules walking to heel. The handler secured Hercules in the police vehicle and drove off with a cheery wave, passing Hesha and Ed on their way in.

Steering Maxine over to them, James said, 'Thanks, Hesha. That roadblock was fast work. Just what we needed. Can you put Maxine in a cell at the station. And get her car towed to the lab for the full forensic treatment? Val and I will be along shortly.'

With a smart salute, Hesha took Maxine away as Ed made a call.

Aware of the peace, now that the helicopter had left and the team had departed, James took a deep breath. *Bloody hell, that was close.* He wafted his sweaty shirt, drained now that his adrenaline was fading.

From the bottom of the lane, Val had watched the action, leaning against the car. As he reached her, she arched an eyebrow. 'Let me guess. We need a statement from Nell?'

Monday 22nd April – 12.30 p.m.

'For God's sake, how can we go off and pretend that everything's OK now?' Mark ranted at Nell.

But Nell remembered how much Mark and Cassie had riding on this new venture, even if they'd been horribly blindsided by these revelations. She'd corralled him and Cassie into the Land Rover's cab, despite his protests.

Cassie had been too shell-shocked to resist Nell's insistence, 'because you *still* have a business to build. And you don't deserve to miss out.' She glanced at Cassie. 'We can't do anything about Maxine, but you *can* make the most of the car's success for your venture.' Having a few interested parties was a great start, but it would take more than that to get them off the ground.

With Rav, Aanya and their parents, along with Svetlana and Hugo in the pickup back of the Landy, Nell followed Colin driving in the gullwing with Dani, to its arranged stand on the East Field.

Despite trying to be practical, Nell's curiosity about Maxine was off the charts. She'd *ached* to jump in a car and be part of the chase, see what happened, hear Maxine's explanation . . .

But Cassie's sudden eruption interrupted her thoughts. 'I don't get it – she was so keen to put me and all those other offenders on the straight and narrow. Yet she . . . she *killed* someone?'

'Was she behind the fraud, do you reckon?' Mark asked.

Nell gave a tight nod. *She had to be, didn't she?* And if Richard was involved, that must be why she killed him, too. Nell swallowed. The team didn't even know about that. Yet. *Was Rav right – had Maxine killed Jack because he'd uncovered the fraud and was blackmailing her? Or were they working together, and she couldn't risk him ratting them out?*

'What am I going to do now?' Cassie's voice contracted as she shot a worried look at Mark. 'Am I part of your business, Mark?'

'You what?' He turned to her, gaping, as if her uncertainty had shocked him back into action. 'Too right. Where am I going to find someone with your experience?'

'Oh my God!' Cassie beamed at him. 'Well . . . when do we start?'

'If Colin's serious about his conversion, I don't want to give him time to reconsider. So how's tomorrow?'

'Bloody hell!' Cassie exaggerated her eye-roll. 'Not even a day off. What the heck am I getting into?'

As Mark grinned back, they fell silent, registering the crowd gathered around the sign – and the empty stand – for the gullwing. At the sight of the approaching car, the crowd began to clap and cheer.

'Blimey . . .' Mark stared, lost for words.

'You'd better get out there and meet your admirers.' Nell shoved them out of the cab, then went to the back of the Landy to help the other passengers down.

While Mark and Cassie collected orders for conversions and handed out business cards, Neeta and Rakesh drew Nell to one side, with Aanya. They looked worried.

'So it was that woman? Who murdered Jack?' Neeta said. Her

eyes slid towards Aanya then back to Nell. 'Is it over? Aanya isn't going to be questioned?'

Nell nodded. 'Yes, it was Maxine.' Nell let out a long exhalation. 'And yes, I think it's over in terms of questioning.'

'But Aanya may have to give evidence at a trial?' Neeta asked.

Rakesh groaned. 'And that will have the press all over it, won't it? Murder trial of a racing driver?'

'Yes, probably,' Nell said. 'But it'll be several months from now. And the witnesses they call, and what they ask them, will depend on how Maxine pleads. And it would be pointless for her to plead not guilty when she tried to escape, wouldn't it?'

'True,' Neeta said. But she didn't look very reassured.

'More to the point,' Nell added, 'I don't think Jack's affairs had anything to do with Maxine's motive.'

Neeta nodded, glancing up as Hugo approached.

'I know this probably isn't the most auspicious timing,' Hugo said, 'but I have to ask. Nell, your mother wondered if our two families would like to have lunch together?' He smiled at Rav's parents. 'She said how much she was looking forward to meeting you.'

'Lunch?' Cassie overheard, interrupting and gatecrashing with one word. 'God, yes, I could go for some lunch. I've barely eaten in the past couple of days, I've been so on edge.' She looked at Nell hopefully.

'Cassie, you can't abandon your potential customers,' Nell reasoned.

'Of course not. But once we've spoken to this lot, it will thin out over lunch. We can come straight back afterwards.'

With an embarrassed laugh, Nell looked at Neeta. 'Well, what—?'

'I don't know about lunch,' Aanya interrupted, 'but I *do* want to know how *you* knew it was Maxine.'

'Yeah!' Cassie frowned, then brightened. 'Tell us all over lunch, then *everyone'll* be happy!'

Nell glanced at Rav as the private family event ran away from them. He shrugged and grinned, and his family mirrored the friendly gesture.

Nudging her, Rav teased, 'I hope you've got all the info sewn up. Looks like they expect you to have all the answers!'

Nell glanced at the gathering, but Rav nodded at something behind her. 'And they're not alone.' Nell turned – and faced James and Val.

Chapter 32

Monday 22nd April – 1 p.m.

After she'd given her statement, Nell, along with James and Val, stepped outside into the bright sun. The team around the large table on the terrace were sharing a picnic, chatting, and even laughing. The cloud of guilt and worry and uncertainty had been lifted. With the suspicion of murder no longer hanging over their heads, the indelible stain of a fraud accusation expunged and the resounding success of the gullwing's performance, they all felt more optimistic. The buzz was contagious, and Rav's parents nattered animatedly with Hugo and Imelda.

Shannon had inveigled her way in, sitting between Lucio and Colin. To be fair, both men needed a great deal of cheering up, and she was managing an entertaining stream of chatter single-handedly. She glanced up at James. 'Hello, stranger.' But she didn't move, even though her smile held more than a hint of delight.

So James sat with Val, and instantly platters of sandwiches, dainty quail Scotch eggs, individual quiches, salads and miniature pies were passed towards them.

As Nell sat down, her phone buzzed. She checked the text, then showed it to Rav.

Mai: Delighted to announce that Little Smitington Nature Reserve is now an SSSI!

Nell raced Mai's typing bubbles with, CONGRATULATIONS!

Mai: Thanks for all your help. You've all been amazing! We need to CELEBRATE!

'Too right,' Rav said. 'Shall we see if they want to go for drinks later?'

Nell shot him a sidelong smile. 'I have a feeling they'll be celebrating just the two of them tonight.'

'No way? Really?' Rav looked sceptical.

'Yes, way.' Nell arched an ironic eyebrow.

'Hey, Nell?' Aanya called out from across the table. 'You were going to explain things. We've been waiting patiently.'

Nell glanced up as Val and James both shrugged. 'Go on,' James said.

Shannon sat back, folding her arms with a flicker of amusement.

'Right.' Taking a deep breath, Nell wondered where to start. 'I guess the first main insight about how Jack was killed came out when James said they needed a forensic botanist. They needed to compare samples from Jack against samples in the water where he was drowned.' Nell looked at Colin warily, hoping she could gloss over his son's autopsy with some delicacy.

But Colin remained stoic. 'Comparing the water in his lungs with the pond water?'

'Not just the water in the lungs.' James assumed too much interest. 'When you drown, small particles get into your bloodstream and are carried to your organs. The kidney, liver, brain, bone marrow.'

Colin winced, but nodded.

James took that as a cue to continue. 'The pathologist makes slides of those tissues and then the forensic botanist looks for phytoplankton, or microscopic algae. Diatoms are best because they're encased in silicon, so they can withstand the processing procedure.' He nodded towards Nell. 'Nell had the right expertise to ID the diatoms, so we drafted her in.'

When Colin looked at Nell expectantly, she explained, 'Jack's samples and the samples from Little Smitington Pond didn't match. In fact, they were *so* different, they indicated totally different types of waterbodies. I knew from Mai's surveys that Little Smitington Pond was pristine. But according to the species in Jack's tissue, he'd been drowned in water with much lower ecological value, and much higher nutrients. Like a fish pond.'

Nell turned to Svetlana. 'When I read your interview in *Vogue*,

I saw your photos taken at home, on a bridge, over a pond. And I saw you had some huge, very fancy koi carp.'

Svetlana's mouth dropped open. 'Someone drowned him there? After I left?' She shuddered. 'If I had stayed, maybe I would have heard . . . or stopped it . . .' Her face was uncharacteristically mournful before hardening again.

Colin stared at his plate.

The deep, reflective silence was broken when Svetlana shrugged. 'There is something in his beloved fish showing what really happened to him. He spent a fortune on them. Had to have the best.' Her brow crinkled briefly. 'A specialist supplied his beloved Yamato Nishiki.'

Cassie looked up, startled, then laughed self-consciously. 'Oh, I thought you said Jack had a Yam*aha Niken*.' Her face froze. 'Oh.' She stared at James as she recalled where she had made that mistake before and the statement she'd made. 'I thought he was going to show me a motorbike at the party. But he was talking about fish?' She looked confounded. 'Why the hell would he think I would want to see *fish?*'

Svetlana gave a small laugh. 'He expect everyone to find them captivating. Calming. Good for . . .' she wrinkled her nose '. . . *well-being*.' She shrugged. 'And, in the end, they told truth of his death, no?'

'So, let's get this straight,' Dani said, turning to Svetlana. 'After everyone left the party, you punched Jack and left him – what, stunned? Unconscious? – in the drive. Maxine came back, saw that you'd gone and found Jack in the garden, perhaps a bit out of it. She drowned him in the pond and then – what? – drove him to Little Smitington to fake the crash and the drowning?'

All eyes swung to Nell.

'Yes,' Nell said. 'But Maxine would only have seen that Svetlana had gone. She didn't know if she'd return. She had to make it look like an accident.' Nell glanced at Svetlana. 'Your magazine photos showed that your pond is fenced, so it would have been hard to make drowning look accidental there. Maxine might have seen Little Smitington Pond from the road on her way to Finchmere. And she'd want to get herself and her car away from your house.'

'The brake line was only scored,' James said. 'So I think she was trying to give the impression that Jack could have driven the car while gradually losing the ability to brake, justifying why he lost control at the corner and smashed through the fence, across the field and into the pond.'

Svetlana frowned. 'So you think she put Jack in the Mustang, to hide him? His keys would have been in his pocket, easy to find. Then she moved *her* car and came back to collect the Mustang?' She shrugged. 'Clever plan. If I had come home, I wouldn't have checked car. I would not have been bothered if I heard the Mustang driving off. I would just think Jack was going to hotel.' Her glance started to move towards Aanya, but she pursed her lips and gave a one-shouldered shrug.

Nodding, Nell added, 'When Maxine got the Mustang to the edge of the pond, she moved Jack to the driver's seat, scored the brake line—'

'And tampered with the handbrake,' James added.

'And pushed the car into the pond,' Nell concluded.

After a silent pause, Dani whispered, 'Jesus.'

Lucio frowned at Val. 'How does this link up with the fraud, though? Were Maxine and Richard in . . .' he searched for the word '. . . *cahoots?*'

'Yes,' Val confirmed. 'Maxine and Richard falsified the provenance of a few cars.' She paused, then answered the question Lucio had really wanted to ask. 'Fraud Division seem satisfied that the criminal behaviour was limited to just the two of them, so you're no longer under investigation.' She gave the older man a kind smile. 'You'll be invited to talk to those officers in due course because there will be business ramifications. But they'll advise you.'

Lucio nodded. 'I understand. Thank you.'

With a nod at Mark and Cassie, James said, 'Maxine and Richard had a knack of very occasionally finding a car with the right bodywork or chassis to, let's say, creatively engineer it into becoming a more interesting, more lucrative example. I bet, if you put your heads together, you'll see what parts she needed you to tool that might have made the difference.'

Mark and Cassie shot each other, then James, uneasy looks.

'No need to worry,' James said. 'Fraud say they're satisfied you were in the dark. The messages on Richard's burner phone make it clear it was only him and Maxine involved.'

With heavy, relieved sighs, Cassie and Mark sat back.

'But what had this to do with Jack's murder?' Lucio asked.

'Well, it's supposition,' James admitted, 'but we know that Jack was good at finding out things that people tried to hide . . .'

Mark grunted and folded his arms.

'And we know that he'd already set up one opportunity to blackmail Maxine from the unsent emails on his computer. The fact that he'd shelved those suggested he'd found a much more profitable way to blackmail her.'

Nell knew that the technical forensic team would be scouring Jack's computer. And Maxine may even confirm the theory, if she felt so inclined. She shot a covert glance at Cassie, and wondered.

'Jack *knew* of the fraud?' Lucio's eyes flashed. 'And he didn't *say?*' He stared at Colin. 'Your boy was like family to me. And the opportunities we gave him . . .'

Colin gave an unhappy sigh. 'I'm sorry, Lucio. I . . .' he ran a hand through his hair. 'I don't know where I went wrong with him. I'm—'

'Not to blame,' Svetlana cut in sharply. 'He is . . . was . . . an adult. You gave him good start in life. He was lucky. Luckier than most. You can only do that. It is up to him what he makes of it.'

But Colin stared miserably at the table, deafened by distress.

'Hang on.' Dani leaned forward. 'Where did Maxine move her own car to, if she drove Jack in his?' She shot Svetlana a glance. The two women shuddered again.

As James folded his arms and smiled at Nell, Shannon's eyes narrowed.

Nell looked at Dani. 'That's exactly what I wondered. So I drove the route to look for lay-bys or somewhere she could pull over—'

'You . . . *drove the route?*' Dani gave a short laugh. 'Like an undercover cop?'

Nell couldn't help laughing. It did sound absurd. 'Well, I did! And I realised the only place she could park off the road was down the track to Little Smitington Visitor Centre.' Nell glanced at James and Val, unsure of how to describe the next step.

'So, Nell asked us to forensically examine the cars,' James said. His sandwich was too dainty to bite, so he ate it in one and nodded at Nell to continue.

'Little Smitington has several rare species,' she said. 'So it's likely anyone parking there would have seeds or particles of plants on the car. In the tyre treads, for example—'

'Ah.' Mark raised his hand at his lightbulb moment. 'So *that* was what all those odd questions about test drives and visiting Little Smitington were all about?'

James nodded. 'And with everyone saying they hadn't been there, we knew that as soon as we'd found something unique to the site, we'd have our murderer.'

Cassie turned to Nell, squinting. 'So, did you just assume, then? When the forensic officer put that . . . whatever it was . . . in the bag. That any old thing would convict her? What if you're wrong? What if that was something from here?' She wrinkled her nose, unconvinced.

Nell shook her head. 'It wasn't a guess. I saw exactly what it was. It was a bluebell.'

'A bluebell?' Cassie scoffed. 'But they're everywhere—'

'No,' Nell said. 'Around here, it's mostly Spanish bluebells or hybrids. But Mai had eliminated those from her woodland. At Little Smitington, it's only native bluebells. And that's what the forensic officer found on Maxine's car.'

'And, even if that was a long shot,' James looked at Cassie, 'Maxine obviously knew something *could* incriminate her. Innocent people don't tend to do a runner.'

Cassie shuffled lower in her seat, picking her fingers, reliving her disappointment in her mentor. But Shannon was looking at James with something approaching respect. And intrigue.

'And,' James added, 'we've got more forensic samples that the officer managed to extract *before* Maxine fled back there today. So that will add to the evidence against her.'

But Nell heard a tightness in his tone, and knew that he was worried about a prosecution. The samples had been taken mercifully quickly – essential, as it turned out – but not under lab conditions. Maxine could plead contamination . . .

A buzz interrupted her thoughts, and James reached for his phone. His furrowed brow smoothed. He blinked, shook his head and reread the message.

'Well, this is . . . this is *great*.' He glanced at Val. 'Hesha's got a full confession from Maxine.' He gave a short, relieved laugh. 'Not only for killing Jack, but Richard Tyler, too.'

As shock rippled around the table, Lucio gasped. 'She . . . *what?*'

'She's stated that you weren't involved in the murders or the fraud, Lucio. Or any of you.' James glanced around the company and smiled at Neeta. 'So a long court case is unlikely.'

Cassie clamped her lips together, and Neeta and Rakesh took a moment to absorb the news, then pulled Aanya in to a relieved, thankful hug.

As the racing team and Colin returned to the gullwing stand, and Val returned to the office, Shannon leaned back languidly. 'Well, James. Case closed. What are you going to *investigate* now?'

'Oh, I don't know.' He shot her sidelong smile. 'I'd heard something about some gallery opening . . . ?'

'Don't even *try* it. Entry requirement's a liquid eight figures.' Nell noticed Shannon's words lacked any sting, a half-smile tugging at her lips over her glass of sparkling wine.

'Just as well. What's the likelihood I'd be free anyway?' James asked amiably. 'I'd only have to stand you up for a hot date with a cold corpse.'

Chapter 33

Monday 22nd April – 4.30 p.m.

Rav stretched in the borrowed race suit. It was a little tight around his shoulders and chest, a little baggy around his waist.

'Can you move your arms?' Hugo asked. 'That's the main thing.'

Rav nodded, extending his limbs to try to get more comfortable. His face shone with a wide, excited beam. The cars around him revved their engines, filling the air with the evocative scent of racing.

'Good luck, Rav!' Imelda cried above the roar. She leaned over and kissed his cheek, squeezing his arm affectionately.

'Drive like the wind!' Rakesh said, in a rare moment of impetuousness. 'Make us proud, son!' He clapped Rav heavily on the arm and stepped back so Neeta could hug him.

'Just be careful. Don't show off!' she said, cupping his face with both hands.

'He can't help showing off!' Aanya protested. 'And anyway, everything Number One Son does is the Best Thing Ever, according to you!'

Rav pushed Aanya and turned to Nell.

Nell grinned at him. 'Hey, racer! Have fun out there!' He pulled her close and kissed her until Aanya made vomit noises. 'I'll watch from the stand, by the home straight, so I can see your glorious run home.'

Rav grinned and nodded, then shook his head solemnly when Hugo qualified, 'It's *not* a race. This is the glorious parade lap to close the event. Just go steady, no overtaking, watch out for those flag signals we talked about just in case something's up ahead to look out for. And, above all, *enjoy* it!'

Nell watched as Rav pulled his racing helmet on, got in the car and started the engine. As their families took their seats, Nell hesitated.

The cars revved. Rav revved the Alfa and she could imagine his huge grin.

'This is so nice of you to do for Rav,' Nell heard Neeta say to Hugo as they walked to the stand.

The starting flag dropped. Rav roared away, keeping good pace with the other cars as they fell into their prearranged line. As Rav disappeared from view, Nell joined the others in the front row of the grandstand.

'He's made a terrific start,' Hugo said approvingly. 'Brisk pace, he's listening to the engine. You can see that he understands the track rules. Very good.'

'It's *so* cool to see him driving on the track!' Aanya said to Nell. 'But don't tell him I said so!'

The Alfa sped around the chicane, losing a little speed next to the professional racers, but the drivers behind him dropped back, showing they were giving him space for braking and nosing the car carefully around the tight bends.

'And they're being very good to him, leaving him room,' Hugo commentated from behind his binoculars. 'But the speed he's lost has divided the group a bit. Ten cars ahead of him, big gap, then him and twelve behind him. Be nice if he can close that gap and make the line-up of cars more continuous, but no big deal.'

Neeta tapped Nell's shoulder and she turned. 'It was interesting hearing how you assessed that case. Rakesh said you have the analytical mind of a researcher.'

'Oh.' Nell blushed slightly, unsure of how to respond. She was spared having to when Neeta continued.

'But you didn't mention to them that you'd been chased, nearly forced off the road.'

'Oh! Yes!' Nell said. 'Of course! That would have been Maxine. And *she* must have thought we'd worked out it was her.' Nell thought, then nodded. 'Yes, Aanya wouldn't say who she thought had killed Jack. She only said that she knew who it was and wanted to go. Maxine couldn't have known that Aanya believed it was Mark at that point.'

Neeta tutted. 'All that grief, all that . . . *danger*. And it was for nothing.'

Nell winced as the image of her ruined car burned in her mind.

'Aanya wasn't to know,' she said. 'And Rav and I took her seriously. She was scared and needed to get to the police, and that was that.'

Neeta's eyes glistened. 'You've been very kind to her. And . . . I think you and Rav make a very nice couple.'

Nell blushed again, more vividly, as Neeta gave her a warm hug.

'Oh, he's handled the wide corner very nicely,' Hugo commentated. 'Here.' He passed the binoculars to Nell.

She looked at the magnified view of Rav cutting a tight curve around the track. 'Nice lines!'

She passed the binoculars to Neeta.

Neeta took them with a fond smile. 'Thank you, *Beta*.'

In response to her mother's endearment, Aanya widened her eyes comically at Nell. Nell felt a happy glow kindle at Neeta's sweet gesture, and at Aanya's humour.

The binoculars were passed back to Hugo. 'Uh-oh, what have we here?'

Nell's head snapped round to him. Her skin prickled. With the cars too far away to see clearly, she stared at her father. 'What?'

'It's OK, just one of the lead Lotus Cortinas has had a blowout.'

'Right . . .' Nell felt a rush of relief that it was an experienced driver, not Rav who had the incident to contend with.

'Oh, bloody hell . . .' Hugo muttered, adjusting the focus. 'He just spun out and hit a Mini.'

Neeta and Rakesh craned to see, in vain, then turned worried eyes to Hugo.

'What's going on, Dad?' Nell asked. Her voice sounded oddly detached and calm.

'The marshal's got the flag going, warning the cars coming around the bend, but there's a knot of four, no, five cars now who've collided, taking up half the track. The others are following the flag's warning and keeping wide as they go around the bend.'

Oh God. Nell thought about Rav trying to catch up and the neat, tight lines he was keeping. She stood up and pressed herself forward against the low hoarding of the grandstand, as if trying to reach him.

'Oh God . . .' Hugo's words echoed Nell's thoughts.

She tore the binoculars from him and held them in front of her eyes. In her desperation to see, the view swooped wildly over the landscape before she located Rav's car. He approached the marshal, but he wasn't slowing.

Oh no, he's focusing on the line and catching up. He hasn't seen the flag . . . Nell's stomach knotted.

Rav entered the bend at high speed and kept a tight line. As he rounded the corner, he was already accelerating in anticipation of the track straightening out. Nell knew he would have seen the tangle of cars like a sudden, unexpected wall of metal before him. He braked too hard and swerved left, making the back of his car swing out. He skidded sideways, miraculously missing the cars. But his front wheel hit some debris on the track from the crash. It launched Rav's car into the air and flipped it over.

Nell gasped.

Rav's car crunched as it landed on the roof, continued rolling, bouncing off the tyres, the roof, the tyres again and finally landing heavily on the roof, spinning to a stop as his momentum died. Smoke billowed from the engine.

Everything was still.

Nell scrambled out of the bandstand, clambering over the frontage. Her heart hammered as she dashed down the grass bank and into the paddock, making a car driving slowly to its garage swerve out of her way. She screamed at the milling, oblivious crowds to get out of her way, shoving them with outstretched hands.

'Move. *MOVE!*'

As she barrelled towards the marshal's section, she waved her arms at one of the officials, signalling to a parked safety car.

The official understood and jogged over, getting in the driver's side while Nell got in the passenger seat.

The car took an achingly long time to get to the other side of the track. Nell's eyes fixed on the far scene, on Rav, and didn't move from him. She couldn't speak. She felt *sick.*

As they approached, she saw a safety car had stopped the race. Someone stood nearby with a fire extinguisher and an ambulance. A fire engine had parked beside the tangled cars. Drivers stood beside the wreckage. Nell scanned the group of racers, her heart in her mouth.

He wasn't there.

As her safety car stopped, Nell dashed out towards the battered, upside-down Alfa. Liquid puddled around the crumpled bonnet; unrecognisable bodywork peeled away from the chassis.

Nell threw herself on the ground at Rav's door. He was upside down, pinned to his seat by his safety harness.

His frantic eyes met hers through the window. He murmured something Nell couldn't make out. She pulled at the handle of the concertinaed door with all her strength until someone grabbed her upper arms and dragged her back and away while she kicked out.

A voice said firmly, 'Come on, let the crew get in there and help him. Keep back.'

But keeping back was torture. Nell fought her instincts to help as the firefighters moved assertively around the car. Two quickly jimmied the windows open and looped a fire hose through and across the car's bodywork, while two others knelt beside the driver's door, a backboard on the ground beside them.

The firefighter nearest Rav fitted him with a neck brace, then yelled something to the two officers holding the hose. As they pulled on the ends, the car lifted, as if taking a life-giving breath. The firefighter beside Rav slid the backboard in through the window and kept shouting instructions.

Nell couldn't see what the two officers beside the car were doing, and agonised as she saw the officers slacken the hose. Rav was eased out, face down on the board.

A paramedic ran forward with a gurney and helped the two firefighters carefully turn Rav face up on the board, then lift him onto the gurney, then gingerly remove his helmet.

Nell ran to him. A punch of nauseous dread hit her in the stomach. Rav's face was washed out, his skin sheened with sweat as if feverish, his eyes rolling, unfocused. She took his hand.

Hugo was suddenly beside Nell, with Neeta, Rakesh and Aanya. Neeta reached for Rav's other hand with a cry of anguish.

'You can't feel your legs, is that right?' the paramedic said.

'Ugghr,' Rav moaned.

Neeta's other hand flew up, covering her mouth. Her body shook.

'That's OK, just lie still,' the paramedic instructed. She looked around, her gaze settling on Neeta. 'Are you next of kin?'

Neeta nodded, still unable to speak.

'We're taking him to Pendlebury hospital. You can ride with us if you want.'

Neeta and Rakesh nodded and hurried alongside Rav as he was wheeled to the ambulance. Nell stumbled beside them. His trolley was pushed inside and his parents climbed in.

The paramedics sat near Rav's head, starting their checks. Turning to the door, Neeta reached out her hand. Nell raised her hand to take Neeta's, beginning to step inside.

'No!' Neeta pushed her back. 'You've done enough.' Her eyes brimmed with tears of heartache. She reached past Nell to help Aanya in.

The door slammed in Nell's face.

As the siren wailed, Rav was ripped away from her on a tide of blue lights.

Acknowledgements

The more I work with the incredible team at Embla books, the more impressed I am with their talents and creativity: Jen Porter, Jane Snelgrove, Emilie Marneur, Anna Perkins, Paris Ferguson and Cara Chimirri – thank you for pouring so much love and dedication into this book to make it the best it can be. I'm so lucky to work with the most tremendous agent in the universe, Katie Fulford, and the lovely Sarah McDonnell, at Bell Lomax Moreton. And I have to thank Hannah Smith, who's now moved to Penguin Michael Joseph Books, for your belief and enthusiasm for the series in the first place.

It's always a joy to work with Emily Thomas – thank you for your kind, constructive critique and your editorial flair for polishing up a manuscript. I'm immensely grateful to the care and attention of the brilliant (and educational) Helena Newton, and for the eagle eyes of Jenny Page and Robin Seavill. And huge thanks to Laura Marlow and her fantastic team for the audiobook magic – brought alive by the amazing acting talents of Kristen Atherton – and Lisa Horton for such adorable and characterful cover art.

Since I've dedicated this book to my formidable Aunty Glad, I can't help thinking how much she would appreciate this powerhouse partnership of amazing women – and how pleased she'd be to see these opportunities even existing. She, along with my parents, championed education as a key to opportunities, and I don't think they were wrong: without their instilling that education was a gift to be valued, their encouragement, and the general expectation that I'd just get on with it (that Aunty Glad exuded, like a no-nonsense Wodehouse matriarch), I wouldn't have taken the path that led me to the challenge of a research PhD, a career in ecology, and now writing. And all seasoned with the competitive edge of Aunty Glad telling me how marvellously her great-nephew was doing at his private school. Well played, Aunty Glad, well played! ☺

I'm also grateful to the ever-informative Graham Bartlett for advice on the police procedural aspects, especially the transition of Nell from outside amateur to forensic scientist in this book – with the disclaimer than any good bits are down to him, but I'll take the credit for any mistakes. I love his approach to always find a feasible solution! And his response, when I asked his advice on how the breakdown of a working relationship between detectives would be handled, has stayed with me: 'We have to resolve things – we can't let the victim's family down.'

I owe a debt of thanks to my ecology colleagues: the insights I learned from Professor Jeremy Biggs, Penny Williams, Dr Pascale Nicolet, Gill Fox and the late Mericia Whitfield during my research with the Freshwater Habitats Trust are at the core of this book. And I'm also grateful to the hundreds of ecologists I've worked with since, to remediate environmental impacts and survey and translocate species. Your anecdotes and shared adventures are greatly treasured.

Sabrina has particular thanks for her botanical expertise, and also for sharing these books with her mum. No kinder words have been spoken than when I told her that Book 2 was out and she replied, 'Ooh! I'll warn my mother!' They, and my other friends on both sides of the pond, have a special place in my heart. Since we're upping our cocktail game this year, I'll be relying on Brenda, Julie, Alan, Bruce and Bob more than ever during any writing breaks (adding Velvet Falernum to our cabinet – for the name alone!) And hoping to share a few more cocktails with Jo, Rachel, Esther, Mark, Matt (and Lauren, in a few years' time!) and more brunches with Erin and Nigel.

Dad, I knew I had to write a book about cars to get you to read it! But I must be fair, you have read all three so far, and that is a high honour, especially when I benefit from your brilliant eagle eye for tpyos. ☺ This book is an affectionate homage to our many days at car shows and festivals, and all the fun and great memories we've shared – and that Mum has generously tolerated, typically with a good book in hand! Thanks, Mum, for reading and critiquing, and never being short of an opinion. ☺ Your input is so valued, and means more than you know.

My scrumptious husband, Ian – thank you for reading, plotting, devising and enacting the key moments and enjoying a good Murder Brunch. I feel so lucky to share this with you! ☺

And for those who have taken the time to read – thank you, and I sincerely hope you enjoy reading this as much as I've enjoyed writing it.

The Nature of Crime

One of the most fascinating things about murderous research and the forensic techniques used in detection is the new appreciation and applications I discover for ecological work.

My PhD research, with the phenomenal team at the Freshwater Habitats Trust, showed me the conservation value of our unseen – and usually unsung – aquatic heroes: phytoplankton and zooplankton. The abundance and diversity of these microscopic plants and animals at the base of the food chain indicate the whole ecosystem's overall health. And, because the species present in any waterbody will vary according to physico-chemical conditions, the microinvertebrate population can reveal stresses in the environment – from the effects of pollution events, to how far, and how detrimental, the reach of everyday land use impacts are on habitats across the wider landscape.

Understanding those types of impacts and remediating them, as well as translocating populations of various species, became a key part of my work as a consultant. And, as for Nell and Mai in this book, this very often involved a great crested newt, or several!

By pure chance, one of the places I happened to help one great crested newt translocation was the Police College, Bramshill, the principal police training establishment of England and Wales until 2015. And, talking of bygone days, since great crested newts can be identified by their distinctive orange and black belly patterns, some studies actually photocopied poor little (live) newts' stomachs! Fortunately, these days we both know better and can take photos a little more easily.

While ecologists surveying newts need a licence, I'd hope that wouldn't deter childhood explorations. One tip – as amphibians are cutaneous respirators and breathe through their skin, they're sensitive to salt on human hands, so wetting hands or wearing gloves ensures any discovered newts, frogs or toads aren't harmed. I have gone to some lengths for great crested newts, including coming home in such a muddy state after trapping some out of ditches in the path of a pipeline, during a week of torrential rain (of course), that I had to be hosed down in the driveway before I could go inside the house.

The ancient woodland indicator species, the native bluebell, revealed more in this book than just the age of Little Smitington wood. With natives being out-competed and hybridised by the Spanish bluebell, it can be challenging to find areas where only the native species prevails. But the bluebell wood is an iconic spring sight, and often features in citizen science projects – when anyone can add their ecological records to a database – such as naturescalendar. woodlandtrust.org.uk. Such projects are a fun, rewarding and easy way for novices and professionals alike to contribute to valuable environmental research.

I knew all these ecological aspects would play a part in *A Mischief of Rats*. So it was a joy to discover the importance of a particular group of phytoplankton – diatoms – in forensic science.

As outlined in this book, the presence of diatoms in dead bodies is used as a positive confirmation of the death occurring in the water, as opposed to the deceased being moved there post-mortem. But that confirmation was not, as I had initially imagined, merely by finding diatoms in the victim's lungs. Instead, it is the presence of these microscopic plants in bone marrow and tissue such as liver, spleen, kidney, heart and brain that are the diagnostic features of death by drowning, as dying breaths draw the diatoms into the bloodstream, and then the organs.

The microscopic size of diatoms, which enables them to penetrate those organs, isn't the only way diatoms assist an investigation; it's their resilience, too. The process of obtaining tissue samples would dissolve most organic matter. But the siliceous frustules – glasslike shells – the diatoms are enclosed with, make them uniquely tough enough to withstand the preparation processes.

And those resilient shells are also what make diatoms so startlingly beautiful. A Google Images search of diatoms is well worth a quick look.

These kaleidoscopic jewels lurk unassumingly in our ponds and lakes – with their exceptional capabilities to enable ecologists to establish conservation practices, and to allow detectives to solve crimes. A reminder in ecology, as well as law, to always look below the surface, and to not underestimate the apparently nondescript.

Dr Nell Ward returns for her next adventure in

A Generation of Vipers . . .

Coming Summer 2023

About the Author

After spending sixteen years as an ecologist, crawling through undergrowth and studying the nocturnal habits of animals (and people), Dr Sarah Yarwood-Lovett naturally turned her mind to murder. She may have swapped badgers for bears when she emigrated from a quaint village in the South Downs to the wild mountains of the Pacific Northwest, but her books remain firmly rooted in the rolling downland she grew up in.

Forensically studying clues for animal activity has seen Sarah surveying sites all over the UK and around the world. She's rediscovered a British species thought to be extinct during her PhD, with her record held in London's Natural History Museum; debated that important question – do bats wee on their faces? – at school workshops; survived a hurricane on a coral atoll while scuba-diving to conduct marine surveys; and given evidence as an expert witness.

Along the way, she's discovered a noose in an abandoned warehouse and had a survey derailed by the bomb squad. Her unusual career has provided the perfect inspiration for a series of murder mysteries with an ecological twist – so, these days, Sarah's research includes consulting detectives, lawyers, judges and attending murder trials.

About Embla Books

Embla Books is a digital-first publisher of standout commercial adult fiction. Passionate about storytelling, the team at Embla publish books that will make you 'laugh, love, look over your shoulder and lose sleep'. Launched by Bonnier Books UK in 2021, the imprint is named after the first woman from the creation myth in Norse mythology, who was carved by the gods from a tree trunk found on the seashore – an image of the kind of creative work and crafting that writers do, and a symbol of how stories shape our lives.

Find out about some of our other books and stay in touch:

Twitter, Facebook, Instagram: @emblabooks
Newsletter: https://bit.ly/emblanewsletter